ASCENSION

By Brian Campbell, Stephen Michael DiPesa, Conrad Hubbard, Sam Inabinet, Kathleen Ryan, Malcolm Sheppard

Credits

Authors: Bill Bridges (Introduction, Epilogue), Brian Campbell (Signs of the Times, The Revolution Will Be Televised), Stephen Michael DiPesa (Hell on Earth), Conrad Hubbard (A Whimper, Not a Bang), Sam Inabinet (The Earth Will Shake), Kathleen Ryan (Prologue), Malcolm Sheppard (Judgment, Designing Ascension). World of Darkness created by Mark Rein•Hagen.

Storyteller game system designed by Mark Rein•Hagen.

Development: Bill Bridges

Editing: Carl Bowen

Art Direction: Aileen E. Miles

Interior Art: Langdon Foss, Michael Gaydos, Jeff Laubenstein, Larry MacDougall, Jean-Sebastien Rossbach, Alex Sheikman, Drew Tucker

Cover Art: Christopher Shy

Layout, Typesetting and Cover Design: Aileen E. Miles

1554 Litton Dr.
Stone Mountain, GA
30083
USA

© 2004 White Wolf Publishing, Inc. All rights reserved. Reproduction without the written permission of the publisher is expressly forbidden, except for the purposes of reviews, and for blank character sheets, which may be reproduced for personal use only. White Wolf, Vampire, Vampire the Masquerade, Vampire the Dark Ages, Mage the Ascension, Hunter the Reckoning, World of Darkness and Aberrant are registered trademarks of White Wolf Publishing, Inc. All rights reserved. Werewolf the Apocalypse, Hunter the Reckoning, Wraith the Oblivion, Changeling the Dreaming, Werewolf the Wild West, Mage the Sorcerers Crusade, Wraith the Great War, Trinity, Mummy the Resurrection, Demon the Fallen, Dark Ages Spoils of War, Dark Ages Storytellers Companion, Demon City of Angels, Doomslayers into the Labyrinth, Hunter First Contact, Nights of Prophecy, Rage Across the Heavens, The Red Sign, The Shadow Players Guide, World of Darkness Sorcerer, The Bitter Road, The Book of Chantries, The Book of Madness, Blood Treachery, Convention Book Iteration X, Dead Magic 2 Secrets and Survivors, Digital Web, Digital Web 2.0, Dragons of the East, Guide to the Technocracy, Guide to the Traditions, The Fallen Tower Las Vegas, Forged by Dragon's Fire, The Fragile Path Testaments of the First Cabal, Horizon Stronghold of Hope, The Infinite Tapestry, Mage Chronicles Volume 1, Mage Storytellers Companion, Mage Storytellers Handbook, Manifesto Transmissions from the Rogue Council, Masters of the Art, New World Order, Sorcerer Revised, The Technomancer's Toybox, Tradition Book Akashic Brotherhood, Tradition Book Celestial Chorus, Tradition Book Euthanatos, Tradition Book Hollow Ones, Tradition Book Order of Hermes, Tradition Book Sons of Ether, Ascension, and Time of Judgment are trademarks of White Wolf Publishing, Inc. All rights reserved. All characters, names, places and text herein are copyrighted by White Wolf Publishing, Inc.

The mention of or reference to any company or product in these pages is not a challenge to the trademark or copyright concerned.

This book uses the supernatural for settings, characters and themes. All mystical and supernatural elements are fiction and intended for entertainment purposes only. This book contains mature content. Reader discretion is advised.

For a free White Wolf catalog call 1-800-454-WOLF.

Check out White Wolf online at
http://www.white-wolf.com; alt.games.whitewolf and rec.games.frp.storyteller

PRINTED IN CANADA.

ASCENSION

Contents

Prologue	4
Introduction: The Trumpet's Clarion	14
Chapter One: Signs of the Times	20
Chapter Two: Judgment	50
Chapter Three: The Revolution Will Be Televised	96
Chapter Four: The Earth Will Shake	120
Chapter Five: A Whimper, Not a Bang	144
Chapter Six: Hell on Earth	166
Chapter Seven: Designing Ascension	188
Epilogue: Glory Days	220

Prologue

Amanda waits without impatience.

She sits on the shoulder of a titanic rock — wheat-colored, fine-grained, perilously smooth. Her right leg is stretched straight out and arched to follow its curve; the boulder is without feature or foothold, and only the friction of denim on stone prevents her sliding to the ground below. Around her left foot is looped a barber's strop. Her leg bends and twists a little to keep the leather taut as she works. Her knee braces her hands as she guides the weapons along the grit.

Below the massif, David Cho kneels in powder-soft sand and lays a fire against a smaller slab. He makes a nest of dry grass and sage leaves, sets withered fern stalks and oak twigs beside the tinder, reaches for flint and steel. Before he strikes, he prays; before he prays, he looks around. He and Amanda are the only living things he sees. These rocks, in a misshapen circle of twelve — these are the only landmarks in a desert too bare for dunes and too flat for concealment. Water wore this country to its bones long ago. The sea rebuilt it, aeon by aeon, from grit and gravel. When the ocean left, the dust devils invaded, scouring the sandstone into powder, but tonight there is no wind, no water, no clouds in the stark, cold sky.

David draws sparks, catches them in wool, places them gingerly into their cocoon. He watches the first white thread rising, follows it with his gaze, watches it disappear into a blackness full of unwavering, bitter stars. He smells only arid air and acrid smoke. He feels only sand's heat and night's chill. He hears only his breath, the tinder whispering on his fire, and the thin, silken scraping of Amanda honing her knives.

Not her knives, he reminds himself. *Mercedes' knives.*

From the corner of his eyes, so that she might not feel his glance, he studies his companion.

Mercedes' blades are steel, folded, clay-tempered, curved like katana, strong and lethal along their entire length. A Portuguese sorcerer stole them from their native Japan and put them to ill purpose in Spain. Mercedes Gonzaga de Ortiz bani Euthanatos, slew him and took his weapons as trophies. Senex of Cerberus set them in the hilts and handles of his apprentice's own foci — Toledo-made masterpieces whose own blades were broken.

As Amanda works them, starlight flashes black, white and yellow from their edges. Cold iron, pure silver and raw gold have been fused into blade, guard and pommel. The ornamentation weakens the knives, but Mercedes had wanted to kill creatures that steel could not harm. The Old Man would never have done it, so some other smith added to the master Euthanatos' craft after Mercedes abandoned him — after she followed her lover Alexander Gericault to the Labyrinths of the Nephandi. After she entered the Caul and sold her soul to darkness for irrevocable eternity.

Senex balanced these tools perfectly for Mercy. They are uncannily suited to the hands of her Avatar's current incarnation. Amanda flips one in the air and catches it with thoughtless ease. David adds kindling to the fire but feels a chill creep up his arms.

He remembers two photographs of Mercedes as a Nephandus, taken shortly before Senex slew her in 1923.

In the first, she stands on Coney Island by the Ferris wheel, dressed as a flapper. She has a dancer's centered balance — the swaying hips, artful pose, sensuous stance of a courtesan. Yet, compared to the young girls, the housewives, the grandmothers beside her on the boardwalk, her body seems deadened, slack, propped up by habit only. The *barabbus* leans against the rail looking down on masses of day-trippers from the metropolis, and there is nothing in her face but sun.

In the second, Mercy has seen the camera and who holds it — a man whose shadow falls clearly across her pale summer dress. It is Gericault, and she has turned toward him. She smiles, her dark eyes lively. The crow's feet around them make a strange pattern — not the marks of laughter. Smoker's creases surround her mouth. Her cheeks are pinched and sunken despite her voluptuous figure, belying her youthful hands. Passions etch her deeply; that smile is earnest, painful, demanding.

The two photographs were kept in a traveling frame — a small leather folio, cracking with age and desiccation, on the shelves of Senex's study on Cerberus, beside Mercedes' knives.

When David and his cabal, the Second Seven, visited the Euthanatos' college after many years of traveling with Amanda, the Old Man spoke to each alone. He took David last — brought him to the study, listened to him, heard the history of the Ecstatic's journey, taught him old magic and new rotes, gave him fragile fire from an ebon box on the shelves.

When David saw the portraits, he knew instantly who they were. Amanda had been there a thousand times. She had handled the frame, peered curiously at the decaying calfskin. Yet she never realized who the woman was.

He glances up at her again. Her pose is utterly unlike her predecessor's — leaner, taller, without coquetry, intent only on the keenness of the edge. She looks nothing like Mercy. Her hair is blond, her skin light, her eyes blue. But in the lines of her face,

David thinks he sees a resemblance — a strong one — growing more exact day by day.

Perhaps the similarity is imagination, driven by what he knows of her history. All Nephandi and their Avatars who go through the Cauls return, life after life, as widderslainte, mages who Awaken to serve the Corrupted Ones' mysterious masters. So was he taught in the Cult of Ecstasy; so the other Traditions believe; so the Craft-mage lore agrees; so Technocratic research confirms.

Perhaps the change is real, but meaningless. Since Amanda and the Second Seven drew down the wrath of the House of Helekar, they have fought and hid and run and endured and half died and sought refuge in strange havens. Those times have been enough to set the marks of suffering on any face.

He is staring now, and Amanda looks up from her work. Their eyes meet, and he finds hers unreadable — despite his degrees in psychology, his worldly experience, the turbulent years he has known her.

They are there. They are Mercedes' lines, he thinks, sickly certain that her widderslainte nature is surfacing, reproaching himself for not recognizing it sooner. *Senex would have known. The Old Man would have been able to tell long ago.*

His tinder burns through. The kindling, caught to coal, lights the finger-thick fuel, and the crackling calls the Ecstatic mage back to his task. He gazes into the fire, trying to put Amanda, Cerberus and Senex out of his mind. If he and she live through the coming ordeal, *then* he'll investigate, judge and act. Now he must concentrate on preparing himself for what they are about to do.

David descends into reverie. Flames twist, twine, flicker, fill his eyes.

Seconds come in pairs, twinned. In one of each, he breathes slow as a bear in winter, his pulse nearly still, the fire frozen in place and ice cold. In the other, he pants and gasps; his heartbeat is too quick to count, shaking his chest, and waves of heat bathe his body. The fire of that time dances madly, keeping pace with his blood. David chants at both speeds, thinks in both tempos, mediates between catatonia and *status epilepticus*—

And into this precarious equilibrium, the dangerous thought intrudes:

Senex is dead.

David loses his balance, and the fire shows him what it wills.

• • •

First, a memory: Senex works against the House of Helekar openly.

When Richard Somnitz, Voormas' master butcher, tries to kill Amanda, she kills him. His Consanguinity of Eternal Joy marks her for death — declares to Cerberus its feud against her, and hunts her and anyone who helps her. Yet the Old Man's apprentice lives and thrives, slays every assassin sent, decimates the ranks of Helekar, earns the Grand Harvester's personal vow of vengeance.

When Mark Hallward Gillan uncovers evidence of the House's evils, and the Council of Nine turns against Helekar, and its members are forced to flee like hornets from their crushed nest, the Euthanatos Councilor — and Senex's greatest friend — the Rimpoche Indrani Takstang protects Gillan from Voormas' murderous followers.

When Council forces capture Theora Hetirck, youngest mage of the Consanguinity, and carry her to Concordia for trial, the Old Man's protégé, Mitzi Zimmermann, takes up her defense. Mitzi interrogates the girl — exposes the depths of the *Naraka* Voormas' corruption — sets every hand against the House. Worse still, she saves Theora, takes her under her wing, and brings her home to Cerberus. The child of Helekar becomes the Herald of Senex, and everything she knows of the Grand Harvester is laid bare before the enemy.

And when Voormas besieges the Shard Realm of Entropy, Senex himself leads an army to defend it. He cannot defeat Helekar. He cannot undo the damage done to the Shroud, to the Cycle, to the Tapestry. But the Euthanatos sever Helekar's links to its tainted Nodes, and the Old Man himself denies his adversary the hub of the Great Wheel, and wins a stalemate.

The stalemate lasts only days. It breaks without warning or bloodshed. Senex and his people suddenly withdraw. No one but the Master of Cerberus knows why, and he explains nothing.

• • •

A sound… Whispers. Rumors. David has heard them before, and he knows them to be true.

Even after the Horizon fell and the outer worlds are cut off, it is possible to go directly from Earth to Charon. Masters, adepts, apprentices — even knowing Sleepers — travel from the Euthanatos chantry in Arizona to the college chantry Cerberus. A few other portals remain active, if the Old Man's people use them, and though Senex and his allies are discreet, they are not invisible.

The secret slowly spreads.

• • •

A blur… something gold: David's fire. A way back to the slow seconds and out of these visions. He follows the flames but loses them in a sudden, pale flurry.

Something white: drifting snow. Shining swansdown.

Night behind the swirling veil. Black sky, silver stars. Three shapes — Shard Realms, none of them large enough to make a planet closer to the Sun — Pluto, Persephone, Charon.

• • •

Cerberus' first defense has always been its remoteness.

Few Constructs can muster the technology required to carry Scientists to the edge of hostile space. The less organized Traditions count barely a dozen with the skill, will and Arete needed to walk alone, without aid from their destination, into the wastes of the Deep Umbra.

Yet Voormas descends from the Void under his own power.

He coalesces (for even he, powerful as he is, suffers traveling through the nothingness — disintegrates, a little, in the soul storms) on the dunes in front of the Peregrine Gatehouse. His body transforms as the tendrils of his spirit resume the prison of flesh. When the last wound knits whole, he is ten feet tall, six-armed, obsidian-skinned.

The Grand Harvester, manifest for war, turns to the west.

Cerberus' second defense is the Gatehouse Labyrinth — ever-changing, adaptive, designed to challenge friends, to slow strangers and to trap foes in infinite mazes. Its ironbound doors are three stories tall and twenty-one inches thick. They lock from within, have hidden hinges, and meld their edges with the stone when shut. David cannot see them. He looks out on the portal from a tiny, tallow-streaked cage to their right.

Voormas gestures with four arms. The colossal gates swing wide, strike the walls and rebound, shaking.

Another waxy cage: a lantern beside the Labyrinth's exit. Voormas hurtles past, his face contorted, his hatred like nothing the watcher has ever seen before.

David's flame speaks: *The Grand Harvester has not forgotten the Old Man's meddling. He comes to Cerberus to take control of the last portal connecting Earth and Entropy — and he comes, too, to destroy Senex's lifework, to kill his students, to ruin his creation, to annihilate the man.*

The chantry's defenders stand ready in the courtyard. David knows them all. Three Euthanatoi who lived here before the college was built — ancient, potent, frail. Five Hermetic masters — die-hards who followed Lord Gilmore here from the battle of Mus. Archmages all, veterans of the Ascension War. With Senex, they are the nine most powerful entities on Charon — those who were happiest living here, even after the Horizon fell and life became decay. The old Euthanatoi cannot leave; the Hermetics *will* not abandon another home to any enemy.

Voormas pushes through their wards like cobweb, walks through fields of force like water, brushes away death like dust. He ignores them — ignores, also, the scattering refugees, the apprentices, chantry consors, scholars, the wielders of soft magic. The flame senses his curiosity, pulls forth the sum of his thoughts.

This place is not so starved for the stuff of magic as the other dwindling outworlds. When the Old Man is dead, Voormas will find the source of Cerberus' Quintessence. Now he must reach the Master before he can call up and wield the chantry's more powerful defenses.

He charges forward, and the vision changes.

Smoke mingles with long, delicate fringe… gold-glowing shafts, light as air, burning… and then the fire reveals Senex's last stand.

A clean, bare room: a perfect cube. A circle on the floor, drawn in simple, powdered-chalk lines, intricate beyond comprehension: the key of the Labyrinth. Three clay lamps in an equilateral triangle on the floor. David sees through a fourth, pendant at the apex of the tetrahedron.

Senex waits outside his circle, stately in unbleached white, patient, prepared. He looks up, abruptly, at the hanging light. His gaze meets the watcher's, and in a low, cool voice he murmurs, "David."

The Ecstatic whispers, awed, "Sir?"

The Old Man focuses on a point beyond David, speaks words David cannot comprehend in a language his mind cannot hold. Where their memory lingers, only corrupted fragments survive: *Huarvatat quaddis Zophuriel?*

The fire answers in the same ancient tongue — four voices from four lamps, unutterably tragic in their harmonies. David understands none of it; remembers no trace.

Why do you show me this? The Ecstatic pleads, remembering the Old Man's expression, wise and kind and lost, *Grant him that final dignity, and spare me the sight.*

Fire has no pity; the image burns through. Across David's mind's eye, the battle rages on.

It is not quickly lost.

Senex fights.

He knows that every wound and weakness cleft in his adversary will ease the war others must wage later. He is going to die. He is going to lose Cerberus. But he will make this victory hateful to the Grand Harvester, and the scars from it will be deep.

Mercifully, something blocks David's view at last: Choking thick smoke — gray ashes, floating, out of focus like debris in the eye's humors — signs of an inferno. After what seems like hours, the holocaust consumes itself and reveals the scene.

Senex is dying. Voormas stands by his body, covered in gore. Blood is his first focus, his most favored tool. He is using it to channel his power, now. He will make the Old Man the means by which he takes control of the circle, the Gatehouse, the portal, the realm. He will cut off all escape, and finish the lesser beings at his leisure. He stretches forth his arms, his will, to conquer the mysteries of the circle's magic.

There is no magic there to conquer.

The circle does nothing.

Enraged, the *Naraka* turns to his victim. He will keep him alive a little longer — wrest the secrets of Cerberus from its master's tortured mind.

He is too late. The Old Man dies.

The Grand Harvester extends his third left hand. It holds a primitive stone trident — a reservoir of souls. He will gather in Senex's Avatar and spirit, add it to his power, take the memories from there.

He waits — in vain.

His wrath cracks the floor beneath him.

Senex's soul cannot be taken, whispers the flame. *It is bound elsewhere. Sold.*

The circle means nothing, does nothing. It is a decoy; there are no portals on Cerberus.

Voormas storms out and finds the defenders few — only those whom he maimed, slew or froze on his way in, and their spirits have not waited for him. There are corpses. There are suicides. There are no refugees.

Following trails of fear and footprints to the Gatehouse, he finds the building an empty shell. The famous Labyrinth is gone, the portal merely a clear space in the sand.

The Grand Harvester is forced to leave the way he came, world-walking, at great cost, buffeted by shards and the wind from the sun.

David understands at last the purpose of this Seeking. *Senex was the Gate,* he murmurs, and his timesight darkens.

• • •

A vision: a room with a high, tin-tiled ceiling. Four windows, two at each end of the long, narrow chamber. One pair is twilight blue, open to the breeze. Streetlight glares behind the other, prying around the edges of shades pulled all the way down.

David knows the place — the parlor of an old-fashioned apartment built over a used bookshop in Phoenix, Arizona, the inner sanctum of the Euthanatos chantry founded by Senex. Three lamps, shabby antiques bought for the building when it was first wired for electricity, and an elaborate silver candelabra illuminate faded silk sofas, a horsehair-stuffed chaise, wallowing-deep leather chairs… unchanged since the day the Old Man moved west away from New York City and the memory of murdering his most beloved student.

Mitzi Zimmermann works at a tall mahogany table near the yawning windows. Her former pupil, Julia Stanislaufsky, slouches at a marquetry secretaire in the opposite corner. Julia peers into a large laptop screen. Mitzi pores over paper, parchment, crystals and disks scattered across the polished wood in front of her table — letters to and from other mages, other chantries. Senex's lieutenant — his heiress — runs the earthbound side of Senex's legacy.

No, realizes David, seeing her face as she slits open a letter addressed to the archmage. *She's serious, but her eyes are smiling. Cerberus hasn't fallen yet.*

And there the revelation seems to stall. The Ecstatic, from the vantage of the central taper's flame and a small tea light on the desk, observes only the two women working. They say nothing aloud. David listens to the thoughts they amplify for each other as Mitzi reads from her papers and Julia from her email.

They turn up appeals for help, for membership in the chantry, for sanctuary. There are letters from other mages, mostly Euthanatos, carrying requests for news about the siege on Entropy, for casualty lists, for information about absent friends. Often the writers include lists of names of the dead or missing in response to queries from Phoenix. Personal notes are few and hurried.

Hours pass.

Occasionally the correspondence rises to a higher level — offers of aid or alliance from earthbound archmages or prominent cabals. Messages come from Primi, but only two — and as the Euthanatos discuss them, David learns to what time the flame has brought him. Today the New Horizon Council meets in Los Angeles. Chancellor Gillan has called the Nine together to hear Theora Hetirck deliver a report from Senex on the situation on

Pluto. Any letters the Counselors have written, they will save for the Old Man's official Herald to deliver.

Reminded, Mitzi checks her watch. "They'll be starting now," she remarks.

"If they're on schedule," Julia replies doubtfully. She clicks on an icon — a serpent involved in a nigh-Gordian knot — and untangles it with considerable craft. She is rewarded by a plain white window and the words, "Anything that can go wrong, will go wrong."

The mage called Murphy writes from the floor of the old Belasco theater. He couches his play-by-play of the Council meeting in innocent language, purporting to be an on-site review of amateur night at a college-town coffeehouse. It begins with the "*Master of Ceremonies kicking things off*," and the misanthropic Euthanatos spikes his feed with a few personal comments about Mark Hallward Gillan.

The first act — Theora — performs a spoken word piece about war. Julia ignores the tangled account of the report itself. She knows all too well what Senex's Herald has to say. She wants to hear how the Council reacts to it. *Major downer. Doesn't go over well with the crowd. Truth hurts. Picked apart by the Critics.* Murphy tries to disguise identities, interrogation and replies as best he can. After a while he gives up, types asterisks with a promise for details later. He picks up again with:

Emcee asking if audience has any requests. Our sweetheart getting savaged by the audience. Heckled to death. Don't think they're ready for her aesthetic; attacking her artistic integrity… questioning her right to speak for the author. Oh… got her dander up. Giving as good as she gets, now. Short, sharp history of author's works. Has the last word. Emcee graciously gets her out of the spotlight. Next on the bill, a juggling act from

Julia relays the gist to Mitzi, and the older woman shakes her head ruefully.

A door slams elsewhere in the house. Rapid footsteps cross the hall; someone fumbles at the coat pegs. The door of the parlor opens decorously, and Theora, outwardly calm, makes her entrance.

"Hello," she says quietly — pale, harassed, but under control. She carries a large tote bag over her shoulder. Letters and packages pour out as it slides to the floor. The Herald of Cerberus selects a bundle of envelopes and small boxes then hands it directly to her mentor. "The top one — that's from Gillan," she explains. Her tone — as always, when she speaks of her prime accuser — blends admiration with resentment. "It's something new. He didn't have a message when I talked to him before the meeting, so he must have written it during the session. He gave it to me while he was walking me offstage…

"They hadn't… they hadn't finished when I left," she admits, red-faced. "It didn't go very well."

Mitzi gives her time. "We heard. It can wait."

From her jacket pocket, the Herald takes one more message — a rice-paper scroll with a red-ink seal. She offers it with a knowing smile, and Mitzi blushes.

Julia laughs and slips out to the kitchen. She returns with a massive iron kettle and three cups. Bending over her teacher's shoulder to set them down, she snoops shamelessly at the letter, grins at the bold, dashing Chinese script — Raging Eagle's — and pours out tea.

Theora accepts her tea and sprawls in the center of the large Persian carpet, sorting through her mailbag. She tests every letter for treachery. She destroys the dangerous — stacks the merely important in complicated piles around her. Anyone in the chantry with the time and patience can deal with such routine matters. Occasionally she discovers something personal, even essential, and these she passes to Senex's lieutenant at once.

At the computer, Julia finishes riffling through the email and begins surfing bulletin boards, chat rooms and news sites. She reads out new analyses, flames and gossip on the latest Rogue Council transmissions. When the posters exhaust their topic and repeat themselves, she chases down theories of her own — finds a Virtual Adept's 'blog about the Rogue Council's Sphinx symbol, the urban-legend sphinx at the center of the old Digital Web and the mythical guardian of the Batini Mount Qaf.

"Amanda," murmurs Mitzi. Her pupils stop their tasks and listen while she reads aloud. "'Thought I should tell you, M., we saw A. last week. She is still traveling with the 2-7 — but they're no longer seven, and no one was willing to talk about the missing. Dead, I expect. D. and the others in good health, as far as our eyes could see. A. physically well, but warn S. that I think his experiment has begun to…"

She finishes the letter in silence, and neither of her assistants asks to hear the rest.

Bright movement catches Julia's eye: Red letters scroll across bottom of her screen. It's Sleeper news about terrorist activity. She opens the story and skims it. *Police, federal law enforcement called in to eliminate threat… working to stabilize situation… downtown Los Angeles.* Her first impulse is to dismiss it. Simple unrest, probably, driven by Awakening minds thinning, stretching and even puncturing the fragile Gauntlet. Such riots are all too common in these times. And every genuine incident is exaggerated into propaganda — into opportunities for the Technocracy to renegotiate the relationships between civil institutions and the "special branches" run by local Constructs.

But as Julia closes the page, she notices that her link to Murphy has been cut off.

She hunts down an LA television stream and turns up the volume. An anchorwoman narrates, in the absence of fresh facts, geographic details about the embattled neighborhood, and Theora comes over to watch. Live footage comes from the news helicopter — confused, choppy, chaotic — indecipherable to anyone who had never seen phantom structures, open magic or advanced machines.

"The Belasco," confirms Theora.

Julia snorts. "They won't last long against the Council."

Mitzi says nothing. She writes steadily on, and the younger mages reach for keyboard, cell phones and Tarot deck to find out more.

Suddenly, the Old Man's lieutenant starts. She turns her head as if spoken to — looks at a place between the candles and the kettle, watching something. Neither David nor her companions hear a sound, but Mitzi seems to listen to it. Slowly, her right hand rises — holds — hides — the pendant of her necklace, and her grip is white-knuckled around the flat jade disc, a present from Raging Eagle.

Julia and Theora exchange glances and hurry to their teacher's side.

The three leave the parlor together.

They open the doors to the blind alley, to the chantry members' Gate, to all the places set aside for teleporting friends.

They wait.

They wait all night, and no one comes.

• • •

A memory: Albuquerque. Downtown by daylight — office buildings glittering at noon — black asphalt streets radiating heat even onto the sidewalks, the sparse grass, the undercarriages of air-conditioned automobiles. The sun a blinding nimbus overhead — the Red Star a pale pink glow near the horizon.

A monster flowing through the city center. Tall, skeletal, white-hot, violent. Alien — mythic — demonic — no one who fights it ever knows. It is another nameless threat erupted through the thinning Gauntlet; it breathes pestilence; it must be killed to preserve this scrap of Consensus a little longer.

The Second Seven are the first to see the thing. David stretches Time, and they catch up with it; Zach McCoy wields Do through bare fists; Amanda strikes deep with Mercedes' steel. They attack from one side only — desperate to steer the thing away from helpless Sleepers — equally desperate to avoid the notice of the police, the National Guard, the Men in Black, the shining soldiers of the World Advisory Council.

Others join them, help them — strangers. An old woman in traditional Hopi garb, a middle-aged man in khakis and blue button-down shirt, a teenaged boy with blue hair and a keyboard strapped to his arm, a little girl with silver eyes and a wild aura.

Energies crackle through the beast. It slows, not wounded but angry, rolls over to turn around and extinguishes three score Sleepers on the sidewalk beneath it, most of whom had yet to realize it was there. The deaths draw attention, create a panic — the mob surges away from the stricken, but toward the creature — some people begin to *see* — fight their way against the crowd.

Sirens. The WAC soldiers arrive. They fire slugs and lasers and flechettes into the thing. Combat-armored specialists blast

into flight and join the mages — a practical truce, temporary. As soon as the beast is slain the Technocrats will turn on the Reality Deviants. The New World Order will intern the witnesses and send those who show awareness to containment camps. The Tradition mages will flee, taking with them as many of the newly Awakened as they can.

More vehicles — school buses, station wagons, SUVs — careen around the battlefield. Tommy Gundermann drives one Etheric van, keeping the Second Seven's getaway car safe and mobile. Her passengers track creature and WAC movements, communicate with the fighters, snipe a little from the back doors.

The van reaches the beast's wake — shudders to a stop among the fleeing Sleepers.

Father Timothy Hurley jumps out. He pushes through the press to a woman standing, staring at the thing, shaking with terror. He reaches her, turns her around. Her eyes fix on the Chorister's black shirt, white collar, his clear, understanding gaze. Suddenly she realizes that he can see it, too, and she starts crying in relief. She sobs out her questions, shows him the Marian medal at her neck, something else he doesn't recognize in a tiny leather bag beside it.

Father Tim makes the sign of the cross over her, grasps her wrist and tries to bring her back to the Second Seven. The crowd is too thick; they make no progress, and there are sirens approaching from the north.

He shouts at Tommy to leave him. Voices argue inside, but the van accelerates away.

Squad cars, paddy wagons and something on treads close in from the side street. A school bus skids to a halt just ahead of them. Its doors have been torn off front and back; frightened eyes peer out from most windows. A tall white figure with a mohawk wrestles with the wheel. A bizarrely made-up girl in a red lace minidress over leather jeans tumbles off the roof. A young man with a hundred piercings in his face, wearing black lipstick, vaults down beside her. Together they thrash their way through to the priest.

Father Tim feels a moment's doubt. But the alarming girl looks at the lady's pendants, puts an arm around her and speaks to her in good Spanish about the Virgin and Santeria. The terrified woman follows her eagerly to safety. The young man reaches the priest, jerks his head toward the bus and offers a hand tattooed with ankhs and kanji. The Chorister accepts it without hesitation. He clambers in, joins the Hollow Ones in the rescue mission and ministers to their anxious guests.

The beast, the battle and the bus grind on.

• • •

Confusion. Vision and memory mingle together. David's timesight approaches the shattered present.

The vacant lot behind the Euthanatos chantry teems with tents, sleeping bags and humanity — equal shares block party, religious festival and refugee camp. It is 3:00 in the morning in Phoenix, and it's very dark. No power can be spared for the streetlights after official curfew. It is cold, too — night has leached all the sun-heat from cement and asphalt — so David sees the crowd from a dozen scrap-wood fires.

Worried parents, wide-eyed teens, sleepless infants… men and women and children alone, marked by grief; consoling mages, grim mystics, weary emergency workers; busy hands packing duffel bags and plastic tote bins, stacking canned goods, organizing breakfast; televisions showing only news… riots, political summits, prayer services, war…

Flame brings the Ecstatic twelve views of fear, wonder, elation, despair, dinner, dozing, tears, hysterics, dancing, music, sickness, death.

Suddenly, he watches from only one fire, one belching oily smoke from a wire barrel, just within the ring of vehicles encircling the camp. A battered old pickup truck is slowing to stop on the street outside.

Its passengers spill out of the bed and cab and make their way through the crowd.

Amanda leads the walkers, pausing for nothing. David trails along behind her (and the drained expression on his face shocks his later, watching self), delayed by greetings. Other members of the Second Seven stop entirely, introducing the hitchhikers they have brought with them, exchanging news, discovering long-lost friends among the mages sheltering here.

Amanda goes straight to the fire escape of the building — David bends time to catch up, reaches the top almost before she does.

The apartment over "Rare Books" is a nursery, the lunch-counter pharmacy a makeshift hospital. The chantry proper has moved to the roof — exposed to view and buffeted by the wind, but as a watchtower, it holds the advantage of height over every eight blocks in any direction.

An Order of Hermes savant — the head astrology professor from Mus — waits by the iron ladder, beside a telescope aimed at the Red Star. He wrinkles shaggy eyebrows at the newcomers. "Storm on the way — by dawn. Be ready." He demands their birthdays and makes two adjustments to an enormous orrery behind him. "Very good. You're an improvement." He calls out, "They're here," and waves them on.

Julia is first on her feet. Her trademark batiks and silver "art" jewelry are gone. She wears sturdy denim, a thick barn jacket, a belt heavy with revolver, medicine bag and cell phone. She is the same age as Amanda, began her training in the same year, spent her apprenticeship in peace, her years as an adept on Cerberus and in Phoenix's relative calm — yet she is old before her time. Her brown hair is gray-shot, her faced is seamed and thin-skinned. Her demeanor is battle-hardened.

And protective, thinks David. *But that's not new. She stayed with Mitzi even after earning her independence.* Despite the older woman's power and experience, Julia has always done what she could to shield her.

A second Euthanatos takes a position flanking the visitors. The same fierce guardian instinct gleams in her eyes, but Theora Hetirck is flourishing — her hair long, jet-black, glossy, her cheeks glowing with color, her face strangely young. The hopeless creature of the Tribunal record is gone. David discovers something fresh in her. *Not innocence.* After what the House of Helekar had done to the girl, had done through the girl, had made her do to herself, there can be no innocence for her. *Idealism,* he decides. The silver brooch of her office shines proudly on her shoulder.

David-then wonders, *Why was Theora made Senex's Herald? Why not Mitzi, his right hand? Why not Julia, her senior, surely more trusted?* David-now, remembering that thought, pursues it further. *Why anyone? The Old Man was not the type to award titles or trinkets.*

Mitzi Zimmermann, the Old Man's "canary" (*And why was that? Who gave her the name?*) stands, smiles — untouched by the troubles, to his eye. The same fluffy brown hair, pale white skin, thin bones, seeming fragile as old porcelain. She should break under the weight of her long wool coat. Nonetheless, she has no difficulty shouldering the younger women aside. She steps out to greet her guests — solemn, charming, brisk, businesslike. "Thank goodness. We were afraid you wouldn't make it. We couldn't get word to you."

Mitzi welcomes Amanda as an equal, and with trust. Julia, in her turn, stares warily into the widderslainte face — then suddenly grins and embraces her with obvious, honest friendship. David finds it odd to see these offered to Amanda. He remembers that Mitzi and Julia knew her before he did, before the troubles started. *What was she like, in the eighteen months between Awakening and her first encounter with Gericault? Who would she have been if not for Mercy?*

The pariahs of Cerberus have never met; Mitzi makes the introduction. Theora smiles shyly, enthusiastically, up at Amanda, and David understands. To this girl, Amanda is a distant legend — the Old Man's favorite, the greatest breathing assassin, the thorn in Helekar's side, the killer of Richard Somnitz, the slayer bringing judgment to many, perhaps most, of the girl's old cabal. Moreover, she is the widderslainte that wasn't. She overcame corruption even deeper than Theora's own — living proof that redemption is possible. Nascent hero-worship lights the Herald's face. She could love this stranger, *would* love her — but she meets Amanda's flat, stony gaze, those impenetrable, shuttered eyes. David sympathizes — he knows that expression himself. It's not cruel, but it's without heart. He resents it deeply on the girl's behalf. He looks to Amanda and sees she has noticed Theora's disappointment. *Not oblivious,* he concedes, *but untouched.*

"You look exhausted," Julia exclaims, tossing words desperately into the silence. "Shame on us, letting you stand here. Sit down. Have a drink. Have a rib off the fatted calf." She grins. "We saved you kids the VIP suite."

Theora shakes hands with David. "It's only a tent," she mumbles, "but it's private."

"You're just in time," says Mitzi, making room for them at the table. "Once the storm passes, we're holding a meeting. Will you stay?"

Amanda ignores the offered chairs, settles herself on the parapet. "What kind of meeting?"

"A Council of War," Senex's successor says. David sits beside her, accepts coffee and stale doughnuts, tries to keep a polite mask over his disbelief. Mitzi sees past it, of course. "I know. The storms are beyond our ability to fight," she admits. "The Technocracy's Consensus is unraveling faster than they can weave it — we can do nothing to help or hinder them. That rivalry is over. But Voormas — he is more dangerous than either the storms or the fraying Tapestry."

David-now thinks of the Grand Harvester assailing Cerberus, standing red over the Old Man's body. David-then has his own doubts. Helekar is on Pluto, amid Avatar Shards and soul-destroying Void, and there are no portals working past the Gauntlet. "What can we do?"

"There has been a development. It's possible that we may be able to act… I won't say anything more now. Chancellor Gillan has had a — a revelation. It's his to explain. I think that you and the rest of the Seven should hear it."

• • •

An image: a heap of smoldering ashes on a rock. David knows it must be his fire. Yet it seems enormous, warped out of scale and proportion; he seems to have an ant's-eye view of it.

It is burning very low. More time has passed inside the dream than he thought — a dangerous length of time. He must escape the trance, and quickly, before it kills him. He catches a whiff of its fumes and pursues that, the heat, the dim-red light out of the vision. His perspective shifts; his consciousness rises above the smoke and cinders, sees the pyre *as it is* for the first time:

A heap of ashes — not twigs and herbs, but feathers, flesh, and bone — mounded, gathered carefully around and partially over, a pure white dome — an egg.

David stares. *Phoenix,* he thinks dully. *The Euthanatos chantry founded the year the city was founded. The Old Man's soul — not sold, but pledged. He lived for centuries without losing his mind, held Cerberus virtually by himself, opened Gates through himself. Soulworking. And he believed in the Phoenix prophecy, foretelling the End…*

Senex, dying as the Phoenix died, in a blizzard of burning swansdown…

Frantically, he tries to return to the Seeking — knows he has left it too soon, that his guides have more to show him—

• • •

"It's time."

David opens his eyes. The smudge fire, tied to his Avatar's pace, has burned only halfway through. He lets out one long, slow breath.

Amanda slides grittily down the great rock. She lands gently — difficult to land any other way, here — and the sand drifts lazily away from the impact. "David, did you hear me? Are you there? It's time."

The Ecstatic nods but makes no other motion. Soft footsteps approach; her hand appears over his left shoulder. He grasps it tightly and lets her help him to his feet, but his gaze lingers on the flames.

"David—" Amanda's voice grows sharper, more concerned.

The spell breaks. "I'm fine," he assures her. "I… I need a moment."

"You can't have it. Look."

In the sky above shine distant signs. The Red Star, huge above the horizon, is close enough to show a disc. Beside it, invisible, without inhuman eyes, another red light — Mars — conjunct with the pale, blue-green speck called Earth.

Amanda leads the way back up the spine of the tallest standing stone and points. To the east, a ripple moves over the landscape; something unseen disturbs the fabric of Entropy.

"Voormas."

"Yes." Above the distortion, silver fish dance through the sky — Voidships tracking the anomaly. Light erupts to his left — an Etheric discharge. Another flash — a road flare brought by Hollowers — bursts on the right. Other sparks shine out beyond and behind the first two. Their allies to the north and south have seen the Grand Harvester's fortress coming.

David and his companion need no signal of their own.

Amanda draws her knives — Mercedes' knives — artifacts created by Senex, and so hateful to the *Naraka* in his castle. She mutters a rote of destruction under her breath — a formula of the Old Man's making, given to Mitzi to keep for this day — and the magic resonates with her teacher's signature. She is capable of breaching the chantry's defenses. Though she is not the only one, it is agreed that she and David will attack first — and that, too, will mark this place for Voormas' retribution.

Amanda is her own beacon, and everything is as it should be. The House of Helekar walks directly toward the bait, and her doom walks with it.

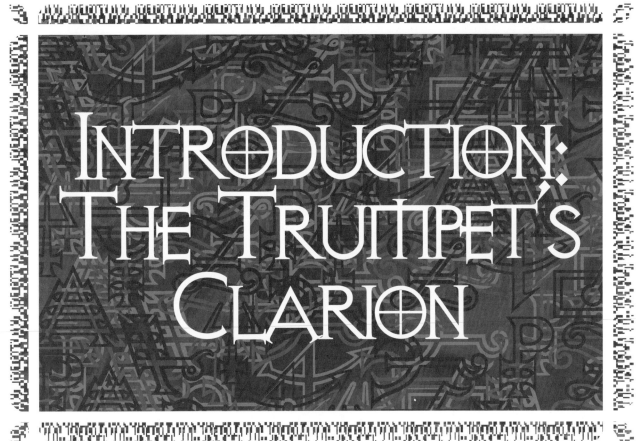

Introduction: The Trumpet's Clarion

> *...the last judgment will be essentially the experience by mankind of awakened conscience and completely restored memory. It will be mankind itself who will judge itself. It will be mankind alone who will play the role of the accuser.*
> —Anonymous, Meditations on the Tarot

The Grand Finale

This book is about an end to things. As we all know, all things must come to an end, and **Mage** is no exception. Stories have beginnings, middles and ends. We've spent the last 11 years telling many new beginnings and middles. Now it's finally time for an end — in fact, we present many endings here, not just one. In a universe as multifaceted as the World of Darkness, one single story just won't do — there are multiple truths and perspectives from which to witness the culmination of history.

Everything has been building up to this book, the final statement on Ascension, the grand fulfillment of the destiny of the Awakened. Every victory and defeat has brought the mages of the present era to this moment, the result of the actions of millennia of reincarnating Avatars. Are their souls winnowed enough of sin to be as light as a feather, or do they tip the scales downward? That's for your chronicle to decide. It's a lot

of responsibility to be placed on the shoulders of a small cabal of mages. But what else is new?

Why Now?

Don't say you didn't see this coming. Mages have fought a centuries-long war for this very moment. If their potent wills can alter reality, then their grandest ideals can never be mere pipe dreams — they must eventually achieve a reality of their own, even if it's one that's warped and twisted by the questionable means used to forge it.

The arrival of Ascension is a promise kept, a long-term loan coming due. It would be pretty cheap to keep the shadow looming on the horizon but ever receding the closer we get to it. Instead of chasing shadows forever, mages must now confront them and win their way to the light. Making Ascension real is the big payoff for years of magic — it's the ultimate act of willworking, to bring one's very vision of the End to fruition. But who's doing the willworking here? Is this something wrought by the Traditions' years of struggle or the endgame of the Technocracy's bid for control? Is it the result of Marauder madness or Nephandi taint? Or is the universe itself finally playing its hand, proving once and for all that a cosmological constant can't be ignored, no matter how much magic is used to gloss over it?

So, the time is nigh. Lay down your cards and reveal your hand. Make your last orders — the bar's shutting down, the establishment is closing. Time to go home.

But where is home?

The Aftermath

What comes after the end? That's for you to decide. White Wolf is ceasing publication of the current **Mage** game and its World of Darkness cousins. Something will rise from the ashes, but it won't be the same.

You might decide that you still want to keep telling stories in this world, the one you've spent years in. Go right ahead. Nobody's stopping you. You can decide for yourself what shape the world takes after Ascension. You can use years of past sourcebooks from all the World of Darkness games to build an elaborate chronicle inhabited by scheming vampires, brutal werewolves and of course, ingenious mages. Using foreknowledge from this book, you can take all of them to the brink of Ascension, and then send them off in a wholly new direction, in an altered — or hauntingly unchanged — World of Darkness.

But if you do that, you're on your own. White Wolf is moving on, creating something new, something even more magical. This is the last **Mage: The Ascension** sourcebook, and every chapter is meant to prove it, paying off the dividends of past metaplot and speculative metaphysics.

All Roads Meet at Ascension: Resolving Metaplot

Mage has years of secretive schemes, plotting wizards and webs of betrayal and deceit to unravel. This book goes a little way toward severing that Gordian Knot, but it doesn't cut it completely — that's the job of each and every Storyteller. While we can suggest the terrible, cosmic crimes committed by Voormas on the eve of Ascension, you have to decide whether the same happens in your game. (Who knows… maybe your characters' cabal has already killed Voormas in your chronicle.) We can reveal our favored candidates behind the Rogue Council phenomenon, but you probably have your own — in which case, feel free to use *your* version.

We don't even attempt, however, to explain it all. There's just too much to tell. Besides, this is Ascension, not the end of a television mystery show where some old bitty gathers the suspects together to reveal which one is the murderer. Even as the universe ends — *especially* as the universe ends — mysteries pile up unresolved. It's up to you to decide which ones to solve, although we give you a number of possible answers for the most popular puzzles we've introduced over the years.

What's more, you might want to introduce one or more prominent (or not so prominent) Storyteller characters from past sourcebooks, some of whom might not have been seen in years. Feel free to do so. We throw in a number of our own favorites here (Dante, Porthos, Senex, etc.), although we just couldn't fit them all (farewell, Czar Vargo!). While you don't want to fill your game with too many walk-on roles, treat yourself and admit those characters you love, even if you can't figure out a plausible way of introducing them. Now, like never before, a few deus ex machinae can be excused.

How to Use This Book

This book is a bit unusual in that it doesn't follow our usual format. Herein you'll find some information that will help you run any Ascension game, along with a number of different "endtime" stories that you can use for the final chapter of your chronicle. They are not meant to be mixed, for each tells its own version of the end, but that shouldn't keep you from making what changes you want to gear them toward your own long-running chronicle.

Chapter One: Signs of the Times suggests a timeline for building up to the Grand Finale itself. You decide whether the end is Armageddon or Ascension. This chapter gives you the worldwide events and the stages in which they occur to get you to whatever end you desire. These events can be spread out over a year or more of roleplaying or compacted into a few sessions — depending on how you want to build up to the final resolution. It gives many suggestions on how the rest of the world reacts to such events as a diminishing Gauntlet — with increasing incursions from the spirit world — and the world governments' reaction to such omens.

Chapter Two: Judgment is as close as we get to providing an "official" story with which to introduce Ascension. It delves deep into years of metaplot to hatch ancient schemes that finally come to fruition now, in the lives of your characters. It builds from the near-mundane post-Reckoning streets to the cosmic realms beyond the Horizon, where Voormas attempts to enact his plan to halt the Wheel of Ages and defeat death itself. All the while, the Tenth Sphere of Judgment ushers in the Final Days.

Chapter Three: The Revolution Will Be Televised gives us a different version of the end, this one determined solely by the Technocracy. The Union's centuries of meticulous planning lead to… well, that's up to your characters to help determine. Their actions go a long way toward deciding whether the future lives up to the Technocracy's original utopian ideals or its Big Brother vision of supreme control.

Chapter Four: The Earth Will Shake shows us what happens when the universe itself fights back, by throwing the biggest, raw physical fact imaginable in the faces of all willworkers — a meteor hurtling at Earth, not just in physical reality but also in the Umbra. Surviving this rude intrusion of objective, undeniable reality will require the characters to gather the aid of Sleepers and mages alike.

Chapter Five: A Whimper, Not a Bang demonstrates what happens when the end of the world takes place off-stage, removed from the eyes of Sleepers and many mages. Magic is steadily dying — and Enlightened Science with it — leaving a completely mundane world in its place. Can the causes be identified in time to save something of wonder and imagination?

Chapter Six: Hell on Earth is the worst possible ending — it's not Ascension at all, but Descent. The Nephandi initiate Armageddon and not even the united Traditions can stop them. But can certain tenacious mages survive and continue the fight in the hellish world of tomorrow?

Chapter Seven: Designing Ascension tells you what to do if you don't like any of the preceding stories, or perhaps you like elements from each but want to brew your own concoction from them. Tips and techniques for building your own version of Ascension (or Armageddon) are provided, including some hints on what Storyteller characters to use and what metaplot to resurrect.

Endtime Stories

The stories we provide herein are suggestions. While "Judgment" is fully fleshed out, the rest of the tales provide general stages and chapters in which events unfold, along with some suggested Storyteller characters. They are meant to be mutable to your needs. Each chronicle is unique, so you'll need to do some work on your own to fully realize these plots in your own game.

When determining which story to run, you need to know the focus of your chronicle. Is it about the age-old struggle of the Traditions to regain what was lost, or is it about the tension between magic and science, Tradition and Technocracy? Is the ultimate evil mere human ignorance or something more palpable, such as demons from Beyond manifesting in the world? Your answers really determine the tenor of your particular Ascension.

Gehenna, Apocalypse, Oblivion, etc.

Mages aren't the only supernatural beings who suffer the scales of judgment. Vampires, werewolves, wraiths and the fae also encounter the end of everything they know. If your game has always ignored these other game lines, you can safely ignore them now. But if you've introduced elements from any of these games before, you might want to also hint at their own demises as your mages struggle to understand what's happening to them.

The disappearance of all vampires can be a spooky event, but only if mages could routinely pierce the Masquerade before. If their undead contacts all of a sudden go silent, it can add a chilling edge to the mounting suspense.

Werewolves stepping out of the material world en masse, marching off to a distant war that they claim will decide the fate of all of Gaia, can also send chills up any willworker's spine. If something is ominous enough to get the Garou to abandon their caerns, then even the most jaded and self-obsessed Archmaster should begin to question the times.

The same for ghosts. Are more and more hauntings occurring as the dead flee the Underworld? Or are ancient haunts now empty of the chilling resonance of the dead? Whatever can put the fear of death into the dead is something even Voormas and Senex should hesitate to dismiss.

Regardless of the type of supernatural being, they're all experiencing the worst of times. This is a sourcebook for a **Mage** ending, however, and that means you should manipulate these other events to somehow shine a light on Ascension. Not some atavistic Gehenna where corpses rises to suck the blood of all the living or a primordial final battle where a dragon corrupts the Earth, but Ascension — where the millennial toils of the Enlightened finally pay off.

Final Words

What a long strange trip it's been.
—The Grateful Dead

Okay, I couldn't help myself with that quote; it's just too appropriate. It has been a long (11 years) strange (three editions) trip (60+ books). Although my current tenure as **Mage** developer began only two years ago, I've been involved in the game from the start, way back with first edition. I remember the rush of creativity we all got when trying to hammer the rulebook into shape for its tight deadline. (It was a tradition to release each new title at GenCon, and we sure weren't going to miss that date.)

There were some odd ideas that slipped into the first edition that were later quietly ignored — many for good reasons, others because… well, they just didn't fit the direction in which the game was now going. Take the Zigg'raugglurr, for example, an alien race from the fourth dimension that I added to the book at the final hour because we still needed more antagonists. They got a write-up of maybe five paragraphs and were maybe mentioned once or twice in successive sourcebooks, but they otherwise disappeared from the published **Mage** universe, written out of the Tapestry. Until now. They're resurrected again for old times' sake in Chapter Five: A Whimper, Not a Bang. See, we haven't entirely forgotten our history and from whence we came. Well, not all of it, anyway.

Mage was the brainchild of Stewart Wieck, his response to Mark Rein•Hagen and crew's innovative game design in **Vampire** and **Werewolf**. With the help of fellow White Wolfers, the game made its release date and went on to make gaming history with perhaps the most versatile magic system ever presented.

The first line developer to whom Stewart proudly handed his newborn was Phil Brucato, who molded the game through its early years, giving it a spin all his own. He oversaw the second edition and then a spin-off setting: the Renaissance-era **Sorcerers Crusade**.

Taking up the reins from Phil was Jess Heinig, who gave the game a new spin and a revised edition, toning down some of the frankly over-the-top directions the game had occasionally wandered into.

And then there was me, reintroducing the conflict between the Traditions and the Technocracy with the Rogue Council, about whom we finally get some answers in this book. So, I've been here from start to finish, even if I did sit out most of the middle acts.

Let's not forget the host of excellent writers who actually produced the words you've been reading for the last few years. Their sheer creativity and talent under deadline pressure is a sign that magic really does exist.

This has been the hardest White Wolf book I've worked on. While it was exciting to finally blow the lid off the secrecy and shadows, it's also been rather poignant. I hadn't fully realized how many stories there were yet to tell until time ran out. But now it's done and in your hands, where it truly belongs. Now you get to complete what we've begun.

Do as thou wilt.
— Bill Bridges
August, 2003

Chapter One: Signs of the Times

Some say the world will end in fire,
Some say in ice.
From what I've tasted of desire
I hold with those who favor fire.
But if it had to perish twice,
I think I know enough of hate
To know that for destruction ice
Is also great
And would suffice.
—Robert Frost, "Fire and Ice"

The Beginning of the End

Humanity is preparing for a grand catastrophe, seeking signs of the End Times. Hysteria builds as the jaded masses look for some scandal to rouse them from boredom and apathy. The mass media eagerly hype any news story that will boost their ratings, drawing sedentary consumers across hundreds of cable channels to intimations of the world's imminent demise. By assigning apocalyptic importance to current events, a new generation elevates its own importance… not realizing that the truth is far worse than it can possibly imagine.

Shocking stories come and go, of course. The mere significance of a year on the calendar was enough to cause an outbreak of panic back in AD 2000, stirring madness (and an endless supply of news updates) over the threats of "Y2K." Fear and paranoia launched inspections for possible computer viruses, predictions of various breakdowns in civilization and threats of new and virulent plagues from distant lands. Within a few years, the real threat of terrorism would lead to imaginative speculation over where enemies would strike next.

In the World of Darkness, shadows are darker than they seem, and the night more deadly than we dare contemplate. Imagine, then, a populace overwhelmed by millennial fever, seeking any evidence it can find of the world's imminent destruction. Humanity suspects that dangerous trends are accelerating — and as is often the case, their fears and legends hold some basis in fact. If reality can be shaped by belief, and the collective fears of billions can shift reality's Consensus, hype can lead to horror. Dreams and nightmares empower the very forces they imagine, especially in unseen realms. It is possible, of course, that much of this hysteria is merely the result of overactive imaginations… or perhaps it is just enough to tip the fragile balances of the supernatural world toward apocalypse.

Nearly every supernatural society has some legend or prophecy of the world's demise. In a purely delusional sense, it gives them comfort, confirming that only *they* will be able to recognize signs of the end of the world. Like their histories, their prophecies put their own kind in the center of it all. The results serve as object lessons for the sinful or inspiration to motivate the real saviors of humanity. Those delusions are about to give way.

Nearly every sect, clan, tribe or Tradition also has an enemy it blames for disturbing the balance of the world when signs begin to manifest. Paranoia has distracted them from action against the mounting signs of apocalypse. In recent years, mystics and visionaries have offered evidence that ancient prophecies are coming true, but only truly epic atrocities can stir cabalists and conspirators from their obsessive rivalries. In a world fraught with enmity and distrust, even mages are quick to blame what they find on the actions of their enemies. Instead of working together to investigate further, the Awakened and Enlightened break down into bitter conflicts, arguing over what is to be done rather than working together for a solution.

In recent years, great catastrophes have heralded the end of Creation. Some mystics rant that this is only the beginning of a new age, a turning of some Great Wheel, but the End Times offer no assurance that the human race will survive the crushing events that follow. Mages are mortal, as vulnerable to the sting of death as unaware Sleepers are. Yet for the Awakened, the horror of Armageddon is much greater, for they can often see what ordinary men and women cannot. Nightmares have beset humanity, but pride, paranoia, xenophobia and overwhelming hubris have prevented mages from taking action. They've been rationalizing the most cataclysmic events of the past. Now greater terrors await them in their future.

Death Comes on Schedule

All things must come to an end. Signs of the world's demise have been building for decades, promising a new age of suffering and destruction. Now is the time for those promises to reach fulfillment. Some citizens of the common populace expect the world to die suddenly, impacted in an instant with an undeniable and overwhelming catastrophe. While such events are certainly possible — perhaps from a nuclear incident, or a meteor crashing into the Earth (see Chapter Four) — the many varieties of Armageddon mages have predicted present more insidious possibilities.

The catastrophic has since become commonplace. Anyone living in the World of Darkness is accustomed to sudden events drastically changing their perceptions of the world. The average citizen might even be somewhat ambivalent when such events occur, content to hide behind the regularity of a work schedule, the solace of cable television, the distractions of technology and the amusements of conspicuous consumerism.

Even mages are not immune to such episodes of sloth and apathy. Governments and agencies take drastic action when they see fit, declaring states of emergency, but they cannot uncover deeper problems hidden in our world — dangers occulted in supernatural realms.

In the chapters that follow, we will present to you five possible ways that the world can end — five among many. This chapter alone lays the foundation for many more. Each dark fate is set against a broader background, an unraveling of the Tapestry of Creation that affects all of the world's supernatural creatures. The world could end in a sudden disaster, of course, but while ordinary men and women search for the next great catastrophe, they have remained oblivious to events in the supernatural world, events more secretive and insidious. Forces once hidden in shadows will emerge into the light of day, and darkness will envelop the world.

Visionary mages already suspect the truth: that the world has been dying for a long, long time. Entropy has been building for millennia, and it's all got to lead up to *something*. Very soon, prophets and madmen will see revelations of what that ultimate destiny might be.

Behind the Curtain

If you've been running **Mage** for years, you're already well acquainted with how to begin an epic chronicle based around magic. The wonder of an initiate's Awakening, the rivalries of a city's occult scholars, the pervasive threats of rival cults, deviant willworkers and soul-crushing collectives — such stories have been told in epic detail. Beginning a chronicle about mages is now relatively easy. Deciding how to *end* such a chronicle, finally and definitively, is much harder.

The easiest mistake to make in such a story is overkill. You could, of course, unleash a drastic event that plunges the world into despair *right now*, but that would rob the heroes of your story of their significance. An "Armageddon chronicle" is best savored, and it's far more compelling if the events that launch it are insidious — so subtle that your players don't realize the significance of recent events. There's no need to do something drastic to launch Armageddon, because *it has already begun*. Events in the last year — and in some cases, the last 10 years — have foreshadowed what is to follow.

The world might end in fire or in ice, a slow death that requires years of suffering until all light and life is extinguished. Whether the events that follow are overtly supernatural or occulted from mankind, as sudden as a firestorm from the heavens or as insidious as an alien invasion, the particulars depend on the theme and mood of this, the final chronicle. There are so many ways for the world to end that one of them becoming real is inevitable.

As the Storyteller, you must decide how the world ends, whether by fire or ice, catastrophe or treachery. No matter what conclusion you prefer, forces are already in motion to ensure the supernatural world's destruction. This chapter describes — sign by sign, step by step — events that have led and will lead to Armageddon. This story must begin with a quick summary of apocalyptic events that have already occurred, while showing more than has been seen before. From these rends in Creation, the Tapestry of reality unravels.

Any good story has a solid ending; the time has finally come for a definitive ending to all stories set in the World of Darkness. Armageddon or Ascension, like similar concepts of Gehenna and Apocalypse, has no real meaning if it is an un-quantified idea in the distant future, a subject for theory and rhetoric. Horror is personal, and the time for horrific revelations has arrived. Take heart, though. You might linger over the events of this section as long as is necessary, unveiling each new vision and tragedy with sadistic delight. No matter how the end comes, the first signs of the world's destruction remain the same. The final signs, and final judgment, are up to you.

Signs of the Past

Before the world's mages can rush toward their annihilation, it would be fitting for at least a few of them to take a quick look over their shoulder, glimpsing the horrors lurking behind them. Hindsight is 20/20, bestowing a clarity of vision that even exceeds the insight of a magical visionary. If there was a time to avert the world's imminent doom, it has passed. The Nine Traditions will make last-ditch efforts to save the world, but they have squandered their opportunities while satisfying their foolish pride. Bitter recriminations of Traditionalists and Technocrats have obfuscated more critical events. Now that we can look back at the terrors of the past few years, we can see them with new eyes, recognizing them for what they are. Such nostalgia is far more comforting than contemplating what is to come. Here is how the end began.

The Red Star

Our fates lie written in the stars. As part of the fulfillment of ancient prophecy, a new star appeared in the Umbral heavens. Its arrival corresponded with the birth of a great prophet, a messiah of critical importance to a vastly different society of supernatural creatures: the Garou. Werewolves who stepped into the spirit world (especially the Penumbra) could see this new star blazing with crimson light in the heavens, as real as the manifestations of spirits or incarnations of their totemic gods.

Mages in the Penumbra could see this new phenomenon as well, but were far less likely to understand its significance without consulting a select few packs of werewolves. Disparate visionaries interpreted its meaning in vastly different ways, often for the comfort of confirming their own beliefs. The Garou have more specific interpretations. Their future might ultimately lie within the claws of the pack that captured the "Perfect Metis," a creature born on the night the Red Star first appeared. He is a paragon, a visionary… and a weapon they could have since turned to their own ends. (More details are available to those who consult the **Werewolf** book **Rage Across the Heavens**.)

Denial and rationalization have been useless; the fulfillment of prophecies continues unabated. As Armageddon approaches, the Red Star will become more visible in the heavens, *even in the physical world*. At first, an Enlightened few will notice it. (In game terms, it is only dimly visible at first to people with at least one point of Arete or Awareness, and even then, only with die rolls.) As this apocalyptic phenomenon grows in strength, scientists will scramble for explanations of what they are witnessing on their finely tuned astronomical equipment, speculating that a new star might be forming in the orbit of Saturn. By then, of course, it will be too late. The jaded and ambivalent will dismiss it as another anomaly science must interpret — but soon, they must accept even greater madness. Each time an impossible act occurs, it makes the next miracle or tragedy more plausible. Consensus then shifts toward chaos.

When There's No More Room in Hell

The dead now walk the Earth, their true forms hidden from those who would not understand. The Avatar Storm has shaken the pillars of Creation, shattering the barriers between worlds. Those who study the dead, including many Euthanatos, speak of a Maelstrom that has ripped through the Underworld, flaying souls and destroying empires built by the Restless Dead. A few years ago, souls that escaped this catastrophe fled into the physical world, seeking bodies that could shelter them against the storm — the undefended bodies of the recently deceased. Forces hitherto unknown then empowered ordinary men and women with extraordinary power, directing alliances of imbued hunters against the walking dead… and eventually, against other supernatural creatures as well. (Further enlightenment is hidden in the **Hunter** core rulebook.)

Ghostly spirits have since learned to animate dead bodies, walking among us as zombies. In the early days of their awakening, the very forces that obscure supernatural activity drove ordinary people who saw such things mad. Just as the sight of a werewolf in its true form can cause spontaneous outbursts of temporary insanity, when the dead walk, ordinary humans can only rationalize, flee or collapse as the once defined barriers of their world crumble. The recently reanimated are terrible to behold, but over time, the resurrected have gained abilities to masquerade as human… even while inhuman appetites lurk within them.

Imbued with forces we have yet to comprehend, a few human hunters have taken arms against the night, acting on visions they had of these shambling dead. Training themselves in countless raids against lesser zombies, these hunters have become what they first shunned — growing in power until they are as supernatural as the monsters they destroy. Their conviction has since allowed them to see other supernatural creatures, confirming that they are not alone in their world. It hasn't taken them long to reload their weapons and put other anomalies in their sights.

The story is not merely of interest to those who study the dead. Imbued hunters act on powerful visions, and as the End Times advance, their vision will become clearer. In fact, their power is growing. If the world is coming to an end, then hunters might turn their attention to more powerful creatures, including sorcerers. When encountering a mage, a hunter's instincts might tell him to blame these deviants for the troubles at hand… or perhaps, desperate for answers to the visions that torment him, he'll turn to the most powerful mages as the messiahs of a new age. If finer distinctions cannot be made, the outcome of either eventuality could be unreasoning violence.

Ancients Awakening

Vampires have their own intimations of doom. Within their separate supernatural societies, Kindred and Cainites are aware that the oldest of their kind — the Antediluvians — are awakening from millennia of static slumber. The first of these titans to return was the father of all Ravnos, an Ancient whose children hid among tricksters and deceivers. His noblest (and distant) offspring hid among the itinerant peoples of the Earth, including the outcast tribes of the Rom Gypsies. Such trivia would ordinarily be inconsequential to practitioners of magic… but the awakening of the Ravnos Antediluvian from centuries of torpid slumber brought outbreaks of plague and warfare to his restingplace in India. Sorcerers might struggle to conceal their magical conflicts, but with each Ancient awakening, the true face of evil will be unmasked, and mankind will recoil from monstrous revelations. (This terrifying timeline was first unveiled in the **Vampire** book: **Nights of Prophecy**.)

For days, supernatural strength obscured the sun around the tainted land where the Ancient awakened. From the mystic East, a circle of Cathayan vampires rushed to oppose it, waging war openly like titans against the immortal… and further spreading outbreaks of insanity. These crimson gods pushed each other to the brink of destruction… but it was mages who finally destroyed them. Amalgams of Technocrats — including "Shockwave Contingency" Iterators of the Technocracy — responded to the incident with a devastating pyrotechnic bombardment. The mass media rapidly fabricated rationalizations for the event, guided by Syndicate spin doctors and Ivory Tower conditioning. The incident was passed over as yet another aberration of inhumanity in the Third World.

Openly, mankind might desperately deny what evidence it sees of the horrors around it, but in the deepest recesses of the human mind, people know what lurks in darkness. Lies on network news can never completely silence dark and doubtful suspicions, fears that awaken only in the middle of the night, made manifest through dreams and nightmares. As the Ancient Ones rouse from their torpid state, they begin to exert their formidable psychic and supernatural power upon populations of vampires… and to some extent, the masses of humanity.

When these gods return, they do not need to stride the Earth as giants to ensure their ultimate victory over herds of humanity. As the world spirals downward into deeper horrors, ancient vampires will begin to creep into the collective unconscious of humanity, appearing at first behind the shadows of sleep. Their names perch unspoken on the tongues of innocents; their true appearance is hidden in the minds of powerful dreamers, fully recalled when these titans are seen for the first time. The Ancient Ones have no need to destroy everything in their wake. With each crimson resurrection, chaos and fear will echo among the Masses, and Consensus will shift once more, slowly accepting the fact that *ancient gods now walk among us*. One has awakened. Twelve will follow.

Stormwardens and Psychopomps

Mages have been distracted by other revelations. In the recent past, a cabal of mages undertook a hazardous journey to a Technocracy base in the Arctic. A self-proclaimed "Rogue Council" set them on their course. Behind a safely anonymous façade, the Sphinx, this Council has not only announced a new manifesto for insurrection, but also offered insights into hidden atrocities. Secrets lay buried in the ice, and a handful of witnesses have unearthed them.

Deep within a Union Construct, a Progenitor scientist had performed an exceedingly dangerous experiment. Using heretical Enochian rites and occult lore gathered during the Second World War, he summoned otherworldly entities into our own dimension, fusing them with human subjects who had demonstrated psionic potential. Strangely enough, these cosmic forces were unusually compliant to his request, as though waiting for this signal to return. The lone survivor of this experiment developed the ability to control spiritual forces… and alter the boundaries between the realms of flesh and spirit. (The results of this raid depend on the last story in the book **Manifesto: Transmissions from the Rogue Council**.)

Enemies of the Technocracy would no doubt be quick to condemn the Union for such an experiment, but it was based on explorations conducted half a century ago, not by a world-shaking conspiracy, but by a handful of troubled visionaries. The demented cabal that realized these deviant dreams was sentenced to Gilgul long ago, its members' once-Awakened souls silenced forever. And indeed, a legacy of dreamers has held this same potential. Within the Nine Traditions, a select few individuals have demonstrated the potential to guide destiny in such a fashion. They are currently known as Stormwardens: mages with an immunity to the Gauntlet's deadly barriers, along with a modest ability to actually control it.

The Progenitor's experiment has tapped this same potential, re-creating the Anakim, creatures of flesh and spirit. Legends have obscured their origins. Verbena speak of them as "fetches;" scholars of dead magic describe them as "Annunaki." The Awakened and Enlightened can see only a part of what they truly are. With Awakened sight, practitioners of magic might see a true form twitching with spindly limbs and gray flesh. Unable to cope with such outright magic, Enlightened Technocrats might use procedures to see behind a seemingly magical façade, identifying them as alien creatures. Hearing of Enochian magic, religious mages might see them as angels, avatars of a higher power that could save them from the world's destruction.

Regardless of their true appearance, they are immune the shards of the Avatar Storm, like Stormwardens. This new generation possessed by spiritual Psychopomps has revitalized ancient traditions, demonstrating the ability to manipulate souls… and pass judgment. The entity encountered in the Arctic was the first to be seen in centuries. As the procedures for their creation are perfected, the ancient race of the Anakim will descend from the heavens. Whether they are seen as the saviors of souls, heralds of the End Times or outsiders with an alien agenda, the arrival of the Anakim presents vast and terrifying possibilities… all of which conclude with the end of the world.

Signs of Unrest: Dreams, Nightmares and Rumors

The past cannot be changed, but in the present, madmen and visionaries are attuned to the horrors at hand. Even the common populace shows signs of xeno-

Elementary Consensus

Here's a 25-cent definition of part of our story so far: Consensus is reality as mankind collectively imagines it. In gross terms, if humanity believes that an act of magic is impossible, it is considered "vulgar," and forces of Paradox punish the mage who attempts it. There is a very good reason to keep the supernatural hidden, then. If enough humans witness and believe that monsters are real, or that the impossible is actually possible, Consensus could theoretically shift. This evolution happens with technology all the time: the first cloning experiments were (by this example) very hard to perform, but if scientists can replicate such experiments repeatedly, a Progenitor's chances of pushing the envelope of genetic engineering are stacked a little in his favor. In the same way, when humans witness an act of magic made real, the chance of replicating this feat becomes slightly more possible.

In game terms, a shift in Consensus could manifest in any number of ways: The difficulty for a given Arete roll might be a little lower, the effects of a phenomenon like Delirium might be reduced, or the Gauntlet rating might be slightly reduced. As the chances of success at vulgar magic increase, more Sleepers will witness such events — theoretically a vicious cycle. Paradox punishes those who stray outside the limits of reality, but in very broad terms, if enough people believe something is possible, the boundaries of reality might change. In other words, witnessing one impossible act can actually make it easier to believe in the next impossible event to come along.

Some believe that Armageddon is the erosion of reality itself, a time when all magic becomes progressively more possible and supernatural forces more obvious. Others contend that if the amount of supernatural activity in the world increases, and Paradox cannot contain it, other cosmic forces might rush in to purge such aberrations. The Avatar Storm, for instance, could theoretically destroy the Gauntlet, allowing outside forces to enter our world... or it might be gathering to eradicate everything magical in the world, leaving only what exists in "static" and unchanging reality. A shift in Consensus could even make grand catastrophes more probable — your reality might vary. This is merely an elementary definition of "consensual reality," a foundation that will be undermined by the events of Armageddon.

phobia and paranoia. Plagues and terrorist atrocities are all too real, of course, diverting civilizations' resources away from hidden horrors... but behind the scenes of mundane reality, other tales are told. Ordinary humans cannot see these events for what they are, but a perceptive few have seen signs of the End Times. They act as conduits for the collective unconscious, acting on behalf of all humanity.

The human mind, it would seem, is unprepared to deal with obvious evidence of the existence of the supernatural. If humans were not capable of such epic demonstrations of denial and rationalization, after all, they couldn't believe in the illusion that they control their own world. Or could it be that the hysteria reflected in the mass media — the passing obsessions about the threat of Y2K, of terrorism, of outbreaks of strange new diseases from distant lands — are indicators that humankind already suspects that it is helpless to avert greater catastrophes?

Supernatural forces work to obscure the most obvious supernatural phenomena from human perception, such as the Delirium hiding the predations of werewolves, madness allowing denial of ghostly incursions, or even Paradox bestowing outbreaks of insanity. When presented with hysteria that human reason cannot rationalize, humans sometimes reinterpret what they see to fit their own beliefs. Such rants and ramblings seem insane, of course, but they often hold shards of truth — especially for mages who can interpret what is really happening.

A series of unimaginable catastrophes and paranormal events is destined to take place throughout the narrative to come (although you must decide the exact trajectory and acceleration of the world's descent into oblivion). Such tragedies are foreshadowed by subtleties and limited encounters with the paranormal. They ultimately proceed to outright and obvious demonstrations of humanity's helplessness. Appropriately enough, Sleepers can see the early signs only through dreams, visions, reveries and nightmares.

Religious Visions

When everything goes to Hell, it is inevitable that the most zealous will see only what they really want to see, interpreting events to confirm their own deeply held beliefs. Mages also deal with personal paradigms on a day-to-day basis, so it is not unusual that they might also see apocalyptic phenomena in a way that reaffirms their own religions or philosophies. Behind any timeline of apocalyptic events, there should always be a certain amount of "background noise" from confessions and protestations of religious visions.

Some find that the easiest visions to construct in this fashion are Judeo-Christian ones. If a mage sees the statue of a saint weep blood or the face of Christ appear on an otherwise commonplace background, who can really challenge the validity of such a claim? Such personal perceptions are not merely random occurrences. At a time when or a place where apocalyptic phenomena are about to occur — or are currently taking place — any mage could have a religious vision to confirm the significance of that event.

In any given place in the world, visions might also correspond to the dominant religion. This doesn't have to mean that any one religious vision of apocalypse is coming true, of course. When forces outside the world we know, beyond our understanding, invade this world, we have no frame of reference for describing them. Therefore, the human mind plays tricks, reinterpreting sensory data to fit a system of belief it understands on a primal, faithful level. Even ordinary people have these types of visions as the End Times advance, beginning with the Awakened, Aware, oracular or attuned and then proceeding down the scale of spiritual enlightenment.

Prophetic Dreams

Some Technocratic analysts and practitioners of magic speculate that the collective belief of six billion humans determines the boundaries of reality, a collective reality known to experts as Consensus. As the world moves toward a global community, widespread perceptions draw the line between the coincidentally possibly and the blatantly magical. A few occultists and analysts take this a step further, stating that the "collective unconscious" is in some way attuned to Consensus. Although the conscious mind recoils from revelations of the supernatural, the unconscious mind knows that the occult world is out there. Such insights surface as legends… and dreams.

The end of the world will no doubt shift this Consensus. Once-impossible events will become real, and with each impossible occurrence, the next catastrophe becomes more plausible. Overtly, mankind might deny such things with the declarations of scientific "experts" and clever journalism, but all this analysis and technobabble cannot silence dreams. Powerful minds might even tap into the shifting tides of Consensus, gaining glimpses of the inevitable from beyond the wall of sleep. An ordinary human might refuse to accept, for instance, the intrusion of an astral power or totemic Incarna in the physical world, but visionaries gain hints of such events while the rational mind rests. Marat said that the sleep of reason produces monsters — perhaps in the End Times, unconscious Sleepers might reason more clearly than they can in a waking world cloaked with lies and deceptions.

Mages are affected even more strongly by these insightful perceptions. They might not remember such dreams when they wake, but in the midst of using their analytical skills (or die rolls for such Abilities as Cosmology, Occult or Enigmas), they could remember dreams they have had before (perhaps manifesting as flashbacks or interludes). It is even possible that someone attuned to the Primordial forces of the world (such as a mages with the Dream Background) can consciously tap into this wellspring of knowledge through focused meditation.

With these paranormal possibilities, eternity's end does not have to be announced through a drastically improbable event. Behind the scenes of Creation, dreams and nightmares might erode the very foundation that defines what is "impossible," showing how Consensus is shifting, how subtle supernatural and spiritual forces are affecting the world and the ways in which prophecies are being fulfilled. When the first signs of Armageddon occur, they might be witnessed openly by the Awakened and Enlightened… and secretly by those Sleepers who play a role in this dark destiny.

Virulent Paradox

Outbreaks of madness afflict Sleepers who encounter the supernatural. Mages undergo a far more extreme process. When a mage pushes the boundaries of reality too far, Paradox pushes back — a concept with which even initiates are intimately familiar. In concentrated quantities, it can even bring madness, as a paradoxical mage deviates from the world around him in rapidly growing episodes of insanity.

Some prophecies hint that a mage who can overcome these distractions and deceptions can ascend beyond the world we know into a higher plane of reality. He would then escape the confines of consensual reality — and thus define a very literal interpretation of the word "Ascension." Then again, other legends have spoken of mad mages eventually succumbing to "twilight," becoming so removed from the reality around themselves that they "ascend" into a very different world, one that confirms their own delusions as the final arbiters of reality. As the End Times advance, legends are destined to become real, including interpretations of these two ideas.

This book offers five ways in which the world could end, but the possibilities really are limitless. Armageddon can do more than destroy the world; it can destroy a mage when the criteria for Paradox shift. A mage might have his own interpretation of how the world will end — and if he does, Paradox Backlashes might actually confirm such beliefs. "Angels" might plague a sinful mage, even if they are merely hobgoblins of his imagination. Escapists might find the one true way to reach another, better place, even if they never realize they have stumbled into a Paradox Realm. An eternity of bliss might merely be a moment of overwhelming Quiet. Any mage defies reality, after all, merely by the act of performing magic. If he strays too far, his personal destruction could be different from the signs of the apocalypse that others witness. For the delusional, an ascent to an eternal reward might be indistinguishable from a descent into madness.

Paradox passes judgment, and the force of judgment will no doubt be overwhelming in the End Times. It would be a cruel irony for a mage to ensure his own destruction by an incautious use of magic, perhaps in some desperate attempt to save the world. His fate is a fitting one if this demise neatly wraps up his own personal paradigm of the world's collapse. No Sleeper needs to ever see a pagan warrior ascend to Valhalla or the soul of a Euthanatos descend into oblivion. In the early stages of Armageddon, such final judgments can occur occulted from the rest of this timeline.

Variations: Taking Others Down With You

A deviant mage might not have the luxury of escaping the rest of humanity's fate. Later in this chapter, certain representatives of humanity (let's call them "the Chosen" for now) might be able to witness magical events that others cannot. Whether by virtue of Awareness, oracular ability or a latent ability to perform magic, they could share the same fate as mages with a similar paradigm. (See "The Third Sign," later in this chapter, for more details.)

If such is the case, more virulent manifestations of Paradox can actually *cause* one of the timelines we've offered in other chapters to advance (if within only a limited area). The same sinful mage we mentioned earlier might draw angels, avatars or Anakim from the heavens to carry Sleepers around him to similar judgment. A scientific genius might open a gateway for explorers to descend into the Hollow World; a Nephandic cult guru might lead others into Hell.

Such events could eliminate deviant mages long before the coming of Judgment Day. Perhaps all their alternatives will be gone by then, and only one paradigm of magic will judge the Masses on that day... or perhaps these forces will silence the masters of magic forever, trapping Creation in lifeless stasis. From one botched act of magic, a willworker can doom himself for all eternity. It is far too soon for such resolutions, however. We have yet to see the first signs of Armageddon.

Signs of the Future: The First Apocalyptic Phenomena

As Creation unravels, the impossible will gradually become more real. The supernatural is destined to emerge from the shadows, tainting the safe and sane world defined by human hope with alien agendas. It is just as likely that such forces are not antagonistic toward humanity, but to the monstrous and devious forces that prey upon the Masses instead. It might be that a Reckoning is at hand, a final judgment for creatures and creators lurking at the fringes of human perception. Either way, supernatural forces will be at work, and they must gradually grow in strength. If ice, not fire, envelops the world, then the next step in the world's demise is supernatural forces creeping further into the human world.

Whether Traditionalist or Technocrat, Marauder or Nephandus, a mage is empowered to witness, understand and even affect supernatural phenomena that ordinary humans cannot. While the catastrophes to come might be of global (or even cosmic) proportions, the early stages of an Armageddon chronicle should involve isolated and localized events. Mages are invariably drawn to such phenomena. How this happens depends (as with everything else magical) on a mage's medium and paradigm, be it revealed in an Ecstatic's trance, foreshadowed by an Orphan's tarot casting, detected by an Etherite's scientific experiment or disseminated as data from a Void Engineer's failed Dimensional Science procedure. Transmissions from the Rogue Council (or directives from a Technocratic Construct or Control) are another possibility, but by no means the only one.

Experts mobilize Technocracy amalgams. Mentors enlighten Tradition mages of their dreams and visions. Marauders are naturally drawn to chaos through coincidence and misadventure. Nephandi are drawn to human suffering by depraved and heightened instincts. Visionaries have a vast array of reasons to investigate anomalous phenomena, if only to satisfy their own curiosity. Through the filter of their own perceptions and paradigm, they will witness the signs of Armageddon.

The First Sign: Incursions

Since before the dawn of recorded human history, the spirit world has remained separate from the physical world. Legends speak of a time before time, when a cosmic event separated the realms of flesh and spirit. If acolytes and initiates actually listen to the recitations of the Tradition instructors, they have learned many different versions of the same story, telling of a great "Shattering" that tore the two worlds apart. The boundary between worlds was once gossamer thin, and allegedly any man or woman could pass through it in sacred areas infused with magical energies. What has happened before could happen again.

To support these tales, followers of light have interpreted legends of faerie rings, junctures of ley lines or natural formations surging with feng shui energy as magical anachronisms from that earlier, more spiritual time. According to legendary stories, travelers could once use these magical nexus points to travel between worlds. Scholars of entropy (or agents of darkness) might counter that profane areas desecrated by blasphemous acts and atrocities allowed darker forces to enter our world. Many masters of archaic lore, including the mystics of various Houses within the Order of Hermes, claim that such events are merely less common than they were millennia ago. The formal term used to describe these unexpected travails between worlds is *Shallowing*.

Sons of Ether and Virtual Adepts scoff at such antiquated notions, preferring to study more quantifiable cases of sudden disappearances. As part of their scientific enlightenment, they seek Awakened explanations for alleged alien abductions, the formation of crop circles and widespread outbreaks of cattle mutilation. Yet all of these perceptions spring from the same source: supernatural events that temporarily breach the Gauntlet, the barrier between our world and its alternatives in the spirit world.

Mages have since become painfully aware that the structure of the Gauntlet is changing. As the End Times advance, even the most powerful willworkers find it dangerous to cross over into the Infinite Tapestry. Unless a mage can manipulate spirits to aid him (or die for him) as he passes through the spiritual Gauntlet surrounding this world, the great forces marshaling there will flay his very soul.

In fact, this barrier is now sufficient to keep the world's Masters and Oracles trapped outside Earthly reality. Such paragons have only begun to realize the true significance of the Avatar Storm and its effect on the Gauntlet. Many have speculated why the Gauntlet is stronger now than it ever was before, and a few have suspected the truth: This barrier is not merely composed of ephemeral spirits. At the height of the Reckoning, *living souls* bolstered the Gauntlet. Some might even dare to consider these shards as Awakened.

Only a few Masters realize this, and as an intimation of Armageddon, they would herald the End Times by uttering this fateful truth: *The Avatar Storm is composed of disincarnate Avatars.* Mages who cross the barrier between this world and the Otherworlds draw these shards toward them, for the only forces that can flay the very soul of a mage *are the shards of another Avatar.* These "Avatar shards" now surround our world… and their presence heralds greater transformations in the Gauntlet surrounding Earth.

Avatar Shards

Greater forces are at work. The disparate sects of the Celestial Chorus recite a common truth in many different voices: All souls are reflections of one harmonious source. While the Choristers represent a host of various religions, many are aware of the myth of *the One*, the wellspring from which all Creation came. When the One became many, it was divided into Nine Spheres, nine cosmic truths reinterpreted through the many varieties of magical practice.

Masters of magic trapped outside reality have begun to suspect deeper truths behind this story. Masters and Oracles have become disconnected from the Earth, destined to never return to the world we know, but some have learned much from their attunement with the infinite. Some visionaries witness "Avatar shards" adrift in the Void, Quintessential fragments drawn to the physical world, where they long to become incarnate. When the world was in balance, these shards would drift in the Void outside our world until drawn to the proper incarnation. Some theories posit that this could be the origin of magic in our world. As shards of the One, they drifted toward one world, where they empowered a chosen generation with the might of magic.

Only a few Oracles have dared to draw the same theory from these spiritual events: that shards of spirit from the Void might play a role in the Awakenings of mages. The very word "quintessence" refers to a "fifth element," a linguistic artifact of a time when all of natural Creation was said to be formed from earth, air, water and fire. Therefore, supernatural creations were considered to exist outside nature. All magical energy — such as Blood, Gnosis, passion and Glamour — holds a variant of this essential Quintessence.

Whether a mage requires this outside impetus or holds the potential within himself is a matter for debate. Yet, the recent experiment to draw one of these shards into an Enlightened agent (deep within an Arctic Construct) has shown that Avatar shards can bestow new possibilities to human hosts. Just as the word "Arete," in a sense, means "potential," it is possible that a human with the potential for magic can also awaken to great power when united with this quintessential essence.

Generations of willworkers have disputed whether all Sleepers have the potential for working magic, whether mages are destined to inherit such power, whether cosmic forces pass judgment on those who receive such gifts — in short, the origins of magic itself. The answers await us in the very act of our world's destruction. As the End Times advance, Avatar shards are descending to the Gauntlet in a vast and cosmic horde, desperate to get through to the realm of flesh before magical evolution reaches its ultimate conclusion. They are no longer there to keep alternatives to reality out of our world. *They are gathering in strength, attempting to get into our world.*

Some mages have already theorized that these Avatar shards are incomplete, or "un-Awakened," each one a separate entity seeking an Awakened host that can make it complete. A handful of Tradition Masters speculate that once spirit and flesh are united, the resulting creation could then hold the potential to return to its origins, rising into the heavens to return to the One source of all magic. Those that fail to reach this goal — this Ascension — might be destined for less desirable fates. The force of the One has been scattered across Creation, so now destiny, they say, must come full circle. All that has been shattered must be made whole… or dissipate into oblivion.

A heavenly host now waits on the doorstep of our world, on the fringes of Earthly reality. The combined force of all these Prime razors battering at the Gauntlet is finally *wearing through it.* In certain places, they have wormed their way through, creating holes into the spirit world. At first, these rifts in the barrier between worlds are only temporary, causing paranormal events that only a few Sleepers witness. Yet as humanity begins to suspect that the supernatural is real, as mankind realizes that alternatives exist to the world they know, the Gauntlet weakens. Consensus shifts… and spiritual creatures wander from the spirit worlds into material reality. The walls of reality are falling; the center cannot hold; incursions from the spirit world into the physical world fulfill the First Sign of Armageddon.

Shallowings

In spiritually significant places of the world, the Gauntlet between this world and the Otherworlds occasionally gives way, if only for an instant. For spirits that can materialize (using the eponymous Charm), it is an opportunity to fully manifest in the physical world — especially if the Gauntlet suddenly becomes weak (or practically nonexistent). When such freakish fluctuations occur, a spirit that can't materialize might find itself outside its natural element, lost and disoriented on the wrong side near where the Gauntlet once was.

As the Gauntlet begins to give way, isolated spirits might cross over into the physical world. Accordingly, individual Sleepers might encounter them, and be totally unprepared to respond to, or even interpret, what they see. As the first signs of Armageddon are revealed, ordinary people (or those with a minimal amount of attunement or Awareness) might *reinterpret* what they see in terms their mind can survive. Consider the dreams and visions mentioned earlier; now imagine them physically manifesting. Perhaps if enough of these events occur, these same kinds of witnesses might see spirits for what they are. That way lies madness.

The first instances of spiritual contact should be isolated, perhaps even ridiculed. An innocent citizen might *think* he's seen some otherworldly phenomenon he can't explain, but articulating it to other Sleepers would be nearly impossible. Mages (and werewolves) have a distinct advantage over the Masses: they are aware of vast hierarchies of Umbral spirits, possessing the Arete (or Gnosis) to define what they are.

Imagine how the average person would react to a sighting of a Bane or a Nexus Crawler… or a Paradox spirit. This doesn't mean the sensory data would conform to textbook (or sourcebook) definitions of spirits. A sighting might not rely on sight, for instance. A Sleeper might first notice the presence of a Wyld spirit by smell, sound, sudden glimpses of infrared or ultraviolet phenomena, symbolic (or Platonic) representations of what the spirit represents or if all other descriptions fail, a purely mundane manifestation with unexplained, anomalous or frightening complications.

Madness might force observers to reinterpret what they see (or smell, hear, etc.) to fit their own philosophy. Religious souls might witness revelations. Scientific scholars might attempt to quantify impossible phenomena. A recluse might scream from his rooftop that thousands of animals have infested his walls. A hedonist might succumb to alien sensations and new addictions. Children might encounter imaginary friends. Weaker minds might simply collapse. Isolated unfortunates become victims to these First Signs. As a more dangerous corollary, dangerous minds might interpret them as signs that such forces have *chosen* them, concluding that such an impossible event encountered them for a reason.

When ordinary Sleepers encounter the supernatural, it is inevitable that a cabal of mages will investigate one of these phenomena. Tradition mages might make tentative explorations. At first, their motivation to investigate might be to resolve such hysteria before someone more brutal (like an amalgam of Technocracy agents) rushes in to solve the problem with extreme methods. If the Technocracy finds out, it will mobilize forces to contain the surrounding area — or at least, send in the survivors of the last Tradition raid. Local law enforcement or representatives of the government might respond to such reports themselves, but they will honestly be unprepared for what they encounter.

Storytelling Incursions

A few humans will adapt to these unusual circumstances, possibly even gaining a glimpse of what these spirits really are. Perhaps they possess some low-level and previously undetected supernatural ability (may be as a result of having the Awareness or Occult Ability, or a Merit that makes them mediums). For added fear, such encounters could show a progression of events, as the rules of reality shift to favor spiritual forces.

Such a story might begin when a cabal tracks down an ordinary person who is obviously rationalizing an encounter with a spirit (preferably one that characters know can materialize). The description might involve religious mania, low-grade delusions or pop-culture occultism. Whatever the message is, it contains references that a mage can interpret as a description of a spirit. A similar event later occurs in the same area, but this time, the witness has succumbed to absolute madness. Whether through psychometry, speaking with spirits, Hermetic knowledge or analysis of magical resonance, the investigators then realize that a spirit that cannot normally enter the physical world has now found a way to do so. Reality has shifted slightly, if only temporarily, in a limited area.

Then launch another spiritual incursion, one in which a seemingly ordinary person can define what she has seen perfectly, perhaps with a clarity of detail normally reserved for mages with the Spirit Sphere. Fluctuations in the Gauntlet that allow such events should be temporary, at best. If mages can track the spirit to where it entered this world, they realize that the nearby Gauntlet appears weakened. Yet by the time the cabal confirms as much, the breach might then suddenly and inexplicably repair itself.

If a similar investigation takes place much later in the story, other forces might come through. A curious mage attempting to interact with this shattered barrier could coax an unexpected result: getting cut by Avatar shards, receiving a backlash from a tendril of the Avatar Storm in the physical world or even worse, realizing that his tampering has allowed something else to come through the rift. Spirits lead the first incursions; eventually, Avatar shards will follow.

Variations: If you're not afraid to "cross the streams," hunters work particularly well with this sort of story. Trained by continually slaughtering zombies, vampires and werewolves, they are often at a loss to explain what happens when a materialized spirit appears. Hunter-net is full of accounts of werewolf hunts and ghost slayings, but put one of the imbued up against an ephemeral entity like a Bane, Epiph or totem spirit, and he will suddenly find himself at a loss.

Primordial mages understand such spirits intimately. Hunters (and other Sleeper investigators) encountering such new phenomena will find themselves confronted with an opportunity to investigate an enigma. Lacking the Spirit Sphere, they might rely instead on sudden and overwhelming acts of violence to destroy what they cannot understand. When the first of these Shallowings occurs, it might be amusing to have imbued hunters receive visions of the same event… and use very crude methods to resolve it. This is sure to draw the attention of the cabal's enemies, government investigations or Technocratic reprisal — though such concerns won't matter very much soon.

Technocratic Variations

At this stage, a cabal of mages might find an area of spiritual incursions where the Gauntlet has temporarily been breached. A Marauder might be drawn to a witness's madness; a Nephandus might seek a troubled soul whose faith has been shaken. If Tradition mages can't scry where an incursion has occurred, they're certainly likely to notice the responses of groups like the Technocracy. The Union cannot mobilize the overwhelming response it once could, but a spiritual invasion motivates Loyalists and rogue Technocrats alike. (If the story include elements of **Manifesto**, this would be a good place to introduce Panopticon, a Technocratic organization that cuts across Convention lines to unite in defense of the Technocracy's ideals.)

Wherever reality gives way, the Union attempts to send in its agents, like an immune system for the world's reality. Some outsiders might consider its responses extreme, especially when "Reality Deviants" (or even innocent witnesses) get caught in the crossfire. The Union, however, has been fighting for centuries to defend (what it sees as) Consensus: the reality created by humankind. The alternative is chaos. More precisely, the alternative is the events that follow, the early stages of Armageddon.

When a spiritual incursion occurs, a Tradition mage might find it suspicious that the Union has gathered an unusually high concentration of personnel in an extremely limited area. Through Awakened sight, it is obvious that someone is using a bit of Syndicate spin doctoring (or NWO mind control) over the local news. Iteration X patrols might increase for a limited period of time. While the Union doesn't have the centralized organization it once did, autonomous amalgams might requisition resources to move on any "Incursion Areas" where a Shallowing has occurred.

Now consider a follow-up story in which evidence of the same sort of activity has occurred, but the Technocracy isn't there. Tradition mages might be tempted to solve the situation by themselves… before the Union uses its own heavy-handed measures. The real threat at that point would not be the Technocracy (since it has other places to concentrate its resources). After this, the next crackdown might occur at the behest of local law enforcement, government agents or the military. Such agencies might also seal off an area where an incursion has occurred, but they will be far less prepared than either the Traditions or Technocracy.

When Sleepers respond to supernatural events, including local law enforcement and government agencies, they present different complications than Technocratic investigators do. Mages are mortal, after all, with lives outside of Tradition gatherings and ritual ceremonies. The sorts of complications that result should foreshadow the fact that ordinary Sleepers are slowly *becoming aware* of what is going on, even if they don't understand it. That's a theme that should grow as the early signs of an Armageddon chronicle occur. In fact, it's even possible that an incursion or Shallowing will occur in a place where a mage's loved ones or family lives. These Sleeper relations might even be among the first witnesses, forcing mages who have hidden their true natures for years to seek acceptance.

Futher Incursions: The Dead Return

Haunts resonating with death energy might also experience similar fluctuations. Wraiths have been trapped outside the lands of the Quick for years now. In a chronicle inhabited by Euthanatoi or other scholars of death, a stray encounter with a ghost can heighten tension at this stage of your story. The Maelstrom has eradicated much of the Shadowlands that ghosts frequent, and many Euthanatoi suspect this by now. Yet as the barriers of reality are tested, a spirit might find a way to slip through the cracks. Entropy has an odd way of defying expectations, after all.

Storytelling: Using whatever incarnation of ghostly lore you prefer, this story line begins when you release a lone ghost into your chronicle. (Purists might prefer to adapt the spirit-creation rules; inventive types might adapt recently published sourcebooks about ghosts; anachronists might resurrect out-of-print books about wraiths. For the sake of this story, it really doesn't matter.) The spirit has seen first-hand the destruction wrought in the Shadowlands, and he might be able to communicate this to someone in the cabal with the Spirit Sphere. The apparition is probably quite weak, perhaps fading away as the mages encounter it.

When humans begin to witness other ghosts, they might make the same rationalizations described previously... or such events could confirm privately held beliefs they have harbored for years. For all appearances, witnesses might actively deny that anything supernatural is involved. The brave few who dare make such disclosures could be ridiculed on the local news, in supermarket tabloids or as they relate such stories while drinking heavily in local bars. Nonetheless, a few visionary individuals break this mold, daring to question commonly held beliefs. They gain more courage as they find more evidence that *they are right*. In fact, near the end of this stage, a few humans begin to see these spirits as they truly are (perhaps by virtue of the Awareness Ability).

Consider the impact of a chronicle in which more people begin to believe in the existence of ghosts. Now contemplate what happens when Consensus shifts, as magic involving death and resurrection becomes more believable... and more plausible. Once a few humans believe the supernatural is real, of course, the shifting boundaries of reality should make it easier for other spirits (ghostly

or otherwise) to return. While this isn't a necessary series of events, it could be the beginning of grand revelations about the existence of the occult world — or the impetus to launch a massive backlash against all magic or supernatural activity in your chronicle. It really depends on how you decide to describe your chronicle's version of Armageddon.

> ### Further Prophecies
>
> In any chronicle, dangerous stories are easier to detail when the Storyteller has an outline (or timeline) of how events proceed. The critical path presented here — from incursions and invasions to the world's annihilation — represents the early stages of an Armageddon chronicle. Each reveals signs of Creation's ultimate destiny. Of course, these details shouldn't preclude you from detailing other events, elaborating with one of the stories in the next five chapters or using this launching pad to leap off in an entirely different direction. Whatever catastrophe you have in mind, it becomes more probable if you can foreshadow and prepare for it.
>
> Prophecy is a powerful method of foreshadowing these signs. In fact, a prophecy doesn't need to disclose *everything* that is to occur. A simple chronicle might involve choosing a series of events for these four signs (or seven signs or more, depending on the length of the chronicle). If you can create a narrative, poetry or trail of clues that foreshadows these signs, good roleplayers will do all they can to build their own rationalizations, hierarchies, theories and explanations of what is happening (just as Sleepers will, oddly enough).
>
> A chain of six or seven events is more than enough to support a final chronicle, one that gives direction to the story at a time when some characters would otherwise succumb to fatalism, suicidal last-ditch attempts to save the world, degeneration into madness, apathy or ambivalence. Giving the heroes a hint of what is to come empowers them, giving them an edge others don't have… and thus making them important in the events that are to follow. If all else fails, they can take what they know to mages who are more powerful than they are. (Even then, that should prevent them from building a bomb shelter and checking out of the story.) Bestowing prophecies is merely one of the simplest methods of motivating your plot; for other tools to use while taking apart Creation, see Chapter Seven: Designing Ascension.

The Second Sign: Invasion

Your mage might have cursed the inconvenience (and later, the retribution) of the Gauntlet each time he passed through it, but truthfully, the barrier was there for a damn good reason. A willworker is extremely fortunate to have the ability to pass through the Gauntlet to worlds outside his own. He is even more blessed that other entities to do not have the ability to cross it into his own world. Certainly, some charmed spirits are able to materialize in the realm of flesh, but never permanently… at least, not until unforeseen acts of Armageddon change everything.

Incarnae Awaken, the Chosen Gather

Powerful supernatural forces have remained hidden from humanity since the dawn of time. Whether astral, Umbral or trapped in the Underworld, these various entities are ranked in assorted hierarchies and pantheons. A master of Cosmology might be familiar with only a few of these spiritual orders. Shamans (and werewolves) might be familiar with the spiritual servitors of Incarna. Hermetics and Choristers might study the celestial hierarchies of angels. Astral travelers, Ecstatic escapists and Akashic masters of Mind might have read of the courts of Preceptors and Umbrood dwelling outside reality. Verbena, of course, might simply seek the pantheons of ancient gods, eager to interpret what they find in the guises of deities they understand.

The Avatar Storm has isolated Earth's reality from its alternatives, but in moments when the barriers shallow, cosmic forces might reach across this schism. If judgment is at hand, Umbral forces might choose individuals to act as their avatars. The thought of even one hierarchy or pantheon acting in this way can produce disturbing results, especially when ordinary men and women are chosen for such contact. Considering the diversity of beliefs mages hold, a more extensive series of events could seriously undermine reality as we know it.

As spiritual activity mounts, a few ordinary people might find ways to commune with these seemingly "godlike" powers. This communion could be as incidental as humans having dreams about astral courts, or it could be as overt as groups of ordinary humans actually worshipping such powers. Cults form in remote regions. New drugs open gateways of perception. Sacrifices are offered to propitiate cosmic forces. Rituals performed by Sleepers might have unexpected results when the barriers between worlds give way. One word describes Sleepers who encounter such vast and terrifying powers: *the Chosen*.

An ordinary human making contact could then believe in her destiny as one of the Chosen… or she might collapse from the strain in a bout of insanity. It is unlikely that such an individual would actually be bestowed with great power, unless the "Chosen One's soul" was imbued with *something* allowing her to overcome her former limitations. That is unthinkable, of course — until you consider *an Avatar shard bestowing such power*. Keep reading.

Anakim and Psychopomps

Transmissions from the Rogue Council have suggested a possible invasion from outside the world we know. Revelations from a cryptic source called "the Sphinx" have led many mages to the same enigma. Mergers of flesh and spirit are creating higher beings. Alien outsiders have chosen to possess a handful of willing human vessels, granting them spiritual abilities unknown to the modern world. Yet the Anakim have walked the Earth before.

In ages past, spiritual "Psychopomps" guided Avatars to carefully chosen individuals, granting them sorcerous and magical power. Whether their purpose was to shepherd souls to Ascension, fulfill forgotten destinies or further some other cryptic agenda remains a point of debate, at least among occult historians. In the Dark Fantastic age of the 15th century, Psychopomps silently went about their work. Even during the height of conflict between the Order of Reason and the Nine Traditions, this heavenly host chose vessels for their celestial power. Less than a century later, mages began to notice the presence of these spirits… and soon thereafter, the Psychopomps fled our world. (If further details are required, consult **The Infinite Tapestry**.)

Centuries later, at the turn of the millennium, a secret and sinister experiment in a Technocracy Construct applied forbidden procedures to summon a swarm of alien spirits, forcing them to merge with dozens of meticulously selected Enlightened psychics. The technicians never realized the power these spirits possessed. Almost all of test subjects died; only one survived. The capabilities of this one survivor, Peter Wu, exceeded all expectations. His powers have since been tested under scientific (and martial) conditions. A few witnesses to his abilities have concluded that if one of these spirits merges with an Enlightened agent (or Awakened mage), the subject transforms into a greater being, one with power over souls… and the barriers between worlds.

Technocracy supervisors have since disavowed all knowledge of this experiment, claiming it to be the work of rogue agents, deviants who have summoned up something they cannot put down. Yet a few arrogant Technocratic analysts have managed to access evidence of this experiment… and have drawn disturbing conclusions. Some have even suggested that by "harvesting" more of these spirits, they might breed a new generation of soldiers. They are seriously mistaken, since they operate under the delusion that the experimenters actually *controlled* these entities.

What Dreams Are Made Of

The first invasions into the physical world will inevitably be seen by witnesses who don't understand what is happening. When such forces manifest, Sleeper witnesses must struggle to redefine what they see. Then again, such incursions don't have to take place in the realm of flesh. Visionaries proficient in the ways of spirit know of other realms just outside the one we know. Much has been written on the subject of Dream Realms, by authors referring to such disparate concepts as Chimerae, Oneirae and the Dreaming.

Chimerae allow strange new revelations of reality. By some accounts, powerful dreamers allegedly create pocket realms around their sleeping bodies, dimensions that malefic spirits might infest or inhabit. (Some speculate that certain species of vampires have also displayed these "dreamwalking" abilities.) When the barriers between worlds are shallow, dreaming spirits might not want to risk infesting the harsh physical world. Instead, they might choose to find their Chosen Ones in dreams.

Another possibility concerns the Periphery, the area students of spirits know as the realm between the physical world and the spirit world of the Penumbra. In moments of great reverie — or states of altered consciousness — dreamers, visionaries and poets might sense spiritual forces in the Periphery, if only for a moment. For spirits that cannot quite breach the Gauntlet, it might be possible for such outside forces to make contact with such delicate and vulnerable souls.

Dreamers and visionaries would make excellent vessels, conduits or avatars for outside forces. Only a poet might be able to articulate what he saw in the midst of such a reverie, and through words, he would call to others who would understand. A cult of psychedelic scholars might use some powerful chemistry to reach across the boundaries of reality; they would be prepared for contact when Avatar shards claim them. When Sleepers Awaken and the Chosen are called, dreamers might lead the way.

Hermetic Masters and magical scholars would be able to supply an additional, desperately needed data point: Historically, the merger of Psychopomp spirit and Awakened mage was always a willing one. The experimenters believed that they selected Peter Wu… but it is just as possible that the Psychopomps exploited an opening into this world, choosing Wu for their *own* alien agenda. It might be that the alien spirits have controlled the agents who "summoned" them…

Drawing upon the powers of their possessing spirits, Anakim can now control disembodied Avatars. The most obvious application of this potential is mastery over the Avatar Storm, but as the End Times advance, their powers might grow. Hopefully, this new generation of Anakim meets with historical expectations… otherwise, the world's mystics are unprepared for what is to come.

The Heavenly Host

In this stage of the world's annihilation, more Anakim will walk the Earth. One lone Anakim should be sufficient to elicit alarm, confirming that an invasion has begun. To an ordinary human, this entity appears as human as any other citizen of the common populace. Aware humans (such as those with the Awareness trait, or possibly Kinfolk and other half-breeds with immunity to Delirium) might suspect that such an entity is somehow different. Mages researching occult lore might even guess at their agenda. For many, they are simply heralds of the End Times, the agents of change.

Their purpose will soon be apparent; for now, observers must depend on appearances. An Anakim seems slightly out of touch with reality, without demonstrating any outward manifestation of occult origin. When a Psychopomp merges with a mage (or an agent), the Anakim also develops a hidden "true form," one that hints at the higher being's greater power (at least, as interpreted by the possessed mage). As in so many mystic phenomena, the mage's paradigm defines his possibilities. The Anakim's (former) Tradition or Convention provides the most general indicator of the union that will result.

Seeing an Anakim's "true form" is not an obvious observation. (At least one success on an Arete roll is required; the appropriate Sphere should really be left to your imagination.) All mages will see the same true appearance behind a human façade, gaining a glimpse into the Anakim's potential. For instance, the first Anakim of our millennia — a New World Order Technocrat — transformed into a hybridization of human and alien flesh. Further possibilities are yet to come, as evinced by a few salient examples.

Scientific mages who become Anakim (perhaps including visionary Technocrats, Sons of Ether and Virtual Adepts) might draw from scientific lore when developing their new powers. Behind a human façade, the closest approximation of an Anakim's appearance fits with lore of other alien invasions. Anyone who has even performed a casual perusal of such documentation might define the creature as a "Gray": an entity with gray skin, wide eyes and slightly elongated features. Other possibilities include machine men, automatons or electrical avatars.

When seeking Anakim, Etherites and Adepts might use television cameras to filter out misperceptions of an Anakim's human appearance. Technocrats have a wide array of devices for filtering out magical illusions… as well an old standby procedure involving mirrorshade sunglasses. Furthermore, Technocrats might have the clearance to learn that after the Second World War, the Men in Black were authorized to search for such phenomena. It is entirely possible that they have been on Earth before… or perhaps sightings of these "Grays" were merely tricks of Paradox, episodes of madness that hinted at the real threat of alien vision that lay in their future.

Religious mages chosen by Psychopomps assume celestial guises. Whether seen through Awareness or Arete perception, the "true form" of this otherworldly choir might match the Anakim's own expectations of the heavenly host. "Angels" now walk among us, at least according to some definitions of the word. A time of judgment is at hand, and although the Anakim are far from limitless in their power, their immunity to the Avatar Storm gives them a great advantage over willworkers who are unprepared for the world to come.

Mages who are familiar with apocalyptic revelations or Enochian magic (including the Celestial Chorus and certain scholars of the Order of Hermes) might find celestial and angelic sightings encouraging. Some will not see the Anakim as a threat, but as saviors. After all, they have come from the heavens to herald the End Times. And indeed, like many incarnations of celestial Avatars, they have an innate power to bring redemption to the saintly… or damnation to the diabolical.

Shamanistic or otherwise spiritual mages (perhaps including Dreamspeakers, Cultists of Ecstasy or even certain Euthanatoi) selected by celestial entities might gain true forms resembling primordial or totemic spirits. These higher beings appear to the insightful as avatars for primitive gods (or even Incarnae). Yet for spiritualists who have tasted the pain the Gauntlet now has to offer, it might be clear that whatever bolstered that barrier with the ability to flay Awakened souls exists within each Anakim. It is as though that deadly force has fused with human flesh… and now walks among us. It is as though agents of the Avatar Storm are roaming our world, as scouts for the storm.

Verbena Anakim might appear as reincarnations of an ancient power, known to learned masters of lore (and perhaps characters with the Occult or Cosmology Knowledge) as fetches. The Verbena's spoken history long predates written history, though it has, of course, been distorted by bias across the millennia. (In fact, memories of the origins of the Anakim might be accessible only with five successes on a Dream Background roll.) At the dawn of time, the Psychopomps, as part of a higher court of astral entities, sired children through carefully chosen human paramours. The Stormwardens of the modern age are distant descendents of these "plane-touched" paragons.

The Anakim have since returned to the world with the power of the original generation. Part flesh and part spirit, their new incarnations walk between worlds. Awakened Anakim, empowered by the Psychopomps' mysterious powers, are here to fulfill alien agendas. Debates over their true purpose should heat up during the second stage. One prevalent theory is that they are here on behalf of disembodied Avatars, attempting to guide them to "chosen" Sleepers before the arrival of Armageddon… just as Psychopomps guided Avatars to chosen mages centuries ago.

The Avatar Storm has torn the chaos of the Otherworlds from the static reality trapped in Earth's domain. Fearful mages might suspect that the Anakim have arrived to correct that imbalance. Whether their actions will drown the world in an etheric sea, silence the force of magic in the world or trap Creation in a dystopian reality for all eternity remains to be seen. Whatever their purpose is, the arrival of the first Anakim heralds Armageddon. And to further complicate matters, the fulfillment of this sign is by no means the only way in which the world can end.

Variations

Far more unusual variants can advance this stage. The race descending upon Earth does not have to be the Anakim, of course. This elder race is mutable enough to advance any of the five story lines that follow, and mages of different paradigms might see them different ways. Suppose that these Old Ones corresponded to only *one* paradigm; they could then define a religious, magical or scientific theme to Armageddon. This dangerous option warrants careful consideration. For example, if the end of the world has religious overtones and every character in the cabal is a Virtual Adept or Etherite, you're going to be in for a very strange chronicle.

With other paradigms, however, come other opportunities and tragedies. Learned masters of lore have hinted that other alien races might exist on other

The Second Sign: Technocratic Responses

As more shards and spirits enter the world, Technocrats have their own alternatives to dealing with this crisis. Hunting the invaders is one obvious objective; neutralizing Avatar shards is another. Either agenda might be futile, but after centuries of subterfuge, it is unlikely that the Union will not organize the best resistance it can. The Technocracy does not have limitless resources (especially not at this time), which means that it must be willing to sacrifice other objectives to focus on either of these goals. That might give zealous Tradition mages a chance to score "victories" against the Technocracy… and in the process, cripple the Union's chances of at least postponing Armageddon.

Capturing or destroying all Anakim would be an epic task (especially if you believe that other agencies of the Union were responsible for summoning them here). Hunting down Avatar shards is a more effective objective. In fact, observing Psychopomp spirits (perhaps under controlled laboratory conditions) might eventually lead to some understanding of how Avatar shards can be controlled. If a Void Engineer's Dimensional Science is capable of affecting the Gauntlet, perhaps such "technology" can be altered to capture these Avatar shards. Intense mental (or psychic) processes or conditioning might even allow an Enlightened Scientist to absorb these shards without getting cut.

Such innovations depend on inspiration, however. Hidebound, "loyalist" Technocrats lack the creativity to solve these problems. In fact, many are more obsessed with stopping agents who are inventing new procedures for dealing with these new challenges. Inventors who succeed, and survive, tread the edge between Technocrats and technomancers. They might find a way to liberate the world, or solidify the Gauntlet forever. Or perhaps, in their arrogance and hubris, they might try to exploit this technology for their own advantage, endangering the very world they attempt to control.

worlds, each with its own views of reality. Consider these alternative stories:

• The first invasion might appear as an attempt at colonization from a race beyond the stars. The invaders might be the citizens of some Umbral colony that is desperately trying to fall to Earth to avoid becoming entirely ephemeral.

• A greater race, such as the long-forgotten Zigg'raugglurr, infused with the power of one of Nine Spheres, might set itself against the Avatars of the other eight.

• The last fragments of a ghostly Hierarchy could descend upon humanity, breaching the Shroud that has contained the Shadowlands.

• For scholars of the esoteric, the invaders could be a lost race from within Earth itself, such as Atlanteans beneath the seas, Arcadian fae returning to Earth or dero from the Hollow World.

Regardless of the means that these outsiders have used to cross into this world (technological, spiritual, magical, psychic or otherwise), their methods strain the Gauntlet even further. Avatar shards present them with an opportunity — and empower the Chosen to aid them. As the Third Sign manifests, Earth's spiritual defense system will be weakened. Like a disease, an infection, a cancerous corruption or a quirk of evolution, this foreign body threatens mankind's survival… at least, the survival of humanity as we know it. Great powers might rework the world (and reality) in their image; only mages would have the strength of will to oppose such efforts.

The Third Sign: Abductions and Awakenings

From this point on, the possibilities for the world's demise expand, branching out heuristically into forking paths of probability and entropy. Any one of the destinies in the next several chapters might begin around this time. In fact, they might deviate greatly from the events described here. For each of these fates, dozens more are possible. Regardless of the details, the general theme remains the same: The accelerating collapse of the barrier surrounding the Earth allows extradimensional phenomena to take more drastic actions in the physical world.

Rapture

As the barriers between worlds fall, recorded instances of Shallowings and incursions increase, despite all paranoid attempts to disavow all knowledge of them. Government denials, Technocracy quarantines and lies on the eleven o'clock news cannot silence the urban legends and viral rumors of such events spreading like panic throughout the Masses. As the gaps in the Gauntlet grow wider, it should become apparent that such breaches not only allow outside forces into this world, but allow the possibility for certain humans to leave this world. Such might happen by accident… or it could happen because something from outside has a reason to *take* them.

The Awakened and imbued are no doubt likely victims, but some events might be as prosaic as documented cases of unexplained disappearances, "alien abductions," near-death experiences or even encounters with the worlds of the fae… or the dead. A vast array of possibilities arises as a result. Sleeper wanderers stumble into an Umbral wilderness. Lost children hear whispers from predatory ghosts and Unseelie faeries. Seekers after horror never return to the world we know. Whatever the paradigm, the meaning is the same: Humans begin to disappear.

At first, such occurrences should be rare, mere foreshadowing. (Perhaps one or two "missing persons" cases take up an entire chapter in a chronicle, as the characters are called upon to research what they falsely think is an isolated incident.) The locations of such events should correspond to the usual locales for paranormal phenomena. Whether the story demands an isolated stretch of wilderness, an allegedly haunted house or a legendary location like Loch Ness or the Winchester Mystery House should depend on the cabal, cult or amalgam that investigates. Less exotic stories might feature more prosaic locations, such as dark alleyways, tent cities of homeless, playgrounds at midnight, dumping grounds for corpses and so on.

As darkness falls upon the world, such rifts in space and time will become more frequent, drifting toward the more calcified, static places in our world. Spiritual adepts should realize that the Gauntlet is usually impermeable in these locations… but no longer. Whether all hell breaks loose in an isolated laboratory or downtown Manhattan depends on the variety of apocalypse you prefer.

Supernatural investigators might struggle to find a pattern to such events or a commonality in the victims involved. The most common victims show some potential for magic, either because they had some untapped power (such as Awareness) or were *destined to become mages*. Predictive magic (such as tarot castings or Technocratic analysis) has been known to uncover a few individuals with the possibility to awaken with magical (or psionic or Enlightened) ability. Looking deeper, investigators should discover that there is residual evidence (perhaps Resonance) of disturbances in the Gauntlet where these events occurred.

As these events become more common, mages should be drawn to them, whether by free will, curiosity or (as an old stand-by of this genre) acts masquerading as coincidence. As always, where magic happens, mages ask questions. Yet such investigations should also be dangerous. If a human disappeared in such a rift, other forces might have also come through it. A tear in the Gauntlet might allow a swarm of Avatar shards to rush at an incautious mage, lashing out with spiritual damage (just as the Gauntlet normally would). Specific Sleepers attract these Avatars, leading to more unthinkable consequences.

By the time the pattern is revealed, the amount of magic in the world increases. Sleepers begin to Awaken with increasing frequency — an event that's certain to bring back bad memories. Mages will remember quite distinctly (perhaps as a result of a Prelude long ago), the horror and wonder of Awakening to the possibilities of the supernatural. It is as though the forces of reality had passed judgment on these lost souls, accepting them into a higher stage of evolution — or damning them with unexpected destruction. The days of judgment are at hand. When they arrive, souls might be found wanting. The strong-willed gain limited magical powers; the weak-willed go mad.

Congregations of Souls

Each human has a shard of Quintessence within: a fragment of Prime, an active Mind, and (one would hope) a soulful Spirit of some kind. According to some mystics and paragons of the Celestial Chorus (and a previous description in this chapter), all Creation springs from a single source: the One. Creation shattered the One into the shards of reality; the Nine Spheres are merely reflections of this. All magic is but the reflection of the One. All religions are reflections of light from this single source of illumination. Perhaps cosmic events might draw the fragments of this shattered world back together. If so, the results transcend such boundaries as "identity" and "individuality."

Avatar shards can kill, or they might select hosts randomly, but the early signs of Armageddon are more believable if the Sleepers who encounter these shards find them for a *reason*. (What that reason is determines the theme and mood of your chronicle.) And of course, the Chosen destined to receive these Avatar shards don't have to face their destiny alone. As the Gauntlet falls, fate might bring them together, through dreams, visions and nightmares.

Each mage, when he or she awakens to magic, has a natural affinity for one of the nine Spheres. Nine potential mages, brought into one location, might become "whole" in a sense, united as one. Once mages have come to accept the frequency of abductions and Awakenings, the first group of abductions (or Awakenings) should occur. A cult of nine might venture into the wilderness together, only to disappear without a trace. Perhaps they would all Awaken together, forming a cabal with unusually powerful bonds between them. Or perhaps a group of Sleepers who disappeared earlier returns when the Third Sign is revealed, acting as one.

Each cult needs a purpose. A congregation of souls could seek other Chosen, sacrifice Sleepers to rapture or abduction, or seek out more powerful mages (such as Nephandi or Marauders) to lead them. It is equally likely that they are united in one objective: summoning

> ### Variations: Magic Kills
>
> As a sinister alternative, supernatural forces reaching across the Gauntlet might not actually awaken Sleepers at all — they might destroy them. Potential mages, low-level psychics, hedge magicians and similar sorcerers are the first to die in this scenario. As the rifts in the Gauntlet increase, the alien forces gradually seek out mages with greater power. The last Masters left on Earth, the survivors of the Avatar Storm who were not exiled from Creation, are the last hope to stem this incoming tide… or perhaps they are merely the last to die.
>
> How such deadly forces are seen corresponds to the paradigm of Awakened and Enlightened witnesses. Storms wrack the world, or higher powers descend from the heavens. Once Hermetic Masters battled Bygone beasties, from dragons to giants. Marauders might indulge in "zooterrorism" to marshal such forces, and ancient powers might return to destroy the last great sorcerers. Dragons and wizards might battle again, this time atop the skyscrapers of the world. Aliens or angels might transform humanity.
>
> An inventive Storyteller can launch this timeline into any permutation of catastrophe he chooses, especially when the end of the final chronicle is at hand. It is difficult to sustain these over-the-top options for long, however. They either offer quick-and-dirty ways to end a chronicle or trap the Storyteller in a recursive loop in which events must become increasingly improbable to shock the players any further. Caution is advised.

more Avatar shards from the world's Gauntlet, creating a cult of servants to the Anakim. Humans might disappear or transform one by one, or they might create the new apocalyptic cults to herald the End Times. Mages seeking one of the Anakim could follow leads to a cult that is about to form. Those who can see beyond the veil of the world's deceptions might witness gatherings of the Chosen. A new age, the final age, is at hand.

Phenomenon Magnets

At some later stage of the chronicle, mages might take desperate measures to alter the course of history. Once a mage (or a player) believes that the end of the world (or chronicle) is at hand, karma and retribution become less tangible. Why not attempt some mighty magic to heal the world? What have you got to lose? The answer is appropriately poetic: everything.

A mage who acts against what's left of the Consensus could actually accelerate its unraveling. A Paradox Backlash might, in addition to lashing the mage with damage, actually summon one of the apocalyptic phenomena mentioned earlier: incursions, abductions, disappearances, unwanted Awakenings, Avatar shards tearing through the Gauntlet, cult retribution and so on. Such events might affect Sleepers in the immediate area in one of the following ways:

• A Paradox Backlash that would normally summon a Paradox spirit instead allows an Umbral (or astral) spirit to temporarily manifest in this world, weakening the nearby Gauntlet.

• A Backlash that normally inflicts "witches' burns" of aggravated damage might actually draw Prime shards across the Gauntlet to lash the incautious mage... and then set them loose in the immediate area.

• A Backlash that normally affects a mage with unexplainable phenomena (such as milk curdling or a watch ceasing to function for an hour) instead affects a human near the mage, or with some link to the mage... or calls to the closest of the Chosen ahead of schedule.

Variant Awakenings

As the End Times advance, Sleepers attract Avatars shards, which can Awaken them. The criteria by which they are judged might correspond to a recurring theme. In an apocalypse of religious significance, paragons of virtue (or degenerates steeped in sin) might act as catalysts for this change. This last generation of mages could be lost souls who were destined for greater goals but never had the chance to fulfill them.

Stranger resolutions are possible. They might be united as the inheritors of a long-forgotten legacy, the descendents of a lost dynasty or the last remaining offspring of the fae. They might be the Chosen People of one race, nationality or religion. Or perhaps instead of the Chosen, there are actually soulless humans in our midst, empty shells waiting to be filled by forces from beyond. In the last event, imagine a Spirit mage's reaction when she encounters a soulless human for the first time... and then finds the same person later, transformed. The possibilities are as endless as alternatives to reality.

This last generation of the Awakened might have all the powers of a mage, or they might only have one variety of magical power. Maybe the cults who Awaken all share the same Sphere, creating cabals of telepaths, spiritualists or visionaries who seek out sources of Quintessence. Consider a world where mankind, in its own defense, suddenly evolved cultists who could perform only countermagic, hunters who could seek out and nullify those who defy consensual reality. Posit the idea of a generation capable of only communal magic — drawn to each other to perform the one great rite that heralds Armageddon. The breaking of nine seals might bring nine Spheres to the world, granting them one by one to the final generation. The servants of an Incarna or Antediluvian could perform that very act that summons their "god" from torpid slumber, exile or oblivion.

Whatever the motive dwelling in the collective unconscious of these shards is, the humans who possess them would be suddenly infused with great power. Their magic could be minor, consisting of the first rank or two of a given Sphere, or legendary acts of heroism could manifest. With such power comes temptation... and the retribution of Paradox.

Mortal Responses

Don't think for a moment that mortals will be helpless as the final signs are revealed. Humanity has a remarkable ability to adapt to changing circumstances. (If we weren't adaptive, evolution would have turned out much differently.) For every widespread panic, a leader tries to calm the populace. For every plague or scientific catastrophe, a scientist struggles to find a solution. While the vast majority of humanity might be content to listen to countless hours of experts blathering the importance of their own interpretations over cable television and the Internet, any Armageddon chronicle can feature a few heroes with the strength to stand against impossible odds.

With every hero, there are also villains (or at least, misguided would-be heroes). Drastic measures call for drastic action — or (again) well-intentioned, misguided actions. At some point during an Armageddon chronicle, humanity's ability to rationalize away the presence of the supernatural will completely and utterly break down. Witnessing one impossible event makes it possible to accept other unimaginable occurrences. With that in mind, you must decide the point at which even the most oblivious human must say, "Why yes, I suppose vampires do exist." ("Were they here before the angels arrived?")

Once humanity realizes the open and obvious existence of the supernatural, people will respond in immediate and dangerous ways. Isolated humans might attempt to remain rational while the masses panic. Fear can lead ordinary citizens to take arms. Panic stirs governments to pass new and entirely illegal legislation to oppose the forces of the occult and enemies they do not understand. Militaries and law-enforcement authorities, for all their discipline and training, succumb to the xenophobic agenda of all-too-human commanders. And at the top of these chains of command, world leaders have weapons that can destroy their world as surely as any supernatural event could. At some point during this very supernatural series of events, be prepared for the rest of the human race to make their own drastic, last-ditch efforts. The backlash goes much further than citizens stockpiling duct tape and sealing all the doors and windows of their houses. Mages, if they are openly seen as supernatural, can become a target and a focus for all this madness.

Make contingency plans for this part of the story. Plan for it, because once you reveal that monsters are real, *there is no turning back*. Just as in the early parts of the story, you might feel a temptation to immediately resort to overkill, but empowering entire nations with sweeping agendas and dangerous actions can make the heroes relatively powerless. Once again, you must take your time when unraveling these consequences.

It might be best to use an "eleven o'clock news" approach each session. Instead of suddenly bombarding the story with mortal responses, think of what the top two or three stories are on the news that day. For example, consider what would happen if Sleepers begin to Awaken on a grand scale. Once rare events become almost commonplace, it is inevitable that humanity will figure out what is going on, even if they can't see it with Awakened sight. While they might not openly refer to what they find as ghosts, vampires or spirits, they might filter such events through a screen of everyday affairs, couching events in terms the average citizen would not find as frightening.

Examples of such news stories might include:

• A police raid on a suspected coven of witches in New England, suspected of links to a local outbreak of disease.

• One of the Anakim is listed as one of the FBI's Ten Most Wanted. To anyone who is not among the paranoid populace, however, the crimes against him seem falsified.

• A religious leader (actually a Celestial Chorister) appears before the state (or provincial) government, demanding leniency against the practitioners of pagan and alternative religions.

• Stories report a series of freak accidents tied to a local teenager, who is then taken into police custody without charges filed or a formal arrest made.

• Dozens of local citizens with ties to a martial arts dojo (a front for the Akashic Brotherhood) are alleged to have been taken to a nearby internment camp.

• A local software company (a Virtual Adept chantry) is raided by the government for hacker technology (the spontaneously generated effects of several programmers Awakening).

• An open-air rock concert, underground rave or gathering in the desert leads to small cults coming together (and Awakening) during the use of the same illicit drug… or dying en masse from a freak event of nature (Avatar shards swarming across the Gauntlet to destroy them).

In the early stages of an Armageddon chronicle, Technocratic crackdowns might seem severe. It should be obvious to Tradition mages that amalgams of operatives are working overtime to cover up supernatural events, either through abductions, Syndicate spin doctoring, NWO mind control or mundane influence. As extreme as these measures might seem, they are harsh for a reason: responses from a panicked populace or from government authorities can be just as bad or much, much worse.

The Technocracy has developed procedures over time for dealing with such events. Governments, by contrast, should be prone to react to sudden fluctuations in public opinion, skewed polls, general panic and the need to demonstrate their own authority. Don't take such stories as thinly veiled polemics against events in our own world, though. They simply reinforce that everything in the World of Darkness is "darker" and more dangerous than in our own.

Further Signs: Speculation and Annihilation

Beyond this point, many possible futures await; five of them are revealed in the chapters that follow. From here, early stages of any Armageddon chronicle must accelerate toward its conclusion and denouement. Since these are *possible* conclusions, fortunetellers, prophets and scholars of the Time Sphere might see visions that confirm any one of them — even if none of them are true.

Destruction will spread as the End Times advance, but whether it heralds the end of everything or the dawn of a new age remains to be seen. Mages might be slaughtered in hordes or transformed into *something else*. The Awakened might die in the streets or ascend to worlds beyond. Civilization might fall, or a new order might arise to take its place. Chaos can rule all, or all magic can die. Whatever Earth's destiny is, this penultimate stage of Armageddon takes place as the world is overwhelmed with supernatural phenomena. A chronicle in this stage is destined to end quickly as all Hell breaks loose… perhaps literally.

In an Armageddon chronicle, the Storyteller should finally consider how each Tradition, each society and most importantly, each character will react. That last group is the most important. Instead of merely being witnesses, the cabal (as represented by the players) must have the opportunity to act. How they act must determine their final judgment. The rest is all a prelude to that revelation.

Legends of the Fall

Until the presence of supernatural and apocalyptic forces become overwhelming in your chronicle, human civilization is propped up by a façade of lies. Humans cannot survive encounters with the many forms of occult forces surrounding them without lapsing into madness or rationalization. The few things they can understand summon forces that can destroy their memory, force them into submission or kill them outright. Mages, on the other hand, see the forces behind this smoke and mirrors, gaining insights into the primordial, spiritual, visionary or technological truths of the world. They might only be mortal, but they are capable of taking action — sometimes, drastic action.

Each Tradition has its own dreams and prophecies of how this world will end. Individuals must ultimately decide how they will react to the events of the End

Times, but mages who have had extensive contact with the Nine Traditions might be conditioned to react in more esoteric or extreme ways. Each Tradition will have its own method of organizing and reacting to evidence of Armageddon. Behind the unraveling of Creation's Tapestry, each group will have its own drastic solutions to the world's imminent demise. Even among mages, masses panic. An individual mage might turn to the mentors of his sect for guidance… or reject their dictates utterly, when the foundation of civilization and the structure of reality give way.

As Armageddon looms, rivalries and conflicts between the Nine Traditions will intensify. After all, each Tradition has adjusted its beliefs somewhat so that it can work with the other eight… but ultimately, each still believes that its paradigm is the "correct" or "true" version of reality. With the fate of a world in the balance, the End Times might be the best time to assert those beliefs, even at the cost of unity with the Nine Traditions. As horrors approach from outside our world, disparate magical visions might tear it apart from within.

Akashic Brotherhood

One pervasive view in this Tradition has its roots in Eastern philosophies. Perfection of the body conditions the mind and soul, but ultimately, all such material attainments are illusory. The end of the world must bring the annihilation of the self, the eradication of ego. Even an Oracle who ascends to the heavens must ultimately transcend his humanity, becoming one with the cosmos, while the universe is destined to destroy itself. All human life is transient, and if it is fate that all of humanity should be destroyed, so be it.

While this might seem like a fatalistic response, most of the Akashic Masters remaining on Earth share this philosophy. In the End Times, the Earth's imminent demise will trigger large gatherings of Akashics, who will set aside their differences to pursue communal meditation. When resigned to the world's oblivion, they prepare themselves spiritually to meet eternity.

Individual Akashics have the option of resisting this transcendental state of denial. Just as they have perfected their Mind magics, the last generation of the Brotherhood has trained itself in a vast array of martial arts. Otherworldly manifestations arriving on Earth demand a response. Altruistic mages might take up a call to arms to defend humanity against these spiritual incursions. If anything, the peaceful serenity of the last Akashic Masters might very will stir the Tradition's initiates to action, working physically and actively to aid any cabal that decides to make a stand when the walls of Creation fall.

Celestial Chorus

In the End Times, Choristers will prepare for the culmination of religious prophecy, looking for signs of events that confirm that final apocalypse. Regardless of whatever evidence is presented, the last Masters of the Chorus will no doubt try to reinterpret it to confirm their own religious beliefs. If further, more blatant events demonstrate that the Armageddon to come does not fit with the revelations of their own religions, their faith could crumble. Perhaps such loss of belief cripples their ability to perform magic, or in the absence of a spiritual center, they will rapidly shift their paradigm to accommodate the desires of the Chosen… or of new gods descending upon the Earth.

The last generation of Choristers might be far more prepared for what is to come. Many Choristers believe that the world's religions are reflections of the One, and that the Nine Spheres are aspects of the One. Through faith, one might come to accept that the events of the End Times might return humanity to this celestial source. The amount of work to do in such times of trials and tribulations would no doubt be overwhelming. Troubled souls will look for comfort; so will troubled cabals.

Cult of Ecstasy

With their grand command of Time, the few remaining Ecstatic Masters face an overwhelming temptation. They have the power to scry deep into the past, looking for the origins of current catastrophes. Just as vitally, they have the ability to peer into the future, desperately seeking what awaits them. The visions that await such prideful prophets can drive a lesser man mad. If one destiny for the world's destruction is unavoidable, then witnessing it before it occurs is the ultimate act of fatalism. Then again, if many sanity-shaking events are possible, a failed vision can bestow several futures, or a false future. As the descriptions of the final stages of this chapter demonstrate, the further the End Times advance, the more possibilities are presented. Ecstatic Masters might lose themselves in their attempts to see the future, or become aligned with visionaries who claim they can.

One would expect the last generation of Ecstatic initiates to plunge completely into wanton hedonism, living for today. With no future, the pleasures of the present are undeniable. In fact, in a world without tomorrow, a few Time rotes can ensure that a mage is trapped outside such timelines permanently. Cosmic visionaries might even try to use altered states and psychedelia to better understand what is going on. If the Anakim walk among us, can they be reasoned with? Or does the answer lie in other dimensions, perhaps through some astral manifestation contacted through truly epic applications of recreational chemistry?

Escapists might seek answers in other dimensions or future fates, but Ecstatic heroes still have the opportunity to act in the here and now. While it is futile to forecast how the world will end, an Ecstatic might be able to limit his prediction to events in the immediate future. While absolutely losing one's self in pleasure offers an escape, it is still possible for a mage with a love for music, mind-enhancing drugs, and deeply spiritual sex to remind others in his cabal what they are defending. An altruistic Ecstatic can help his cabal find joy, even as the world around him is plunging into despair.

Dreamspeakers

The end of the world offers greater opportunities to study the spirit world than ever before. That's an understatement, since the spirit world might very well be merging with the realm of flesh again. The last Dreamspeaker Masters on Earth, along with the world's other Spirit Masters, are needed now more than ever before. Extradimensional entities will walk among us in unprecedented numbers, and shards of divinity will inhabit the Chosen of humanity. Who better to experience, teach and understand?

And therein lies a great danger: Dreamspeakers are known for their ability to immerse themselves in their work, existing in harmony with nearly any spiritual environment. It is possible that shamans can resist spiritual invasions and possessions, but it is just as possible that they will feel more at home in such a world than other mages, accepting rather than resisting… until, at last, the shards of the Avatar Storm lash out at them. Shards flay the souls who succumb to hubris, even among mages who have the best hope of understanding such motivations.

The last generation of Dreamspeakers must show greater restraint. Initiates and acolytes are "closer" to everyday concerns than Masters and Oracles, so one would hope that would bestow greater sympathy for how cosmic events affect their local communities. One cannot stop the global invasion of an entire race of Anakim (or angels or aliens), but it is possible to work locally to ease suffering, seek understanding and help others cope. Even for speakers in dreams, one of the best ways to deal with Armageddon is not to surrender to the spirit world, but to work in the human world.

Euthanatos

Four words remain unspoken on the lips of every Euthanatos: "I told you so." Entropy must ultimately claim all Creation; all activity to the contrary forestalls the inevitable. No doubt the last Master Euthanatoi will resign and consign themselves to this fact, and possibly revel in it. With the death of all Creation approaching, the final opportunity for resolving the mysteries of death is here. The threat of final judgment does not intimidate Euthanatoi as much as it does other Tradition mages. For those who believe in reincarnation, they have had lifetimes, if not all time, to prepare for their karmic destiny.

As the walls between worlds give way, the most powerful mages might surrender to the temptation to plunge into the Underworld in one final attempt to reconcile their souls with Oblivion. Of course, the Maelstrom might destroy those who surrender themselves to cruel fate. It has been said that only way to truly plumb the Malfean depths of the Shadowlands is to die. Considering the fact that time is running out, it might not be such a bad alternative.

The last generation of Euthanatoi has other opportunities. Many have learned to work with cabals representing many different traditions. Stereotypically, they are known for being able to see the worst case in any scenario, the presence of death when surrounded by life and the many opportunities afforded by chance. All of these qualities suggest that when it's obvious that everyone is doomed and that there are no opportunities, a Euthanatos might actually be one of the most functional mages in a cabal.

Hollow Ones

Screw it! Let's get drunk! The Hollow Masters left on Earth might very well have wasted a lifetime seeking acceptance from the Council of Nine. Now the point is moot. The representatives of other Traditions might take this opportunity to finally and formally accept the Templars, the Ahl-i-Batin or some other anachronistic group — it doesn't really matter. If anyone has a right to be fatalistic at a time like this, it's the few pathetic Hollow One Masters and Oracles who have never achieved the recognition they deserve. The other Traditions probably think the Orphans will spend their final days working with ghosts and vampires anyway — and those groups won't be doing much better than mages as the world ends. Praise the gods and pass the absinthe. It's over.

Then again… the Council of Nine has never really been good for much of anything anyway, other than ostracizing Orphan mages. Organized mages, including the many sects, societies and fellowships of Tradition mages, might stagnate into inactivity, but the Hollow Ones have always had more freedom than such conformists. That means they are more likely to follow their own personal agenda than to succumb to some collective madness in some desperate last-ditch attempt to save the world. The Final Days might actually bring final judgment, a chance for the righteous to ascend to a higher state of existence — a very appealing idea to many Hollowers who follow the Romantic traditions. Hopefully, Orphans who have pursued a more personal path will not be found wanting.

The last Hollow Ones might very well degenerate into hedonistic abandon when the world ends, using it as an opportunity for one great self-destructive orgy, a revel with no consequences. But it is just as likely for individual Orphans to see the End Times with eyes unclouded by dogma or expectations. Orphans have always stood alone. They must now make their peace before they die alone.

Order of Hermes

The answers to Earth's future are occulted in the past. As unthinkable events occur, Hermetic Masters will struggle to quantify new phenomena in the context of hidden events that have happened before. New events cry out for visionaries who can document and analyze them, and scholars who have overcome overwhelming forces before might be fooled into thinking they can command what destiny itself has summoned up. Cosmic forces have returned to Earth — who better to attempt to control them than the paragons of the Order of Hermes?

Legends speak of Renaissance Hermetics who joined with eternity, surrendering to eternal Twilight after attempting desperate and mighty magics to resolve inscrutable problems. If these are the Final Days, perhaps Paradox is not as threatening as it once was. Perhaps its manifestations can even help a Hermetic find his own destiny. The few Master mages left on Earth should be unafraid to show what happens when wizards are finally unmasked and magic is openly at work in the world.

Not all Hermetics are distracted by power over the world around them, of course. As those who are familiar with the workings of the Infinite Tapestry are aware, a few remaining scholars are the last living masters of Hermetic Cosmology. If new phenomena are descending upon the world, then the Hermetics must study, catalog and master them, even as they prepare to face infinity. If a Hermetic can try to understand what is happening, rather than overcoming it, he might learn enough to save himself when Judgment Day comes… or at least accept what is happening.

Sons of Ether

If you think the Sons of Ether are capable of heights of insanity, you should see what they do when the world is ending. Desperate times call for desperate measures, and when you've been spending a lifetime building a time machine, constructing a massive robot or exhuming the dead to reanimate the living, it is time to finally put your theories into practice. Time is running out for all the world's experiments, and the last Etheric Masters have a few desperate plans to save the world through science. Pencils down. Death rays ready. Let's get to work.

The Tradition has always had a plethora of scientific societies, Explorator societies, academic circles and other self-congratulatory mutual appreciation societies. When crises come, opportunities arise for grand debate, grandstanding oratory, contests for attention and most importantly, dramatic experimental demonstrations to prove one's theories. In other words, huge scientific societies excel at wasting time. It is possible a few true leaders might find a way to lead their scientific brethren in communal projects, but such leadership skills often come with the ego and foolish pride necessary to lead such projects astray.

There could be a technological solution to many of the problems at hand, a way to at least ease the world's pain as it dies or bring solace to the insane. A true scientist must be unafraid to experiment, to challenge his own assumptions. The End Times will offer many such opportunities. The last Etherites must learn to truly ground themselves in this new reality — the End Times will eradicate all alternatives.

Verbena

The End Times offer vast opportunities for practitioners of magic. Wild speculation is remarkably easy at such times. Will magic fade from the world, or will it finally be possible to work it openly without retribution? No doubt many pagan religions have already offered a glimpse of the world's demise — are all of them true, or just some of them? ("Are none of them true? What a ridiculous notion.") The Anakim take forms that have been seen in the world before — how long must we wait until they meet with the Verbena to show us what they want of us? ("They will want to meet with us first, of course.") Like the many supernatural creatures of the world and many elder mages, the few Verbena Masters and Oracles on Earth have interpreted recent events to confirm their own importance… and prove that their interpretation of reality is the only correct one.

Verbena also have a reputation as healers, as wise and understanding souls who can find meaning even in times of great tragedy. Such qualities will be tested in the End Times. The wise will not place their own significance in the scheme of things first, but learn to adapt in a rapidly degenerating world. Now it is a time for Verbena to show the finer qualities of pagan beliefs, even if one of them is accepting what the gods have chosen for the world.

Virtual Adepts

Regardless of whatever operating system and configuration you prefer for your machine, it appears as though it just got its final upgrade. The warranty has run out… on everything. Through the computer networks, video cameras and access terminals of the world, one can watch nearly everything happening at once if one tries hard enough. All it takes is attunement to your correspondence point — and for the last Virtual Adept Masters, that's probably a padded chair in front of the largest computer screen possible. Behind a fortress of technology, they are observing as much as they can, coordinating as much as they can as they capture video, chat with distant cabals and collate data.

This means that the last Adepts are very well informed, but like a bleary-eyed Web surfer staring at his screen at 3:00 in the morning, that doesn't mean they understand what they're seeing. While they might insist that their Correspondence rotes ensure they're standing right behind the final defenders of the world, it's really a neat rationalization for sitting your ass in a chair, typing furiously away as the last server is about to go offline. Foolish pride might lead a Virtual Adept to overwhelm himself trying to take in everything. More "733t" Adepts must find a way to put their knowledge to good use, preferably by coordinating the efforts of an effective cabal.

Radio Free Umbra

One of the most dangerous groups in the End Times is a recently assembled one: the Rogue Council. **Manifesto** suggested a timeline for the Sphinx's transmissions. As the events of this book proceed, the events of that book must also advance. Enigmatic transmissions have galvanized the last generation of mages into action. In the early phases of these broadcasts, selected mages received messages that were largely instructional, bestowing hints of supernatural histories, Traditional precedents that have been forgotten, and insights into the motivations of the Primi. And along the way,

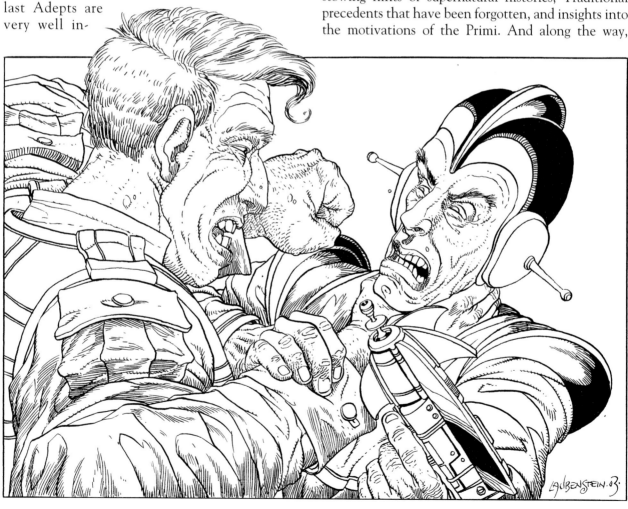

they've tried to rally Tradition mages against the Technocracy. Some grudges never die, it seems.

As transmissions continued, incidents of "reportage" betrayed once-secretive information of corrupt mages and Technocrats. As the Avatar Storm further isolated front-line agents from Technocracy overseers, a few individuals took the opportunity to exploit their newly found autonomy. Freed from the Technocratic collective, they succumbed to temptations of personal power. Such hubris could not be hidden from the watchful scrying of the Sphinx.

These broadcasts and revelations often contained unexplained omissions, however, confirming that the Rogue Council's overseers were far from omniscient. One of the most critical transmissions concerned an Arctic Construct hidden by the Technocracy, where the first of the Anakim returned to the world. Shortly after these events, a new phase of events occurs… and the story continues.

Phase Four: Fading Frequency

A few months after the Sphinx issues its first transmissions, testimonials of triumph are disseminated throughout the Nine Traditions. Stories of victories against the Technocracy are heard for the first time in years… and then, just as suddenly, the messages from beyond cease. Some theorize that the Council has lost its power source or that interference has made further communication impossible. Speculation abounds. Has the Rogue Council decided that its inspiration is no longer necessary, now that the Traditions have started to take action again? Was the Council only interested in starting yet another war with the Technocracy? In Phase Four, self-styled "Emissaries" devote their attention to the final missives, trying to read some deeper meaning into what has happened. Their "Guardian" counterparts insist that this turn of events suggests that some darker fate is at hand.

The fates described in successive chapters offer theories why these messages have suddenly stopped, as well as possibilities for the true origin of the Council. The easiest explanations could correspond to the First Sign of Armageddon. A "Gauntlet of Souls" surrounding the Earth, a network of sentient Avatar shards, might have collectively obscured the Council's transmissions, at least if their origin is outside the world we know. Or, if the broadcasts come from our own world, it might be that the Rogue Council has only just begun to realize the magnitude of threat the Avatar Storm poses. Whatever the reason, fading frequencies force the world's mages to fight again for their own world…

until desperate events galvanize the *Rogue Council* itself into action.

Phase Five: New Activity

As the Second and Third Signs of Armageddon are realized, mages will encounter far greater threats to the world than the Technocracy. Bitter rivalries and petty attempts to avenge the Union's campaigns for reality have distracted the Traditions from greater problems. Old rhetoric about avenging Mistridge or winning the Ascension War becomes irrelevant as the Earth's Gauntlet begins to give way.

After the first incursions and abductions, transmissions resume. Many of the Rogue Council's quirky methods of communication remain the same: notes on windshields, mysteriously delivered magnetic tapes, anomalous manifestations in corrupted computer files and screen savers, hidden meanings in public advertisements and so on. The message is more important than the medium, however, as the Sphinx's agenda seems to change.

The Rogue Council cannot fully explain what happens during the early signs of Armageddon, but invectives against the Technocracy seem curiously absent during this stage. Instead, the Sphinx's enigmas relate to other phenomena, and new activity. Chilling themes recur: clues about missing persons, outbreaks of madness in otherwise "normal" citizens and sightings of a teratological or cryptozoological nature. Many clues can be tracked to the sensitive places where spiritual forces have broken through into our world. The Rogue Council confirms that reality is giving way — but it seems powerless to discern who or what is behind such activity. At this point, any hostilities between the Traditions and Technocracy only serve a diversion from greater troubles.

Phase Six: Omens

The Sphinx seems to have an endless supply of enigmas. Instructional broadcasts about the past soon decrease in frequency. As madness mounts, the Rogue Council must look to the future. Some transmissions concern the movements of individuals — aliens among us — but at best, they reveal where these outsiders have been days after they have moved on. If the Anakim have returned, revelations of their activities are tailored to inspire mages of specific traditions. A Chorister might receive a message of a sighting of an angel, for instance, while a technomage might be more concerned with a story of alien abduction.

The nature of these revelations shifts from past tense to future tense as the next signs are revealed and

Sleepers Awaken. Both the Traditions and Technocracy have limited abilities to predict where mage will Awaken, but the Rogue Council soon develops the ability to pinpoint such future events with chilling prescience. Not all of these individuals can be found, but any given cabal could have several opportunities to find and help these lost souls cope before Avatar shards find them.

Some Tradition mages leap to the conclusion that the Technocracy is trying to capture and condition these individuals, and they're right. This plight might instill some instant sympathy for the Chosen, but in truth, this new generation of Awakened *doesn't actually have to be the "good guys."* The Chosen could be the saviors of reality or a threat the Traditions never expected. If the Chosen are selected by the same criterion, they could be Marauders helping bring Avatar shards into the world, Nephandi corrupting souls or humans transformed by alien agenda. The Rogue Council provides no clues about what to do with these lost souls. It can only point the way. Mages, as always, must find the answers by themselves.

End Time Seekings

This is your last chance to achieve enlightenment… or save the world. Throughout the history of the Traditions, archaic mages have advanced their understanding of magic through spiritual journeys called Seekings (an idea further defined in the **Mage Storytellers Handbook**). Such spirit quests always carry some degree of risk, but they also bestow rewards, including revelations about one's self, the world all around the mage, and the true forms of magic. Any Storyteller who's fond of Seekings might want to expand their role and influence on the End Times.

In many chronicles, mages might be required to perform Seekings just as they are about to gain greater magical understanding (that is, "buy another dot of Arete"). To define the event as something greater than the mere act of amending a character sheet, a Seeking is often a dramatic scene enacted for the benefit of a lone mage. It might be a series of visions encountered during meditation or introspection, or it might be a symbolic spirit quest of a descent into a cave or labyrinth where Guardians bar the way. It might even be a series of events in the "real world" that test the mage's ability to resolve an enigma (or danger) involving magic. If a Seeking succeeds, the aspirant gains Arete; if it fails, the mage might suffer long-term effects of Paradox.

A mage's Seeking realizes the potential of his Avatar, granting him epiphanies into the true workings of magic. Yet a Seeking can be far more than an attempt to seize greater magical power. In fact, the mage's Avatar often initiates this seeking; some believe that such is the case is because it benefits from the mage becoming more enlightened. As the End Times advance, this need for Ascension should gain even greater urgency. "End Time Seekings" should be more than simple attempts to gain magical power. An Avatar should have its own reasons for helping a mage gain more Arete, not to merely "cast spells better," but to define who the mage is destined to be at the conclusion of his life's journey. Such secrets and profound epiphanies of self-discovery are ideal for the final days of the world.

While Avatars drive their chosen mages toward greater accomplishments, mages rationalize their own motivations for attempting dangerous Seekings. Altruists might want to find insights into current catastrophes, thinking that their expanded perceptions and new perspective on magic will give insights into new phenomena. Survivors could take great risks because they believe the time of Ascension is at hand, convinced that increasing their magical power will prepare them for increased challenges. The prideful might even seek out tests that pit them against these new phenomena, deciding that one true hero performing an epic spirit quest can somehow redeem the world, save humanity or avert further catastrophe.

While a Seeking can offer insights into the world, the critical path in its events should be focused on the mage who is attempting it. It might involve new phenomena in the world, but the real goal is to define how the "seeker" works with (or without) magic. Any mage on a Seeking is really attempting to overcome his limitations, as his Avatar guides him to greater magical potential. This spiritual journey illustrates what the mage needs to learn in order to grow. The result is an epiphany that expands the aspirant's ability to harness magical power. Insights into Armageddon are possible, but they should be additional rewards for surviving great risks, not the goal of the Seeking itself. Believing that you are the one hero who can save the world is, to say the very least, the greatest possible act of hubris — the sort of flaw that leads a Seeking to fail.

With this in mind, one of the more unusual varieties of Seeking is one in which the mage does not realize he is being tested… or even that he is in the midst of a Seeking! As the amount of supernatural activity increases (or as cosmic forces that obliterate the supernatural grow), Seekings do not have to be prompted by meditation or introspection. Such epic events might happen in the everyday world, as the environment around the mage takes on mythic (and apocalyptic) significance. Newly Awakened mages might be drawn into these occurrences or actually Awaken as part of them.

If Seekings take on this grander scale, however, the punishments should be as grand as the possible rewards. A failed Seeking might turn a mage into a Phenomenon Magnet (as defined earlier in this chapter), advancing the very timeline he or she is trying to avert. For instance, suppose the aspirant has sought out a rift in the Gauntlet where someone has recently disappeared. A successful Seeking might grant the mage a spiritual insight that allows him to close the breach, but a failed Seeking could actually result in further disappearances… or a guardian spirit leaping through this gateway. As Armageddon approaches, mages do not need to be hermits isolated in introspection. More than ever, they might become the mythic heroes of the modern world.

Even in an introspective Seeking, new supernatural phenomena can appear that relate to a chronicle's apocalyptic timeline — such as Avatar shards, Anakim, angels, demons, cultists and so forth — but they might be there to distract a mage from the real nemesis he needs to overcome: the flaws within himself. A mage who intentionally starts a Seeking to find insights into his role in Armageddon is unlikely to gain an epiphany into his own approach to magic. As a result, he is unlikely to actually complete his Seeking.

Conversely, a mage who can stay focused on his study of magic during a Seeking and can avoid being distracted by new horrors in the world can gain the insight he needs to define his identity and his approach to magic. Once he gains this deeper understanding of his paradigm of magic, he is better suited to take on these new evils, not just with a higher Arete score, but by using methods that make sense for that particular mage. (If you play by the rules that a mage is actually risking a large chunk of experience to attempt a Seeking, the rewards and results should be commensurate to this risk.) If you've developed a style for running Seekings, you have a way to give meaning to a willworker's magical growth. Not surprisingly, this can be very encouraging when the world all around the mage is dying.

The most dangerous application of this concept is actually concluding your timeline, no matter what it is, in the midst of a final Seeking. You might decide in the final session, or final chapter, to use the optional guideline for waiving all experience costs during a Seeking. Yes, this means that a character can rapidly rise in Arete… but then again, if you've tipped off your players that the chronicle is ending, that choice might not be a bad one. In fact, it can make for a fitting conclusion to a chronicle, offering a more meaningful ending than a pyrotechnic obliteration of a world you've invested so much time in defining. The point of an Armageddon does not have to be that the world is doomed. Instead, its theme could very well be that true heroes can overcome ultimate challenges, finding fulfillment even as they attain oblivion, ultimate revenge, unity with celestial forces, transcendence or whatever their destiny is.

Seekings are yet another tool in your kit for building a story about Armageddon, even as you prepare to dismantle the world. You've labored long and hard to build your **Mage** chronicle. By keeping heroes at the center of your story, and showing their magical growth and learning (especially through events like Seekings), all that hard work won't have to go to waste. The world must ultimately end, but if the characters conclude the story dramatically, their final moments don't have to be a hollow death. Through Seeking, one can receive final judgment… and finally reach Ascension.

Chapter Two: Judgment

They asked the soul, "Whence do you come, slayer of men, or where are you going, conqueror of space?"

The soul answered and said, "What binds me has been slain, and what turns me about has been overcome, and my desire has been ended, and ignorance has died.

"In an aeon I was released from a world, and in a type from a type, and from the fetter of oblivion which is transient. From this time on will I attain to the rest of the time, of the season, of the aeon, in silence."

—The Gnostic Gospel of Mary Magdalene

The tenth and final Sphere is Judgment; bliss and damnation are at hand.

As mages progress, they suffer. Thus it always has been, regardless of time, place or culture. Mystical understanding blossomed into the nine-sided jewel of the Spheres, but the singular brilliance of that achievement is hidden behind a veil of pain. The Traditions call the journey the Path of Thorns: a trail that has bled their fellowship to the last drop. Now, we reach the end of that bitter road, to discover why Ascension and Armageddon are one. Their torment is, in the end, the key to victory.

This is the key story for the end of **Mage: The Ascension** — the one that wraps up the major metaplot elements that have been introduced over the years. It's about your characters and your chronicle, and as such, it tells only part of the story. Every Storyteller has final secrets to share. Weave these into what follows and change the plot to accommodate the hidden elements of your World of Darkness. More than ever, the Golden Rule is paramount.

It's a huge story, and it's painted in broad strokes at times, so it's incumbent upon the Storyteller to fill in the details. It's designed to take place over a matter of months, but for flexibility's sake, time measurements (including the exact date of the end!) are only vaguely described. It's important to note that there is a real chance of failure. The characters' actions could destroy humanity's last chance for Ascension.

There are great powers loose in these final days. Voormas. The revealed Rogue Council. An ancient conspiracy that lies at the root of the Traditions and Technocracy. But these are not the decisive elements of the story. *Your* characters, not a secret council of Archmasters, decide humanity's fate.

Let's look at what's led us to this point, but don't forget that all of this has come to pass so that your characters can face a choice: Will they trust the universe or damn it?

A Secret History

The World of Darkness is wounded. It's not an injury you can see or touch, but you can feel it as a subtle *wrongness* that permeates everything. Sleepers cannot grasp the wonder and power that is their birthright. More often than not, faith goes un-rewarded. Even when humanity strives to be something greater, its cunning philosophies and great works rarely break the barrier between what is and what they imagine. Their efforts turn to dust and Entropy claims its due. This taint blossomed into an iron-hard Gauntlet and a narrow collective vision, all because time and again, humankind isn't rewarded in proportion to its efforts.

Only mages manage to escape the cage and realize their desires, but the pull of the Consensus is so strong that they have to work subtly or risk destruction. They can step outside the wounded world and take hold of pure possibility, spinning it into any shape they can imagine. Spells succeed in response to the mage's efforts or fail according to her weaknesses. Some Asian mystics call this idea "ripening karma" and conceive of it as a force that is neither good nor evil, but absolutely necessary. Likewise, the monotheistic traditions of the West reward faith and justice and punish sin. The Greeks called this force *telos*: the completion and perfection of a cycle.

In the World of Darkness, this force has been crippled. Mages touch only its slightest shadow when they work their wills. Few mystics understand its place alongside the Quintessential flow. Meanwhile, bereft of the fullness of this Tenth Sphere, humanity lacks the means to Ascend.

Before recorded history, mystics asked themselves why suffering was so pervasive. Did humanity fall from grace? Why were men and woman born blind to the wonders around them? They studied the problem and went on Seekings to conquer their own blindness.

Isolated cults discovered the principle of Telos under different names and faces. Of these fellowships, two were destined to turn the Wheel of Ages a step closer to Ascension: the Chakravanti of India and the forgotten Ixoi of Europe and the Near East.

The Chakravanti worshipped the primordial Cycle of Creation; it was a collection of societies with no common identity, but a consistent vision. Without directly voicing it, these mages sensed that it wasn't enough to just walk along Creation's path. Sometimes the Wheel needed to be corrected, even if doing so brought on murder, disease and disaster.

The Ixoi

Farther west, groups of Sleepers abandoned the Fertile Crescent. Many of them simply sought better farmland and hunting grounds, but beside them walked refugees from the hell-cities of the ancients. They fled the infernal despots of Bhât, the demonologists of old Babylon and the devil-haunted ruins of places that would be remembered as Gehenna and Babel.

In the shadow of that evil, a few secretly Awakened. Rather than use their power to flee, a hidden fellowship endured tortures so that they could seize the secrets of magic from their infernal masters. Many died, but none revealed their secrets. When their Avatars returned, they inhabited new slaves and won enough continuity to maintain the cult.

In the seventh generation, the sources of this boon revealed themselves: Spirits of divine judgment were behind the fellowship's reincarnations. Where Avatars were shards of the One, these spirits were fragments of an Other: the dark half of the cosmos that lies outside human wisdom.

They were normally banned from Creation, but a wondrous thing had happened — or would happen. In the future, the fellowship would call them through the Dreamshell erected by the One Above. Their emanations flowed forward and backward from that point in time. Taking the shape of bright, winged creatures, they offered the slave mages a gift so that the future summoning would come to pass.

Some asked for wisdom. Others demanded the power to liberate the slaves of the demon-cities. The soul guides (or Psychopomps) taught them the secret history of the cosmos, though the lore was so vast that these mages could only filter it, weakly, through their own beliefs.

The Annunaki gave some of the rebels slivers of their own essence and power. Just as their knowledge was too great for mortal minds, their essence was so potent than many who received it became monstrous or mad. Called *Anakim* by Semitic sages, the imbued mages seized power over the tormented Avatars that raged around the infernal citadels. They brought this soul-power crashing down upon the basalt altars of their captors, destroying nations with their wrath.

The remainder of the fellowship used the confusion to ransack infernal temples for occult secrets. On the Grand Altar of Bhât, they found an artifact whose primitive appearance belied its significance. It would be called the *Knife of Ixion*, a physical fragment of the first tool that humanity used to work its will against the natural order. Bhât's Eaters of the Weak (later reviled as the Nephandi) worshipped it as the first triumph against the One Above. Prophetic Arts revealed it to be vital to the future summoning, so the fellowship took it along into exile.

Exile and Entelechy

The survivors fled to Asia Minor and Greece, cultivating secrecy and magical wisdom as they went. They took the Psychopomps as their patrons, summoning them for guidance. Always cautious of the laws that prohibited them from intervening in human affairs, the emanations of Judgment inspired the fellowship to act as their agents. In spite of the ban, mages would reward the righteous, punish the innocent and render secret judgment upon the works of humankind.

So the fellowship endured and adapted to local cultures. By the Homeric Age, other mages whispered of a House of Ixion in their midst. The fellowship took that name (for the first murderer of Hellenic myth) and infiltrated Awakened lodges and Sleeper courts. In the Troas, they helped the Achaeans destroy a walled city that defied the gods — but spirited its philosophers to safety among the Dorian tribes. When the Dorians swept into Greece, the Ixoi undermined Achaean competition. With small, secret gestures, the fellowship transformed civilizations.

Greek society founded its city-states on the Achaean ruins while its people turned to mysticism and metaphysics. By the fifth century BC, philosophers such as Xenophanes advocated a single god instead of the polytheism they inherited from the Achaeans. This advocacy, in turn, increased the influence of a monotheistic cult called the Celestial Singers. Enamored of Greek thought, the Singers moved to eliminate ecstatic and shamanic elements from their sect. In Asia Minor, this campaign erupted into occult warfare. Wrathful Singers chased Darwushim heretics northeast.

In the East, war between the Chakravanti lodges and the Akashic Brotherhood forced a troop of Warring Hands northwest — into the very arms of the Darwushim. Without being aware of each other's existence, the House of Ixion and the Chakravanti exercised their judgment, bringing the victims of far-flung conflicts together. The Darwushim and the Warring Hands were both purified by battle and suffering. Complementary Resonance emanated from each side as they met and danced a mandala. Fate, judgment and magic combined and called out — and the Khwaja al-Akbar answered.

Shadows of the Perfected One

The Entelechy was the summoning rite prophesied by the Psychopomps. The Khwaja al-Akbar was more than the massed Avatars of the refugees. It was an emanation from the *future* — a future when Ascension had been achieved and the Cycle of Creation, including the Sphere of Telos, was realized. But as soon as it touched the imperfect Consensus, it fragmented across the past and future. Partaking of a fraction of the supreme intelligence, these fragments manifested as the Psychopomps who would contact the Ixoi's ancestors and guide mages for millennia to come. The Entelechy broke down into individual mages. Entropy was inextricably tied to judgment; as the Entelechy ejected the wounded part of itself, its component mages were denied the use of that Sphere.

The survivors taught their fragmented insights to others and formed the Ahl-i-Batin. Those who were part of the Entelechy remembered a brief taste of the truth. Judgment would liberate humanity, but at a terrible price, for they learned that damnation and Ascension were part of the same Unity. The Batini preserved this idea as a part of their most secret doctrine. Even then, rumors inspired a few of them to approach the Devil Kings in search of "secret Unity." Most were corrupted. The Batini responded by mastering subtle methods, so that this dangerous knowledge would never fall into unprepared hands.

The Mythic Age Falls

After the Entelechy, Psychopomp emanations were numerous and powerful. Avatars rushed to incarnations best able to serve the laws of Telos. Ironically, the more perfect union between the mage and her mystic soul quieted the guiding voice. Mages worked their will unchecked by the urge for abstract enlightenment. Ambition led to hubris; hubris was punished by cannon fire and the Ascension War.

The Ixoi were torn by the conflict. As the years flowed further away from the Entelechy, Psychopomp visitations decreased. Judgment's emanations were weak, so the Ixoi relied on their mortal convictions. The majority joined the Order of Reason. Ever adaptable, they transformed into the Ksirafai, "Razors of God" intent on punishing mages who strayed from the path of Ascension. A small Byzantine cult called the Golden Chalice remembered tales of judge-mystics in the East and joined the Euthanatos Tradition.

By the 15th century, the Psychopomps could no longer ride the waning emanations of the Khwaja al-Akbar and departed reality once more. But one mage learned how to circumvent celestial law and summon them from beyond the Horizon: Heylel Teomim.

You Are the Betrayer

Heylel's tortured path convinced him that he could never trust anyone with the secret of creating a true Rebis. All the same, the mage loved learning and, knowing that he would be tried and sacrificed, wanted to posthumously clear his name of infernalism charges. Rather than retain his laboratory, Heylel decided that only his descendants could be trusted to inherit his Arts.

Instead of a physical Grimoire, the Great Betrayer forged an astral book, linking parts of its Platonic whole to the Avatars of his son and daughter. Each part would appear to be nothing more than innocuous Resonance, but when combined, the Quintessential form of the book would come into existence, flowering in the minds of both.

Separated, Heylel and Eloine's children went to foster parents, lived their lives and died. Their Avatars moved from birth to birth, never meeting, always resting in the Sleep of uninspired humanity. The Rebis never called on his children to refute the charges against him; after his Gilgul and execution, his plans for posthumous vindication were themselves betrayed. For his own reasons, Porthos Fitz-Empress, who knew the secret, never revealed it.

Praedictum Apocalypsis and the First Successor

In *The Fragile Path*, Akrites Salonikas warned that, if allowed to live, Heylel Teomim would do more than betray the Traditions. He would graft them on to the Order of Reason. Combined, the Awakened under his banner would turn Earth into a charnel house. He would rule the earth under the name Moloch and cast rebel magi from the Earth. Moloch's dynasty would last beyond his death; surviving mages would return to the world to overthrow his two heirs. Despite the suspect motives of the Council, it was a *good* thing that the Betrayer died hundreds of years ago. It avoided a terrifying future — didn't it?

Yet, so much of what Akrites predicted did come to pass after a fashion. Iteration X projects did, at one time, include machines that "surgically remove imagination and intuition." The horrors of eugenics, the flight of the Masters (some aided by Etheric spacecraft) into other worlds — all of it has happened. Despite being a boon, technomagic and Horizon Council's rejection of the Ascension War destroyed the barriers between science and mysticism. And when Doissetep exploded, *The Fragile Path* was, indeed, the first book burned, for it was with Porthos when he released devastating energies upon the chantry. Execution might have kept the Betrayer from openly bringing Moloch's future, but a shadow of it lingers.

Of the "two successors" mentioned in the prophecy, one has already revealed itself. The "False Heylel" Stormed Concordia with an Orphan army. Brought into being by Technocrats serving the infamous Special Projects Division, it was defeated in the Council chambers by Akrites himself.

One successor remains. That mage carries the Avatar of one of Heylel's children and thus, half of his mystic secrets — and she's a member of your cabal.

What This Means

The Storyteller should choose one player's character, portrayed by someone who can play out temptation but avoid grandstanding. No special traits are required, but you might want to use it to justify a high *Destiny* rating and foreshadow it in Seekings and other stories. This character will be pivotal but not indispensable. In the story, we'll call her (or him; gender is not important) Heylel's Heir.

The Rebis

The future Great Betrayer was an amalgam of two mages: A Solificati alchemist named Julius de Medici and Mia de Napoli, an Orphan. De Medici was convinced that the key to Ascension was the reconciliation of opposites into a single body, soul and Daemon (the Renaissance term for an Avatar). Citing ancient Egyptian legends, alchemy Grimoires claimed that this unification was possible, provided that the mage discovered a "Holy Guardian Angel" capable of sanctifying the union. The alchemist took advantage of the nascent Council of Nine, borrowing books from other Traditions as well as booty seized from raids on the Nephandi. A Babylonian text gave him the True Name of an "angel," and a Hermetic manual possessed a suitable summoning ritual. His own alchemy would take care of the physical joining.

How the future Heylel found his Orphan counterpart is a mystery, but at some point in the rite, de Medici summoned a Psychopomp to bless the alchemical "marriage." The soul guide obliged, and de Medici was given a piece of the *gallu's* essence. With a fragment of the Psychopomp's power over Avatars, he assimilated de Napoli's body and soul.

Heylel Teomim went on to betray the First Cabal. His studies were used against him as evidence of infernalism, but his (mages usually referred to the Rebis as a man) exact method was never discovered. Mages who witnessed his trial claimed he practically invited Gilgul and death. Perhaps he considered himself an Abomination in the end, and he might have known of Akrites Salonikas' prophecy (as recorded in **The Fragile Path: Testaments of the First Cabal**). The Seer of Chronos predicted that, unless he was destroyed, he would corrupt the earth as "Moloch," and that two successors would follow in his wake, ending all hope of Ascension.

Nobody knows what happened to the twins he fathered by Eloine, Verbena of the First Cabal, except that they were spirited away before the witch's imprisonment.

The Razors Turn

After the Great Betrayal, the Order of Reason began the Pogrom, targeting innocent and corrupt mages alike. The Ksirafai began to doubt the purity of their mission under Reason's banner and quietly scaled back their support. In 1716, the last Fulmen (their leader, named after the Latin word for lightning) of the Ksirafai gathered the remaining Razors in Turkey. After eliminating other traces of their existence, they then "defeated" their own Construct. Under the name Dincer Albayrak, the Fulmen presented their "victory" to the Order of Hermes and asked to be recognized as a House under the title of the "Janissaries."

"Dincer Albayrak" found an apt successor in the Syrian Bedouin Caeron Mustai. Sensing a powerful destiny in the 12-year old, "Albayrak" kidnapped Caeron and initiated him into the secrets of the Ixoi. What the Fulmen didn't know was that the Ahl-i-Batin had already found him.

A Batini ascetic discovered him, Awakened him and trained him; the Master's occulted touch meant that it went undiscovered by the Fulmen. Caeron earned the nickname "Sha'ir" from his clan for his eloquence and learning, even though no one could recall where the boy might have found books or time to read them.

Before undergoing final Occultation and erasing himself from reality, Caeron's Batini tutor revealed the secret Doctrine of Unity: that Armageddon and Ascension are one.

When the Fulmen taught him Ixoi history, Caeron came to a horrifying conclusion: his House was destined to bring about the end of the world. The Ixoi were the harbingers of Judgment — and Judgment was the destroyer. He was determined to prevent the end, even if it meant turning away from Ascension.

Caeron guided the Janissaries to full House status, but instead of renewing the Ixoi's mission, he flung the House into political conflict, hiding Voormas' crimes. Recognizing the heritage of the Golden Chalice and Thanatoic doctrine, he dedicated himself to miring the Death Mages in corruption and scandal. Along with his schemes against the Flambeau Primus Porthos Fitz-Empress, his efforts created political tensions that would eventually destroy the Chantry of Doissetep.

Reality on the Brink

Now, in the wake of the Reckoning and turmoil throughout the Tellurian, mages plot and struggle. The Awakened suspect that humanity's final days have come.

Chaotic Prophecy

One sign of the end occurs in the months leading up to our story. Divination magic begins to twist and fail, encountering a cloud of *Storm-Tainted* Resonance that confuses omens and defeats statistical analysis. Mages can usually foretell their immediate future, but predictions about global events and the fate of magical societies become confused. In many cases, new visions contradict previous predictions.

Storytellers should use this complication carefully. Don't deny players the functional aspects of Time magic (such as detecting danger or gathering moderate amounts of intelligence), but do emphasize that the old rules of causality are being rewritten, making it difficult to determine the future fate of the world. Prophecies from the past are somewhat more reliable. The one consistent element of them is that everything familiar teeters on the edge of destruction. Iteration X Statisticians have their "Doomsday Forecast" and the Traditions seethe with rumors of the Phoenix Prophecy and Moloch.

The Harvester of Souls

Why does the Avatar Storm exist? Partly, it happened because of the massive burst of tainted Resonance that arrived with the Week of Nightmares, combined with the successive deaths of Umbra-dwelling magi and the mortal casualties of Project Ragnarok. But in the past, atrocities and disasters have left only small, localized storms. Yet, *this* Avatar Storm is different, encircling most of consensual reality and wrecking the realms beyond, all thanks to the concerted work of several conspiracies. Each of them worked without the knowledge of the others, but to the same end, all to the satisfaction of one mage: Voormas, Grand Harvester of Souls.

Voormas fears death, an ironic thing indeed for a mage in the throes of Jhor. He wants more than just long life. What terrifies the archmage is the end of the Cycle itself, when he will answer for centuries' worth of dark karma.

Long ago, when he was merely a Master of Entropy, Voormas planted a dark seed in the minds of necromantic conspiracies around the world. From the surviving Idran and their vampiric mentors to the supernatural gestalt of the Orphic Circle, each wished to master the worlds of the dead. Voormas took hold of this idea's ephemeral form (what fellow Euthanatoi would call necromancy's *tulpa*) and *twisted* it. Certain cults altered their focus from merely mastering the Underworld to tearing down the Shroud that divided it from the lands of the living. With the Gauntlet gone, Voormas would destroy the barriers between life and death, breaking the axis of the Wheel.

He dedicated his Consanguinity of Eternal Joy to safeguarding corrupted Nodes. He discovered the traces of shattered Avatars there, studied them and waited.

When the Week of Nightmares struck, his plans came to fruition, even though he himself hid from the wrath of the Traditions in a death goddess' realm. The cults' combined efforts rent the Shroud and Entropic energies lashed out around the world. The Resonance sundered the Avatars of dead mages and Sleepers, and Voormas was armed for the last phase of his plan to overthrow Death.

Senex has gone to the Realm of Entropy to stop him. He's taken a full quarter of the Euthanatos Tradition with him to guard the Shard Realm against invasion and, if possible, undo the damage to the Shroud and corrupted Nodes.

Now you know the secret history and the forces that stand on the cusp of change. The final story is ready to be told.

Part One: The Light of the Phoenix

In truth, we welcomed the most appalling destruction. Sensing, even as we mourned our dead, that we were again presented with the most astonishing of opportunities.
—William Gibson, *Virtual Light*

Rumors and ominous dreams plague the Awakened. The Traditions have adapted to the sign of the Sphinx, with some seeing a call to war and others fearing a coming disaster. The Technocracy eschews the grand strategies of the old Ascension War for street fighting and other earthy, bloody conflicts.

The cabal is called by omens, Rogue Council transmissions and prophetic dreams. The Storyteller should customize, elaborate on and add new signs to augment what follows

The Dream

During sleep, meditation or a Seeking, Heylel's Heir dreams. The dream is an infectious one, reaching out to every person with a close arcane connection (two ranks on the Correspondence Ranges chart; see **Mage: The Ascension**, page 209) In all likelihood, this range includes the character's entire cabal. The dream is a side effect of the ephemeral Grimoire that Heylel's Heir carries; it is meant to call out to her twin. Unfortunately, the other Heir routinely uses magic to sever such connections, so he doesn't appear — a contingency that the Grimoire's creator never foresaw.

But this isn't the only element in the dream. Characters with high Awareness ratings and Prime senses detect voices whispering in the shadows: the *Storm-Tainted* Resonance associated with the Avatar Storm.

In the dream, the Heir is covered in blood and wrapped in a white cloth. A giant looms above her in rich robes, standing three times her height, with phoenixes and sphinxes worked in brocade along its collar. Knowledgeable characters recognize the robe's rich, 15th-century cut. The giant's sex is indistinguishable, but it has long, blond hair. Bright twin stars obscure its face. The room has cold, stone floors. Huge tapestries are covered with the sign of the caduceus below a crown: a fusion of common Hermetic and old Solificati symbolism. Heylel's Heir feels exhausted, as if she's completed a great journey on foot. The other dreamers take on their normal self-image, but they feel like they're being watched.

Dreamers can act and ask questions. Unless immediately interrupted, the giant speaks. The language is Latin, but the Heir can understand it (as the giant can understand her) even if she isn't fluent. Other dreamers need to rely on magic or personal knowledge. Use the following dialogue as a model; adapt it to answer the Heir's questions and respond to her actions. Read the accompanying sidebar on the symbolism of the dream to elaborate. As a dream spirit, the giant doesn't actually know the meaning of what it says, but can supplement metaphors with other metaphors. The dream reacts to characters' deliberations, stopping to allow characters to consider its symbols.

If compelled with Spirit magic or attacked, the giant doesn't resist. The twin stars on its face merge into a blood-red sun, and the Heir's swaddling clothes become the purple and ermine of kings. She wears a crown. If she examines it, she sees that it was once broken, but roughly re-forged. One half has her initials; the other, bloody half has the initials MHG inscribed upon it.

Blessing the Child

The giant speaks with two voices.

In a masculine voice, the giant says, "You are Unity, but we split your crown to hide you from the Nine. The Seer told us the path. In you, children, the Holy Guardian Angel of my work will endure and hear its hymns.

"But we have split your crown, so you will not be Moloch. If you are worthy, you will find your brother. Your will is the salamander, the essential fire, and we have given you a forge to heat."

The giant wrings its hands in distress and speaks again, in a second, feminine voice:

"The union is not yours by right. The world's shape was a sundering. After the Garden, the flaming sword *Napea* cut Adam Qadmon into the shards of *Gilgul*. The

Metratron breathed upon Babel and fractured its tongues to keep usurpers from the throne of the Most High. We men and women were meant to be apart in flesh, in mind, in spirit. Even if all the shards of the One were gathered, we would be denied the Garden and the Kingdom. We are not God, husband. We are subject to judgment.

"And my unwanted husband, the other star on this face, would reverse the judgment of the Most High. My child, if your brother is worthy, he will resist you with the wand of Hermes and seek council with the angels in the newly shattered earth."

The male voice: "Without the crown, our children will wither under wrath. Only anointed kings can withstand the winds of Armageddon. They rejoin the *Gilgul* into one body. They destroy the confusion of tongues with their scepters. The crown is the flower of the tree of Ascension."

The female voice: "I would not let my children fall to wrath at the roots, trapped in the Kingdom for the Sleepers' doom. Hold your secret brother close. Embrace him and choose."

Dream Symbolism

Abilities and research will do much to decipher the dream. An Intelligence + Occult or Enigmas roll can be used to supplement player insights.

The Giant: The giant is, of course, Heylel Teomim. The twin stars obscuring his face are his conjoined Avatars. He appears to be a giant because the Heir takes the role of a newborn, tired, bloody and swaddled in white (the color that Heylel wore during his trial), symbolizing one of the Betrayer's children. The masculine voice uses "we" to refer to itself and is Heylel's dominant personality (encompassing his female half within his will). The female voice is an echo of the Orphan that the Rebis absorbed to achieve personal Unity.

Royal Robes: This is the garb of Moloch, earned if the mage overcomes the giant.

The Crown: The crown represents the ritual Heylel used to call a Psychopomp. Joined, it represents the mage duplicating the Betrayer's work. The bloody half of the crown has been stolen from its bearer, MHG.

Holy Guardian Angel: Psychopomp. The "hymn" is the proper ritual.

Adam Qadmon: In Kabbalah, the primordial human of whom all humanity is a part. In Western Awakened circles, the One who shattered into all Avatars. Similarly, the confusion of Babel (emanation from God's messenger, the Metatron) represents wisdom being divided and limited to human (Sleeping) reality. In legend, Enochian is humanity's original language.

Wand of Hermes: A Hermetic mage.

Angels in Shattered Earth: Los Angeles, which is recovering from a massive earthquake that struck nearly a year ago (see **Demon: City of Angels**).

Gilgul: Kabbalistic term for the soul, often used in reincarnation doctrines. The Avatar. Borrowed as the term for the Hermetic rite in which Avatars are "sent to the Creator for final judgment" (which most believe is a metaphor for destruction).

The Sword Napea: The sword guarding the gates of Eden. *Napea* is Enochian for "that which divides," so the sword is that which creates divisions according to God's will.

Tree of Ascension, Kingdom: The kabbalistic Tree of Life. The Kingdom (Malkuth) is the "lowest" of the tree's Sephiroth (Spheres, in this usage), but through it one can rise to the Crown (Kether), the Godhead (or Tenth Sphere).

Anointed Kings: Without the crown of the Betrayer's ritual, the Avatar Storm will kill mages in the end, with "winds of Armageddon."

Phoenix Prophecies

The DVD arrives a few days later, stamped with the mark of the Sphinx. As is usual for a Rogue Council message, there are no arcane connections to any deliverer. It appears alongside the rest of a character's DVDs or in a prominent, mundane place.

The DVD has one track. It begins with the following title:

CLEARANCE ULTRABLACK
Unauthorized Viewing Grounds for Summary Reeducation
Panopticon Field Interrogation Archive
Amalgam: PTFAP-3
Interrogators: D. Washington (NWOGrayOp), M. Romanow (ItXStatArmature)
SecDetail: Bioroid BlackOps 345 and 346, HITMarkV B24, class 3 Primium psi-inhibitor implant.
Subject: "Phoenix" Attakai. RD Profile: Clairvoyant, Telepathic, Precognitive, unknown paranormal activity (see track).

After the title, an opening shot reveals Phoenix, a bedraggled woman sitting in a steel chair in a white room. A silver bead appears to be implanted in the middle of her forehead. This is a Primium inhibitor designed to nullify magic use ("psionics"). She is shackled; an IV drips a clear fluid into her arms. Panopticon agents Dorje Washington and Mila Romanow are off camera, but their voices can be clearly heard as they question their prisoner.

ROMANOW: Are you ready to tell us your real name yet?

PHOENIX: I don't have a name, just a title.

WASHINGTON: An empty identity is a virtue. Why not just release what you know as well? Then we can clean you up. The drugs in your system make dishonesty… painful. Why prolong the agony?

PHOENIX: I only tell the truth. Unpleasant truth is still truth. It's my purpose.

ROMANOW: Then tell us. You're in regular contact with terrorist elements, where you provide psychic intelligence—

PHOENIX: Prophecy… Behold, my terrible angels are loosed.

ROMANOW: Whatever, dear. Your contact is one Mark Hallward Gillan.

PHOENIX: Behold, my terrible angels are loosed — or will be. The final day is not a day, but a torch flaring from future to past.

WASHINGTON: What "terrible angels?"

PHOENIX: The light comes again in glory to judge the quick and the dead. And you will never see them through your single, crippled eye. But the last princes will have two brilliant eyes. Two! Brilliant! Eyes! Those two will become legion!

ROMANOW: Discard the metaphors. Tell us exactly what you mean by "eyes."

PHOENIX: Eyes of the spirit, Mila.

ROMANOW: Washington, how does she know my name?

PHOENIX: They said you were stupid and shy, until the serpent came to you and offered power, Genius dripping from its fangs. Mathematics. Enlightenment.

WASHINGTON: She's overpowered the inhibitor. Security to the prisoner, now.

ROMANOW: I never told anyone…

Two pale Men in Black run in, guns drawn — and freeze in place. All background noise ceases, as if time's been stopped for everyone but the prisoner and audience.

Phoenix looks directly at the camera.

PHOENIX: Go to the Council. Tell Mark that we need two eyes. Three. A thousand. The Ahl-i-Batin's terrible angels are loosed; they won't be satisfied by a few Awakened spirits. Teach them all to see with many eyes! I will see you again, but not in this body.

She methodically pulls off the IV needle and breaks the shackles as if they were made of cardboard. Then she whispers something inaudible into the ears of each Man In Black.

Sound and motion rush back into the scene, but the Black Suits fall to the ground, twitching. A gun held by trembling hands enters from the left side of the shot.

ROMANOW: Bitch. Hands on your head.

WASHINGTON: If you lie down and stay quiet, you'll live.

PHOENIX: *ABBAI KSA.* Be still.

The gun drops and the hands vanish from the shot.

PHOENIX: I know their words of command — their "conditioning." I was a poet; they taught me the verses that chain your minds because, before you were born, they forged each link. We served your masters. Where are they now? They control the spirit of a ruined world and an army of the blind.

Free yourselves. Free the Sleepers. Learn to see. Enigma will take you where dogma cannot.

Phoenix looks up for a moment, then walks out of the shot. The track ends.

Traditionalists with at least two ranks of Occult will recognize the phrase, "Lo, my terrible angels are loosed" from the Ahl-i-Batin's Doctrine of Unity.

The Council Convenes

Well-connected Traditionalists discover that the New Horizon Council (currently chaired by Mark Gillan) is meeting in Los Angeles in about a week's time to hear Senex's Herald, Theora Hetirck. Surprisingly, an Emissary caucus plans to attend. See Chapter Seven for a list of default Councilors. If Gillan is not involved with the Tradition Council in your game, Hetirck asks him to attend because of his experience with the House of Helekar.

The Technocracy also knows of the impending meeting after piecing together Phoenix's interrogation with its surveillance operations. Under Correspondence and Time wards, Panopticon plans and equips for a massive Contingency Five strike. The chance to decapitate the Traditions is too good to pass up.

The meeting will take place at the Belasco (337A South Main Street). The boarded up theater is enchanted with a constant Mind/Prime Effect that conceals it from the notice of any being with four or fewer Willpower dots. Consequently, Sleepers assume that the building was demolished in the late 1960s, shortly after Ecstatics purchased and ensorcelled it. Before its supposed destruction, the theater "degenerated" into burlesque shows and prostitution. Stagehands saw scantily dressed ghosts wandering backstage. Now, the old workers act as consors, and the "ghosts" (actually minor passion Umbrood) are chantry guardians.

The neighborhood surrounding the theater fared badly in the 2003 earthquake. Already poor, it now hosts a shantytown that's swallowed the remaining intact, iron-barred houses. Essentially lawless, its inhabitants share a rough sense of faith and superstition out of desperation and the previous year's angelic visitation. Even though the Consensus has some force, vulgar magic enjoys a -1 difficulty bonus.

The Ecstatics and their consors returned the Belasco to its gilded glory, then enhanced it with the work of new carpenters, sculptors and painters. Woven with the heraldic devices of each Tradition, huge tapestries hang from the ceiling in place of curtains. On stage, nine antique chairs surround a white birch table. Despite its humble surroundings, the chantry's a luxurious place — a bit of Awakening in the middle of a desperate city. The Belasco still isn't the most luxurious chantry in the world, but recent strife forces the Council to accept a more humble venue.

Contingency Five

As Traditionalists gather to debate their purpose, the Technocracy plans its attack.

Under the cover of psionic and electronic countermeasures (a 20-success Time and Correspondence **Ward**) Panopticon Task Force Corona gathers its troops into a Quantum Imaging bay at Nellis Air Force Base, Nevada. The task force is a temporary cluster of Technocratic personnel, dedicated to this mission. It includes six HIT Marks, 30 un-Enlightened soldiers (from the Sleepytown ROTC; see the **Mage Storytellers Handbook,** pp. 175-177) who have been conditioned to accept Technocratic procedures, a dozen Awakened Void Engineer Marines, four Alanson-hardsuited Iteration X military engineers and two NWO psychics. The commandos will separate and pursue stragglers halfway across the world, if necessary. A GPS link to the

> ### Protocol
>
> Any educated Tradition mage knows how to comport themselves in front of the Council. Traditionalists have a strong ethic of tolerance, but they draw the line at pointless, disruptive behavior. The new Council is less formal than the old, which means that Mark Gillan is content to tell rude mages to shut up before calling a motion to Censure.
>
> The Council is given a set period of time to discuss the day's agenda, during which it might ask for comments from the floor. When the time has passed, unfinished items are moved to the next session and the floor is open to petitions and statements. For all floor remarks, a speakers' list determines who can talk on a first-come, first-serve basis. The only exceptions are granted to Heralds, who might question the Council for points of clarification. Group presentations must be arranged with the Chancellor Pro Tempore's secretary ahead of time.

Quantum Imaging teleporter allows them to teleport to new engagements after a brief delay. Quite simply, Panopticon plans to kill the Tradition leadership with a single hammer blow, permanently ending organized opposition.

The operation is headed by General Augustine Aleph, an NWO Man in White who is rumored to be among a handful of Technocrats who receive orders directly from Control. In Act One, General Aleph stays behind the scenes, providing Enlightened support for Corona operatives.

Fortunately, unexpected complications keep the Technocracy from bringing even more force to bear. On the day of the attack, Nevada-area mages are inundated with Rogue Council transmissions directing them to raid the facility. This follows up a series of communiqués that drew Emissaries to the region in large numbers, under the loose direction of an Orphan named Johnny Meyer. The Advanced Energy Commission Construct intended to support Task Force Corona, but the immediate threat of intruders forces them to leave the mission alone. Storytellers might run the raid as a side story, but bear in mind that even though the AEC doesn't want to draw too much attention to itself, the Construct will guard Nellis with everything up to and including tactical nuclear weapons (and as an isolated test site, they can get away with it, too). Rogue Council transmissions call for harassment, not destruction. After a point, mages *must* retreat or face destruction. Use **The Fallen Tower: Las Vegas** to flesh out the information here.

Our main story assumes that Tradition infiltrators succeed in reducing Panopticon's effectiveness. If they fail, additional troops, weapons and the assistance of a Master of Forces (General Oscar Martin) combine to make escape unlikely.

In Session

Unless they drop in very late at night or early in the morning, the player cabal has about an hour to meet and greet other attendees before the Council sits in session. Consors will provide a list of the meeting's agenda. There are a number of minor issues on the table, but the two that stand out are Herald Theora Hetirck's report on the status of the Realm of Entropy and a petition "from a group of mages adhering to the principles of the so-called *Rogue Council Manifesto*." Add any other issues you wish.

When the hour is up, Mark Gillan enters from backstage and says, "All rise. The Council of Nine is now in session." He remains standing as the other Councilors take their seats.

After the Councilors announce their names and titles, they move on to business. Except for the items detailed forthwith, go through the agenda in any order you wish. Use Council protocol (including the speaker's list) to determine how much input your characters have.

When you feel the time is right, Theora Hetirck enters from backstage. The Euthanatos is widely hated because she was a minion of Voormas. After being remanded to the custody of the archmage Senex, Hetirck was pronounced rehabilitated, and she now serves as the earthly representative of her former jailer. Most attending mages scowl when she speaks.

Hetirck's Report

Theora speaks to the audience in a formal, emotionless voice:

"Councilors, Chancellor, members of the assembly: My tutor, Senex bani Euthanatos bids me to speak to you on his behalf. It is with utmost sadness that we report that the attempt to undo the corruption of the Realm of Entropy and Earth's Primal sphere have failed.

"We achieved some of our objectives. *Naraka* Voormas has been denied his Nodes. Evidence uncovered in the Shard Realm has allowed us to track down and bring Requital upon each member of Consanguinity of Eternal Joy who was... found deserving of death by the Council at Concordia. Yet, we have been unable to renew the Gauntlet between the living and dead worlds. The Storm continues to seethe. Were it not for our anchor to an Shallowing, we would still be in danger of rapid discorporation.

Forging the Crown

Obviously, the cabal will want to meet Mark Gillan. This event can happen at several points.

Mark Gillan is backstage before the Council meeting and on stage while it happens. The characters could disrupt the Council session, trick, sneak or otherwise force themselves into his presence. Gillan's been plagued by mages wanting to secure one special favor or another. Not only does he avoid meeting anyone before the session, he also relies on a small jade statuette of Kuan-Yin (a gift from Raging Eagle) that provides him with 15 successes of protection from mind-altering Effects or powers.

During Panopticon's attack (see pp. 65-66), Gillan sees to the safety of Council members. After the Tenth Seat is taken (see p. 66), Batini mages offer to assist the assembly if Gillan comes with them. He agrees, and characters meet him at Arx Karagoz. Even if they meet him earlier, he will arrive at the Batini fortress slightly before or after the cabal once the Batini offer to lead him to the Tenth Seat.

When they're together, Gillan and Heylel's Heir begin to radiate *Storm-Tainted* Resonance. Days before the meeting, Gillan had the same dream as the Heir, but he won't reveal this unless the Heir does.

If the Heir touches Gillan (the "embrace" of the dream), the mystic circuit between the two is complete, for Mark Gillan is the other Heir of Heylel Teomim.

A Grimoire in the Soul

Both mages (and anyone else who uses telepathy to share the Heirs' thoughts) see the tall, androgynous figure of Heylel Teomim in a woodland clearing. The sounds and smells of industrial civilization are absent, as the Grimoire was "inscribed" shortly before he betrayed the First Cabal. Even though he speaks Latin, witnesses can understand him perfectly. The Heirs recognize him as the giant in their dream.

"My children," he says. "My descendants. You are the dream of Unity.

"I write this in the ether to seize the vindication that Akrites tells me will never come. Yet the Seer says I must write. I hope that Chronos has tricked him with false futures. I hope that Porthos, to whom I've revealed the existence of this subtle Grimoire, will not betray me. Yet it seems written in the stars that his jealousy over my Eloine will rule his heart. At my future trial, he will say nothing of this book, and I will be condemned as a Diabolist, among other things.

"So the Seer tells me. But I don't want to die.

"I did not consort with Ildabaoth, the Rex Mundi or any other manifestation of the Void. I will not bow. True Will is the highest law and our ultimate guide on this Path of Thorns. But lore formulated long ago in the black land of Khem tells us: 'As above, so below.' Our will is Below, chained to matter. What is the mirror of our will, Above?

"I found the answer. Our Daemons are consorts of Holy Guardian Angels, called *gallu* in ancient lore. The corrupter of this world imprisoned us beyond their reach, but we might use True Will to climb the Tree of Knowledge and meet those which crown us. They are our true divine reflections; even the dream of the Daemon must submit to them. Thus I have completed myself, under my True Will. I am my own Philosopher's Stone.

"This lore is dangerous. Without a pure heart, the Holy Guardian Angel reflects your own darkness. Keep it secret, my children. It is a secret for the true Council — the one that rules justly. Tell no other, be they your cabal brothers or even Sleepers who might profane the sacred names and call down doom with an ignorant ritual."

Heylel smiles and produces a book from beneath his robes. He opens the book, smiles and says, "Thus do I share with you all the precious things that I have learned."

The Alchemy of Unity

(Grimoire: Arete 6, contains the rote **Holy Union**)

He turns the book toward the observers. It rushes toward them, engulfing them in its pages. Alchemical symbols, Latin script, diagrams and illustrations flash through witnesses' minds. They are not translated. Each page passes by so quickly that anyone but the Heirs find it difficult to remember what exactly was described. If their characters read Latin, players of other observers may make a Perception + Occult roll. Every two successes allows the witness to absorb enough of the text to make use of one level of the Grimoire's Arete instruction capabilities. Every success also grants one fact about the Grimoire's contents apart from Heylel's general mystical insights.

- The "Holy Guardian Angel" or "Divine Will" is a being from beyond the Horizon.
- The being responds to magic similar to the Hermetic Arts, but with an ancient origin. It is too powerful to be bound with Arts that do not meet with its approval.
- The Grimoire teaches one how to summon it but does not provide its name.
- The Grimoire discusses absorbing some part of the "Divine Will."
- The being can directly affect Avatars. It can sunder them, unite them or guide them to specific incarnations.

The Heirs absorb the entire text; Time magic can slow the progression of the pages, while Mind magic impresses them into memory and translates them. In addition to revealing how to cast the ("Holy Guardian Angel") Psychopomp-summoning rote called **Holy Union** (see Chapter Seven), the Heirs can use their memories of the Grimoire to raise their Arete as high as 6 (see **Forged by Dragon's Fire** for rules on Grimoires). **Holy Union** is missing the necessary True Name that must be called.

As noted, the Grimoire can teach the character Arete ranks 2 to 6 without requiring a Seeking. Charge experience point costs as usual. If you don't charge for Arete gains (see the **Mage Storytellers Handbook** for this option) the character may gain a new Arete dot after paying an equivalent amount of experience points for raising the Spirit, Life or Prime Spheres. As noted, other characters must be able to read Latin.

Storytellers should note that this is intended to allow characters to gain Arete at an accelerated pace. They'll need it.

The Grimoire repeatedly warns the reader that she must purify her desires and see beyond her limited ideas of magic, or the "Holy Guardian Angel" will twist to fit her preconceptions. At the same time, the tone of the writing reveals a kind of creeping arrogance, saying that, "A united Will is the natural master of lesser Wills." After mastering the manual and the rote, the mage should rule over colleagues and Sleepers alike after the fashion of a philosopher-king.

Reactions

Only a few minutes pass as the revelation unfolds itself. Mark Gillan is deeply shaken. He now realizes why Porthos Fitz-Empress (who must have known that he was Heylel's descendant) took pains to keep him close by, at the center of Tradition affairs. Was he the archmage's trump card or a focus for his guilt?

Gillan does not want to reveal the nature of the ritual to anyone — not even the New Horizon Council. He doesn't feel that the Council is the "true Council" yet. Because of the Sphinx symbols in the dream he shared with the Heir, he feels that the New Horizon faction needs to solve the Rogue Council mystery (and accommodate the Emissaries) before he trusts their mandate, much less the words of an ancient traitor and apparent megalomaniac.

"The Dark Gauntlet has more than just thinned — in several places, it has simply ceased to exist. By now, you are all familiar with the phenomena of spontaneously reanimated dead. In the deep Umbra, there are rifts that lead to the Labyrinth of the Unmaking itself.

"Our mission was not one of hubris. Anything the *Naraka* would have been able to accomplish, we assembled Euthanatoi should have been able to reverse. But the state of the Tapestry itself has changed. As my master said, 'Reality has not bent like a green tree under the stresses of the last decade — it has broken like withered wood. It is dry and aged. It could be consumed by a stray spark.' The Chakravanti say that this is the Age of Kali, the final era of the cosmos. We have never disputed this, but the fall of our chantries and Voormas' actions have hastened the fall.

"As some of you might know, Sleeper astronomers have tracked a so-called 'stray Kuiper belt object' called KX76. Scientists are unable to determine its exact mass or composition, only noting its luminous, red color. We now know that this is a material extrusion of the Umbral body tentatively identified as Anthelios, the Jewel of Shiva and many other names. This Anthelios is surrounded by Umbral Storms and dangerous Umbrood. All we know is that it burns with Entropic energies — and something else. We can't identify it. We believe that Anthelios' partial manifestation in conventional reality is a sign of the end. Nephandi have changed their rites to include its worship, and it is mentioned in several prophecies.

"Unless an evil hand breaks it, the Wheel will always turn. Time, space humanity — they will renew themselves. Voormas is on the move. The invisible world is thick with his curses, and we believe that he is moments from confronting us for control of the realm. We will protect the invisible world; the visible world, on *this* side of the Gauntlet, is your concern. You must keep the Wheel safe.

"Senex advises you to prepare yourselves. He says, 'You cannot save yourselves, but only flesh and matter end. Souls endure.'"

Chancellor Gillan opens the floor to discussion. The assembly does its best to savage Hetirck, questioning her legitimacy as Senex's representative. Councilor Moro will confirm that she does speak for the Archmaster. Hetirck calmly invites doubters to test her honesty with magic.

Theora knows that Voormas somehow engineered the thinning of the Gauntlet between the living world and the Underworld, but even as his slave, she never found out how. She knows where Voormas is (an Asian hell realm) and that corrupt ghosts and powerful magic tests the Entropy Realm's defenses daily. It's only a matter of time before the mad archmage attacks. She also knows that Voormas was prepared for the Avatar Storm, such that he cast certain spells to maintain an arcane tie to the Earth and prevent disembodiment. (See **The Infinite Tapestry** for details about this Umbral hazard.) The Euthanatoi on the Shard Realm duplicated the Effect by threading their spells through Ravanna's Navel, the Tradition's Bangladesh Shallowing.

The Rogue Seat

The second item on the agenda is the Rogue Council Petition. Whereas Theora walked on from backstage (where the chantry's private rooms are), Alexei DesJean is forced to walk up from the audience.

"I'll be brief, yeah?" he says. "Many of you think we're *les chimeres* — professional agitators. You think the Rogue Council is some kind of hoax our caucuses put together for some reason — revenge, shits and giggles (*pardonez moi*, Chancellor), whatever. So you hid from the Sphinx dreams. You haven't heard the new word from *les Nouvelle Invisibles*.

"The word is that we get a seat. We want representation. We want the Tenth Seat."

Already strained from Hetirck's gloomy address, the assembly's composure frays even further. On the Council, Yves Mercure snaps up to heap contempt upon DesJean's "primitive" demand — an unfortunate turn of phrase that causes several members of the assembly and Dreamspeaker representative Netsilak to glower. Nu Ying leaves, saying, "Inflamed tempers don't lead to wise decisions. I'll wait for calm at my lodgings."

When the tension dies down enough for DesJean to be heard, he responds. "Excuse me, I should rephrase myself. We don't *want* the tenth seat. We *have* the Tenth Seat." He points to Xoca, who grimaces in pain for a moment and spits blood at a space two feet in front of him.

The blood stops in mid air, spattering along a curved line three feet off the ground. An invisibility spell falls, and the Tenth Seat ripples into being in front of Xoca.

"All we want," says DesJean, "is to slide it up to your table."

Xoca passes the seat up to DesJean while a stunned assembly looks on. The Tenth Seat of the old Council on Concordia was lost after the False Heylel attacked the realm. Lord Gilmore recognizes it and quickly confirms its authenticity with Prime magic.

The uproar intensifies into a near melee, as DesJean gives the seat a slight suggestive push toward the Council table. Chancellor Gillan manages to rein in the anger and confusion just enough to organize coherent questions. Under questioning, DesJean will reveal that a Rogue Council transmission led his cabal to the Tenth Seat, and he enters it into the record, as follows:

SPHII724.I.03

Date Received: 4/1/03   **Physical Evidence:** Book
Format: Book   **Recipient Tradition:** OoH
Primary Recipient: Phillip Morcant
#Witnesses: 4   **Identities:** Alexei DesJean/C of E and Akashic, Janet Wolf/Etherite, Aaron Dogon/Akashic, Xoca/Dreamspeakers
Sphinx Present? Y   **Sphinx Form:** Cover engraving
Tracking Attempted: Y   **Tracking Successful?** N
Delivery: Altered copy of *The Fragile Path*
Transcript: "We hooked up with Xoca for a raid on a Grayface-fronted printer. Word was it was a clearinghouse for Grimoires that the Technocracy had snatched to destroy. They'd pulp them and recycle the paper for Neuro-Linguistic Programming readers, MBA textbooks — that kind of shit. Nice of them to recycle.

"We hit it hard, but the Technos had already torched most of the stash. We nabbed a few minor texts — copies of the *Kitab*, things like that — when Phil noticed one pristine book left in a pile of ashes. It was a copy of *The Fragile Path*, but the Sphinx was new. Phil already had a copy from his apprenticeship. He compared editions. In the Sphinx text, Salonikas' prophecy has this additional text:

In the shadow of Moloch, magi will purify themselves, cutting away old ties to Reason. The Persian sect will fall, leaving their quiet secrets in the desert. Those who fled the world will lead the refugees to the buried treasures. While Babylon burns, they'll seize a throne from a desert caravan. The Persians stole the throne that it might not be profaned by Moloch's first successor. It is reserved for the new magus, who has two starry eyes, many souls and listens to the invisible ones. The vision is unclear. This is the second successor or the savior. Enigma takes the new king where dogma cannot.

So we went to Babylon — Iraq. Aaron's good with military protocols and the Union seemed to be keeping its hands out of the war. Turns out some Brit marine opened up an underground chantry thinking it was some kind of bunker. We used a little mojo to look like coalition logistics troops, cased the joint and came back with the Tenth Seat.

"I don't know who killed Aaron — there were a lot of bullets flying around. Let's just say that the payoff better have been worth our blood. We listen to the invisible ones. Our time has come."

Under Attack

Twin revelations about Senex's failure and the Tenth Seat destroy the assembly's self-control. Mages argue, threaten each other and "step outside" for impromptu certámen bouts. This outside disruption allows Task Force Corona to determine (via scientific "scrying") that the Council is in a state of "maximum tactical incoherence." Strike teams teleport to positions at each entrance, with Sleepers covering the HIT Marks as they storm the chantry and take aim at the Councilors. Technocratic probing (by cloaked NWO psychics) reveals a **Ban** (20 successes) woven into the building that prevents co-location. While they can't teleport directly into action, it also means that Traditionalists can't teleport out, making the Belasco a death trap. To allay concerns that they could be coerced into dropping the Effect, the **Ban**'s casters (the only mages who could drop the Effect without using countermagic) are not present.

The Technocrats are here to kill politically oriented mages and devastate the Traditions' "command structure." They'll take prisoners as it's convenient, but for the most part, this is a search-and-destroy mission. Elements of the task force can follow retreating mages to almost anywhere on Earth, but they face minor delays as General Aleph coordinates teleportation Effects with Paradox wards and Nellis Air Force Base's Quintessence supply. This means that teleporting characters have one to three turns of "breathing space" before pursuers appear.

If mages stay and fight in the shantytowns around the Belasco, nearby Sleepers are in grave danger. Their homes collapse, they get caught in the crossfire of

bullets and spells, and the emergency services don't respond unless fire sweeps the neighborhood — a definite possibility. On the other hand, magic and Enlightened Science are easier to use, and the ruins and slums provide excellent cover for hit-and-run tactics.

Storytellers should modify the difficulty of the fight by controlling how effectively Councilors and other Storyteller characters assist the cabal. For the most part, this battle should force the characters to flee. Determine how many Councilors you want the task force to kill, but make room for heroic characters to intervene. The result will determine how organized the Traditions are — and how hard it is to influence them — in the next act. During the attack, the Council tries to flee outside the building and its teleport **Ban** (getting onto the roof or into the sewers also removes one from the **Ban**). Lord Gilmore briefly defends the assembly with a few *very* impressive Forces Effects, but like the others, he believes that it's more important for the Council to survive.

Councilor Blass sends the survivors who get out of the building through a prearranged chain of teleports as fast as she can. Each goes to an armed cache and a squad of consors. Gillan charges nearby mages to stay behind and split pursuing forces before retreating himself. Unless the characters intervene, you should leave Gillan untouched. Assume that he's dogged by Corona operatives until the Batini come to his rescue.

Forewarned

Smart characters will realize that the Phoenix DVD might have fallen into Technocracy hands, and they might warn the Council of the threat of an attack. In this case, a prepared chantry could withstand the assault. The Council adjourns and relocates in a week's time. The theft of the Tenth Seat and contact with the Ahl-i-Batin still occurs at the Belasco in the cloud of general confusion created by the seat's unveiling.

The Poet's Arity

At a critical point in the battle (when the Traditionalists — especially the players' characters' cabal — effectively resist the assault), activate the task force's backup: duped LAPD and National Guard members who believe that they're supporting an antiterrorist raid in the midst of a riot. If nearby Sleepers aren't already panicking, NWO operatives sow terror and anger throughout the shantytown with Mind Effects. If task force elements pursued the characters out of town, they use their Panopticon privileges to press local Technocratic personnel into service.

Unless a character moves it, the Tenth Seat stands on the stage, seemingly impervious to fire and force. As Union reinforcements roll in, a nondescript man and a woman (cloaked with four *Arcane* dots each) appear out of nothingness on either side of the Tenth Seat, lift it up… and vanish. At battle sites, accidents happen to Corona fighters. Technocratic science goes awry. Soldiers shoot each other. An apparent slum dweller kills an Awakened commando with her bare hands. After all, the Ahl-i-Batin are subtle. Throughout the fight, the 10 Batini *khilwati* never cast a vulgar spell.

Outside the Belasco and at battle sites around the world, the tide turns. As the cabal contemplates its response, the thieves of the Tenth Seat appear, their hands held up to indicate that they're unarmed and friendly. This is Farouk al-Faris (see page 91) and his accomplice, Alia.

"We have come to help you and ask you to receive our hospitality," says the man in a light Egyptian accent. "We come courtesy of the Hidden Sha'ir."

"These days," says the woman, "he's called Frater Iago — and other names. Will you come?"

Arx Karagoz

If the cabal won't come, the Batini offer an amulet covered with the Enochian sigils for the Ophanim: a common focus for Correspondence Effects. They tell the characters that if they change their minds, one of them can invest a point of Quintessence to send a brief message.

The Technocracy is still a threat. Panopticon commandos have been thinned enough to allow the characters to pause and decide what to do, but if they wait too long, they stand a good chance of being followed and attacked. If the characters attack the *khilwati*, the Batini teleport away but drop their Arcane long enough to be tracked to Moroccan ruins, where the remnants of the 10-Batini force will incapacitate and abduct the cabal.

Otherwise, the Batini use "thousand-pace strides" (Adept-ranked Correspondence Effects) to transport the cabal to the Moroccan ruins, where they take time to erase their Resonance. The second Effect takes them to the *khilwati* headquarters: Arx Karagoz. Knowledgeable characters realize that the name uses the Latin term for fortress and the name for traditional Turkish shadow puppetry. The colliding languages and subjects suggest some cynical joke. Upon arrival, no immediate location cues are evident. *Masked*, *Shadowy* and *Crackling* Resonance sears the mystic currents around the castle. Characters are offered refreshments, then led through chambers decorated with labyrinthine Arabic designs. As they approach the final chamber, the Resonance deepens.

The Chantry

Arx Karagoz is a three-story Byzantine-style citadel in the outskirts of Istanbul. The place is an *Arcane*-ridden chantry; Hermetic, Batini and Thanatoic magic use is coincidental here. Its collected Backgrounds are: *Chantry* 3, *Arcane* 5, and *Resources* 3. On the floor of a lightless basement chamber, the chantry's Node manifests as a labyrinth of inlaid marble and onyx tiles. Mages gather Quintessence by blindly walking the maze, relying on natural abilities or magic. Tass gathers in shiny black stones in the labyrinth's center.

The chantry has neither supernatural guardians nor an otherworldy realm of its own. There are no consors, as the Batini are ascetics who care for the place as part of their spiritual practice.

Iago's Mask

16-point Artifact

Except for the joyless smile, the mask looks like an ancient Greek funeral mask, made of weathered bronze and tied with a black silk cord.

Worn by the Golden Chalice's leader, the mask conceals the wearer's identity and stifles arcane bonds. An Entropy 5 Effect mutates onlookers' perceptions to overlook distinctive dress, body language, accents and speech patterns, replacing them with the "Iago" template (a graceful robed figure with a hollow voice). It also conceals the wearer's Resonance from detection. The Effect works retroactively. If breached once, subsequent exposure will alter onlookers' memories to forget that they saw or heard anything unusual. As an Entropy Effect, it bypasses most protection against mental control by altering the ephemera of events (what some would call its imprint on the "Akashic Record") instead of individual minds. A Correspondence 3 Effect suppresses any arcane connections except for bonds to a Talisman or Familiar.

The wearer can mentally command any of these powers to shut down for a turn.

Chapter Two: Judgment 67

The doors open, and the circular chamber has a dais at its center. On it, a masked, robed figure sits on the Tenth Seat. Some Euthanatoi might recognize the smiling iron and gold mask; it is traditionally worn by "Iago," leader of the Golden Chalice.

"This is not my throne," the figure says, in Phoenix's voice. "It belongs to one of you."

The Earthly Phoenix

With a gesture, the figure dismisses the Batini, and the doors close behind the cabal. "Iago" takes off his mask. The face is Caeron Mustai's.

Hermetics instantly recognize the mage; see page 91 for his description. **Tradition Book: Order of Hermes** and **Mage Chronicles Volume 1** provide background information.

Caeron tells the cabal his story — and reveals his sins. He answers questions as he speaks, hoping to communicate the gravity of the situation with his confessional style.

What follows is sample dialogue. Don't just read it aloud, though. Steal choice sentences and use it as a general guide for what to say and how Caeron says it.

"I should have died for my sins against Doissetep," he says. "But I am the chief maggot of an order of maggots, devouring silent burrows from the dead flesh of this world.

"When the false Heylel appeared, I knew that my Janissaries could seize that corpse of a chantry. And then what? The Order? The Council? And yet, even as I led cabals to war in the hallways and betrayed us to the Technocracy when Porthos repelled us, I knew that the other politicians and traitors were better than me. They wanted power; I wanted to thwart Ascension.

"When I studied under the hidden Imam, he told me Ascension was Armageddon. He told me it was a wrathful thing, heralded by terrible angels. I believed that if I forced humanity to always Sleep, I would save it. So I was complicit in Helekar's corruption and shared our secrets with the Technocracy. The old Ksirafai lines of communication let me betray us, even as it told me the truth.

"I broke the seals around Fitz-Empress' Sanctum. He only looked up a moment to smile before unleashing the magic coiled within him. He struck with a mote of light. Did I die then? I only remember limitless brilliance, then the Sphinx, which spoke to me in Porthos' voice. It said, 'I forgive you.'

"I awoke on Earth. The Sphinx sent me prophecies and orders. It spared me to prepare the way and redeem myself before Telos comes. I hid myself, taking the face of the Orphan Phoenix to share its warnings. I became Iago to purify the Traditions. I destroyed House Janissary so that none of my successors would use Ksirafai secrets to betray us.

"We can only save humanity by destroying it. Unity is Telos: the end of the Great Cycle and annihilation of everything we know. The Avatars of the Storm feel it coming. It's why they strike anyone who reaches out into the Otherworlds. Ascension is for embodied souls. The whole person finds the one; body or spirit alone will fail.

"The Awakened suffered because I denied it. They suffer again because I embrace it. I was only returned to Earth to prepare the way. You are here to complete it. Two of you will guide humanity to Ascension. You will wear Heylel's crown. I do not know which of you is one half. I found the other in Mark Gillan.

"The Sphinx — the Rogue Council — has this message for you: 'The True Name you seek is engraved on the Tenth Seat. Through Holy Union, you will not create the path to Ascension, but explore it. Enigma will take you where dogma cannot.'"

Decision

Caeron Mustai carefully places the mask on the Tenth Seat then lets out a long breath.

"I'll see where Enigma takes me," he says, before whispering a spell. Then, the room shudders with power as Caeron crosses the Gauntlet. Drawn by his enlightenment, the strength of the Storm is so powerful that what happens is visible in the physical world. Twisted, sharp and etched with tormented faces, the Avatar shards cover the archmage. He smiles just before the Storm tears him apart.

The doors open. Two *khilwati* escort Mark Gillan into the room. The Hermetic looks at the empty throne with grim satisfaction; Caeron promised that he would "accept punishment for his crimes." If Gillan and the Heir haven't already "opened" Heylel's hidden Grimoire, the Storyteller should ensure that it happens now.

Mark Gillan doesn't want to be a "king" of anything, much less lose his individuality by merging with the Heir. He *hated* Caeron; the archmage succored Helekar and threatened his life. All the same, he knows that they have to do something with the power and occult knowledge they've suddenly amassed. The Traditions need it; Panopticon's assault proved that they can no longer assume that the Technocracy will leave them alone.

If the Avatar Storm crosses the Gauntlet, the Awakened are doomed. When the Heir and Gillan

Caeron Mustai tells the cabal everything he knows. Supplement the information in the sample dialogue with these other facts:

• He does not know the true nature of the Rogue Council, but he trusts it because it gave him a chance to redeem himself. The council contacts him in dreams and sudden, waking visions. These visions led him to the cabal and to Mark Gillan. The visions weren't specific enough to pinpoint which member of the cabal is destined to "take up Heylel's mantle."

• He does have a complete knowledge of the history of the Ixoi. He knows that **Holy Union** creates a hybrid creature. Legends call it an Anakim — a monster. He knows that the Stormwardens are descendants of the original Anakim.

• The Avatar Storm is ravaging the Gauntlet with its collective desire to seek embodiment before the end. He doesn't know exactly what will happen when the barrier between worlds falls, but if the Storm smashes into the material world, only mages protected from the Avatar Storm will survive. Stormwardens, Anakim and masters of the handful of Storm-shielding spells that exist will survive.

• He *is* responsible for the destruction of the Janissaries. As descendants of the Ksirafai, they could betray the Traditions to the Technocracy at will. He led the Orphic Circle (see **Hunter: First Contact** to learn more about this necromantic cult) to the Ksirafai library knowing that the Circle would use it to distract the Euthanatos — and as Iago, he ensured that the Euthanatoi would destroy his former House.

• Arx Karagoz and its 15 Batini *khilwati* are Mark Gillan's and the cabal's to command. Because of Caeron's Ahl-i-Batin training (he is their "Hidden Sha'ir"), he is reckoned a Murid (Master) in that "lost" Tradition. Anyone who chooses to take up Iago's mask might also command that faction's twin cabals, the Alpha and Omega Protocols (see **Tradition Book: Euthanatos)**. Even though they follow the characters, the cabals are not passive. They fight for Ascension and will act to encourage their "commanders" to make the right choices.

To Caeron, the cabal members are now generals in the final battle for Ascension. The archmage doesn't know everything, however, and he passes on one critical mistake: He assumes that the Rogue Council wants an earthly representative — a "king" of the Awakened who will guide humanity to Ascension in the last days. The ruler would merge his Avatar with Mark Gillan's, acquiring the "two eyes" mentioned in the dream and the Sphinx transmissions.

"open" the Grimoire, both learn the possible variations of **Holy Union**. The spell can shield mages from the Storm, but the risks are tremendous. Unless "purified," the Psychopomp mirrors the mage's own weaknesses and drives her insane. Through his contacts (including Rogue Council transmissions, if the events were an ironclad secret), Gillan knows what transpired in "Alien Avatar," the story that concludes **Manifesto: Transmissions From the Rogue Council.** Technocracy scientists in the Arctic successfully created an Anakim; the mad creature nearly destroyed the mages who encountered it. The spell has a fatal flaw; how will they correct it?

Ultimately, Gillan (and the Storyteller) will suggest that the characters research, then attempt the ritual. If they succeed, they can pass on the correct method to the Council. If they become monsters, he will enlist the Traditions to destroy them. Unless he is stopped, he returns to the Council. He won't tell the Traditions about **Holy Union**, but he does warn that the Gauntlet might fall. He takes two Batini with him. Through them, he'll keep track of what happens at Arx Karagoz.

Of course, the Heir and his allies might just overpower Gillan and cast Heylel's version of the spell, fusing the two Heirs into a single being. The Rebis will be a corrupt thing; the story then shifts to opposing it. Advice for running this variation can be found in Chapter Seven. Ideally, the characters will *all* undergo the purification Seeking (which follows) and empower themselves, resisting the temptation of other mages' Avatars.

Casting the Spell, Sharing the Secret

There is no set time listed for the characters to use **Holy Union** or to share it with other mages, but they *must* do so for the cause of Ascension. Otherwise the Avatar Storm will destroy the Awakened after burning through the Gauntlet.

The Tenth Seat reveals the correct True Name for each Psychopomp, so at first, any mages initiated into **Holy Union** will need to stand before the seat and reveal the True Name to the caster. Those who have already purified themselves through the Seeking can advise others, increasing their chances of success. Of course, the cabal can transmit the ritual without mentioning the required True Name, but mages who then cast the spell without the proper Name corrupt themselves.

Part Two: The Last War

Only the fortunate warriors, O Arjuna, get such an opportunity for an unsought war that is like an open door to heaven.
—The *Bhagavad-Gita*

The characters have been thrust into the center of a renewed Ascension War. Arx Karagoz, the Batini and the Euthanatoi of the Golden Chalice are theirs to command. Three months pass; the war's players take their places. At this point, allow the characters to test their newfound influence. Their new allies can decisively end several of your chronicle's outstanding conflicts. Keep in mind, however, that the Batini and the members of the Golden Chalice have their own agendas. The *khilwati* are ascetics; they need time to devote to their own spiritual discipline. These are their foci, and losing touch with ascetic practice erodes their effectiveness. Likewise, the Chalice has several outstanding missions to accomplish. Together, these factions keep the cabal informed about the state of the world.

Otherwise, Storytellers should encourage the players to take their characters through research and small, personal stories — such as those suggested by the unfolding events listed in Chapter One — so that the tremendous conflict to come seems mightier by contrast. Remember that successful Seekings are necessary for characters to empower themselves with **Holy Union**; give the characters time for this.

At the End of All Worlds

In Pluto's Umbra, the Realm of Entropy rocks with the battle between two archmages. Long sequestered in an Asian hell realm, Voormas turns against his demonic hosts. With the iron soul of the Yama Queen Tou Mou, he claims the *Pasupatta Astra*: the spirit weapon of Shiva, the Destroyer. Using Quintessence from the murdered god, he presses the attack. His lieutenants are *Yamasattvas*: ancient liches descended from the blasphemous Idran. Spectres, walking dead and *pretas* formed from Voormas' Jhor are the foot soldiers in this war. Curses are their artillery.

Senex of Cerberus rallies his forces: Euthanatoi he called from the mortal world to defend the Realm of Entropy. Even though the archmages are realms apart, the reach of their magic crosses spiritual boundaries. Ghosts and oathbound companions are their allies, but he refuses the aid of other Traditions. Senex's divinations tell him that they are needed elsewhere. The Euthanatoi are outnumbered; in the walking Castle Helekar, Voormas advances step by step, realm by realm. Through its ties to the Golden Chalice, the cabal receives regular news of the Umbral war.

In the aftermath of each exchange, blighted domains sprout like a cancer. These are the Hive Realms (see **The Infinite Tapestry**), flaws gnawed into the fabric of reality by their demonic inhabitants. Spirit-walking Nephandi who survive the torrent of destructive magic note this progress.

By the third month, Castle Helekar batters at the gates of Entropy. Senex destroys the Bangladeshi gate to the realm, but not before dismissing the other survivors. They tell the New Horizon Council that the Realm of Entropy has fallen.

A Hopeless, Glorious Struggle

Storytellers can run the final battle as a side story. All magic is coincidental. In the realm, Entropy Effects and purely destructive spells garner a -3 difficulty bonus. You can run this story with "disposable" characters as a high-fantasy one shot or even allow the regular cabal to participate. In the latter case, Senex detects the subtle threads of destiny around the characters and gives them safe passage when defeat is nigh. In fact, he will *force* them to return if necessary.

In the Realm of Entropy, Senex's forces are headquartered in the Ghost Citadel, a black stone reconstruction of the Great Zimbabwe fortress. Voormas commands Helekar from the middle of the Hell of Being Skinned Alive, where iron knives ride an endless, howling wind. The obscure Shen Bridge connects Voormas' stolen Yomi hell to the Astral Umbra. A further journey leads to a natural Anchorhead: a pit surrounded by a jungle of blue leaves, where the suns shine over the blackened ruins of Mayan pyramids. This is the wreckage of Vali Shallar, once the home of powerful Dreamspeaker and Akashic mages. From there, Voormas' forces secure the Anchorhead so that Helekar might walk through and on to Umbral Pluto.

Senex's defenders cannot win. Voormas is powerful. The *Pasupatta Astra* is a potent weapon, and the *pretas* (Jhor Hobgoblins) and wraiths at his command continually batter at the Realm of Entropy's defenses. Yet in the end, this isn't why Senex's forces lose. At times, the assembled Euthanatoi drive off attackers and even prepare offensives of their own, but a singular event turns the tide against them.

Forces greater than the archmages watch the battle. As Voormas prepares to enter the Realm of Entropy, Senex confronts him. They are evenly matched, so the master of Helekar pauses. Then, in a sudden burst of flame and ashes, Senex's secret patron appears. It is the Psychopomp known as Phoenix.

Phoenix explains that the battle can have only two conclusions that will preserve the integrity of the Wheel. Senex can allow Voormas to pass — or he can use the realm to destroy the world, saving it from further corruption.

Senex will not euthanize the Earth. He chooses defeat and the threat of Voormas' corruption. Even though destruction is the safest path, the Old Man values hope; he puts his faith in the future.

Voormas does not kill Senex. The Old Man quietly releases his life; the Wheel turns.

War and the Flood of Souls

Over the course of the battle, the Avatar Storm grinds into the Gauntlet. Globally, Gauntlet ratings drop by one per month. If a regional Gauntlet was already rated at 1 to begin with, a new Shallowing forms, but local Gauntlets rated at 2 or more before the event leave a last, fragile wall between worlds. For Tradition mages, this is an unexpected boon; for the Technocracy, it's a nightmare. Technocrats battle new hauntings and possessions around the world. The Pogrom kicks into high gear; new recruits and funding are poured into seizing Nodes and Shallowings.

Other Technocrats concentrate on the phenomenon itself. Under Ragnarok Command, they study the Storm, desperately rejecting previous models to find a way to contain it. Scientists with the Void Engineers and Iteration X quietly entertain radical theories. What if the "Dimension Storm" is related to human consciousness — or even inner Genius? These theorists dare Room 101, but they come closer than ever to understanding the Storm's true nature.

Regardless of affiliation, the Syndicate and New World Order activate some of their deepest ties with Sleeper governments, just in case. Evidence is suppressed, programs debunking the paranormal flood the airwaves and vocal, accurate proponents of the occult vanish.

While Traditionalists enjoy some benefits from the fraying Gauntlet, educated observers see the event for what it is. The Storm is tearing away reality's barriers. The swelling crisis brings former rivals together. Rogue Council Emissaries send their experienced warriors to defend other mages from the Union, but they ask for Spirit magic and Umbra lore in return.

Marauders discover that the weakened Gauntlet is a mixed blessing. Some of the Mad Ones are pushed into final Quiet and vanish from the planet. Others call ancient beasts and powers to the fringes of the Earth, and wait.

Then it all breaks down.

The Astral Layer Falls

In the fourth month, part of the Gauntlet collapses.

Avatar Shards attuned to the Astral Umbra break through, destroying the barrier between reality and the realms of thought. These Avatars belong to the Pattern Essence, and they fly through the world in search of compatible human beings. Unlike the Avatar Storm, these shards don't strike mages of other Essences, but the invisible winds can tear Pattern mages to pieces. Many find refuge in Shallowings and along ley lines. It doesn't scour the Earth all at once, though. Mages can use Prime to sense and evade coming "Avatar fronts." Where the Avatar Storm roils, magic goes awry, as *Storm-Tainted* Resonance twists Effects.

The orderly constructs of thought — such as machines, science, mathematics and metaphysics — merge with their ideal counterparts. This is a boon for Technocrats and technomancers. Magical Effects and even normal Abilities gain a -1 bonus to difficulties. Sleeper scientists and philosophers report new breakthroughs. On the other hand, Astral Umbrood make their first tentative steps into the world. Unused to the flesh, they move quietly. A statue in an ancient temple moves for an instant, as its god remembers the stone it once inhabited. Machines either work with unheard-of precision or go haywire, as their spirits adapt to unfettered access to their material counterparts. For the most part, these events look like strange luck or accidents. Some Sleepers turn a blind eye out of terror or sheer disbelief, but in densely populated areas, the Consensus still provides a rough shield. In the presence of at least 100 Sleepers, manifestations are muted.

Avatar Shards merge with Pattern Essences of thousands of Sleepers. This jostles many of them into Awakening but makes them vulnerable to the Storm. A handful throw off the Consensus every day. Over the next month, approximately 10,000 Sleepers Awaken into the Pattern Essence, a figure that increases as time goes on.

The trickle of new mages becomes a flood. As thousands of Orphans work miracles and die from bizarre, horrible wounds, the Technocracy is strained to its very limit. Slapdash cover stories blame plagues and terrorism while the Union hides the bodies and recruits compatible survivors. Incompatible survivors are imprisoned in secret camps. There are too many to condition, so most are kept under guard and fitted with Primium implants to suppress their "psionic talents."

The Storm Mages

Orphans who evade the Technocracy and the Storm often find their way to the Traditions, fleeing to safe locations that Council mages claim for themselves. Cloistered mages usually take the newcomers in. Even in the midst of the crisis, the Traditions hunger for new apprentices.

When mentors talk to their new charges, enlightenment spreads both ways. These newly Awakened mages share a unique power: They can discern the proper True Name for any Pattern mage's corresponding Psychopomp. Storm-Awakened mages relay the information in visions, automatic writing and other intuitive media. Each defines what he knows in his own way. Some dream of an angel of judgment; others, a mandala centered around the mage. This knowledge is triggered by the presence of other Pattern mages, and it never provides anything but vague insight into what the True Name could represent. This baffles Traditionalists; your characters' cabal must provide an explanation.

In fact, the Orphans' knowledge comes from the same force that drives the Storm through the Gauntlet: Telos. As the cosmos approaches its end and the power of judgment swells, the Tenth Sphere leaves its impression on the Storm's Avatars. Rising Telos created the Tenth Seat as its first step, and the Storm Orphans are a further indication of its rising power. Accordingly, these Orphans can also be identified by the single dot of *Storm-Tainted* Resonance they carry. Their magic is haunted by cacophonies of whispers, shadows and

---

The Failing Gauntlet

Even though the Gauntlet is falling apart, spirits don't just materialize out of nowhere. Spirits are still made of ephemera: dream-stuff that is invisible and intangible. Spirits with the **Materialize** Charm can appear automatically, spending Essence as usual. They just don't have to pierce a nonexistent Gauntlet to do so. Other spirits might be able to affect the physical world, but the age of separation between matter and spirit means that Umbrood are largely unused to their new freedom. Over time they take a more active hand, as gods appear to their worshippers and demons return to plague the living in a slow rising tide.

Otherworlds beyond the Penumbra require a guiding spirit or Apprenticeship in the Spirit Sphere to locate and travel them. They don't exist in a direction human beings are capable of perceiving, much less traversing, but the correct guide allows the seeker to *will* a path into being, even if she's a Sleeper. If you know the way, the highest mountains can lead to Astral Spires, and the darkest caves can drop to drowned Stygia. In the days to come, theologians, philosophers and mystics vanish along these hidden paths. To many, these disappearances confirm legends of the Rapture.

As noted, the presence of 100 or more people in a single, coherent community generates a very weak Consensus; a Gauntlet of 1 to 3 exists in these areas. These communities also support a dominant paradigm. Otherwise, all magic is coincidental.

As aspects of the Avatar Storm wash across the Earth, mages find ways to predict and evade it. Prime senses can see an oncoming Storm; combined with the second rank of Time or Correspondence, magic can sense future and distant Avatar Storm patterns. Unfortunately, Time remains unreliable and fails to predict Storm fronts for more than two days in advance. Storms won't usually harm mages with an incompatible Essence unless they stand directly between the shards and a suitable host. As more of the Gauntlet erodes, Essence becomes less and less meaningful. Regardless of Essence, mages with active Prime senses can make a Dexterity + Occult roll (difficulty 6 at first, +1 for each additional turn), giving them time to find a better means of escape. Nodes and ley lines deflect it; the Avatars can't track human beings near strong flows of Quintessence.

Storytellers should decide when and where the Avatar Storm will strike with an eye toward the state of the Gauntlet and the endurance of mages. As the Gauntlet's layers fall, the Storm gets thicker. As a rule of thumb, you might wish to have it strike a given location once a week at first. Eventually, the frequency increases to once every day or two.

The Technocracy fares somewhat better than the Traditions. Primium acts as an effective shield (soaking Storm damage equal to its countermagic rating) and Ragnarok Command's satellite network can observe the global Storm and pass telemetry on to any interested amalgam.

strange sigils: the presence of a higher power on the verge of manifesting.

Thanks to this enigma, your cabal can spread **Holy Union** initiations beyond Arx Karagoz and the Tenth Seat.

Return of the Wild

Two months after the Astral Gauntlet collapses, the Middle Gauntlet follows, unleashing the Spirit Wilds upon the Earth.

Avatar shards attuned to the Dynamic Essence flood material reality. Just as Pattern shards attacked Pattern Essences, the Dynamic shards seek Sleeping and Awakened Dynamic souls. New mages Awaken, *Storm-Tainted* and able to call up the true names of Psychopomps attuned to mages of the same Essence.

Spirits of nature awaken from their slumber. Attuned to their natural cycles, many of them are barely noticeable, but in paved, polluted and wounded parts of the earth, the spirits' rage swells, and bizarre accidents claim humans who walk too closely. Again, crowds can enforce a weak Consensus, keeping the most bizarre phenomena away from major cities, but in the wilderness, animals' roused spirits let them act with new intelligence.

The Triatic spirits — Banes, Pattern Spiders and others — have never had counterparts in the material realm, so their influence is subtler. Few of them become the Drones and Fomori of werewolf legend. More often humans are inflicted with new cancers and palsies as their bodies mirror the corruption, stasis and madness that infects their auras.

The combined effect is disastrous. Paralyzing plagues grip offices. Polluting factories collapse as decades of spiritual rot take hold on the bricks, mortar and workers. In the north, wolves use their new intelligence to feast on human meat and "correct" the natural order.

The greatest difference lies in the skies. After the Middle Gauntlet falls, the Red Star blazes in the sky, visible to all.

Contingency Six

The Technocracy can't rely on subtle tools anymore. Ragnarok Command's attempt to understand the worsening situation skirts the edge of Reality Deviance. Most agents blame the superstitionists for sundering dimensional barriers.

A further blow strikes when all Void Engineers receive this transmission:

Authorization: DSEATC Tychoides Kepler
Priority: Alpha. Override all projects.

Orders: Assemble all available Interstellar Voidcraft and proletarian assets (specialists and colonists) at launch sites. All personnel will board vessels. All vessels will converge at Copernicus installation (coordinates HR 5460, HD 128621, WDS 14396-6050B). Neutralize all remaining physical assets as per General Order 111243 ("Destroying Assets to Prevent Deviant/Xenosapient Capture").

Detailed orders are forthcoming. Personnel should settle all earthbound affairs before arrival. Do not make plans contingent upon your return.

Not all Void Engineers follow these orders, but most do. After handing over some of their equipment to the other Conventions, they destroy the rest, including teleporters and other gear that could be used to travel to off-world Void Engineer installations.

With the loss of the Neutralization Specialist Corps (the Convention's earthbound "alien busters"), the Technocracy scrambles to contain omnipresent supernatural activity. Finally, a month into the fall of the Middle Gauntlet, a single message from Control appears at all Constructs, initiating Contingency Six: the mass internment and neutralization of all Reality Deviants. This contingency requires more open activity — and more subversion of Sleeper institutions — than ever, but the New World Order is prepared. It makes a few adjustments in the corridors of power. In Washington, Beijing, Moscow, Pretoria and elsewhere, national governments claim emergency powers.

World leaders declare that terrorists using advanced technology have launched a worldwide crusade against civilization. The terrorists belong to a coalition of millennial cults called the Nine. Under an uneasy alliance, these cults have stolen secret drugs (especially hallucinogens) and weapons from the developed world to pursue a common, destructive goal. Presidents, prime ministers and generals reveal that for the past three decades, they've monitored the terrorists and appointed a special body to respond to it. This World Advisory Council will direct military and intelligence services from around the globe. Citizens are advised to stay in their homes and report any suspicious activity, especially if it concerns the occult, because the terrorists recruit through such circles.

The World Advisory Council

The World Advisory Council is a public think tank and semi-official alliance of intelligence services, including those of countries that are officially enemies. For over 30 years, the WAC has disseminated bulletins about the threat of "millennial cults." Naturally, the most important officials — senior spies, generals and politicians — are New World Order operatives, with a mix of other Conventions filling out the hierarchy of analysts and advisors for its Sleeper membership. With some prodding from Technocracy operatives, it was a simple matter to convince governments to give them the task of organizing antiterrorist operations. It is chaired by Panopticon leader General Augustine Aleph, but only a few highly placed Sleepers are trusted with evidence that he exists, much less leads a shadow government.

> **US Presidential Address**
> My Fellow Americans,
> America has always taken the lead in fighting for peace and liberty. Some of these struggles have been public; others have been secret, but no less noble.
> Over the past three decades, we have worked with our allies to contain a terrorist threat so dangerous that, before now, publicly acknowledging its existence would have endangered the lives of millions. These terrorists come from all walks of life, but all of them hate liberty and what our great society has been able to achieve. These cults do not belong to any nation and are spread among many religions, but all of them hate democracy and hate progress. In their hatred, they have come together to overthrow our most cherished institutions. Ironically, to do this, they have had to infiltrate and steal from our most secret defense projects. Now they have struck. But America is strong; with the help of our allies, we are ready to fight back.
> In these past few months, you've seen some horrifying things. The terrorists use biological and chemical agents to attack our infrastructure, including mind-altering drugs. In response, I am compelled to activate National Security Directive 58, authorizing the temporary relocation of our citizens. I regret to say that in order to preserve long-term freedoms, we must abide by some short-term restrictions.
>
> **Chinese Premier's Speech to the Communist Party**
> Report all strangers and strange activities; they are signs of the counterrevolutionaries' operations. The People's Liberation Army is ready to defend the dictatorship of the proletariat. As always, we will prevail. Question local troublemakers, especially if they claim to have supernatural powers or a history of mental illness. The rebels are using religious organizations to shield themselves. We must close all churches, temples and monasteries. Public displays of irrational piety are a threat to the People.
> Cooperate with World Advisory Council agents; they are in full command of the Emergency Education Camps. Keep their liaisons fully informed, so that we can coordinate our actions with similar efforts in other nations.

Capture and Internment

Front-line amalgams are deployed to the worst trouble spots to track down Reality Deviants. Using the standing treaties of organizations like NATO, the WAC acquires military and law-enforcement powers. As its agents, Technocrats are authorized to capture and imprison "suspected terrorists" in any coalition nation. Sleepers are either released or transferred to conventional authorities. Mages are "tagged" with dense Primium spheres, implanted into the skin. These "psionic inhibitors" come in several strengths; each time a tagged mage attempts an Effect, he must overcome the inhibitor's countermagic. A field amalgam is issued inhibitors that provide one to five dice of countermagic. Agents follow up with conventional sedatives to provide an extra margin of safety.

Most of the camps were built by governments during the Cold War to imprison dissidents or relocate citizens in case of an emergency. Now, Panopticon supervises them with the help of local military personnel. Agents assess prisoners to determine whether they would make effective Technocrats. Mystically inclined, strong-willed prisoners are executed, as amalgams don't have the time or personnel to crack the hard cases. Otherwise, prisoners keep their psionic inhibitors and stay drugged between tests and interviews.

The Hollow Revolution

A month after Panopticon begins Contingency Six, prison camps in Utah and Siberia fall. Rapid Correspondence Effects and warding transport the attackers to each camp's perimeters. Teams of black-clad killers use magically enhanced guns and explosives to blast through the opposition, then teleport out with as many prisoners as possible. The wrecked command posts in both camps bear the same spray-painted stencil: a Sphinx with "The Hollow Railroad Was Here" emblazoned beneath it.

The word spreads through occult circles: The Darklings are done with posing; from now on, they'll use their magic to forge culture into a spear, headed for the heart of the Technocracy. The Hollow Revolution attacks many fronts. Rabble-rousers haunt the speakeasies that appear in the wake of WAC curfews. The Hollow Ones have always been attuned to the spirit of the age; Sleepers take notice of what they have to say and begin to protest against lost freedoms and missing friends.

In North America and Europe, cliques follow tides of demonstrators, surfacing at camps and World Advisory Council installations to wreak havoc. Their numbers swell with the Orphans that they've freed and mages who've managed to evade Technocracy jailers. Most cells need a thief to acquire gear, a front-line soldier and a mystic capable of dealing with the Umbrood. Teleportation and synchronicity transport them from one combat zone to another. The Hollow Ones' Railroad Riders (see **Tradition Book: Hollow Ones**) manage transportation. The Hollowers light a spark, and in the hands of the Traditions, it quickly grows into an all-consuming revolutionary flame.

Counterattack and Retreat

The Technocracy drops the last degree of restraint. After the 10th camp is hit, the Union unleashes its most advanced tools. ARC helicopters, drones, hardsuited marines and Aurora fighters attack suspected Warpath hideouts — even in the middle of crowded cities. Governments chafe under WAC guidance after these operations claim noncombatants. As the Avatar Storm triggers further Awakenings, Sleepers begin to make the connection: Humanity is changing, and the World Advisory Council is doing its best to suppress it.

Ragnarok Command is overloaded with missions as the spirits grow confident enough to manifest in force. Panopticon is a constant drain on its resources as it presses the Union to provide more troops and equipment. Still, the offensive works. Mages are harried by the Avatar Storm and the Awakened war machine that pursues them.

Mystics find refuge in developing nations. The Union's grip is loosest in parts of Africa and Asia. Mages set up ramshackle chantries in the empty parts of the world. While doing so affords them some protection, it also means that the Technocracy can use indiscriminate weapons far from prying eyes. When such refuges are discovered, they are usually obliterated.

One anomaly is Australia. The Void Engineers who used to monitor the Outback are gone; in the desert, mages find not only safety but pre-prepared provisions and shelter. In 2003, Rogue Council transmissions summoned the Emissaries to Australia's deserts. There are enough provisions to sustain several hundred people for months. The Emissaries have even found Nodes that were never catalogued by Void Engineer surveyors.

War Council

At some point, the cabal should gather mages together to renew Tradition unity and share the secret of **Holy Union**. Arx Karagoz's Ahl-i-Batin have the means to spread the word very quickly, but the Traditions are scattered in the aftermath of the Council attack. The most logical place to meet would be at Arx Karagoz.

Otherwise, mages come to them. After the Middle Gauntlet falls, they brave the Storm and the Technocracy to come to Arx Karagoz. The chantry's Ahl-i-Batin call them. *Khilwat* al-Faris (see page 91), tells the characters that the signs are undeniable; it's time for them to bring the Awakened together at Arx Karagoz. If the cabal rejects the suggestion outright, then the Traditions are lost. Without **Holy Union**, scores of mages fall to the Avatar Storm and can't form a unified front to resist the Technocracy.

As Caeron Mustai's former servants, the Batini have many contacts in the Rogue Council movement. The cabal would do well to invite these Emissaries to the table. You can send the same cabal that attended the Belasco meeting or choose your own. The Emissaries take up the fight started by the Hollow Ones, but they aren't alone. Regardless of affiliation, the Traditions fight for their very survival, but without a larger strategy, the Technocracy and Avatar Storm will divide and conquer them.

Politics

As Chancellor of the New Horizon Council, Mark Gillan agrees to the meeting and brings the survivors of the Council with him. It's risky, but Gillan wants to ensure that there's a bloc that moderates the other Heir's influence. How successful this is depends on who survives. The Akashic, Etherite and Chorus representatives who convened at the Belasco would actually welcome a strong leader. The Dreamspeakers, Cult of Ecstasy and Virtual Adepts either distrust authority or prefer local leaders. They oppose any kind of "president" for the Traditions.

The Verbena and Hermetic representatives might be open to new leadership, but they are suspicious of anything with the stink of Heylel Teomim attached to it. Gillan hasn't told them about the origin of **Holy Union** or his own connection to Heylel Teomim. Of course, if Gillan tells them, he immediately becomes a suspect as well. Therefore, the balance of power hangs on a knife's edge. If Gillan exposes the origin of **Holy Union**, he could turn the Council away from the only solution to the invading Avatar Storm and ruin his own position. He can oppose a power play only by undermining the very thing that can save the Traditions.

On the other hand, Emissaries like the connection. To them, Heylel was a hero — the first rebel, willing to do what it took to keep the Council focused on its goal. If the Council rejects Heylel's work, the Emissaries (goaded by Rogue Council transmissions instructing them to "follow the one who holds the Great Betrayer's staff") can act as an alternative avenue to disseminate **Holy Union**. Unfortunately, such an act could alienate New Horizon followers, leaving the characters with a much smaller, more desperate force to fight with.

It's up to the cabal to find a political solution. The following are a few ways to do so:

Demonstration: By exerting direct control over the Avatar Storm, mages who have undergone **Holy Union** can prove that their methods are effective. The Council is as desperate as it is contentious, and it needs to find a permanent solution before the Storm consumes everything. This tactic is effective only if more than one character can show that the spell works. Even then, visible corruption effects will earn the distrust of the Council.

Espionage: The cabal now commands some of the world's greatest Awakened spies and assassins. They can uncover blackmail material with which to coerce reluctant Councilors. They can even remove those Councilors, if they dare. If they're aiming for leadership roles, the hardest target will be Catherine Blass of the Virtual Adepts. She's sufficiently disciplined and cautious to make blackmail attempts impossible and assassination troublesome.

Submission: Characters can demonstrate their willingness to work with the Council by proving their loyalty. This proof can take the form of an official oath, but only if the characters endanger themselves for the Council's sake. Handing the Council the Tenth Seat will demonstrate their sincerity. Aside from this, the New Horizon Council is constantly seeking other symbols of the old Council of Nine's authority. They've already recovered the Lotus Sword; finding another Tradition Blade would cement their trust.

Calling off the Hunt: Using the Golden Chalice, the cabal can end the last vestiges of strife between the Order of Hermes and the Euthanatos. Both sides are tired of the conflict and would like a way to end it. The Chalice first discovered House Janissary's treachery; Thanatoic assassins relied on them to sniff out the rogue Hermetics. The Golden Chalice can just as easily put the Euthanatos mages' fears to rest by claiming that further vigilance is unnecessary. This has to be played carefully. If the characters have let everyone know that they hold Iago's mask, it will be dismissed as a false gesture and the Euthanatos will try to repatriate its wayward sect — by force, if necessary. If the cabal presents itself as a third-party negotiator and success follows, the two Traditions will heed any future advice.

War and Survival

Mages are angry.

The Technocracy murdered their friends, families and lovers in the Pogrom, and they endured it, because the Union's front-line operatives were good people duped by a corrupt body. They lost their leaders and most sacred places, and they endured it, because it was more important to keep the spark of Awakening alive. They fell from being the priests and kings of humanity to scrambling for the last, waning sparks of wonder, and they endured that descent out of respect for the Sleepers who truly ruled the world.

They are done with mere survival. If justice can't be done, then let it be vengeance. If Armageddon is nigh, let it be the purifying flame of a battle, and not the slow rot of a world choked by hopelessness.

Even dedicated enemies of the Sphinx see the need for resistance. The Union isn't backing down. New mages — the lifeblood of all magical societies — are being abducted instead of initiated.

The Traditions desperately need a way to organize their forces to predict the Avatar Storm, train the growing flood of Orphans and resist Technocratic attack. Your characters' cabal can be an invaluable help here, as their hidden chantry and Correspondence-trained magi can link far-flung cabals more effectively than any other organized force the Traditions have. The Golden Chalice can teach cabals the subtle art of guerilla warfare. Finally, al-Faris can contact the Ahl-i-Batin, and the lost Tradition will fight this battle beside them.

Conclusions

Unless the cabal botches things, the meeting should end with the cabal gaining a measure of official responsibility for the Traditions. There aren't really any right or wrong answers, but there is a possible compromise. The cabal can coordinate the defense of the Traditions, but let the Council guide its efforts. Rogue Council Emissaries will accede to the idea, as long as it doesn't stifle their proactive efforts against the Union. Naturally, if the cabal members are Councilors themselves, it makes things that much easier.

Unless the cabal steps up to help the Traditions, the Traditions will fall. Panopticon and the Storm will destroy them. They need to share the secret of **Holy Union** and unite the Traditions' forces. Only they have the means to do so.

Rise of the Underworld

Seven months after the Gauntlet first weakens, its last layer is smashed open by the Avatar Storm. A Maelstrom follows it. The whirlwinds of the Underworld merge with the world's weather patterns. The skies rain bones, blood, burning iron masks and other effluvia of the dead. In minutes or hours, these artifacts melt back into ephemera, until the horror repeats itself in another cyclone or tidal wave. The Shroud separating the Underworld from the living Earth is gone.

Ghosts are intimately familiar with the living world, and they waste no time returning. The dead rise from their graves or return to the places and people they loved — or hated. The weak aura of Consensus in major population centers manifests as denial; Sleepers refuse to believe that the dead walk.

Primordial Avatars seek out salvation in compatible Sleepers, and a new wave of Awakenings adds to the thousands already roused by the Storm. Every day, hundreds of people Awaken to their magical birthright;

the Technocracy can't contain them all. Already strained by the growing Awakened population and pervasive spiritual activity, the weak pretense of terrorism disintegrates. Days after the first graves empty, the United States strips its sanctioning from the World Advisory Council. Other nations quickly follow suit. The ruse is over; these are the End Times.

A Final Stand

The Technocracy abandons its camps and gathers its forces for a final strike on the Traditions, General Aleph believes that if the organized center of superstition can be crushed, the Union can then turn its efforts to reeducating the Awakened Masses. Granted, it will require social conditioning on an unprecedented scale, but once accomplished, it will renew the Gauntlet and snatch Mass Ascension from the precipice of defeat.

HIT Marks and futuristic weapons augment equipment acquired from the world's militaries as Panopticon leads lightning raids against Tradition strongholds. The cabal is lucky; unless it does something to attract attention, Arx Karagoz's *Arcane* rating conceals it from the offensive.

The Avatar Storm is nearly unavoidable. Unless they possess the Questing Essence, mages who aren't protected by **Holy Union**, the *Stormwarden* Merit or magical protection must find refuge near Nodes or constantly flee the spiritual currents — except in Australia. There, the Storm begins to subside, even as strange phenomena rise from the Outback. If the characters are directing the Traditions' efforts, they can organize an exodus to the Outback. Its Nodes and supplies make it the best place to hold out. Otherwise, scattered remnants of the Traditions are cut down as they flee.

Evil and Madness Lay Low

Where are the Nephandi and Marauders? Traditionalists and Technocrats both ask this question, but they are too consumed with the war to find out the answers.

The Mad Ones gather and wait. The fall of the Gauntlet is a great gift. They wait for the collapse to take its toll and the forces of Order and Balance to settle their differences. The winners will be too weak to oppose them when they rise up to free the Tellurian from the chains of law and moderation.

Of course, every Marauder interprets this opportunity differently. Geoffrey, General of God, sees the warring Archons of the Demiurge fight among themselves, and he prepares his army to destroy the survivors in the name of the Lord. The ragged mages of China's Broken Army Star see the unrighteous Confucian and Communist social orders collapsing, and they eagerly await the right time to teach the true meaning of the Tao. As Wyld forces rise, each mage's Quiet cooperates toward this end.

The Nephandi are missing.

When the Red Star appeared, they felt a sudden pang of terror. The Eye of Ildabaoth wept; representatives of their masters called them to crusade for the Void. Carved into human flesh or whispered in the blasphemous Dragon's Tongue, the call to arms' words varied, but the message was the same.

An interloper wishes to claim the mantle of the Destroyer and forever bar the Dark Lords from returning. He will kill the Void; the Fallen must do everything to prevent that, or their own sweet extermination is threatened. So the Nephandi use their Arts to travel to the battle — to Umbral Pluto, where their enemy plots to extinguish Anthelios.

Armies

General Aleph commands 4,000 Enlightened Technocrats, 8,000 Extraordinary Citizens and 20,000 Sleeper soldiers. He has no other reserves. This is an all-or-nothing fight to which he commits every Technocrat that he can muster. Many of them are scientists, not warriors; dozens are freshly conditioned from the internment camps. Ragnarok Command's amalgams refuse to participate so that they can dispatch aid to Sleepers and defend against threats from the Deep Universe. See Chapter Seven, for systems you can use to determine the shape of the conflict.

Twenty ARC-2 helicopters, four Aurora transatmospheric fighters (see **Guide to the Technocracy**) 1,000 hardsuits (see **Convention Book: Iteration X**) and 500 HIT Marks are at their disposal, along with dozens of conventional vehicles and satellite support. The Auroras each carry six Polydimensional Neutron Devices (commonly known as "spirit nukes"). Aleph will use his air power to obliterate major concentrations of Traditionalists, followed by Sleeper soldiers, then teams of Extraordinary Citizens led by Enlightened amalgams. These forces gather over a week's time. If the characters have been paying attention, they can muster their own defenders right away. Panopticon is preoccupied with its own maneuvers. In any event, the Technocrats *want* the Traditions to gather their best and brightest, so they can fall together. The dilemma for Tradition mages is that if they stay apart, the Union can hunt them down at its leisure. If they unite, they risk everything but have a slender chance of victory.

What resistance can the Traditions offer? That depends on your characters. If they don't take an active role in organizing the Traditions, scattered Emissary cells dot the Outback — easy prey for Aleph's army. Assuming they use the whole week, the characters can gather up to 3,000 Tradition mages and 5,000 allied Sorcerers, armed with whatever Wonders they can find. If the cabal takes less time, decrease the Traditions' strength proportionately.

Through popular culture and religion, the Celestial Chorus and the Hollow Ones can most effectively mobilize Sleepers. The Hollow revolt primed Sleepers to stand by their side. The Chorus has the ear of thousands of faithful. Few of these allies will be skilled soldiers, but given enough time, the Tradition and Craft could raise as many as 10,000. The other Traditions can bring 5,000 more.

War and the Dreamborn

Chapter Seven offers guidelines for running full-scale battles.

Australia's spiritual landscape is unique. Despite the Gauntlet's fall, it retains an earthbound realm, protected from the tremors of the magical universe. The mages who study such things call it a *Sleeping Land*; Australia's is known as the Dreaming. For full details, see **Dead Magic 2: Secrets and Survivors**.

The Dreaming rises to shield its land. In the weeks after the Shroud's fall, the Storm winds quiet down, but other stranger, phenomena arise. Primary among them is the rise of the Dreamborn: the once-slumbering spirits of the Outback's mystical landscape. Long ago, their physical bodies calcified into the land, but now Uluru (also called Ayers Rock) shifts, and the land around it quakes — something repeated on a lesser scale at sacred sites throughout the country. Viewed with Spirit senses, the Dreamborn are vast creatures, suggestive of their mortal descendants. They are simultaneously humans, the land and the animals of their own story cycles, etched with convoluted marks of power — the Songlines that keep their memory. The Eaglehawk,

Lightning Men and others hunger for the Quintessence that their slumber denied them.

The Dreamborn possess incalculable power — enough to match and perhaps exceed the Technocracy's weaponry. For game purposes, each one manifests as a Paradox Backlash targeting concentrated sources of Quintessence that do not belong to the land or initiates of the Dreaming — typically, a two-point Backlash per point of Quintessence. Avatars brimming with Prime Energy are included — unless they are protected by **Holy Union**. Those mages are marked as belonging to another power; the Dreamborn will not touch them.

If the Traditions can hold out against the first wave, the Dreamborn's rise proves to be a powerful benefit. Storms smash Technocracy craft out of the air and swallow battalions into the earth. With each incident, the Outback's Nodes strengthen; their Quintessence refreshes twice, then three times as quickly. But when mages completely drain a Node, the Dreamborn weaken or turn to reclaim their power. Mages can discover this by talking to Dreaming-initiated informants or [if their players succeed at an Intelligence + Occult roll (difficulty 8)] after witnessing the power of the Dreaming for themselves.

If the Traditions are well-organized and frugal users of Quintessence, they gain the upper hand. Storytellers should decide how well the cabal enforces this goal by running a few battles, then using narrative techniques to describe the rest of the war. When the Traditions begin to win, they receive a new warning from the Sphinx.

To Storm the Tower

To conventional dating techniques, the huge rock painting looks thousands of years old, but despite its Aboriginal style, the sphinx and binary code mark it as a magical transmission. If the characters don't encounter it directly, it comes to them as a photograph or video transmission of the rock wall — perhaps one from a battle site.

When decoded, it says the following:

If you destroy the Union, you destroy yourself. Instead, defeat the Technocracy by saving it. Meet Control in the White Tower. Go to the Fortress of Government at Midnight. In the Assassin's Hour, say you seek and serve Nowhere. Give Holy Union to Project Ragnarok. You need only meditate upon them and it will be done. Enigma will take you where dogma cannot.

Fallen Utopia

Characters with two of more dots of Cosmology know that the Fortress of Government is an Astral Realm (see **The Infinite Tapestry**) that extends from the Vulgate to the Epiphamies (the "top of the Fortress"). Getting there is easy; without a Gauntlet, mages can will their way there via any government complex large enough to get lost in. As they travel, mundane offices become the Fortress' Corridors of Power. Hallways twist and transform into every form of government that ever existed.

At night, the Fortress grows corrupt. Hostile Umbrood servitors (and mortal politicians who've wandered here since the Gauntlet's fall) challenge the characters, asking for identification, authorization and bribes. Storytellers can use a combination of roleplaying and Abilities such as Law, Leadership and Subterfuge. Once they reach the top, the characters can see the whole symphony of human bureaucracy play out below.

In the hour astride midnight, the corridors are completely dark. This is the assassins' hour; spiritual reflections of political killers stalk the halls. At this level, Assassin Umbrood (see page 93) are divided into ideological camps, not nations. The cabal is an unknown element, so the spirits try to ascertain their affiliations. Taking a side is extremely dangerous, as the other factions will temporarily ally to eliminate the side with the "unfair advantage."

Of course, clever characters (including those helped with Linguistics and Enigmas) will realize that in Latin, "nowhere" is Utopia. The assassins respect characters who declare this affiliation. Naturally, regardless of their side, they're the *real* defenders of that principle. They can lead the characters down the correct corridor, though they all swear that it can't be found at midnight. Nevertheless, it's there — and it's the only time that it appears.

The Utopian hallway is dusty and cobwebbed with the work of tiny, sickly Pattern spiders. No Umbrood will follow them. At the end of the hall is an ornate set of wooden doors, inscribed with the rose and cross. When opened, they lead to a hill surrounded by what appears to be French countryside. Below the blazing Red Star and ringed by seven walls, the White Tower of Languedoc glitters in the astral night.

The Chamber of Command

The gates are ajar. When the characters walk through, silver and gold metal flows out of the ground, forming armed, robotic monstrosities twice the height of a human being. They follow the characters but do nothing to impede their progress. Circuit patterns crawl across the inner walls, then vanish without a trace. The place's power becomes more noticeable with every step toward the center. *Paranoid, Regal, Secretive* and other

Resonance is plainly apparent. The characters feel as if they're being watched by thousands of eyes, and human-looking shadows and ominous sensations punctuate every moment.

The tower has a rich 19th-century interior. Empty laboratories and staterooms lead off from a huge central staircase. Finally, at the top, two brass bound doors carry the gilt seals of every original Convention, except for one. The wood is slightly scarred around the former resting-place of the Craftmasons' sign. The doorknob is a bit dusty, but it turns easily.

Inside, a grand circular chamber holds 10 seats: splendid wooden thrones inlaid with screens and the silver webbing of sensors. They surround a glass table, which acts as a giant screen. Maps of the Earth and Umbrae float inside it, and coded gibberish scrolls by each map as arrows point to sectors, Constructs and even individual Technocrats. In the center, a translucent dodecahedron glows softly and spins slowly.

The only inhabitant is a boy with black curly hair. No older than 10, he sits on the table, swinging his legs. He wears a dull orange jumpsuit with "DSEATC" stenciled on the breast pockets. This is Tychoides, head of the Void Engineers. As the characters enter, he's toying with a flaked obsidian hand ax. This is the Knife of Ixion, an artifact of critical importance to the destiny of humankind.

The Clothes Have No Emperor

Tychoides inhabits a cloned body that hasn't fully grown, but his Enlightened faculties are honed to near perfection. The characters could kill him, but his mind and Genius would simply co-locate to another body. He would consider this evidence that the characters don't deserve the opportunity he wants to share.

"Do you have any questions?" Tychoides says as he gestures to the empty seats around them. If asked, he tells them about the true nature of Control.

The Consensus has always dreamed of secret masters, giving them the names of gods, angels, saints, enlightened adepts and eternal kings. This was also the dream of the Order of Reason, but it was always kept in check by the Craftmasons. The Convention valued common labor to deified rulers. Like all the Conventions, they believed that there were higher mysteries for the elect, but that their role was to hound every worker to Ascension in the Great Craft. But the other Maximi — the rulers of the old Conventions — had different ambitions. In the late 17th century, the Craftmasons were disbanded and their history was reduced to a footnote in the Union's annals. The remaining Maximi began their slow evolution into Control.

Eventually, few in the Order could remember their masters' names. They only knew that the rulers of Reason were nearly omniscient, able to pry into disloyal thoughts and sense the smallest inclination toward inefficiency or rebellion. The Order instituted a harsh regimen of discipline to prevent disloyalty and sloth. Social conditioning and bureaucracy took hold, by the 19th century, the Maximi were renamed the Invisible Collegium. High-ranking scientists and politicians were rumored to be members, but they would confirm nothing. Over time, some of those who were rumored to be Invisible Masters would vanish. The rank and file of the Order of Reason assumed that they had been summoned to the Collegium's secret chambers to continue their work.

The truth of the matter was that under conditioning, thousands of Enlightened minds projected their wills toward the idea of an all-seeing, hidden leadership. At first, the rulers of the nascent Technocracy reveled in the power this idea gave them. They saw themselves as the apex of Reason's philosophy: humanity rendered godlike by human will alone.

Then they began to fade.

After all, invisible masters don't need bodies or personalities. As the 20th century dawned on the Technocracy, Control's humanity had vanished. Only ephemeral bonds remained, collecting the Union's subtle paranoia and crystallizing it as orders from on high. As other agents and Scientists grew influential, conditioned will followed suit, stripping them of their humanity and substance. The Technocracy annihilated its greatest minds.

For the past 100 years, the true ruler of the Technocracy has been the fears and aspirations of its members, forged into a palpable shape by what might be the greatest magical ritual ever created. When the Avatar Storm struck, Control weakened, just as the Technocracy believed it would. When the Union fell prey to Tradition terrorism, Control returned to save it, just as the Union hoped it would. These were not the stated desires of every Technocrat, but a collective, subconscious urge that social conditioning forged into the truth.

Only two Conventions could fully resist this urge: Iteration X and the Void Engineers. Under Tychoides' direction, his Convention undid social conditioning and relocated its leadership to deep space. Iteration X was saved by the Computer, a toolmaker god who hoped to use humanity to complete itself. It instituted the Machine Cult to prevent its Technocrats from giving birth to a rival god.

Why is the master of the Void Engineers doing this?

"The Technocracy failed, but Technocrats must not," he says. "They can't repair the Gauntlet or save the world for Reason, but they can save it from Madness." He tells the cabal that the Mad Ones plan to defeat the final battle's victors, then consume the world with their own chaotic paradigms. The Traditions and Technocracy *both* need to be strong for the struggle ahead. Nevertheless, Tychoides won't force anything. He is bound to the Technocracy by history and legend. If the collected will of the Union detected his influence, it might consume him just as it did the old Maximi.

"I don't want any part of your 'Ascension.'" He nods to the empty thrones. "I wonder how much it would resemble theirs. There is enough wonder to be found in men, women, base matter, the energies of stars and in all created things."

He points to the table, and the maps vanish, to be replaced by a white star surrounded by a translucent shell. Lines of stellar power trace the shell's outlines.

"There is another universe. We found the gate here. My explorers will keep their bodies and minds and map the new Void.

"I leave this universe and the Technocracy to you." Tychoides places the Knife of Ixion on the table. "A gift from the Ksirafai," he says. "They called it Ixion's Knife. In the old, secret lore of the Order, it was revered as the first tool used by men to defy the gods."

Tychoides walks across the table to the floating gem. He explains that this is the Grand Viasilicos, the ancient Wonder by which the Maximi communicated with the entire Order of Reason. Now, it is the center point of the illusion of Control, where the central, self-dominating will of the Union gathers before issuing its instructions to the Enlightened everywhere. It still retains its old powers, in that it can be used to issue orders.

"Tell them anything you want," he says, then walks away.

Choices

If the characters do nothing, then when the Marauders attack, there won't be enough organized opposition to stop them. They must call off the Union's assault, then share **Holy Union** with Ragnarok Command. A mere thought accomplishes this, but the mage must be familiar with the ritual. Furthermore, the mage needs to be able to couch it in technomagical terms or else her transmission violates social conditioning, wreaking havoc upon the Union. Doing so requires cooperation between a technomancer and mystic, or a brilliant flash of insight. The Enigmas, Occult, Science and Hypertech Abilities will assist characters, but Storytellers should also reward clever explanations from players with success.

By sitting in any chair and willing it, characters can relay orders to the entire Technocracy. Panopticon is especially susceptible to this transmission. Ragnarok Command's devotion to Control has eroded due to the high concentration of Iteration X operatives and because their investigations into the supernatural have weakened their collective social conditioning. The Union's collective consciousness can interpret general commands (such as "call off the attack"), then transmit them to senior amalgams as specific instructions, These are relayed though normal channels and have all the appearance of authentic orders.

The Grand Viasilicos presents two dangers: one for the Technocracy, and one for the characters. Contradict social conditioning too much, and Paradox courses through the Technocracy; *every* conditioned agent gains one point, which contributes to a Quiet Backlash. Such are the consequences for shattering a magically imposed worldview. Commands (including simple information) such as "accept the truth of mysticism," or "surrender to the authority of the Traditions" qualify. Storytellers should consult the **Guide to the Technocracy** to work out what other orders would violate the Union's core directives.

With every message, the cabal risks being incorporated into the Technocratic mass mind. Each character can issue a number of messages equal to her Arete, at the cost of one *permanent* point of Willpower each. The mage feels part of her essence drain into the Grand Viasilicos. Clever phrasing helps a little, but Storytellers should count run-on sentences and convoluted orders as two or more messages. After using up her allotment of messages, the mage's player must make a Willpower roll (difficulty 8). Failure causes immediate discorporation as the mage is subsumed into the psychic construct of the Technocracy. The Viasilicos can't be moved; it's now the metaphysical center of the realm as well as a Wonder.

Ideally, the cabal will persuade the Technocracy to call off the assault on the Outback and prepare for the Marauder invasion. A thoughtful cabal can pave the way for an earthbound dialogue between Panopticon forces and Tradition mages.

The last vestiges of the Ascension War end, but Ascension requires one last quest.

Part Three: Wandering Stars

I come into this world, I accept evil, I resign myself to death.

— Zoroastrian proverb

The Gauntlet is gone. For good or ill, the spirits have returned. If the cabal managed to avert total war, the Traditions and Technocracy bury their dead, repair their strongholds and guide the thousands of Storm-Awakened mages. A month after the end of the war, a tenth of humanity throws off Sleep — and the numbers still rise. Millions have died witnessing magical conflict, as those newly Awakened in the path of the Avatar Storm or at the hands of Umbrood. Nations either stand on the threshold of collapse or have fallen into desperate anarchy. Surviving Sleepers distrust the Awakened. The oppression, horror and warfare that followed their rise to the public eye inspire some to cleave to the old law: "Thou shalt not suffer a witch to live." Even Technocratic science is viewed with suspicion — a fear that inspires calls for a simpler society and sometimes, Luddite violence. Is this the new age of wonder?

Light years away, the Dyson Sphere known as the Cop vanishes.

The Avatar Storm wanes. Mages with **Holy Union** and Sleepers weaken it when they host Avatar shards. One inconsistency troubles mages versed in Avatar lore: The Questing Essence is missing.

The Sphinx

At the end of the month, the last Rogue Council transmission arrives. Each member of the cabal receives it in the language and medium he favors. Virtual Adepts find it waiting on their laptops; Hermetics discover an Enochian scroll tucked into their library. In all manifestations, it bears the sign of the Sphinx. It reads as follows:

Thank you for your trust. Will you trust us one more time?

When the characters finish reading, Dante is there, even if it entails being many places at once. This was a simple enough task when he was a Master, but as an Oracle, it's a part of his nature.

To a Broken Refuge

Inspecting Dante with supernatural senses reveals an aura unbound by a body. Streams of power connect him to the ground, the air and into the subtle dimensions of the Umbra, where they weave into the Tapestry of all things. Yet he is still human. The colors of sadness, hope and wonder course through his subtle body. Characters do not feel the consuming power of an archmage around him, but a sense of completeness — interaction with everything on the subtlest level.

Any attempt to interfere with Dante's purpose fails without fanfare. Still, he never influences the characters' decisions with anything but his words. He asks that they bring the Knife of Ixion with them. They'll need it for reasons he can't explain.

"I wish I could tell you everything you want to know," he says, "but other forces make that too dangerous. Will you come with me to Horizon? Your answers are there."

If the characters try to press him on what he knows, he repeats his reason: There are other powers that would sense the truth even as it was uttered. He — and the Rogue Council — can give a full account only in the safety of the realm. Dante will only bring the cabal with him. He will, however, give the characters up to a day to settle other affairs. If they choose this option, he will transport them at a predetermined time of their choosing. Then, with a thought, they appear at the gates of Concordia, the ruined capital of the Nine Traditions.

See **Horizon: Stronghold of Hope** for a look at the realm in its prime. The Diamond Wall is blackened with soot; the Gate of Correspondence is cracked, throwing its Arabic designs and silver circuitry askew. Insurmountable **Bans** prevent co-location. Dante quietly walks toward the Council Chambers in the heart of the city. The broken wonders of the last Council of Nine are everywhere: The skeletons of zeppelins lay in the wreckage of temples made of living blue wood. Prehistoric creepers choke the alleys; feral cats chant nonsense Enochian and Gaelic as they prowl for food. Skeletons clutch broken staves and ray guns.

Dante leads them up the broken steps to the hallway called the Janua Sapientae. The old gates are sealed, and nothing more than mirrors or empty frames remain. Then there is the green-domed Chamber of the Table Cenacle, where the Rogue Council awaits them.

The Rogue Council

The tapestries are shredded. The statues that once adorned the chamber are ash. But the Table Cenacle and Ten Seats of the Spheres remain — including the Tenth Seat, which returned when the characters appeared in Horizon. The Saxum Oculorum's crystal has been carved into the shape of a Sphinx: a crude, chiseled archetype for the seal that accompanies each Rogue Council transmission. All of the seats but two are occupied.

Chapter Two: Judgment   83

In the Seat of Entropy, a hundred human shadows converge into the image of Senex, the Old man of Cerberus — the Council's newest member. In the Seat of Forces, the figure fluctuates between images of the gods of thunder and fire, elementals and angels of wrath, before settling into the form of Porthos Fitz-Empress. In the seat of Life, three bloody-handed goddesses part to reveal Nightshade of the Verbena.

A host of golems, robots and arcing electricity become the phantom of Alexis Hastings. Bearing a diamond sistrum, Jou Shan of the Akashic Brotherhood emerges from a coiled water dragon. A shaft of light and a host of singing voices rise, then fade into Sister Bernadette of the Chorus as she takes the Seat of Prime. The Dreamspeaker Ihuanocuatlo emerges from an obsidian mirror. Lastly, crimson and ashen-skinned figures converge at the Seat of Time. The naked man and woman bear the faces of Marianna of Balador and Akrites Salonikas, and the figure in the seat shifts between both shapes.

Dante takes the Seat of Correspondence. The Tenth Seat belongs to the cabal.

The Way of the Sphinx

Dante tells the cabal that they can ask anything they wish. See Chapter Seven, to uncover the truth about the Rogue Council. There are no more secrets — only a final task to ensure Ascension.

As powerful as Dante is, he can't protect the Rogue Council's Avatars from Telos. Despite their bond with the Oracle, they remain discorporate. Telos will annihilate them. Even so, the mages who these Avatars once embraced have transformed them. They choose enlightenment for all, even if it means sacrificing their chance to rejoin the One.

Two things bar the realization of that goal. The first includes the Marauders, who will try to fragment humanity's destiny with unchecked Dynamism. If the Technocracy has avoided destruction and spared the Traditions, this concern is well in hand. Side by side, the two societies can fend off the attack. Only the cabal can counter the second obstacle: Voormas, Grand Harvester of Souls.

Helekar's master thwarts Ascension out of compassion — and fear. By unhinging the Wheel of Creation, he hopes to re-create the world in his own image: a Destroyer that never kills; a Black Mother who never gives birth. This would be the supreme act of *necrosynthesis*: unity between the life and death principle. Voormas' Tapestry would be world without growth, but without loss. The dead and the living would be a part of one indestructible whole. Awakening would be impossible.

Ascension and destruction are one. This is the secret of the Red Star, the so-called "Eye of Ildabaoth." It is Telos, the Realm of the Tenth Sphere — what Voormas intends to destroy.

The Fallen and the Tenth Sphere

The Euthanatos were not the only mages to oppose Voormas — but they hardly had common cause with his other enemies. The Nephandi left Earth, swarming to waiting Hive Realms and hellish vessels bound for the Entropy Realm. The Dark Lords call them and the princes of the Hive Realms gibber and punish, pointing to the enemy that threatens their very existence. As disciples of destruction, they miss the ironic truth: They have always served Telos. The somnolent Malfeans are Judgment's oldest manifestation — its destroyers.

Early mystics encountered the Neverborn on their quest to understand natural cycles. They did not see the fullness of Ascension in destruction. They were terrified, and they looked for a way to placate these unknowable beings. They dreamed of punishment and conspired to avoid it by destroying themselves — Descending. While they hid their souls in the Void, they would send sacrifices to placate the Neverborn. The Nephandi developed a dark theology to explain their nightmares, but as victims were bled upon their altars and Avatars were warped, the visions of damnation only became stronger. The irony was that the more they tried to avoid Judgment, the more they did to invite its full wrath. The Cauls mark them as Oblivion's own; they've cut themselves off from the Psychopomps who could save them.

The Tenth Sphere is not merciful — it is annihilation *and* liberation. Its dark Malfean half represents the former; the Psychopomps, the latter. Yet the Rogue Council *doesn't know this*. It serves the other half of the ultimate truth.

Now, the Malfeans sense a force moving against them, defying their purpose, and their dreams call Nephandi to defend the locus of their power. The sudden resurgence of their masters catches many Nephandi by surprise, especially when, against all likelihood, the Hive-Dwelling schismatics join them in the crusade to defend the Red Star. Then again, a few of the Fallen scholars have now begun to see the parallels between the Hive Realms, the labyrinthine strongholds of the Underworld's spectres and the so-called "cracks in the Umbra" reported by Archmasters who visit the edges of reality. The ultimate truth of the matter is left for Storytellers to decide.

The First and Final Focus

Despite his immense power, Voormas can't assassinate Death alone. He needs Quintessence and Awakened will to perform the ritual. Senex's work to purify the realm and Helekar's old Nodes slows Voormas down (the Old Man's Avatar believes that he'll be ready in two lunar months), but he will ultimately bypass the wards and curses laid down by Euthanatos defenders. This leaves him needing Awakened will — a requirement fulfilled by the *Pasupatta Astra*.

In the *Mahabharata*, the *Pasupatta Astra* is Shiva's weapon. In the poem, the Destroyer gives it to the hero Arjuna, warning him that with a thought or glance, the weapon can destroy worlds. The weapon's form or nature is never described, but Indian mystics claimed that it was more than a knife or trident. It was also a *doctrine* that Shiva used to lead the world to the end of time. Modern mages might call it a meme or paradigm capable of binding thousands to a single purpose. Voormas used it to this end; every Questing Avatar from the Avatar Storm is bound to the *Pasupatta Astra*. Voormas carries it in the form of an ephemeral trident to assist his ritual magic. Soon, he will direct thousands of Avatars toward the destruction of the Red Star.

The Rogue Council doesn't know whether Voormas could succeed, but even the attempt would be disastrous. Telos will rise up only when a sufficient number of humans are Awakened — a "critical mass" that will rouse it. Voormas prevents that by binding millions of Questing shards in the *Pasupatta Astra*. Even if he fails, he condemns those souls to destruction; the Tenth Sphere will only exalt or damn embodied Avatars. Either way, he needs to be stopped.

The ephemeral *Pasupatta Astra*, however, is only one aspect of the weapon. The characters acquired the other when they took the Knife of Ixion from the White Tower. In truth, the *Pasupatta Astra* is one fragment of a very old tool. The First Focus was crafted before the Sundering; human hands worked matter and spirit into a single instrument.

The Greek Ixoi described it as a pit of flame; their Chaldean brethren claimed that it was a bronze sword. It's true shape was a high mystery, known only to the Masters of the Craft, but even then, this understanding was incomplete, for it might have taken any shape before the Sundering. All sects agreed on the one truth that with it, the first murderer slew his kin. This crime defied the natural order. As a result the worlds shattered and the murderer was condemned. In the spirit world, Ixion was bound to a wheel of fire. On Earth, humanity was bound to cycles of Sleep and fitful Awakening.

Stolen Essence

The archmage spent centuries searching for the *Pasupatta Astra*. He discovered it questing in the deep reaches of the Apex of History (see **The Infinite Tapestry**), but the guardians of the ultimate weapon refused him. Despite his aspirations, he wasn't a god. As an enemy of the Wheel, he was no Arjuna. The Presence that Voormas identified with the true Shiva cast him back to the Spires time and time again.

In the Ten Thousand Hells of Asian legendry he found the solution. Yama Queen Tou Mou was barely a shadow of Kali, but she was divine. He approached her, offering to synthesize his Awakened power with her own, but he kept his own council. At the culmination of the Tantric rite between archmage and the goddess, Voormas released the souls bound to her. His necromantic skills were insurmountable; the stolen souls that made her a match for the archmage dispersed. Perverting the spiritual union between Shiva and Shakti, Voormas devoured her remaining essence. He returned to the Apex of History with the stolen spirit of a goddess. His divinity confirmed, he claimed his prize.

As Above, so Below. For sundering the worlds, humanity was cut off from its natural magic. The Knife of Ixion and *Pasupatta Astra* remain. One might counter the other, but not even the Rogue Council knows how it might be accomplished. Still, fate ordains it. This last quest cannot succeed unless the First Focus is reunited.

The Shattered Dark

After explaining what they know, the members of the Rogue Council ask whether the characters will go to oppose Voormas. They cannot compel the characters for the same reason they can't simply do it themselves: Direct intervention would destroy the value of free will. They can only communicate and advise. If they do any more, humanity's choices become meaningless and Telos dismisses its accomplishments. Such is the nature of Judgment.

If the cabal refuses, Voormas completes the ritual. The horrific results of that are left for the Storyteller to adjudicate. As we warned, it is possible for characters to fail. Whether or not they choose to go, they have the ruins of Horizon to scrounge for equipment and resources. Allow characters to accumulate up to 10 bonus dots worth of material Backgrounds each, including

Quintessence, Wonders and Familiars. The Storyteller determines exactly what forms these items take. For example, a character can easily assemble a made-to-order library and a great deal of Tass, but he will have to decide carefully between Wonders left by previous inhabitants. Artifacts might lack instructions, malfunction or otherwise complicate the plot as the Storyteller desires.

The cabal can study here as well. You might wish to allow characters a full season of study using the system in **Guide to the Traditions.** The magical nature of Horizon makes study go faster. In addition, the Rogue Council and Great Library's effective trait values are *Mentor* 6 and *Library* 6, respectively. Millions of occult texts and the Avatars of the greatest esoteric masters cut study time to days or hours.

When the characters feel ready, Dante opens a portal into the Deep Umbra. Horizon vanishes, and the broken vistas of the Deep Umbra unfurl before them. Reality is falling apart.

The Chambers

The battle between Senex and Voormas strained the fabric of reality, so new Hive Realms and other fissures into the Unmaking stretched and grew at the seams. The Nephandi's cabals used byways through the cosmic rot to attack the Entropy Realm. Voormas' liche-generals repelled attackers from the gates of conquered Cerberus,

and the archmage allowed himself enough time away from his final rite to scourge the enemy with his own curses. The Deep Umbra sagged under the collective weight of this power… and snapped. The Fallen were trapped, buried in their own spiritual caverns. Jupiter, Saturn, Uranus and Neptune seethe with Storms in the middle of a vast plain of broken reality.

The normal boundaries between the Realms of Matter, Time, Mind and Spirit no longer apply. They have combined and broken into an infinite number of connected realms — the greatest labyrinth in existence. But the power of the Spheres continues to fuel the realms. Time distorts the passage of events so that years might pass over a few seconds in baseline reality. Mind creates the realm from the mages' own dreams and nightmares, Matter embodies it, and Spirit connects and binds it to the power of their Avatars. Each realm is a materialized Seeking… or something even more dangerous.

Worlds of Enlightenment and Damnation

Unlike typical Seekings, each realm is experienced by every member of the cabal. The Seekings are still keyed to specific characters, however. The rest of the cabal can help one character overcome her flaws. Then, when she succeeds, she can opt to either leave the labyrinth (and can proceed to the ruins of Cerberus or home again) or use her newfound insight to find a portal to a new Seeking Realm. The next Seeking Realm challenges a new character's spirit. Thus, once everyone has had a successful Seeking, the entire cabal might move on to its final destination. Of course, it's also possible to *abandon* your comrades. A successful Seeking imparts the esoteric insight needed to bypass the rest of the realms. Only a mage who has had a successful Epiphany in her own realm can find the gateway to the next. If he leaves or fails the Seeking, the cabal is lost. Instead, they can use Spirit magic to break through the local Pericarp and enter the dark side of the Labyrinth: Harrowing Realms.

Each Harrowing Realm is inhabited by Nephandi, demons, Hive Dwellers, spectres, Banes or an unholy combination of each. When the barriers between the Sphere Realms collapsed, these creatures were trapped in their spiritual "tunnels." Some Nephandi were immediately disembodied in a rush of accelerating time. Others were fused with their allies. Maddened Fallen prowl realms in the bodies of the demons they once summoned.

Even though they are trapped, the influence of the Mind and Spirit Realms gives the inhabitants a terrible power: They can seize the Avatars of visiting mages. In a mockery of a Seeking, the Avatar takes physical form here, but the pervasive power of the Unmaking traps it

> ### Other Battles
>
> The cabal is fighting the central struggle for Ascension, but not the only one. On Earth, the remnants of the Traditions and Technocracy fight the Marauders. Fantastic beasts, high technology and titanic force contend. The Marauders want to liberate the world by tearing it apart. By driving everyone mad, they'll free them to explore their own personal universes — what a sane mage might call the ultimate prison. The intensity of the war is on par with the Battle of Australia. If the cabal ended that conflict without decimating the Technocracy, the combined forces of Reason and Tradition win the day. This makes for an exciting story in its own right, so Storytellers might wish to play it out.
>
> Thanks to the Sphinx, several cabals take parallel paths, taking the brunt of Voormas' defenses so that the players' characters' cabal can reach Helekar. Amanda Janssen's Second Seven is one such cabal (see the Prologue). Add others as you see fit.

in a nightmare scenario. These are anti-Seekings, controlled by the inhabitants of the realm. The enemy can either twist the symbols of a normal Seeking or set up a mindscape composed of its own evil beliefs. The Fallen will target one mage at a time, attempting to force the victim to deny her Avatar or contradict the lessons she's learned thus far. For example, the Avatar might be cast as a plague-bearing child, so that its mage will forget compassion and recoil away.

If the victim succumbs, the penalties are terrible: She *loses* a dot of Arete and all of her stored Quintessence bleeds away. She betrayed her own Avatar. The inhabitants of the realm will usually try to strike shortly afterward, hoping to imprison the susceptible mage, break her spirit completely, steal her essence and use it to try to escape the realm. If the cabal can resist temptation and destroy the creatures anchoring the realm, it falls away into another Seeking Realm, keyed toward the last victim of Avatar Harrowing.

Despite the influence of the Time Sphere (which allows the Storyteller to take as much time as she likes playing through each realm), the realm cannot accelerate time to the point that it would vault the characters past the appointed time of Ascension or destruction. As the end approaches, the Sphere's "range of motion" shrinks along with its prophetic properties.

Baring the Soul

The Harrowing concept originated with **Wraith: The Oblivion**. For more advice on running them, consult the **Wraith** core book, **The Shadow Players Guide** and **Doomslayers: Into the Labyrinth.** One difference is that a mage's Harrowing features the Avatar as a separate entity. Instead of a Shadow (a ghost's "dark side"), the director of the Harrowing is a Nephandus or demon, so the cabal can confront and destroy their tormentors. Just be careful not to let the characters punch through Harrowings with brute force. Each Harrowing Realm is similar to a Demesne (see **Guide to the Traditions**) in that it obeys the will of its inhabitants.

The Destroyer of Worlds

Past the realms of enlightenment and suffering, two worlds loom. The Realm of Entropy on Umbral Pluto is a black sphere silhouetted against Anthelios: planet of the Tenth Sphere. The gray mist that surrounds it is the wreckage of Charon, a moon destroyed in the battle between Senex and Voormas. Together, it looks like a pupil contracting in a fiery eye. The worlds are getting closer. Then, a small moon appears from behind the planet. It's Cerberus: Senex's chantry and the gatehouse to the realm.

Cerberus is deserted. (Senex sent every survivor home.) Only the bodies of Voormas' minions remain. Some of them still twitch in magical half-death, but their souls are gone. Characters can rest here, as there is fresh water, food and medical supplies, despite the battle for Pluto. The invaders didn't care about the needs of the living, so they left these resources untouched.

The tang of destructive Resonance hangs in the air. It's a simple matter to follow it to the gate where it hangs most strongly — but with it is a hint of Dynamism. The simple oval, opened by Cerberus survivor Mitzi Zimmermann, allows characters to pass through its smoky exterior to the Entropy Realm beyond.

Castle Helekar

Voormas' fortress stands among the ruins on scorched Mahaghat Plain, resembling a gaunt stone man, the towers of its arms raised in a defiant prayer. The sky is nothing but the blood color of the Red Star. As they approach, the characters feel the hum of concentrated *Storm-Tainted* Resonance emanating from the castle's crown. A 30-success **Ban** prevents scrying or teleportation or shortcuts through the local Umbral periphery within a mile of the fortress.

Howling, sharp-toothed creatures pour from the gates at Castle Helekar's feet. These are Voormas' *pretas*: Hobgoblins formed from centuries of Jhor. Each looks like a caricature of the archmage himself. (See pp. 94-95 for details.) Among them, characters can see the withered, mauled bodies of Voormas' lieutenants — victims of their master's Jhor. They attack the characters immediately, trying to devour their flesh and with it, their body's Quintessence. The flying greater *pretas* try to envelop airborne characters, then drop into the swarm. The characters have to keep moving, lest they risk being overwhelmed by sheer numbers.

If the cabal prevails against these enemies, then Castle Helekar joins the battle. An ancient 20-success Matter/Entropy rote makes the structure immune to decay and its walls tougher than modern tank armor. It can strike twice per turn, and its fists and feet cover a 30-foot diameter. Anything it strikes takes at least 20 levels (not dice) of bashing damage and, if it crushes a character under hundreds of tons of rock, is sure to kill him outright unless he's protected by magic. The fortress is directed by the bound ghost of its architect, but it's clumsy (four dice for attack purposes).

Even though it's nearly impossible to destroy, the fortress can be entered through its doors and windows. It's incredibly fast for its size, so players must make a Dexterity + Athletics roll (difficulty 7) to enter. Failure means being crushed against a moving parapet or wall. Storytellers should either determine the amount of bashing damage based on story needs or roll one die, using the result as the damage dice pool.

Castle Helekar does have another weakness: Voormas hasn't had time to protect its power source. It draws 10 points of Quintessence per turn via a Correspondence-Prime Effect that Senex originally created to provide for the realm. Ten successes of countermagic can cut this power off, stopping the fortress dead in its tracks. It won't fall, however. Enchantments allow it to stay frozen in any upright position where its feet touch the ground.

Voormas

None of the fortress's momentum is imparted to its inhabitants. The corridors twist and buckle as it moves, but magic reduces the effect to a gentle swaying.

This was the Consanguinity of Eternal Joy's fortress. As such, it's filled with gruesome reminders of the sect's place in Tradition history. Human bones are ever present, but not as ritual tools. They've been crafted into practical things such as walking sticks or inlaid in doorways. The walls are engraved with paeans to the gods of destruction in Greek and Sanskrit. A fine, metallic ash flows down the hallways, moving with the breeze, but the stone and bone doesn't look careworn at all. Only the dueling chamber's cracked and blackened marble bears witness to the powers wielded here.

Voormas is the only inhabitant. By the time the characters enter, he has assumed his Avatar form. He awaits them on the battlements — the spiked "crown" on the head of the statue-fortress. In one left hand, the *Pasupatta Astra* blazes with red and gold light. In his presence, the cabal hears a great wailing sound: enough screaming voices to fill the whole realm. The howling resolves itself into chanting in hundreds of languages, with the tongues that each listener understands standing out from the rest.

Shivasakti, thou art the divine Father and Mother
Grant me thy devotion, destroy the evildoer
and the withering Wheel of Ages from whence evil issues.
Wear the garb of Maya; conceal the truth in thee
Let our desires become ultimate wisdom
Let our accomplishments lie eternally.
Fix form out of formlessness with thy miraculous power
Conquer all death and fate beneath thy heel
and let stillness be the eternal law.

This is the *Worshipful* and *Destructive* Resonance of the *Pasupatta Astra*, multiplied by thousands of Questing Avatar shards. The trident is a "placeholder" in reality — an icon representing the supreme doctrine of the Destroyer. The souls enthralled by it lend their power to Voormas. He intends to loose that massed magical will upon the Red Star, snuffing it out, "destroying Death" and eliminating Telos. The dirge of worship is a sign of the ritual's progress. Luckily for the characters, the *Pasupatta Astra* is committed to this task, so Voormas can't use it to snuff out their lives.

Death Gods

The archmage musters as much magic as he can spare to kill or repulse the characters. If he senses a weakness, he destroys a character in as horrific a manner as he can fashion, all the while claiming that his cause is just. After all, the Nephandi oppose him. The cabal's been sent by servants of the Red Star, a legendary omen of evil. When appropriate, Mind spells and superhuman Manipulation back his argument. He wants nothing more than to create a world where humanity isn't chained to karma or death — a vision of Ascension.

Voormas needs three things to successfully perform the ritual: Quintessence, the Realm of Entropy and the *Pasupatta Astra*. Aside from defeating him in direct combat (which carries its own complications), the cabal can stop the ritual by neutralizing the necessary ingredients. The spell is actually quite simple, but an enormous undertaking. Quintessence directed through the Entropy Realm is absorbed by the *Astra* and channeled by the legions of captive Avatars. These Avatars serve as Voormas' ritual partners for a massive Entropy Effect designed to destroy the Red Star and all of its metaphysical aspects.

The Quintessence cost is enormous. Without that power, the ritual would be too difficult to perform. The realm is still linked to nine powerful Nodes, cultivated by the Consanguinity of Eternal Joy, preserved by Senex and reclaimed to power the ritual. Unlike the arcane connection that animated Castle Helekar, the link to these Nodes is secure: 50 successes have to be overcome to bring it down. The **Ban** around Castle Helekar keeps Voormas rooted to the realm; characters would have to physically force him out of the realm. Alternatively, the cabal could overcome this Effect. Voormas will try to kill characters who attack his standing magic. Failing that, he'll bulwark them with his own Awakened skill.

Finally, there's the *Pasupatta Astra* itself — the chink in Voormas' armor.

For all his wisdom, Voormas doesn't know that the *Astra* is a fragment of the First Focus. Now that the Gauntlet has fallen, the two halves of the artifact can finally merge, returning to their original, innocent state. Strengthening the arcane connection between them does so. Voormas' **Ban** doesn't cover this magic because he didn't anticipate this particular threat. A 14-success Correspondence 3 Effect accomplishes this goal. The archmage might sense and counter it, however, even if he doesn't understand its purpose.

Another method is simpler. The *Astra* and Knife of Ixion must collaborate to kill a single person, binding the First Focus to its original purpose: murder.

Doom

This is the last battle for reality. The characters fight it as they wish, but each choice they make has consequences. On the other hand, they might make a choice we haven't anticipated. Take what you see here as a framework from which to create your own conclusion.

Killing Voormas stops the ritual, but has a terrible price. The archmage is cursed such that his killer inherits his madness. See Voormas' description (pp. 94-95) for details. Steeped in Heylel's **Holy Union** and corrupted with the will to remake the universe in his image, the murderer becomes the true Second Successor of Akrites Salonikas' prophecy. Earth's remaining mages must oppose him. That story is left for you to tell.

If the characters reunite the First Focus, the *Pasupatta Astra's* trident vanishes. The material shell that was the Knife of Ixion crumbles to dust, paying the price for an ancient violation of cosmic law: the first backlash that sundered the worlds.

The Questing Shards of the Avatar Storm burst forth from the remains. Without **Holy Union**, witnesses are instantly annihilated. As a wave of power, the Avatars sweep through the broken realms and to the Outer Horizon. The barrier crumbles. This is the end.

Ascension

These are the final moments of the universe. All the barriers are broken; the Outer and Inner Horizon dissolve before the racing fragments of the One, questing for human hosts. This is the last tide of Awakening. At last, on the broken Earth, everyone is a miracle worker.

The Awakened create wonders and destroy monuments. Cities are raised from the dust, then sundered in the birth pangs of power remembered. But the newly Awakened were all Asleep once; most of them remember the humility and compassion of mortal days. The last miracles are not born of fire and water. Progenitors heal shamans who bear wounds from their common war with Marauders. Little gods repair Enlightened ma-

Chapter Two: Judgment 89

chines. At night, a red glow lights the world: the purifying fire of Telos' Red Star.

When the last fragment of the Avatar Storm finds its host and the last living mortal throws off ancient Sleep, every will sings to the subtle places of the universe. Only the Neverborn recall the ancient chorus, and they, too, throw off the last throes of torpor. The terrible angels are loosed to do their duty. They consign illusion to the Unmaking by turning it into truth. They destroy the barrier between science and mysticism, sacred ground and simple earth.

The Mad Ones are expelled from the cosmos; every Quiet births a universe that lives and dies according to its merits. The worshipful Fallen are consigned to the Hells of their dreams: what they always truly desired. Judgment annihilates the last barriers; humanity claims the right to reward and punish itself.

Technocracy triumphs in all its forms. Gray Men exult in submission to the Control of their own will; transhumanists find the key to Singularity consciousness. Every technology is immanent.

Others find their Unity, their Akasha, their True Ether, their uncorrupted tongue of Enoch, all integral links in the chain of reality. That Entelechy conquers the last barriers of magic and Paradox. Joyously, they move back through Time and create themselves. Thothmes, Bhât, the Himalayan War, MECHA, Concordia — all are part of the thread that is cast back through the ages to pull history again, to the moment of Ascension.

There is always the One, but diversity — the Cycle and the Other — is never excluded. There are uncountable paradigms, but they don't chain belief or power.

In the end, they are games.

Appendix: Players in the Last Act

A number of important characters play roles in this story. To avoid redundancy, many characters that have been covered in recent **Mage** books aren't listed here. Space consideration prevent us from listing standard statistics for minor allies and antagonists, so see the **Guide to the Technocracy**, **Guide to the Traditions** and other templates for details. Keep in mind that canonical characters should be seen as placeholders for other figures who matter in your own game. Take a look at your chronicle's roster and see where they might fit in.

Caeron Mustai: The Repentant Phoenix

He has so much to make up for.

The founder of House Janissary (and the last Ksirafai) kidnapped Caeron when he was a child, never knowing that the young mage had already been initiated into the Ahl-i-Batin by al-Khidr, the Occulted Green Man of Batini myth. Al-Khidr appeared the night before Caeron's kidnapping and told the boy that a new part of his destiny was at hand, then he revealed the inner mystery of the Ahl-i-Batin.

Caeron thought little of the secret until he learned the arcane secrets of the Ixoi. He combined the knowledge of his two Traditions and learned the terrible truth: that Ascension was a destructive force whose time was at hand.

Therefore, the ruler of House Janissary denied Ascension. He used old Ksirafai ties to leak information to the Technocracy. He hid crimes and undermined the Council of Nine with his willing tool, Getulio Sao Christovao. He helped only the Batini, a Tradition he considered to be composed of his spiritual ancestors. Arx Karagoz was a refuge from his sins; a place to purify himself until he was ready for new treachery.

Then Doissetep's Winter ended in thunder, and Caeron expected to die. Instead, he had a vision of a phoenix, struggling to rise from its own ashes, and a sphinx holding the souls of Doissetep's victims. Then he saw the future and his purpose.

The first Rogue Council transmissions were prophecies. He disguised himself as an Orphan named Phoenix. He sought out all the old secrets of his House. He passed

them on to the Rogue Council, and subsequent transmissions led mages to hidden Nodes and old lore. In another guise he penetrated the Thanatoic Golden Chalice, Ixoi who long ago disagreed with the Craft's decision to join the Order of Reason. He engineered a purge that cleansed the last bit of treachery from the Janissaries.

Image: Caeron can look like anyone, but his natural form is that of a handsome Middle Eastern man with long, black hair. A thin scar bisects his face, indicating where magic tore him in half before his patrons intervened.

Roleplaying Hints: You must redeem yourself to find peace. When you were steeped in sin, Ascension was simply using you as an unwilling tool. Now you know that it's inevitable — and glorious. The virtuous will be rewarded. You are not among them, but you're prepared to face whatever torments await if it means ensuring that humanity is exalted instead of just destroyed.

Farouk al-Faris: Leader of the Khilwati

Farouk al-Faris doesn't enjoy the profane acts that defending Ascension requires. He's been a thief, a murderer and a con-artist, but his successes have never brought him joy. He prefers asceticism and simple living. As such, he's representative of the *khilwati* of Arx Karagoz: humble, efficient men and women who eat and breathe secrecy.

Al-Faris served the Hidden Sha'ir for 20 years. Of all his schemes, Caeron's connection to the Batini was his most innocent. They were his people, trained to avoid the fallout of his secret treachery. He hopes that, in the end, he can preserve these Batini so that if he was ever held accountable for his crimes they could bear witness — and tell the terrible truth about Ascension.

The *khilwati* will stand by their master's wishes, but the Hidden Sha'ir proved that weakness can claim the mightiest. Caeron denied his destiny; al-Faris and the rest will do their utmost to ensure that your players' characters stay the course, even if it means twisting the intent of their orders.

Caeron Mustai's legacy served these Batini well. They have contacts throughout the Traditions, and they make a peerless network of spies and messengers. Their magical specialties enhance their secret identities, safe houses and social ties, which they've accrued by decades of intrigue.

Image: Farouk is a slightly gaunt Egyptian who dresses in a robe and skullcap unless his work requires a disguise. He has a quiet voice and unassuming manner, as befits a man who's spent his life offering himself to Unity. Other *khilwati* share his tendencies. Half of them are Caeron's Bedouin cousins. The rest, like al-Faris, come from all over the world.

Roleplaying Hints: The *khilwati* prefer silence, humility and inaction, but if something is to be done, it should be done well and anonymously. Glory is another temptation from Iblis. Nevertheless, sometimes it's better to exploit others' flaws than to correct them. God has given imperfection a purpose, too.

Tradition: Ahl-i-Batin
Essence: Questing
Nature: Martyr
Demeanor: Architect
Attributes: Strength 3, Dexterity 4 (Precise), Stamina 4 (Tireless), Charisma 3, Manipulation 4 (Wise Speech), Appearance 2, Perception 4 (Excellent Hearing), Intelligence 4 (Mechanical Aptitude), Wits 5 (Lightning Intuition).
Abilities: Academics 3, Alertness 5, Athletics 4 (Endurance), Awareness 5, Brawl 4 (Blinding Strikes), Dodge 5 (Rolling), Enigmas 5 (Paradoxes of Ascension), Etiquette 3, Linguistics 5, Medicine 4 (First Aid), Meditation 5 (Moving), Melee 4 (Knives), Occult 4 (Arabic), Stealth 5 (Disguise), Survival 4 (Desert)
Backgrounds: Avatar 2, Arcane 4, Contacts 4, Destiny 2, Influence 3. (All of Arx Karagoz's Batini benefit from their chantry.)
Arete: 4
Spheres: Correspondence 4, Mind 3, Prime 3, Time 3
Willpower: 8
Quintessence: 6
Resonance: (Pattern) Geometric, (Primordial) Shadowy

General Augustine Aleph

In the beginning, Man created the State. And the State created Augustine Aleph, and it was good — or would be, if he could remember which state, when and how. Citizenship is meaningless now. Any military in the world will let the general into its secret installations and assume that he's come from the very top. As his command became universal, his distinctive identity diminished.

General Aleph has been a member of the Technocracy for nearly a century, though the years when he must have worked as a front-line agent and even his original name and face have faded from all memory. His black uniform makes Technocrats and Sleepers tremble and obey, but it has no nationality and no insignia. Only the recent addition of Panopticon's eye strengthens the popular rumor that Aleph is the face of Control. It's a reputation worn by a handful of individuals in the Union, but Aleph — like Choe Yo'ng and the other rulers of the World Advisory Council — knows that it's false.

He has risen here because something nameless has pushed him, stripping away more of the man he used to be with each new power or secret initiation. Now, Augustine Aleph is a vessel for something greater. At night he dreams of an ancient door. Behind it is Control: the people who remember his name and purpose. But the general fears that if he takes that walk or reaches for more power, those people will flay the rest of his identity from him. There is precious little left, so he remains the consummate general, representing all nations, delivering precise, anonymous death to the enemies of Technocratic hegemony. Now that he commands Panopticon (a mission given to him in a dream), he senses that he's on the verge of an apotheosis. He'll either attain supreme power at the cost of his identity, or he'll learn the truth about his past. In either case, he's eager to proceed.

Image: Permanent procedures ensure that General Aleph appears to be the highest ranking person in any military organization except for heads of state. When he uses this authority, personnel records confirm his command and memories twist so that men and woman he's never met remember decades of work under him. In all cases, he's seen as the man who command's a nation's secret weapons and spies. He's a fit, pale man who speaks in an agitated sounding baritone and looks to be in his late 50s, but any of these details can be changed to suit a particular mission.

Roleplaying Hints: You've given everything to the Technocracy — even your name. You can see the secret movements of conspiracies in the world, but your role is that of the hammer, not the scalpel — you smash down or cut away the secret world when it threatens to reveal itself. You have an intuitive mastery of mind control and the exotic physics of space and quantum power. This mastery aids you immensely in your operations, as you can shield advanced technology from the Paradox Effect for selected missions.

Most of all, you want to return to the normal life you suspect you once had or to find some glorious enlightenment in the final, invisible layer of the conspiracy. The Traditions are the last hurdle to overcome. You intend to break them and seek your own destiny. If doing so means taking to the field personally to force a final resolution, you'll do it.

Convention: New World Order
Essence: Pattern
Nature: Perfectionist
Demeanor: Director
Attributes: Strength 2, Dexterity 3, Stamina 3, Charisma 5 (Commanding), Manipulation 5 (Subtle), Appearance 3, Perception 4 (Global Awareness), Intelligence 5 (Master Strategist), Wits 5 (Adaptable)
Abilities: Academics 3, Alertness 3, Awareness 5 (Paranormal Threats), Brawl 3, Computer 4 (Military Systems), Dodge 3, Drive 3, Enigmas 3, Etiquette 3, Finance 3, Firearms 4 (Handguns), Helmsman 3, Hypertech 5 (Teleportation), Intimidation 5 (Threats of War), Investigation 5 (Counterespionage), Leadership 5 (Military), Medicine 3, Occult 3, Science (Physics) 5 (Quantum), Subterfuge 5 (Espionage), Technology 5 (Military)
Backgrounds: Allies 10, Avatar (Genius) 4, Cloaking 4, Contacts 10, Destiny 4, Influence 9, Requisitions 10,

Resources 7, Rank (Panopticon) 5, Secret Weapons 5, Spies 9

Arete (Enlightenment): 7

Spheres: Correspondence 5, Forces 3, Matter 4, Mind 4, Prime 5, Time 4

Willpower: 10

Quintessence (Primal Energy): 20

Resonance: (Pattern) Hierarchical 2, (Pattern) Synchronous 2, (Primordial) Liquid

Assassin Umbrood

These spirits stalk the Fortress of Government (see **The Infinite Tapestry**) by night and represent secret murder as a tool of rule. By day, these spirits are innocuous servants of the Corridors of Power, but as the halls darken and corruption reigns, they throw off their disguises and prepare for bloody work.

At the lowest levels of the fortress, the assassins represent specific nations, terrorist groups and militias. Spirits wear the masks of CIA hitmen and Wahabist bombers. As characters ascend, the assassins become purer archetypes. Technocratic explorers would be amused to find replicas of their own Men in Black battling Guy Fawkes effigies. Finally, at the Epiphamies, the assassins represent the types of government. The forces of Republican Democracy, Anarcho-Communism and Hereditary Monarchy fight in the darkened corridors, each trying to block the attempts on their own officials.

Naturally, the "victims" re-form on the following night, making the struggle as endless as it is pointless. Visitors are in danger because they might be mistaken for enemy agents. Aside from this concern, the Umbrood often try to recruit characters to act as scouts or decoys.

If their missions are spoiled, they'll lash out against those "traitors" or "counterrevolutionary elements" that they hold responsible.

Image: By day, the spirits are minor clerks or receptionists — easily overlooked by mages in search of Boons. By night, their appearance changes according to the level of the fortress and their own affiliations. On the highest floors, they take the form of famous figures representative of their political system. This causes some embarrassment (the spirits are supposed to be subtle killers), so most wrap themselves in dark cloaks and masks. Most gather in groups of four to six to plot the night's intrigues, though some very large operations (such as a complete re-creation of the assassination of Julius Caesar) might involve over a hundred killers.

Willpower 5, **Rage** 7, **Gnosis** 5, **Essence** 17

Charms: Blast (Weapon), Death Fertility, Disable, Iron Will, Track

Abilities: Brawl 3, Dodge 2, Etiquette 3, Firearms 4, Investigation 3, Melee 4, Politics 4, Subterfuge 4

Pretas

Voormas' legion of Hobgoblins surrounds Castle Helekar. Characters can also encounter them during the battle for Pluto and alongside the archmage's other minions. There are two kinds. All of them look like distorted homunculi of Voormas himself. They number in the hundreds.

The majority of them embody different kinds of deaths. The Hobgoblins suffer deep cuts, oozing bullet wounds, lesions and broken bones. Some are animate clouds of ash and bone chips. Voormas has feared death for a long time, so every variation of his anxiety is represented. One *preta* in a hundred looks like the traditional image of the hungry dead, with curling tusks and distended bellies. These Hobgoblins ceaselessly shake bone rattles, and the sound inspires howling and wailing from the masses of lesser Hobgoblins. These beings are actually ghosts who've been twisted by their master's Jhor. They are much stronger than the rest, and they can sprout great crow's wings at will to fly at particularly evasive quarry.

Use the *pretas* as a running threat. Characters who keep moving can fight them off. Traits for greater *pretas* follow the slash.

Attributes: Strength 1/5, Dexterity 2/4, Stamina 1/4, Charisma 2/2, Manipulation 1/1, Appearance 0/0, Perception 2/4, Intelligence 1/2, Wits 2/3

Abilities: Alertness 3/3, Athletics 0/3, Brawl 2/4, Dodge 1/3, Intimidation 2/4

Health Levels: Lesser: OK x2/Destroyed. Greater: OK x10/Destroyed.

Voormas, the Grand Harvester of Souls

Voormas' obsession with cheating death has reached its apex. Now he plans to destroy the Wheel and replace it with himself. The universe would halt in its tracks, and Voormas would guide it down a course free from suffering, loss and decay as Shiva reborn. An eternity of half-dead Stasis is a minor price to pay for eternal existence.

Voormas served the gods for centuries, always testing himself to conquer his fear of the afterlife — a sliver of bad faith that dogged him while he used the skulls of priests as begging bowls. The Euthanatos confused his fervor with genuine faith. Voormas became a talented death mage, but his fear remained, intensified by his growing understanding of the Wheel. Something was wrong with the cosmos; karma was more apt to punish than reward. Each turn of the Wheel was thicker with chaos. A lesser mage would have been satisfied with life-extending spells, but the Grand Harvester knew that those mages were simply a bulwark against ultimate destruction. He had to throw down the Cycle and steal the thrones of the gods.

Voormas learned to channel the powers of Kali and Shiva, hoping to remake himself into the Tantric union that heralds the end of worlds. Now that he's seized the *Pasupatta Astra*, he can finally break the Cycle and save the Tellurian from untold destruction. This plan has been lifetimes in the making, first revealed to him by the *dakini*, soul-guiding goddesses that he encountered in the deepest reaches of the Realm of Entropy. With their help, he learned to secure Nodes and discovered that Yama — Death — would reveal himself in the form of a red star.

As ruler of the Consanguinity, he fostered the death taint in his followers. Good Death became a thing of the past, as serial killers and venal mages seeking immortality flocked to his side. His servants would still obey him after the Traditions hunted him down. Ghosts bearing his commands flitted from the Thousand Hells to innumerable cults, checking their progress. Then his triumph came, embedded in the Reckoning, and he knew it was time to act. His closest servants were rewarded with lichedom: a spell stolen from the mind of an Etruscan necromancer.

With Jhor flowing through his heart, he sees signs of his death everywhere. Soon he will be a god: an incarnation of Shiva who refuses to destroy.

Image: Voormas is a withered, ancient man of South Asian descent who hobbles on a cane made from a child's skull and spinal column. When violence or high ritual calls, he becomes the *Shivasakti Ayavatara*: a 10-foot-tall, six-armed androgynous creature that combines the attributes of Kali and Shiva. Its black iron body, fangs and taloned hands make quick work of lesser enemies, but he takes few chances with other mages. Spells cast from a screamed mantra, burning lotus, skull or sword dispatch them.

Roleplaying Hints: You will never die. As a god, you will crush Death and Fate and replace them with universal laws more to your liking. Yet you see the

Fighting Voormas

Voormas is a formidable enemy. (See Chapter Seven for general notes on how to run a villain of this caliber.) Aside from the Knife of Ixion, Voormas' weakness is his unyielding attachment to his own life. If forced to choose, he will generally protect himself over attacking. One secret preoccupation is the magic that keeps him alive: an Entropy 5, Life 5, Time 5 Effect built to 30 successes. Using countermagic on this spell will drive him to distraction. He'll drop a few offensive Effects to enhance his chances of success as he bulwarks it against further attack. Mind Effects that present him with images and sensations of his own death also unnerve him, causing him to make critical mistakes or even pause to center himself.

The Storyteller should think of other situations that remind Voormas of his own mortality. Simply attacking him or showing him simple images of death won't do it. He's too hardened with Jhor. These tactics have to provoke his fear to a degree that his Thanatoic background and considerable powers can't dismiss.

phantoms everywhere, proclaiming your demise. Yama taunts you; you'll only know peace when you kill him. The souls of the *Pasupatta Astra* already worship you in anticipation of the unchanging Age to come, and the Nephandi are your most insistent foes. These facts confirm the rightness of your cause.

You use heretical Tantric magic along with your own unique necromancy. Your spells work on the premise of self-deification: claiming the divine attributes that are rightfully yours.

[Attributes before the slash represent the *weakest* version of his Avatar form. The strong form adds at least four dice to unarmed or melee combat pools, soaks lethal and aggravated wounds and radiates an aura of fear (roll Willpower, difficulty 6 to overcome; at least three successes are required). Voormas might have 20 or more successes worth of additional Effects prepared. These spells do tax his concentration, just as they would for any other mage.]

Tradition: Euthanatos
Essence: Primordial
Nature: Curmudgeon
Demeanor: Deviant
Attributes: Strength 1/8 (Crushing), Dexterity 1/6 (Multiple Strikes), Stamina 2/7 (Tough), Charisma 3, Manipulation 6 (Reasoned Words), Appearance 1/0, Perception 6 (Intuitive), Intelligence 6 (Wisdom of Age), Wits 6 (Prepared)
Abilities: Academics 5 (India), Alertness 4, Awareness 6 (Entropic Magic), Brawl 6 (Pressure Points), Cosmology 5 (Entropic Realms), Dodge 4 (Dodging While Striking), Enigmas 5 (Cosmological), Etiquette 3, Intimidation 6 (In Avatar Form), Investigation 5 (No Tools), Leadership 5 (Over Followers), Linguistics 6, Medicine 4 (Ayurvedic), Meditation 6 (Mantras), Melee 6 (Swords), Occult 6 (Thanatoic), Stealth 6 (Shadowing), Subterfuge 5 (Easy Liar)
Backgrounds: Allies 10, Arcane 7, Avatar 8, Destiny 6, Dream 3, Influence 3
Arete: 9

> ## THE CURSE
> Whoever kills Voormas might inherit the death mage's madness. His Jhor is so powerful that it can actually survive his death. In this case, it leaps to the Awakened being with the closest sympathetic tie. In most cases, this would be Voormas' killer. Voormas' madness is a strange variation on the usual death-taint, though, as he's obsessed with death because he fears it, not because he loves it. This madness manifests as sadism (anger at his mortality), his *pretas* (reflections on how he might die) and an obsession with Arts that cheat or command death.
>
> In game terms, Voormas transmits Jhor appropriate for a 10-point Paradox Backlash. The victim's player may make a Willpower roll (difficulty 8) to reduce the effects of the Jhor; each success reduces it by one point. Unfortunately, the mage's current Paradox total adds directly to the Jhor. The victim inherits Voormas' terror, but she will act it out according to her own paradigm. Keep in mind that the killer will undoubtedly have access to the *Pasupatta Astra*, giving her the means to continue Voormas' work. The cursed mage becomes the "Second Heir" predicted by Akrites Salonikas and an enemy of Ascension.

Spheres: Correspondence 4, Entropy 7 (see **Masters of the Art**; assume that Voormas can target any number of creatures in his line of sight with a single success and that he can create Effects that "jump" from one target to another), Forces 5, Life 5, Mind 4, Matter 3, Prime 4, Spirit 5, Time 5
Willpower: 10
Quintessence: 24
Resonance: (Pattern) Enduring, (Pattern) Preserving, (Primordial) Black, (Primordial) Divine, (Primordial) Murderous 2, (Primordial) Rotting. Voormas has the most severe form of Jhor. Combined with his magic, this Resonance complicates attempts to defeat him.

Chapter Three: The Revolution Will Be Televised

"…we are honored to have with us a revolutionary of a different caliber. He has revolted, resisted, fought, held fast, maintained, destroyed resistance, overcome coercion. The right to be a person, someone, or individual…. All that remains is recognition of a man, a man of steel, a man magnificently equipped to lead us; that is, lead us or go."
—The Prisoner, Episode 17, "Fall Out"

History and Destiny

This story begins as others do. At the end of the 20th century — as one millennium ended and another began — a cosmic event called the Avatar Storm swept across the boundaries of Creation. For visionaries who challenged the very limits of reality, other dimensions beyond human perception had once offered limitless adventure. Surrounding the Earth, a mathematically impossible boundary separated the precise and ordered world of conventional reality from all its alternatives. The boundary still exists, but it is growing weaker. Although this phenomenon is known by many names, it is most commonly referred to as the "Gauntlet," since those who pass through it, whether through shamanistic rites or advanced technology, are invariably punished. Void Engineers sometimes call it a "Dimensional Barrier," even though they cannot quantify exactly how it functions.

Should this barrier fall completely, the threshold that separates the relatively safe world of Earth from myriad alien alternatives would be eradicated. Science would hold no meaning; sanity would be irrelevant without a common frame of reference; forces beyond space and time could descend upon the helpless populace of Earth in one rapacious feast. In the Final Days, some who dared to cross this threshold have never returned to our world. A few idealists describe these journeys to a higher (or different) plane of existence as a literal "Ascension." Others would typify it as a descent into madness, for hordes of Marauders wait outside these barriers to bring chaos back into the world.

Beyond the barriers, mages and madmen are still trapped in a Void outside the world we know, at the mercy of ancient and alien forces that are growing in strength. Whether you think of these outsiders as coming from "hyperspace," the "Deep Shadow" or the "Deeper Universe" is merely a matter of semantic distinction. Something is coming, and the vanguard of its invasion is already here. Should the barrier between the possible and the impossible falter, all of humanity would be helpless against the manifestations of a vast and uncaring cosmos.

The Last Celestial Masters

For centuries, mystics, visionaries and inspired scientists have explored this boundary surrounding the Earth. The most extensive and coordinated exploration has been conducted by an alliance of Technocrats, a technological secret society that predates the passing curiosities of the Knights Templar or Bavarian Illuminati. This one Union is defended by a legion of operatives in a wide variety of uniforms: black suits, jumpsuits, space suits, business suits, lab coats and even cybernetic armor. Their enemies vilify them as Orwellian fascists set upon creating the ultimate dystopia, soulless scientists in black hats and mirrorshades. Yet hidden within this society, visionaries see the last defenders of a grand ideal for mankind: the agents of the Technocratic Union.

At the turn of the millennium, the Technocracy was ascendant, its Iterators and managers watching humanity from outposts outside our world… and watching the heavens carefully. The Technocracy maintains a web of conspiracy so vast that it occasionally takes credit for "controlling" reality itself, but perhaps that's too grandiose a term. More precisely, it *enforces* reality, waging war against all who would suborn it for their disparate visions.

Their tools are advanced and experimental technology, decades ahead of mankind's cutting edge, but too visionary to use for anyone who does not understand Enlightened Science. Their watchwords were once simple to indoctrinate and chant: *One World, One Truth, One Reality*. One vision was set against all contrary alternatives, like the barrier surrounding the "real world" we know.

Now the barrier surrounding Earth is faltering, and the center cannot hold. Throughout the 20th century, a series of "space stations" called Horizon Constructs existed in the hyperspace surrounding the Earth, carefully poised on the edge of the Horizon. Regular shuttles, bursts of encrypted communication and Iteration X patrols connected this network of extradimensional fortresses. From these vantages, the highest-ranking operatives of the Technocracy directed agents on the surface below them for decades, using surveillance and coordinated tactics against a common enemy: mages who did not subscribe to the Technocracy's dogma.

Each act of magic performed by these Reality Deviants undermined Consensus, the reality that humanity desired — at least, as the Union interpreted it. Men in Black and heavily armed cyborgs stood on standby, ready to lead strike teams against hidden cells of enemies organized through "chantries" and archaic "Traditional" societies. Yet just as they looked to the world below, they trained their telescopes on the Void above, knowing that somewhere in the night, someone or *something* was watching them as well.

Their campaign for reality depended on hunting down any who did not support their vision, a crusade first called the Pogrom by Iteration X. Each skirmish was justified as part of a centuries-old conflict called the Ascension War. In the final years of the war, a handful of Tradition mages found a way to cripple three Horizon Constructs, knocking them out of the heavens. Paranoia spread through the network of Horizon Constructs, empowered with fear that the network of defenses poised on the edge of reality might falter. It-X Statisticians rapidly made predictions. Ivory Tower analysts collated data. Syndicate directors debated the implications. Systems crashed in the heavens, as agents down below braced themselves for a massive retaliatory shock wave. The Technocracy's bulwark of defenses surrounding the Earth gave way.

And then a wave of propaganda followed, declaring that the Ascension War was over. The Pogrom ground to a halt as the Technocracy shifted its resources against less obvious agendas. High-tech crusades against Reality Deviants abruptly stopped. Perhaps the number-crunchers realized that they had attained the critical mass to consider all reality as static. Or perhaps they anticipated a more immediate and imminent catastrophe. Amalgams of agents once enlisted to fight on the front lines of the Ascension War soon had greater autonomy to investigate other "threats to reality." The crusade to abduct and "process deviant mages" as recruits to the Union became a dated objective, an issue raised by the more radical factions of Iteration X, but largely ignored by the other Conventions.

A few exceptions to this reformation have survived and evolved. One is Panopticon, a multi-Convention Methodology that has evolved to handle the new troubles sparked by the Rogue Council transmissions. Originally quite small, it could become increasingly effective as the End Times advance and its assets increase. Without recognizing distinctions of rank or Methodology, all its agents submit to one system of rank. These steadfast survivors have been largely limited to requisitioning old gear and scrounging what they can, however, with a little help (and occasional resentment) from the Conventions. Loyal to higher ideals, Panopticon agents patiently await the time when their Masters on the Horizon will resume control.

In the meantime, strike teams of Technocracy agents have mobilized against other threats. Independent intelligent analysts began to choose their own targets… and priorities. The sudden change in dogma was once unthinkable to many, but not as shocking as the events that followed. A catastrophe occurred, in a way even the most talented analysts could not predict: a new development in the Avatar Storm. Forces trapped outside the Gauntlet fought their way *inside it* and finally breached it. Weakened by attacks by Tradition mages, the network of Horizon Constructs attempted to delay this incursion but could not halt it. Alien forces infiltrated the Earth, and chaos returned.

It was the end of an era. And it heralded the end of the world.

Guides to the Technocracy

Now a reckoning is at hand. Tradition mages have seen the Technocracy as a towering monolithic society, but cracks and fissures have widened deep within. In addition to countless personal conflicts, ideological arguments between Conventions and brute force attempts to seize power, a fundamental schism has threatened the Union's security. A conflict had been building between agents on the "front lines of the war for reality" and their Masters and managers in the skies above them. Routine indoctrination, social conditioning and psychological evaluation conducted by their superiors had kept such outbreaks of insubordination to a minimum… but in the more remote sectors of the Union, including the exploratory ships of Void Engineers, outbreaks of independence threatened the Union.

For decades, directors and supervisors in Horizon Constructs had made policies and issued directives for the amalgams and cells serving them. Yet the agents on the front lines of reality, down on Earth, saw that such policies did not always account for what they *really saw* day by day and night by night. To complete missions and high-level objectives, amalgams of Technocrats occasionally had to bend the rules, sometimes stepping outside official procedure to accomplish their supervisors' agendas. The risk of punishment was great, but with the fate of reality hanging in the balance, it was a risk and a sacrifice worth taking.

In the aftermath of the Ascension War, Horizon Constructs that once reinforced troops were suddenly cut off from the so-called "real world." Unable to directly interact with events on Earth, the highest-ranking representatives of the Union struggled to reestablish surveillance and communication with agents in the field — with only limited and infrequent results. They could watch and wait, but sudden and unexplained technical failures (perhaps manifestations of Paradox) interfered with the most autocratic attempts at dominance. Therefore, isolated cells of Technocrats had greater authority than ever before to conduct operations on Earth. Conditioning gave way to survival instincts.

When transmissions did come through, they spoke bluntly of the need for immediate action. The most authoritative of these transmissions came from a collective entity known as Control, a higher authority that seemed to transcend the very structure of the Union. Through any technological device — speaking through radios, watching through televisions, monitoring through computer screens — its Voice gave imperatives to agents in the field. Its identity transcended any one language, culture or gender, as though it were composed of the very collective that so many higher-ranking Technocrats idealized. Caught out in the cold, Technocratic agents heard… and could not help but obey.

The source of the transmissions had been cleverly concealed, and even those with the highest security clearance questioned its origins. As the empowered debated, a few Enlightened souls saw the answer to this mystery. The truth will soon be revealed… and for beleaguered agents, the truth can drive men mad.

The Past Unearthed

Modern propaganda about the Technocracy has secured its true origins and original motivations. Scholars such as Terrence Whyte have written of raids on magical strongholds centuries ago, as far back as the early 12th century, but such tales have been distorted to justify endless crusades on modern chantries. Historians have documented the emergence of the Victorian Technocracy and the conquests of the Proctor Houses, but certain stories of the Union's origins have been suppressed. Unknown to most modern Technocrats, the original Ivory Tower was the White Tower of

Languedoc, the grand lodge for a 14th-century secret society of the Order of Reason.

In a meeting chamber atop the tower, the Inner Circle of this Order of Reason endlessly debated conflicting visions for reality. Their names have been erased from history, for in order to master the world, they would have to hide from all supernatural rivals. The founders of Nine Conventions spoke of history to come. Their agents, the Outer Circle, had been recruited from lodges across Europe, recruited for their gift of Enlightenment. Unaware that their souls held the same Avatar possessed by true sorcerers and mages, they were instructed in Enlightened arts that emulated the sciences of the time. From the White Tower of Languedoc, the Inner Circle of Daedaleans used hidden sorcery to commune with lodges and refuges across Europe and around the world. As has been detailed more fully elsewhere, they communicated with distant lodges through a network of Viasilicos — crystals shaped like five Platonic solids — and secretly employed scientific practices far beyond what the common populace suspected.

Some of these Renaissance sciences have since been forgotten, such as their various attempts to prolong human life through alchemy. Yet the Inner Circle has kept them hidden for centuries: first in their fortresses and lodges, centuries later in their Horizon Constructs… and later in colonies hidden deep within the Void. Far from Earth, their descendents have continued to grow in power, aided by elders preserved through alchemical processes that would never work on Earth. From the distant reaches of space, they have rarely asserted their control… but their power is growing.

The Beast Awakens

Earth has recently been menaced by far more immediate and far less philosophical concerns. Imperatives from a Rogue Council on Earth have tried to resurrect the Ascension War. Inspired by invectives and propaganda, Tradition initiates once again unleashed a hail of gunfire against Men in Black, believing that every shot fired would help save their world. Yet as the Technocracy was focused on the threat of these Reality Deviants, its analysts remained oblivious to other threats to the world. In 1999, a great awakening confirmed the Technocrats' worst nightmare: Our world harbored ancient and unaging evils far more powerful than the mortal Masters and Oracles who performed mere acts of sorcery.

In India, a vampiric creature thousands of years old arose from torpid slumber to unleash chaos. Like a god, he traveled with destruction in his wake. The Technocracy responded by dealing death from above. Tactical air strikes coordinated by Iteration X focused incendiary, pyrotechnic retribution against the undead atavism. The legions of vampires descended from this god went mad when he returned, slaughtering each other in an orgy of insanity. The vampiric cultists who could claim direct descent from him all but passed from the world — only a few dozen remain, and they are hunted as a weak and fallen cult. Yet this outcome was nothing compared to even more drastic consequences: *The Technocracy had seen ancient vampires unmasked.*

These epic events were dutifully recorded for further analysis. Technocracy analysts had been marginally aware of the existence of various supernatural groups before this event, of course. Union amalgams had reported firefights with werewolves, for instance, and Void Engineers had repeatedly driven incursions of ghosts and spectres back into their extradimensional planes of existence. Yet these monsters had, for the most part, struggled to remain hidden from mankind: their very survival relied on their secrecy. Quite simply, the Technocracy had never seen supernatural activity on this scale before. This creature, named Ravnos, had no desire to remain hidden, but to unleash epic power against all those who opposed him. The data gathered from this one event placed a thousand other lesser occasions in perspective. Beyond the Horizon, Technocratic Masters evaluated their agenda once again.

Concluding the Time Table

With this new information, analysts and statisticians added new depth to their predictions. Since its inception (and indeed, centuries before it), the Technocracy (and the societies that led to its creation) had adopted the policy of planning its agendas years in advance. At any given moment, the Technocracy had (at the very least) a Five-Year Plan and Ten-Year Plan for its agendas and objectives. The highest ranking Technocrats, it was said, had access to more visionary goals, such as the near-mythical Fifty-Year Plan revealed to them in segments and excerpts, so that the full vision could not be passed down to front-line agents. Collectively, such projections and plans were known as the Time Table.

During the Ascension War, most Time Tables were composed based on information concerning forces that threatened humanity — more precisely, mages who endangered the common populace and the reality it created [Consensus]. Because of repeated attacks on Technocracy strongholds, the Time Table was often a reaction to threats posed by Tradition mages, disparate Crafts of independent mages, malefic influences of Nephandic mages and wildly unpredictable possibilities posed by Marauder mages.

Other supernatural creatures, including "monsters" such as vampires and werewolves, were largely considered impossible by most of humanity. Since they worked strenuously to hide their existence from mere mortals, they posed little threat to Consensus. As long as they remained hidden and did not try to seize the Technocracy's resources, they were represented by a set of minor vectors, variables and trends in the Time Table.

The first awakening of an Antediluvian vampire challenged this strategy. Vampires were no longer content to remain hidden — their influence was now obvious and epic. Perhaps media spin can reinterpret carpet bombing as essential to defending freedom or democracy in the Third World, but the sudden and unexplained deaths of hundreds of thousands of humans in India was harder to rationalize… especially after many of them had been completely drained of blood. As humanity became more aware of the presence of the supernatural, it slowly became more aware of alternatives to conventional reality… and thus would magical energies of all kinds grow stronger.

Factoring in events in India, statisticians and analysts recompiled their Time Tables. It did not consist of a Fifty-Year Plan, nor did it entail a Ten-Year Plan. By all projections, the world was destined for destruction *within five years*… unless the Technocracy mobilized agents to stop the most significant trends. In a wide array of scenarios, there were countless ways for the world to end; therefore, one of them was inevitable. Burst transmissions disseminated this information to as many Horizon Constructs as possible, but the chain of command had been disrupted. The defense of reality was now in the hands of front-line operatives, who would have to take drastic and independent action to stop the world's destruction.

Asserting Control

Far from the concerns of Earth, Technocratic colonies remained trapped in the Deep Universe, remote realms of the spirit world isolated by a great void. Their citizens have become entirely ephemeral, wholly spiritual in substance — even though many of them still believe that they are flesh and blood. Each colony is idealized; some Iteration X intellectuals even consider each to be a Platonic ideal. Whatever happens to Earth, presumably, these colonies will live on.

One of the most remote realms is an artifact of an older time: the distant realm harboring Control. Its existence is maintained by the collective effort of the "Inner Circle" of the Technocracy, now exiles from our world. Through combined effort (and communal procedures), they have broadcast thoughts and words directly

to Earth, sending transmissions from beyond the Far Horizon. Since the Avatar Storm, this council has been shut out from reality, trapped in its realm of the Deep Umbra. They are equivalent to the Oracles and Primi of the Nine Traditions, but some are far older and far more potent. Rumors speak of them as "Old Masters." As often happens, the rumors hold a quantum of truth.

This Inner Circle of the Technocracy is a collective: it can transmit only through consensus. Its minds include "Technocracy Oracles" who have left Earth to achieve a higher state of Enlightenment, relics from before the time of the Victorian Technocracy. A few are relatively recent promotions, paragons of the Victorian Age who reflect new and dangerous attitudes. Its oldest and most potent minds are *Daedaleans*, 13 paragons of the Order of Reason who ascended into the heavens centuries ago. Deep in the spirit world, occulted in a distant colony, they have become completely spiritual. As gnostics who have escaped their prisons of flesh, they are creatures of pure reason. Existing outside of time, their council reveres the Enlightened minds who served as the architects of the original Order of Reason. Their very existence is a contrast to a dystopian and dictatorial society vilified by modern mages. The Technocracy is a bleak consequence of the original Daedalean order, a shadow lengthened by a brilliant light.

Throughout most of the 20th century, this Inner Circle elected to remain outside the Ascension War. As the conflict drew to a close, a majority of these minds attempted to circumvent a schism in the order, broadcasting directly to specific amalgams. In the wake of the Avatar Storm, they have become curiously silent. Younger minds on the council have diminished in strength with the growth of the Avatar Storm; older, stronger minds have been struggling to assert their will. Their collective is watching reality, waiting to act and waiting until it is time for the communal Voice to speak.

A Deeper Schism

Just as the Inner Circle worked within the original Order of Reason, a secret society exists within the Technocracy that defends many of the same ideals. It does not have absolute control. If anything, it contests for control with other organizations within the Union, such as Panopticon, Invictus and other projects detailed elsewhere. Its members are aware of the true origins of the Union and have survived within it by hiding their true agenda. Like the original Daedaleans, they commune through a network of Viasilicos, or "seeing stones." Each of the conspirators of this society is Arcane, with a natural resistance to all attempts to monitor his activities.

One of the most influential was an academic named Terrence Whyte, who has helped obscure the true origins of the Technocracy by extensively documenting and disseminating evidence of the historic raid on Mistridge in 1210. While supporting the eradication of all contesting magical philosophies, these "21st-century Daedaleans" have waited for the more xenophobic factions of the Technocracy to clear the world of their natural competitors. Once that is done, they can support the agenda of the original Order of Reason: to make men masters of their own world. For the sake of dogma, they call themselves Unionists.

Yet at the highest levels of the Technocracy, conspirators with a different goal for the Union oppose them. They also support the eradication of Reality Deviants, but for a different reason. Once all overt, "vulgar" magic is gone from the world, the only methods of willworking that will survive are those that can disguise themselves as mundane influence. More precisely, only their Technocratic science will "work," and all magic will fail. By working their Enlightened procedures through technology, they are supporting a supernatural edge that will allow them to control the Masses. If they can shape minds through mass media, if they can reshape bodies and minds through Progenitor genegineering, or at least reformat them in the image of Iteration X ideals, then their secret society will have uncontested control of the world. That is the theory, at least. Obedient to the chain of command, they regard themselves as Loyalists.

Recent events have changed their plans. The Avatar Storm has isolated powerful conspirators who seek to conquer the world through Technocracy. High-ranking officials can no longer direct agents in the field. As supernatural activity becomes more overt, hidebound Technocrats will be increasingly powerless to oppose such forces. Their tactics of tracking and conditioning Reality Deviants have been honed to perfection during the height of the Pogrom, but they cannot direct sufficient firepower to overcome spirits invading the physical world, Stormwardens immune to the Storm's flux or Psychopomps leading alien entities into the physical world. They will direct their troops to fight to the last man, but the redemption of the world does not lie in the brute-force tactics of warfare.

Technocratic agents caught out in the cold are now aware, more than ever, that there are far more dangerous and more powerful entities than mortal Tradition mages. The Ascension War has distracted them from more important battles. The Awakening of an Antediluvian has proven the true threat vampires pose; the increasing visibility of the Red Star has shown that the spirit world has begun to break through the Gauntlet and infest the physical world. The Walking Dead have shown that Hell cannot hold them, and the spirits of the dead are returning to the land of the living. Now overwhelmed by supernatural activity, they have little choice but to declare the Ascension War a victory — if only to bolster the morale to face the other horrors of the night. The war is over. Now other revolutions will begin.

> ### Unearthing the Past
>
> Prior to Chapter I, a paramilitary group claiming to be descended from the Knights Templar makes an Enlightened discovery in Languedoc: a subterranean chamber holding a collection of rare books, which are believed to be encrypted texts relating to a 15th-century secret society called the Order of Reason. (The chamber has no passages to the surface; finding it relied on applications of Correspondence magic.) The discovery of rare texts related to the practice of magic rapidly results in the tomes changing hands very quickly… thus disseminating this information throughout (and outside) independent branches of the Technocracy. (See **The Red Sign** for more details.)
>
> Before this discovery, the existence of the Order was nearly mythical, its existence a heresy within the Union that required immediate brainwashing (or more precisely, "social conditioning"). Propaganda relating to the origins of the Union has since been called into question, specifically the eradication of a 13th-century "magus" chantry called Mistridge. One of the chief proponents of this official history was a New World Order instructor named Terrence Whyte.
>
> A backlash in the New World Order then leads to a surge in academic activity. Proponents of a new revised history insist that their organization should be called the Ivory Tower. Tension between this Convention and the others increases, as representatives of Iteration X insist that patrols should be launched against previously ignored supernatural activity. The schism between Horizon Constructs and front-line amalgams widens, as servants of the Ivory Tower are distracted by ideological debates… while the amount of supernatural activity on Earth increases. Through their dogma, they argue for the "rebuilding" of a metaphorical ivory tower, bolstering the Unionist cause.

Chapter I

Technocratic amalgams have done far more over the last century than hunt down and condition deviant mages. Agents have pursued limited campaigns against other supernaturals as well. One of their most extensive campaigns has enlisted the most independent Convention: the Void Engineers. Using applications of Dimensional Science, Engineers have patrolled the boundaries of physical reality. When ghosts have made incursions into human cities, they have sent operatives to erect barriers between worlds. For every demonic manifestation, for every extradimensional horror that has crept into physical space, an armed marine of this Convention has been ready to stand and fight it.

At the start of Chapter I, a dedicated team of Void Engineers issues a warning to any amalgam that will listen: Patrols have detected an increase in supernatural phenomena. Extradimensional entities (or "spirits," as deviants would call them) have broken through the Dimensional Barrier (what Tradition mages call the Gauntlet). Such entities occasionally manifest in our world, but these new sightings do not correspond to previously encountered phenomena.

The team has followed standard procedure, attempting to increase "barriers" surrounding our world — a rather vague reference unfamiliar to anyone who hasn't studied Dimensional Science (or learned the Spirit Sphere). It then worked with other Void Engineers to covertly hunt down anomalous phenomena. Because the team has been cut off from its usual reinforcements, however (most notably, the nearest Horizon Construct), it does not have the resources to stop all of these invasions. It is shifting its priorities to researching these events further, attempting to find a pattern.

This information is promptly passed up the chain of command. In many of the largest cities, the highest-ranking representatives of each Convention have formed an advisory board called a Symposium. Since the Avatar Storm, these representatives have had greater authority (and less oversight from their own superiors), but they do not have the resources to force absolute loyalty and obedience. More amalgams have "gone rogue" in recent months, and the Technocracy cannot monitor the activities of agents as thoroughly as it once did.

This doesn't curtail political conflict within the highest ranks. In many Symposiums, representatives of the Void Engineers are promptly accused of failure, and resources are shifted toward representatives of other Conventions. Ivory Tower intelligence analysts and Iteration X comptrollers stand to benefit, as they lead their own operations to stop these incursions. Progenitors typically remain defensive, fighting to make sure their funding for research is not cut, but some of their field researchers are assigned to study these new invading organisms. Most Symposiums will then assemble teams of agents to combat this new menace, complete with charismatic Syndicate reps to lead them. (If you've been using **Guide to the Technocracy**, the characters' relationship with their supervisor might also change because of local politics.)

In other areas of the world, the five Conventions have learned to work together more effectively, partly because of a new organization called Panopticon. As an extremely loyal and dedicated branch of the Technocracy, Panopticon measures all agents by the same metric: a system of rank. Panopticon amalgams tend to represent a broader spectrum of agents than the teams assembled by isolated Symposiums. This increased loyalty requires closer contact with supervisors, however, which invariably leads to closer scrutiny, more thorough critiques and more frequent brainwashing sessions (Mind procedures euphemistically referred to as "social conditioning").

From the characters' point of view, anyone not working for the Technocracy might notice signs that local agents have had a sudden change in objectives. Technocracy agents suddenly receive new directives. Almost overnight — the night that the Void Engineers' report goes out to local Union supervisors — surveillance of Reality Deviants decreases. If a cabal was under current investigation by the Technocracy, the hunt stops immediately. Awakened observers might notice signs of Technocratic teams mobilizing around a few key locations; Enlightened agents might be assigned to one of them. Some of these sites are areas where a great deal of Primal Essence is focused, such as sacred sites and the junctures of ley lines.

In game terms, most of these locations are areas where the Gauntlet rating is low. A few sites, however, do not fit this pattern. Instead, they are moderately or highly populated areas. It is as though the spirits are searching for something… or someone. Mages and Technocrats then scramble to figure out what they're looking for, but not before innocent Sleepers begin disappearing and innocent witnesses see things they couldn't possibly imagine.

Anomalies: An increase in the sighting of paranormal phenomena quickly leads to active investigations. Tracking down "extradimensional incursions" becomes the most common mission for collaborative amalgams. Talented teams of agents (including the characters) should have the authority to conduct one of these investigations on their own. (**Guide to the Technocracy** has plenty of details on assembling this amalgam.)

In the background, Men in Black question witnesses of spiritual phenomena; Iteration X sends patrols into ordinarily peaceful neighborhoods, driving through streets in black vans or vehicles citizens might describe as "unmarked police cars." Many of these supporting agents are sympathizers and proles — that is, ordinary agents who do not have Arete ratings. (If your chronicle assumes this secret society has far-reaching influence, the patrols might actually include police, government agents or military personnel.) Even then, the Technocracy has only a fraction of the personnel necessary to search all these areas, as some spirits slip through the cracks.

Once the data has been gathered (and the characters make their reports), statistical analysis (and Entropy Sphere procedures) confirms patterns to these incursions — although curiously, not all of them fit the same profile. Citizens are witnessing extradimensional entities in our world, and the most common cause is a rise in breaches in the Dimensional Barrier, the "self-defense system" for Earth's reality. Contact with these phenomena soon leads to outbreaks of temporary madness. Advanced cases are directed to (recruited) psychologists for debriefing, mental health care and social conditioning.

Analysts and statisticians assemble all this testimony. A few descriptions match some of the "spirits" encountered by Void Engineers, possibly including "animal spirits" summoned by deviant shamans and "ghosts" contacted by Euthanatoi. Others are totally new to this realm. (In game terms, this might include the sorts of spirits werewolves normally encounter in the Umbra. Picture how an average person will react to an Epiph or Wyldling, and you'll have an excellent witness for an amalgam's investigation.)

On Earth, high-ranking Void Engineers face punishments that will hinder their career. The few who try to provide a mystical description of how the "Gauntlet" works are sent to Psych Ops for treatment. The usual Dimensional Science procedures are not working. It is as though this barrier has altered its properties again, which calls the Convention's competency into question.

In the last year, the number of injuries the Void Engineers have sustained while investigating this barrier has increased. After the other Conventions start exploring these "incursion areas," agents are attacked by phenomena that they have never experienced before. On at least one occasion, a supernatural "storm" manifests in the physical world, as the Avatar Storm punishes agents who look too closely. (It lashes out with aggravated damage at agents who find these breaches, as though the agents had crossed the Gauntlet itself.)

New Propaganda: On the Horizon, a group of academics within the Ivory Tower soon posits a new theory that this Dimensional Barrier was strengthened by the Order of Reason. The propaganda insists that the Technocracy has abandoned the original ideals of the Order, which has led to the current course of events. Furthermore, revised history insists that the Order was established to protect the Masses from supernatural forces, including extradimensional activity and sudden "primal storms" (that is, anomalous events deviant mages would ascribe to Paradox). Radical intellectuals will try to broadcast this propaganda to the front lines, with mixed results.

Rival Technocrats immediately accuse these intellectuals of disloyalty, but because of the Avatar Storm, they cannot sufficiently mobilize troops to raid the Horizon Constructs where many of these intellectuals are stationed. Iterator Simon Magnum calls for their immediate execution. Ivory Tower agents directing espionage activities (including much of the Operative Methodology) call for reeducation and social conditioning instead. Because of the difficulty of communicating with the front lines, this information leak remains limited… at least for now.

Lockdowns: In response to the deadliest and most frightening incursions, teams of Void Engineer Dimensional Scientists mobilize to areas where the "barrier between worlds" have given way, accompanied by marines from this Convention. In teams of five or 10 agents, they're sent *through* these rifts (with Spirit 4) to patrol for further incursions. (Your agents could easily be assigned to act as possible reinforcements, defending the area where this experiment takes place.) Casualties are high as the Avatar Storm responds; most teams are left with one or two agents who aren't seriously wounded.

In the physical areas surrounding these experiments, Ivory Tower operatives establish "lockdown" areas, claiming that this activity actually represents an "invasion." Some amalgams search for witnesses; others look for signs of further incursions. Iteration X is on standby, ready to bring in deadly forces should either the first or second line of defense fail. The Syndicate uses what influence it can for some spin control on mass media, perverting reports to fit the ratings requirements of the eleven o'clock news. The Technocracy has limited resources, however — especially now — so each lockdown vastly decreases the chance of Tradition mages (and rogue Technocrats) being monitored in other areas of the city. Priorities shift.

Later in the investigation, psychologists sort through data regarding the witnesses of these events. In the past, the Technocracy has used predictive procedures to track down individuals who might "Awaken as mages." The Union actively recruits some of them, of course, while others are used as bait to capture Reality Deviants who come after them. By comparing the profiles of potential deviants with the parameters of witnesses, analysts soon discover that an unusually high correlation exists between the two groups. In other words, many of the Sleeper witnesses were *potential mages*. High-ranking representatives use this fact to justify these operations as successful — the spirits have (unintentionally) helped them track down recruits for the Union.

A Softer Touch: In some limited instances, independent amalgams and Tradition cabals might pool resources to investigate on their own. Innocents are in danger, not only from extradimensional forces they cannot understand, but from brute force solutions used by the Technocracy itself. Once a lockdown is established, Ivory Tower rivals need to use quick-and-dirty Mind procedures to process witnesses, using some of the same conditioning techniques normally reserved for captured Reality Deviants. Iteration X prefers to use firepower, in which case, bystanders could be wounded in the crossfire. Where "reality has been compromised," hidebound Technocrats respond with excessive measures. After all, the cost of such responses pales compared to the consequences of failure.

Rogue Technocrats might find an incursion on their own, one strange enough that it doesn't fit within the Technocracy's "statistical analysis." Such a discovery presents an opportunity to question witnesses, hunt down an extradimensional creature, and track its path back to where the Gauntlet has been temporarily compromised. If the team has sufficient skill, it might be able to solve one of these minor incursions on its own. If it fails, the Technocracy will call in a lockdown, and it will want to find out more about the rogue agents who discovered this anomaly. The common populace will suffer, even as Horizon representatives claim to be "protecting" them.

System: The **Mage Storytellers Companion** includes rules for using spirits in **Mage**. The best way to "stat out" a spirit incursion is by adapting those rules. Charms such as Break Reality, Solidify Reality and Shapeshift are malleable enough to account for all sorts of unexplained phenomena. The one Charm an "incursion spirit" should have, though, is Materialize. It can't go home, so it will do what it can to adjust to (or prey on) the realm of flesh, as filtered through its alien agenda. This spirit doesn't have to be a deadly one either. (Those threats are best saved for encounters much later in the chronicle.)

Threat Dossier: The Call of the Wyld

Spirits that were previously unable to Materialize manifest in the physical world during Chapter I. As an example, consider what happens when a new variety of a Chimerling breaks through into our world.

Mirror Chimerling
Willpower 3, **Rage** 5, **Gnosis** 10, **Essence** 18
Charms: Break Reality, Re-form, Shapeshift
Assignment: Code Violet

Witnesses making contact with this extradimensional entity (Subject B-113) report sudden sensations that defy all scientific explanation. A temporary cover story compares these sensations to the influence of a hallucinogen, but the entity actually exhibits a limited ability to alter the structure of reality. We suspect that it is attempting to steal the identities of citizens it has killed.

Your assignment is to track its movements, document the identity of Sleepers that have witnessed it (for later debriefing), and if possible, eradicate this entity before further damage is done. We cannot provide reinforcements immediately, due to more extensive outbreaks in other parts of the city. Do not jeopardize your loyalty by failure.

Chapter II

At some point in Chapter II, Control ceases all transmissions. This silence in itself is not remarkable, since messages from this cryptic source are normally infrequent. Concurrently, some agents (including yours) should encounter some of the phenomena mentioned earlier in this book (the beginning of Chapter One: Signs of the Times): disappearances, abductions, sightings of new and unidentified phenomena and so forth. Independent supervisors respond by forming their own battle plans… until the Horizon Constructs interrupt with their own detailed and frequent directives.

Clarity

The Avatar Storm, along with the destruction of three Horizon Constructs, has disrupted the higher-level organization of the Technocracy. For prolonged periods of time, front-line agents have doubted the degree of involvement of their superiors. The amount of surveillance and communication from the Horizon has varied widely, sometimes by region, allowing more agents to go rogue, certain reports of disloyalty to go unanswered and dangerous supernatural events to go unnoticed.

At the start of Chapter II, this trend comes to an end. Many front-line operatives have been busy with lockdowns and spiritual incursions, but Horizon supervisors have had their own issues to address. By diverting resources from other projects, such as coordinating hunts for Reality Deviants, administrators and technicians of the Technocracy inevitably restore surveillance and communications. They still cannot send troops and reinforcements to Earth, but they can advise — and watch — operations on the front lines. Once again, there is an "eye" watching from the top of the Technocratic "pyramid."

This endeavor, Project: Clarity, draws significant resources from other agendas, but its success does not need to be announced right away. Since the Avatar Storm, the powers that be have occasionally observed lapses in loyalty that they could not act on right away. As systems go back online, one top priority is following up on investigations into rogue agents.

Loyal Panopticon supervisors soon receive detailed messages from their superiors with instructions to coordinate further lockdowns. In some cases, they are instructed to relieve other Technocracy agents of command; these individuals are then assigned to more hazardous missions. Shortly thereafter, the Technocracy reactivates Project: Invictus, a coordinated effort to purge Reality Deviants hidden within the Union. Rogue Technocrats soon find themselves hunted… by teams assembled by their own organization.

A Shift in Power: Eventually, Masters and managers on the Horizon resume broadcasts as if the Avatar Storm never happened. Agents in any amalgam will suddenly find themselves reporting to higher authorities. If they were performing missions for an Ivory Tower Supervisor, they soon receive broadcasts from a manager one rank higher. Some Progenitors sequestered in laboratories suddenly lose their funding and are sent to support amalgams in distant cities. Cyborgs receive downloads from sources with which they were previously unfamiliar, and Syndicate reps must contend with a "corporate reorg" and give detailed reports to managers they have never heard of. (In the parlance of **Guide to the Technocracy,** Supervisors must once again submit to the commands issued by Masters.) Horizon immediately asserts its authority… and disgruntled front-line agents do their best to hide any signs of dissatisfaction. The chain of command is re-forged.

From a Tradition mage's point of view, it is possible that her cabal has made contact with a rogue or independent Technocracy agent. They might have even cooperated at some point, if only to keep more powerful (and less understanding) superiors from interfering with their activities. At the start of Chapter II, all such deals are off… at least for now. Such contacts disappear for a while, but not before finding a way to notify the cabal that "transmissions from our superiors have resumed." Disloyal agents might be hunted down, and their contacts in the Traditions marked for surveillance.

Disloyal Agents Eliminated: Restored surveillance allows intelligence analysts to look for new instances of anomalous activity. Contacting agents on the front lines, they rapidly assemble dossiers of various occult groups. For instance, the agents of Project: Redlight (see **The Red Sign**), continue to transmit a great deal of intelligence very quickly regarding the activities of vampires. A few successful operatives are "rewarded" with missions to research new threats regarding Antediluvians. After disclosing a vast amount of contradictory material regarding archaic history documents, these pawns are quickly eliminated in a vampiric Jyhad. These cells of agents are soon thereafter regarded as compromised.

Disparate amalgams compile similar dossiers on ghosts, werewolves, the walking dead and other phenomena. Completely isolated from these threats in hyperspace Horizon Constructs, Union supervisors attempt to prioritize these threats, occasionally sending teams of agents to an untimely demise. Not surprisingly, these missions are often given to agents whose loyalty is considered questionable. Because the Horizon Constructs cannot retrieve agents for social conditioning, they cannot simply "correct" minds that have been corrupted by a taste of freedom. Oversight committees have already scheduled some of these agents for "deletion," but managers hope that by sending disloyal agents against supernatural phenomena, they might learn something before expendable agents are killed.

Within a few days, a collective of moderately competent bureaucrats attempts to create a color-coded "ROYGBIV" threat system to evaluate the danger of various missions. (*"Your mission is to eliminate a pack of werewolves in Central Park and abduct their leader. The threat level of this operation is Code Blue."*) Through this system, Code Violet missions are considered the easiest operations. By contrast, the last survivors of Project: Redlight suddenly find themselves enlisted in a series of Code Red missions to find further evidence of Antediluvians. Agents soon confirm that the supervisors who devised this system do not fully understand the level of threats involved, and lives are lost.

Many of these missions are only partially completed. As disloyal agents are systematically sent to their deaths, enthusiasm for waging war against other supernatural threats begins to wane. As a result, the schism between the front lines and Horizon widens even further, and more agents go rogue. On the Horizon itself, Ivory Tower academics rant that this attempt to restore the Union's original ideals is a gross misinterpretation of their polemics. Enemies in Iteration X respond that the dissidents' revisionist histories are in error, calling instead for the restoration of the Pogrom.

Tracking the Anakim: A few of the more unusual dossiers concern theories of an alien invasion. A standard background dossier relates publicly known rumors regarding alien abductions, events in Roswell and legendary Men in Black questioning witnesses of such events. Teams of agents who receive these assignments typically regard them as a punishment, but after hearing about teams sent on Code Red assignments, any dissatisfaction with such missions are kept concealed. Citizens interrogated after various lockdowns have related a vast amount of barely credible evidence of what they have encountered. Investigations into this latest "invasion," on the other hand, can be traced to testimony given by Men in Black.

A handful of sightings concern extradimensional entities that have learned to disguise themselves as ordinary citizens. (Ivory Tower analysts can confirm that similar subterfuge has been used by the walking dead and certain species of vampires.) Agents of the Operative Methodology have established procedures for seeing through these disguises, of course. Several agents have reported seeing "gray-skinned humanoids" masquerading as ordinary humans. These witnesses are brought into local safe houses for questioning, and many mysteriously disappear shortly thereafter.

Most agents are entirely unaware of the origins of the invasion: a failed experiment in a Construct in the Arctic. A small population of humans with psychic potential had been exposed to extradimensional phenomena, resulting in the creation of an agent who could actively control the barriers between worlds. (Some would be tempted to call him a human/alien hybrid.) A small cabal of Tradition mages attempted to exterminate this individual (and the results depended on a story found in **Manifesto**).

Since then, Men in Black have found other individuals *near Technocracy lockdowns* displaying similar abilities. These invaders have escorted Sleepers across the Gauntlet, and in some cases, escaped capture by stepping outside our dimension without fear of retribution from the Avatar Storm. Perhaps through some mass delusion, all Technocrat witnesses claim to have seen the same "real appearance" behind this human façade. As incredulous as it might seem, most of these beings have the features of six-foot-tall "gray aliens," complete with wide eyes, spindly limbs and gray skin. The hunt begins for these individuals, who are assigned a codename for lack of a better term. Official files refer to them as the Anakim, the same term used in experiments whose records have been expunged.

Dimensional Science: Void Engineers are sent to repair rifts in the Dimensional Barrier. The technology to repair this barrier is highly experimental, depending on procedures that representatives of other Conventions consider almost mystical. Therefore, Earth Defense Corps personnel are watched more closely than many front-line amalgams. (Secretly, the Void Engineers have responded to this interference by developing proscribed technology to actually reverse social conditioning).

In the past, agents who fail to adequately defend the Dimensional Barrier have been reassigned to patrols into deep space. Not surprisingly, these explorers take pride in their status as outcasts and exiles… and then develop more extensive procedures for reversing their former conditioning. With a drastic increase in the number of extradimensional incursions, the Union cannot simply reassign these personnel, especially since journeys into the Void have become one-way trips.

Attempts to investigate and repair breaches in the Dimensional Barrier soon meet with spectacular failures. Manifestations of the Avatar Storm punish investigators working from *within the physical world.* When technicians fail to seal a gateway, strengthen the barrier or enter these rifts, massive elemental and electrical disturbances lash out to wound or destroy intruders. (In game terms, a failed attempt to manipulate the Gauntlet during this chapter doesn't just accrue Paradox — it wounds the mage or Technocrat responsible as though he had crossed over into the Umbra.) Some of these rifts unexpectedly heal themselves, but Engineers are at a loss to explain why.

An open dimensional rift is a threat to any Awakened or Enlightened soul who goes near it. (It's a good thing, then, that your agents are assigned to help contain one of these areas.) Some loyal Technocrats regard these freak events with an eye toward justice, taking them as signs that the Void Engineers involved have crossed the line from the realm of science to the domain of mysticism. Any sufficiently advanced technology, after all, resembles magic… but some sufficiently advanced technology might be interpreted *as* magic. A few technicians attempt to resign in protest, only to find themselves blamed for incursions in their assigned areas.

New Cults, New Gods: As rifts open in the Dimensional Barrier, extradimensional forces reach out for weak minds on Earth. Some gather humans with magical potential, bringing them together through dreams and visions to remote and unwatched corners of the Earth. Avatar shards Awaken such initiates, and revelations from outside reality guide them to perform rites of summoning. Marauders, Nephandi or even demons act as the shadowy leaders of these cults. Whatever the

Threat Dossier: Targeted Anakim

Manifesto included new rules for Anakim. For a start, these mages have the ability to cross the Gauntlet without taking aggravated damage, and they can cloak their true forms behind a mortal façade. Finding an Anakim requires investigation. Capturing or eliminating one is far more difficult, since it has the ability to "escape" across the Dimensional Barrier with the Spirit 3 Effect: **Stepping Sideways**. Aside from Peter Wu in the aforementioned sourcebook, here's another Anakim to set loose in the world. (The Storyteller should fill in his appearance and goals to best fit the chronicle.)

Darren Bright

Background: Darren was raised a devout believer in a fringe Christian sect in Arizona. His Awakening at age nine brought him to the attention of the Celestial Choristers, but their paradigm never really stuck with him. He much preferred the more judgmental, wrathful religion with which he was raised over the mellow paeans to the One that his fellow Choristers sang.

He retreated to his family's compound and gathered Sleeper followers, intent on Awakening them through the evocation of an angel. Instead of an angel, they summoned a Psychopomp, a spirit that possessed the all-too-willing Chorister. The merging of essences, however, resulted not in a more enlightened being, but in a slightly deranged religious fanatic who now felt that he was an incarnate angel.

Image: Darren certainly looks like an angel, complete with robes, wings and occasional halo. He's even cultivated a Jesus-style beard and long hair.

Roleplaying Hints: It's very hard to convince you that you aren't an angel — your Anakim powers are like nothing known to mages. Hence, you must be an angel, right?

Faction: Anakim
Essence: Primordial
Nature: Fanatic
Demeanor: Child
Attributes: Strength 3, Dexterity 3, Stamina 2, Charisma 3, Manipulation 5, Appearance 2, Perception 3, Intelligence 4, Wits 2
Abilities: Alertness 3, Athletics 2, Awareness 2, Brawl 3, Cosmology 2, Dodge 2, Intimidation 3, Occult 5, Subterfuge 5, Technology 1
Arete: 3
Spheres: Correspondence 3, Mind 2, Prime 2, Spirit 3
Willpower: 8
Quintessence: 5
Paradox: 1
Resonance: (Dynamic) Frenzied 1, (Entropic) Disintegrating 2
Anakim Powers: See pp. 198-199.
Corruption Flaws: Phobia (being caged), Insensible to Pain.

Assignment (Code Blue)

Surveillance has tracked the movement of a self-styled "cult leader," an advisor to the new generation of Reality Deviants in our city. His abilities allow him to exit our dimension at will, crossing the Dimensional Barrier to a realm where he can "teleport" across large distances. His exploitation of magical forces assists him in hunting down potential mages and perverting the laws of time and space to reach them quickly. He is using his charismatic (and possibly psychic) influence to recruit these deviant citizens into a cult, in which they might combine their abilities to summon further extradimensional incursions.

A psychological profile made one year ago verified his work with an agency called "The Bright Foundation," responsible for a (failed) summoning of an alleged "angel" into a private compound 10 miles from our city. You will know him when you see his true form: He is an Anakim, appearing to Enlightened witnesses as a Raphaelite angel. (File on relevant artistic style appended.) Your mission is to find him, track him and gather further intelligence. Once you observe him entering an area that is not populated by witnesses, terminate him with prejudice before he can form a new cult. Should you fail, Shockwave is willing to accept collateral damage among the surrounding populace to ensure his confirmed elimination.

motivator is, they are united in perverting these rifts in the Gauntlet. It should not be difficult to spare one amalgam to seek out one of these new cults and investigate. (Such a mission could make for an effective chapter in your chronicle. See the "Targeted Anakim" sidebar for one approach.)

Laboratory Conditions: The first rifts in the Gauntlet occur in "mystical" or isolated areas. As defined in Chapter I, later waves occur in places where it is normally very strong, such as a downtown area in a large city... or a scientific laboratory. Some segments of the Technocracy are not devoted to ideology, but to the advancement of science (or as some moralists would suggest, advancement at any cost).

Experimental Technocrats, such as reclusive Progenitors, might be drawn into this new series of events when a rift in the Gauntlet appears in one of the most spiritually barren and calcified places on Earth: a Technocracy laboratory. Although this entity might act (if only in terms of game mechanics) as a "spirit," its manifested form could make it look like the sort of genegineered or scientifically anomalous beastie that draws the attention of scientific agents. Medical personnel then attempt to capture it, or Iteration X cyborgs can hunt it to extinction... despite the protests of Progenitors and other visionaries.

The Schism Widens: Faced with many failed missions during this stage, mid-level agents begin to disregard broad and draconian policies sent from the Horizon. Rank-Three Technocrats — such as Progenitor Research Associates, It-X Programmers, Ivory Tower Intelligence Analysts, Syndicate Chairmen and Void Engineer Commanders — continue to direct agents in the field, but they refuse to report everything they find to their superiors. As a result, Horizon managers file reports of insubordination against independent managers... but they cannot send troops down from Horizon to capture and retrieve them for psychological evaluation and social conditioning. It is a stalemate, at least until something happens to knock a few pieces off the chessboard.

Highly loyal operatives on the front lines (also referred to as "Loyalists" through internal propaganda) immediately use surveillance to observe amalgams held under suspicion, sometimes under directives from their superiors. Cries for a renewed Pogrom are answered with propaganda over the "security of reality itself," which is then used to justify a different set of atrocities. Although Horizon command can't mobilize troops, Syndicate managers can still manipulate computer files, mass media and wealth — all three resources are allocated to bolster directives from the Horizon. Project: Invictus, a recent attempt to purge "deviance" within the Technocracy itself, soon secures an unprecedented amount of funding.

On the front lines, a growing number of agents maintain their allegiance to "disloyal" supervisors. Cut off from Technocracy resources and oversight, they maintain organized and independent cells of operatives. (Technocracy Supervisor "coordinators" — as defined on pp. 81 and 206 of **Guide to the Technocracy** — are essential for keeping these cells of amalgams together.) In addition to their dissatisfaction with the Horizon, many of them are motivated by transmissions made by dissidents within the Ivory Tower.

Some rogue agents begin to accuse Horizon managers of seizing power merely to support their own personal objectives. Others argue that the real purpose of their Union should be to once again "make men masters of their own world." Believing that they represent the original ideals of the Union (and unknowingly, the Order of Reason), they formally declare themselves as "Unionists." Caught out in the cold, they prepare themselves for a revolution against their former masters.

A separate sect of rogue Technocrats finds reasons to work with other technomancers, including Sons of Ether and Virtual Adepts. To escape the scrutiny of clear channels of surveillance from the Horizon, they rapidly develop alternative networks of communication. Virtual Adepts develop "private spaces" in the Digital Web, enable mystically encrypted chat rooms and email servers and hack their way into suborning (and improving) obsolete or abandoned Technocracy technology. In private communiqués, some of these dissidents and exiles agree that overt demonstrations of magic might attract unexplained phenomena. As Traditionalists argue over prophecies, destinies and signs of "Armageddon," "technomancy cabals" go into survivalist mode, preparing themselves for the worst.

A Scholar Disappears: An academic debate over the origins of the Technocracy leads to a fierce political struggle. Several high-ranking Technocrats disappear, including Terrence Whyte, the author of many polemics on the origins of the Ascension War. Some theorists postulate that he joined with a Void Engineer ship for a voyage to the Far Horizon. Tradition mages, if they hear this story, might deduce that he was actually attempting a Seeking.

CHAPTER III

Forces from outside our world have infiltrated our reality. Whether they will destroy it or repair it depends on your point of view. The compilation of a final Time Table suggests that Armageddon is at hand, but Technocrats have little need for mysticism or prophecy. Loyal

Technocrats might even be suffused with optimism at this point. The first casualties in this alleged Armageddon have been disloyal Technocrats, Void Engineers dabbling in "mystic procedures" they cannot explain to their contemporaries and independent mages who were foolish enough to tamper with dimensional rifts.

Fluctuations of the Avatar Storm in the physical world are only the beginning of a wider array of supernatural phenomena. At the start of Chapter III, quanta of extradimensional matter begin to drift into our world, seeking living beings that fit certain parameters. Each incursion is accompanied by a meteorological disturbance. Storms rage, electrical activity disrupts technological equipment, and darkness falls. Behind these cosmetic effects, agents who can monitor primal forces track subatomic activity that defies explanation.

On the front lines, agents communicating with their contemporaries begin to refer to these manifestations as "shards" or "quantum shards" (perhaps hoping that their parameters can indeed by quantified by some as-yet-undeveloped metric). Independent Technocrats — as well as deviant technomancers, Etherites and Virtual Adepts — need a common term for them as well; they make analogies to "dark matter." Reality Deviants would go so far as to call them "Avatar shards," but that description implies a spiritual, soulful or even intelligent component to this activity. Further analysis is required.

Pogrom Restored (New Awakenings): Early analysis confirms that "quantum shards," like the extradimensional entities that arrived before them, seek out individuals with paranormal or psychic potential. Recent statistical analysis (including high-powered procedures attempted on the Horizon) suggests that some of these "contactees" might have the potential to become Technocrats themselves… or deviant mages.

Some of these "Chosen" subjects are currently under investigation for possible recruitment into the Technocracy. Others are acolytes and servitors of deviant cults. (In game terms, some might also be humans with Numina, psychic powers, abilities as mediums or even a few points in the Awareness Ability.) Within a few weeks, technicians find ways to track the movement of these quanta (perhaps with "manar," as defined in **New World Order**) and discover that contactees are *Awakening as mages.*

Men in Black move into position; Shockwaves of Iterators are on standby; Syndicate representatives prepare for recruitment, containment or elimination of these new victims. The Pogrom is restored, but only against newly Awakened mages… and Tradition mages who come looking for them. The Technocracy soon discovers that more of these Awakenings are taking place than it can monitor. In some cases, operatives face opposition from independent cabals chasing down the same lost souls. In far too many cases, these "Chosen" initiates attempt to use their newly developed abilities, only to learn about Paradox the hard way.

Dark Matter (Shards Hunt Victims of Paradox): Unionists witness firsthand what this newly discovered "dark matter" can do to unprepared victims. As a new generation (perhaps the last generation) of mage initiates attempts to understand its new access to deviant abilities, the number of Paradox Backlashes in the world increases. In severe cases, shards seek out victims of Paradox… and punish them with the same virulence as the Avatar Storm — by now referred to as "Dimensional Storms" within the Union.

Tradition mages working outright acts of magic are targeted by this same effect. Theories written by dissident Ivory Tower academics — soon disseminated through Unionist cells — describe this effect as reality itself passing judgment on those who have deviated from reality. It is clear that the shards have a criterion for selecting those who benefit from their effects and those who suffer. Some Progenitors describe these quanta as an "immune system," but they are unsure what disease it is attempting to cure.

Race Against Time: Independent amalgams pursue methods of containing this "dark matter." They can do so only by coming up with new applications of Enlightened Science and contravening established procedures. To survive this new manifestation of the Dimensional Storm, they must find a way to isolate, contain and protect themselves from "dark matter" before Loyalist Technocrats discover their activities. If an amalgam can figure out how to survive an encounter with Avatar shards, or even manipulate them, it will have a significant edge later in this timeline.

One possible answer depends on shadowing and observing Anakim. Witnesses have seen these extradimensional entities manipulating or directing quantum shards, but the Anakim do not appear to need apparatuses (that is, magical "foci") to do so. Observant Men in Black respond that these psychic powers rely on Mind influence. Other technomancers attempt to devise new technological procedures for replicating these effects. Research begins. (It won't be finished, however, until Chapter VI.)

These phenomena exist outside the limits of Technocracy dogma, so agents must invent new terminology to even describe it. Some try to base their solutions on

theories of "primal forces" or definitions of "Dimensional Science," but without a standard to measure these forces against, all these interpretations degenerate into a torrent of technobabble. Technocracy dogma has also described nine types of "influence" (rather like "Spheres"), but these shards do not correspond to *any* of them. Although their movements can be tracked with the Prime Sphere, they are not Prime; although they affect and are affect by the Gauntlet, they are not Spirit; they are not ephemera, spirit matter, ectoplasm, Quintessence or any previously encountered substance. (Analysis of this anomalous data will not be complete until Chapter V.)

Rogue Agents: Faced with supernatural forces they cannot fully understand or oppose, some absolutely conformist Technocrats go insane. Inspired by such heroes as Secret Agent John Courage, they exist outside the dogma and rallying cries of Loyalists, Unionists, dissident academics, technomancers and anyone else who represents "a side." ("You set me free, Mr. Anderson.") Instead, they experiment and innovate new procedures. Some destroy themselves trying foolish feats like stopping bullets, splitting themselves into dozens of identical agents and superheroic flight. Shards seek them quickly, and the results are spectacular, violent and tragic. Given absolute freedom but denied the training to learn to use it wisely,

operations led by these rogue agents resemble suicide strikes more than campaigns.

Reality Hardens (Optional System): As the amount of visible supernatural activity in the world increases, Paradox strengthens to defend humanity. One way to represent this effect is by increasing the lethality of a Paradox Backlash. Instead of using a chart in the revised core rulebook to calculate damage, resurrect the rules used in **Sorcerers Crusade**. Here's a simplified version: Each "success" rolled on a Paradox Backlash immediately inflicts a level of aggravated damage. This might sound harsh, but then again, it's as deadly as crossing the Gauntlet... and at this stage, the shards that empower the Gauntlet have drifted into the physical world.

Chapter IV

Here's a syllogistic irony for you. Any mage who has been trapped outside the Horizon for more than three months after the Avatar Storm cannot manifest in the physical world. As Avatar shards have worn away at the Gauntlet, however, these razors of primal energy have torn rifts in the barrier between worlds, allowing spirits to manifest in the physical world. Therefore, mages (and Technocrats) trapped beyond the Horizon — who have also become spirits — *might also find new ways back into the physical world.* Much of Chapter IV deals with the consequences of this change.

The chapter starts with the first appearance of a Master or Oracle in the physical world, followed by the revelation that he is merely a spirit (using rules detailed in **The Infinite Tapestry**). Such invaders cannot stay in the world for long, but they can interact with and advise mages. (By the time Chapter VI starts, they should be much easier to defeat, leading to a few easy, yet significant, victories against Tradition Masters.) More importantly, this new revelation allows Horizon Loyalists to send reinforcements from the Horizon. Sneak attacks and lightning raids follow.

Storytelling Changes: As the End Time advances, the Gauntlet and the rules that govern it continue to change. Storytellers might find these transformations easier to convey if an actual physical event occurs at the same time, denoting that something far subtler (and perhaps even more philosophical) has happened. Instead of telling players "the Gauntlet rating decreases by two temporarily," it helps to show what happens when the Gauntlet weakens.

For instance, the Union might have found one gate that is more enduring or obvious than the others, kept under guard by Iteration X troops. When your agents are sent to study it, a massive fluctuation could then lead to transmissions from the Horizon occurring on all communication equipment in the area. A bridge, boardroom or surveillance chamber on the Horizon might be visible through the gate. A hologram might walk through a temporary gate between a Horizon Construct and a front-line safe house, and so on.

In the largest lockdown areas, an Avatar Storm might manifest as a physical storm, with dark clouds, rain, high winds and other meteorological phenomena that scientists cannot fully explain. Even if this storm occurs only in the area where your characters' amalgam or agents are present, it is enough of a signal to grab their attention and launch speculation… and action.

The Gauntlet Weakens: In Chapter II, Project: Clarity restored Technocratic communication and surveillance. As Armageddon draws closer, weakened barriers to reality temporarily restore travel between dimensions as well. Some facts do not change: Any mage traveling from the physical world to the spirit world still suffers aggravated damage (unless the traveler is using one of the solutions detailed in **The Infinite Tapestry**). Spirits with the Materialize Charm, however, do not suffer this penalty. Mages trapped in the Void might not realize it, but they can actually learn this Charm (since it depends on a Trait called Gnosis; see pg. 113 of **The Infinite Tapestry**.) Innovative Void Engineers and Virtual Adepts studying this system might think of this solution in less spiritual terms, perhaps by "writing code for a workaround."

Void Engineers eventually develop a Dimensional Science procedure that opens a temporary gateway (or conduit) from the Horizon to Earth's surface. Agents relying on this form of transport still suffer side effects, possibly including the phenomena called "disconnection" (again, see **The Infinite Tapestry**). In addition, they cannot stay in the physical world for more than three months. That's more than enough time for an amalgam *from the Horizon* to carry out a mission… even one as dangerous as returning a disloyal Technocrat to his supervisors for a loyalty review. The consequences of capture are much greater than the threat of powerful Mind procedures. Any agent returned to the Horizon for more than three months adapts to his surroundings, enough so that Earth itself becomes an alien environment.

Virtual Adepts, cooperating with rogue Technocratic agents, soon master similar "subroutines" for opening rifts between the Void and Earth. A Master mage or Technocrat with the proper rote (probably employing Correspondence 5 and Spirit 4) can replicate some of these procedures. The good news is that by the end of the timeline, several agents have documented these new procedures. Any breach in Horizon security would be a powerful weapon later in the timeline. Opening a gate from the Earth to a Horizon Construct, however, is far more difficult. (For instance, imagine overcoming a 30-success **Ban** and **Ward** against Correspondence and Spirit Effects in the Construct.)

The bad news is that if the Dimensional Barrier is breached thus, other forces on the other side can take advantage of the opening. Void Engineers won't open gates without a squad of Enlightened marines and soldiers nearby. A lone Virtual Adept, on the other hand, might allow a spirit to enter the realm of flesh, or even worse, lead to abductions or disappearances of innocent citizens. Therefore, most mages are wise enough to not make these rituals common knowledge. After all, some Marauders and Nephandi exiled from this world have been struggling to get back in. Independent agents fear that cults on Earth might help these exiles to return… and their fears are justified.

Tradition mages are distracted by higher concerns. Masters and Oracles on the cusp of Ascension face a difficult choice. Should they return to Earth to shepherd more souls on the path to Ascension, or do they continue to quest for enlightenment, finding their destiny in the stars? Egoists remain utterly focused on attempting to master all aspects of reality (perhaps straining to reach Arete 10 or mastering all Nine Spheres). Altruists might use this opportunity to advise mages on Earth, but they do so by risking their own destruction; amalgams might be sent to destroy these apparitions. Other Masters will undertake epic Seekings on the Far Horizon, pursuing ideals so lofty that they have little to do with petty struggles on Earth. Those truly guilty of hubris believe that undertaking these vision quests will save the world. They are the most likely to die.

Securing Reality: Forces on the Horizon do not traffic in mysticism and archaic philosophies. High-level managers on the Horizon argue the Technocracy's "mission statements" — the Precepts of Damian — but they can all be simplified into one primary objective during Chapter IV: *securing the Earth.* For all the various theories of "dark matter" and "quantum shards," it is clear that overt acts of magic, such as blatant acts of Enlightened Science, not only endanger the people who practice them, but innocents around them as well.

Whether the commands originate in a Syndicate boardroom or Autocthonia, the Technocrats' true agenda does not change. Loyalists soon hold to the ideal that while overt magic is dangerous, covert procedures are essential. The Technocracy has spent over a century perfecting procedures that could manipulate reality while incurring a minimal amount of risk. Its technological tools are accepted by the Masses, as they bring health, longevity and wealth (at least for those who can master them). The Loyalists' final Time Table is then unified in one purpose: creating a world where subtle acts of Enlightened Science will work, and all alternatives (including all forms of magic) will fail. If innocent lives must be lost in this campaign, then the ends justify the means, for all of reality is at stake.

Reinforcements Arrive: Aligned in purpose, Horizon Constructs send troops down to the front lines in one final push for the War for Reality. Rogue agents are hunted. Reality Deviants are eliminated. Hidden chantries and headquarters for rogue cells are destroyed after their locations are confirmed through Project: Clarity. Strengthened by reinforcements, Loyalists begin hunting "deviants" in their own organization. Project: Invictus is revealed, and a massive housecleaning takes place.

The war for the hearts and minds of the Masses is far more difficult. Syndicate and Ivory Tower influence in local governments are strained to their limits, as mass media outlets are denied any revelations of the purpose behind these attacks. Fearful of imagined evils, the Masses invent rumors about what is actually happening: stories of terrorist attacks, alien invasion, signs of Revelation, verifications of Nostradamus and stranger theories. Reality is strained, but Paradox responds by punishing the most overt practices of magic. As Tradition mages desperately attempt to defend themselves with vulgar acts of magic, they wound themselves with (now deadlier) Paradox Backlashes.

The eleven o'clock news effect (mentioned in Chapter One of this book) might kick in at this point as stories about witchcraft, paganism, shamanism, and devil worship proliferate in the mass media. These reports are not just or fair, nor are they rational. They are the results of a panicked populace looking for a quick solution to a problem they cannot possibly understand. Citizens begin to argue that magic is real, and that it is a threat to those who do not practice it. The occasional sighting of a team of policemen, agents, soldiers or rescue workers making a raid against a deviant cult might be excused under such circumstances, if only by the fearful. The most frightened segments of the populace accept that drastic measures are necessary if their safety is at stake, and if it's really for the "common good."

Delirium and Madness (Optional Rule): It is possible that you consider so many open acts of magic to strain the credibility of your chronicle. Once ordinary people can prove that "magic is real," **Mage** becomes a very different game. An invasion from the Horizon might shatter any illusions about the existence of the supernatural, in which case, the final sessions of this story could be drastically different from all that came before them.

As an alternative, reality might undergo another subtle shift as a backlash against so much Paradox. This interpretation depends on the concept of "Delirium." Long before the dawn of human history, supernatural forces have obscured the presence of occult forces. Werewolves in their true form, ghosts that have crossed the Shroud and even the walking dead bring about instances of temporary insanity in those who witness their activities.

By extending that idea further, you could choose to apply the effects of Delirium (as mentioned in such games as **Werewolf** and **Hunter**) to witnesses of vulgar magic. In general, how an average citizen responds depends on his Willpower. Strong-willed individuals cope better than weak-willed ones. This effect, however, applies only to vulgar magic (or blatant acts of Enlightened Science). Coincidental or subtle effects do not require this solution.

Chapter V

A sudden assault from the Horizon rapidly alters the landscape of reality. Sneak attacks lead to massive casualties, as chantries and safe houses alike are compromised. Horizon has been waiting and watching, preparing for a final push in a renewed Ascension War. If enough major victories are scored, the war for reality might soon be over.

Yet other forces have been watching and waiting as well, hidden in the night. For decades, Void Engineers have sent their ships into the Deep Universe, where their agents establish colonies and strongholds. The Gauntlet has prevented these outposts from sending transmissions to Earth or attempting to return to physical reality, but now "clarity" has been restored. Some truths have been hidden for centuries; the oldest of these exiled outposts is far older than the Technocracy itself. In Chapter V, Control resumes its transmissions. Its ideology supports many of the theories posited by Whyte and other dissident academics. The Unionists will not receive physical reinforcements, but this is a moral and ideological victory.

Asserting Control: New phenomena are occurring, and visionaries and heroes oppose them. The xenophobic secret masters of the Technocracy, the Loyalists, seek to dominate humanity, but even from their perspective on the Horizon, they lack the ability to fully defeat these new threats. As they tighten their grip, more of reality slips through their fingers.

All hope is not lost. Rogue cells of Technocrats and a new generation of Daedaleans might find a way to save the world… through Enlightened Science. On the Horizon, dissident academics in the Ivory Tower have remained in contact through the same network of Viasilicos used by the original Order of Reason. (In fact, one of these "seeing stones" once rested on the desk of Terrence Whyte; see **The Technomancer's Toybox**.) Avatar shards, the Anakim and new manifestations of Paradox and Delirium threaten the reality the Technocracy has struggled to shape. Only visionary minds, like those of the original philosopher-scientists, have a chance to solve these dilemmas. The Technocracy has no established procedures for these phenomena, which means that the technomancers who want to invent them must rebel against their Masters to save the world.

One amalgam could easily pursue a series of missions against this background of shifting realities. If the characters have been willing to defend the common populace against the Loyalists, the wave of attacks in Chapter IV has probably hammered their morale. Such devotion can then be rewarded by moral support from beyond the Horizon when the campaign is at its darkest moment. One transmission from Control, through as simple an apparatus as a radio, telephone or television set, would confirm that they are not alone in the revolution. In fact, Control could offer them direction just as it seems that their conflict with the Loyalists is drawing to a close.

Destroying Deviance

Humanity might struggle to deny the existence of the supernatural, but the Masses still fear it enough that

outright acts of magic are punished. Enough anomalous activity has occurred by this time that mankind cannot help but believe that the supernatural is real… and take action. In Chapter V, Avatar shards, Avatar Storms and semi-automatic weapons fire from local authorities all eliminates "enemies of reality." At this point, one dramatic event to demonstrate mankind's triumph over occult forces could seal this timeline. This event could be the capture of a major mage like Dante (or an ephemeral mage returning from the Void), the slaughter of a dragon in Central Park (see the sidebar), or some similar triumph of science over magic. United by fear of an unknown enemy, the goal of a Technocratic New World Order could easily become true.

At this stage, the Pogrom against Tradition mages resumes, but Technocracy agents aren't the only ones who are hunting them. Fearful of the existence of the supernatural, local authorities and government agencies should also act against Tradition mages. Mages are mortal, after all, so mundane authorities can alter their lives without having to alter reality. As mankind scores victories against magical forces, Consensus should shift against overt and archaic applications of magic. Occasionally, Technocracy agents might also hunt a particularly dangerous mage during this time, but other than a few media-worthy assaults on the paranormal, they can focus on greater threats… including rival Technocrats.

Silence in the Eye of the Hurricane

Avatar shards have bestowed great power to Sleepers who were destined to become mages… and possibly even destined to play a role in Armageddon. Some survivors have been recruited (or hunted and abducted), but many of these initiates — the last generation of mages — will eventually destroy themselves trying to marshal forces they cannot understand. Without Technocracy indoctrination or Traditional training, they have the power to summon up forces they cannot put down. (In game terms, these "initiates" might even have unusually high Arete or Avatar ratings to further this theme, perhaps around Arete 4 or even Arete 5.)

Quantum shards, dark matter, primal shards — by any name, they are new and unpredictable phenomena. When Armageddon begins, Avatar shards give potential mages a final chance to experience what they've been denied. The cosmos gives, but it also takes away. As the End Times advance, newly Awakened initiates (and recently Enlightened agents) will start to experience more virulent Paradox Backlashes. When a Paradox Backlash occurs (perhaps with five or more points of Paradox), sudden manifestations of the Avatar Storm can reach across the Gauntlet to flay them with spiritual wounds. (In game terms, when an "initiate" stacks up five points of Paradox, a Paradox Backlash occurs, and the damage rolled is aggravated. See the optional rules for this effect at the end of Chapter IV.)

If you like, ordinary Sleepers may see a vastly different, and possibly coincidental, reason for why these individuals suffer and die, such as diseases, deadly accidents or car crashes. Anyone watching with Enlightened sight (that is, anyone who can use Arete or Awareness) should be able to see that Avatar shards are inflicting the actual damage. At this stage, a handful of deaths are sufficient as long as Avatar shards are acting as the instruments of justice. This (relatively minor) event confirms that the shards can now kill, regardless of the condition or status of the local Gauntlet.

Now that humanity suspects that the supernatural is real, reality's backlash against overt acts of magic intensifies. Almost at random, similar Paradox Backlashes affect specific mages and agents, including experienced willworkers. In these cases, however, the "backlash" does not inflict damage — *it reduces the victim's Arete*. (Roll for a Paradox Backlash; subtract one point of Arete per success.) Avatar shards don't

> ### Threat Dossier: It's Time to Kill the Dragon
>
> Once humans begin to suspect that the supernatural is real, Reality Deviants and magical anachronisms will have a harder time hiding from the Masses. After Sleeper witnesses confirm sightings of modern monsters, the Technocracy has an opportunity to eliminate such threats without interference. Here's an example of a typical mission from Chapter V.
>
> **Reptilian Anomaly**
> **Willpower** 8, **Rage** 10, **Gnosis** 8, **Essence** 26
> **Charms:** Airt Sense, Create Flame
> **Assignment (Code Blue)**
> *Within a few miles of a major metropolitan area, a group of cultists has gathered around a site pulsing with Primal Energy. Surveillance confirms that they are performing some type of societal or communal ritual, but it has gone terribly wrong, summoning an incursion spirit across the Dimensional Barrier. Dark forces sleeping in the Earth have therefore manifested in our world. Without an appropriate frame of reference to define this reptilian anomaly, the few witnesses sane enough to observe it have described it as a "dragon." Iteration X is mobilizing a Shockwave; your agents must detain this entity until reinforcements arrive.*

always mete out these effects during every Backlash, but they *can*. And again, this effect doesn't need to be widespread. A handful of "silenced" mages and agents should be enough to encourage paranoia, as long as it's evident that Avatar shards were responsible.

Any agent using surveillance methods (such as Correspondence/Prime procedures) can track when these events occur, but they cannot find a reason. These occurrences are always presaged by the arrival of multiple Avatar shards converging on their target. A handful of incidents should be sufficient — any more, and agents (especially your characters) feel utterly helpless, running from any phenomena they do not understand. (Just to be sure, it would be wise not to "randomly" target your characters with this effect.)

At the same time, the Technocracy mandates the use of coincidental (or "subtle") procedures. Since they have trained for over a century to hide their activities behind a technological façade, Technocrats are far less likely to draw the vengeance of Avatar shards. Because their subtle influence does not appear as overt magic, they can also escape scrutiny by the Masses. In fact, media spin reveres experts, scientists and soldiers as heroes during this time.

Other Trends

Transmissions from Control: Control resumes its transmissions at the start of Chapter V. It seeks out scattered survivors of the Loyalists' massive attack, attempting to unify them in the defense of humanity. Their goal is not to isolate a self-sufficient Technocracy in a new Ivory Tower on the Horizon. Their goal is a far older one: to make humans masters of their own world. Yet the society they started has become corrupt. Unable to control the Masters who have taken their place, they will assist the revolution to destroy the Technocracy's Loyalist overlords.

After extensive discussions in briefing rooms and rogue Technocrat bunkers, two solutions emerge. The first is to find a way to grant immunity to the hazardous effects of Avatar shards and the Avatar Storm. The second is to "open the floodgates," using Dimensional Science to tear open rifts in the Gauntlet at key locations. If Avatar shards can now silence (or slaughter) mages, they might theoretically purge (or destroy) all magic in the areas where they are channeled. Doing so would be catastrophic in those key areas, but it would theoretically keep the shards from continuing to wear down the Dimensional Barrier.

If those "key locations" are Horizon Constructs, the Loyalists' masters would lose their Technocratic advantage. The network of Horizon Constructs would be disrupted even further, giving front-line agents greater autonomy. (Tearing open a rift thus is a process that can be attempted with Spirit 5, but it should require at least 20 successes and a communal roll to pull off… as well as technological devices crafted by Void Engineers.)

Unfortunately, Unionist agents do not realize that the Loyalists are also pursuing a similar solution: opening gateways on Earth to direct the shards at Unionist strongholds. After all, if they're sequestered in their Horizon Chantries at the time these shock waves hit, they will be immune to the effects of widespread Avatar Storms in the physical world. Earth could be cleansed of magic, but the Horizon would (theoretically) remain safe.

Tradition mages might question whether this act would affect sources of Quintessence as well — but Technocrats are not Tradition mages. Loyalist managers have begun to receive transmissions from Void Engineer colonies, and they are evaluating whether they can harvest these colonies as sources of energy. It's a flawed plan, but if the final Time Table is resolving, both sides of this conflict will consider such quick solutions.

Conflicting Frequencies: Transmissions from the Rogue Council (see **Manifesto**) might also resume at this point (if the story has incorporated that timeline as well). Which side the Sphinx might support is purely the purview of the Storyteller. Perhaps the mages behind the Rogue Council are clearly enemies of the Loyalists, so they would have a common cause with the *Unionists* working to free humanity. (This might even by a plot by Unionist Masters to expose Technocratic corruption!) They'll have a tough time convincing Tradition mages to work with Technocrat revolutionaries, however.

Eventually, the Sphinx reveals that several groups are working on variants of the same project: flooding selected locations on Earth with Avatar shards. Both Loyalists and Unionists eventually pursue this plan. Both sides of the revolution would then look like "bad guys," each racing for the same final solution to Armageddon. Tradition mages who've made it this far into the timeline might be tasked with stopping the "floodgates" from opening.

The Voice of Reason

The timeline could easily end with mankind destroying a supernatural horror, realizing the existence of magic and joining the hunt for Reality Deviants. Acting on fears of helplessness in the face of magic, mankind would rise up… aided by secret Technocratic Masters. Yet this surge still wouldn't resolve the conflicts within the Technocracy itself. If the schism has played a role in the story up to this point, Chapter VI must resolve that conflict.

At the end of Chapter V, Control broadcasts a warning about the critical mass of Avatar shards building around the world. Unless its energy is channeled, the wave of extradimensional forces will build until it washes over the Earth, obliterating the Dimensional Barrier. Whether this event will heal the world or destroy it is a matter of great debate. As a result, Unionists and Loyalists race for solutions to this problem… each acting for their own advantage.

Chapter VI: Endgame

On the final day of this timeline, one final wave of reinforcements breaks through the Horizon: the first real tempest of Avatar shards in the physical world. In the location where this final invasion takes place, the result is an Avatar Storm so violent that it purges its Awakened (or Enlightened) victims of their Arete. (In game terms, it first inflicts aggravated damage as though the victim had passed through the Gauntlet, then it triggers a Paradox Backlash, and *then* it erases the victim's Arete.) It won't remove all magic from the world, but it will cripple its victims sufficiently to end this conflict.

Some analysts would argue (if they survived) that the results are what humanity ultimately wants, if only on a subconscious level: a world purged of magic. It is perhaps inevitable that some radical group would *willingly* channel these shards into this world. Directed at selected targets, Avatar shards could then serve as the ultimate weapon of Armageddon. If no one channels this energy, the day will come when these shards will wear down the Gauntlet so far that they break through the barriers of reality on their own. Fear of exotic paranormal events empowers this final catastrophe.

With the Technocracy rapidly fragmenting, Loyalists and Unionists compete to be the first to invoke this "final solution"… before someone else beats them to the punch. If one faction can find a way to survive this storm, or direct it against its enemies first, it could very well act as "doomsday weapon" in the War for Reality. The world is now a chessboard with two opponents — the Unionists and Loyalists — and the first one to achieve checkmate can finally "control" reality unopposed.

Once this "perfect storm" occurs, it shouldn't merely be an abstract philosophical concept or pure game mechanic. It has to look like *something*, if only to Sleeper technology that can measure it. It could be a wave of cosmic radiation flooding through the weakened Dimensional Barrier; Anakim might walk among the Masses in the area, silencing all who practice magic; its effects could be borne on a plague, infecting victims for reasons mundane scientists cannot deduce. Whatever the means of transmission is, it is even possible that Paradox (or optionally, Delirium) might cover it up as a mundane occurrence instead of a supernatural one. Regardless of its appearance, if no single faction can channel this tempest, then its final manifestation is an Avatar Storm sweeping across the Earth, flaying Awakened (and Enlightened) souls with equal impunity.

The most important move in this endgame is the location of the first gateway that floods the Avatar shards into the realm of flesh. Chapter VI is a race against time. Four major outcomes are possible:

— If the last wave of Avatar shards floods a Horizon Construct, it could then spread to others, compromising the entire network: The Unionists win.

— If the storm is channeled through a gate on Earth and the Horizon remains untouched, only Loyalists on Horizon survive with technomancy: Loyalists win.

— As an alternative, the Unionists might find a way to protect themselves from this storm, as the Loyalists cut off all their sources of Quintessence. Directed by Control, the survivors could actually build a new Order of Reason.

— The shards break through the Gauntlet before anyone can act, and the world of flesh is overwhelmed by the spirit world. As in the dawn of time, the two become one. Everybody loses.

Launching the Revolution: At the start of Chapter VI, a scientist (or supervisor) who has found a way to exploit the Avatar Storm contacts your characters. He gives them the knowledge they need to open the gates, close the gates or shield Enlightened agents from the Avatar Storm. With this head start, the characters must choose what to do with this deadly knowledge — the future is in their hands. If they've been given orders and can pull off their objective before their enemies do, they will tip the balance in this endgame. For added drama, they might be informed (by Control, the Rogue Council, Secret Agent John Courage or whomever else you prefer) that the other side is also racing to open the floodgates and will be ready to unleash its Final Solution at a specific time. If the heroes do not act quickly, their enemies will.

Loyalty Triumphs: If the Loyalists "win," all alternatives to their vision for reality are weakened on Earth. The dominant variant of "magic" left is technomancy: coincidental applications of technological magic, as developed on the Horizon. Any act of magic that appears openly supernatural summons further Avatar shards. Since the Loyalists control the only functional variant of "magic" on Earth, they reassert their control as the secret masters of the world. This outcome might lead to a denouement in which we see what the world is like in a few years… in a dystopia under one absolute Technocracy.

Humanity United: If the Unionists open their gates first, the Horizon Constructs are purged. A chain reaction weakens the network as the front-line agents free themselves from the oversight of their Masters. Loyalist Technocrats, unable to cope with the fact that an overwhelming supernatural act is occurring, might go insane, into Quiet or simply expire in a final act of Paradox Backlash. Much of the energy of this final storm will be dissipated, but unfortunately, some of it will still leak into the physical world, weakening outright forces of magic as well. The storm then cuts off sources of Quintessence in the world, extinguishing the energy needed to sustain a network of Horizon Constructs. Magic weakens, but the Unionists survive.

Survival: In theory, if a Technocrat can devise a defense against Avatar shards — perhaps by watching and learning from the Anakim, adapting Dimensional Science or even following a ritual detailed by Control — he can survive this final wave of the Avatar Storm. The answer doesn't need to be complex. (It might be only a Spirit 5, Prime 5 procedure requiring many successes, but that's a rare combination of Spheres for a Technocrat!) The harder part is choosing the technology to represent this effect. A bomb shelter is an obvious defense against a storm, but more fanciful invasions involving radiation waves or Anakim ghosts require more elaborate solutions.

Everybody Dies: If no one "wins," and neither side opens a gate to channel this worldwide energy, the Dimensional Barrier eventually falls. The resulting storm actually flays all souls, and every mage and Technocrat on Earth is purged as the spirit world floods into the physical world. The only Enlightened survivors are then the colonies and a handful of mages and Technocrats on Seekings. Perhaps the protagonists' amalgam escapes on a Void Engineer starship toward a resolution in another realm. The characters might appear before representatives of Control, escape to a Technocracy colony or attempt a final Seeking on the Far Horizon… one that leads to Ascension or utter annihilation.

Denouement

The Earth might be reclaimed by the defenders of old ideals; it might be transformed in a dystopia ruled by the Loyalists; it might be purged of all magic, becoming a realm where even technomancy ceases to function. (See Chapter Six of this book for rules on diminishing magic.) You must decide which outcome best suits your chronicle… and which side the protagonists are on when the revolution ends.

Unfolding this story, chapter by chapter, is like broadcasting the final season of a television program that's been running for years. Humanity will be watching, of course, even if the Masses don't understand the real significance of what is occurring. In a final surrender to technology, the most hopeless citizens will observe these historical events with passive acceptance. Experts enlisted by mass media will rationalize what they cannot understand. The revolution will be televised — but even during Armageddon, only the Enlightened will see the truth behind apocalyptic events. This is the Technocracy, signing off.

Chapter Four: The Earth Will Shake

…One sees that all that the astronomers have to do is to discover that stars have sex, and they'll have us sneaking into bookstores, for salacious "pronouncements" and "determinations" upon the latest celestial scandals.
—Charles Fort, *Lo!*

Most notions regarding Ascension and Armageddon are intrinsically anthropocentric, in that the universe is seen to hinge upon the decisions made by humans that could lead to salvation or damnation. As mages develop their abilities, they have access to perceptual modes that reveal that the universe is much larger and more complex than the sum of its material contents; these same abilities can extend the consequences of their actions well beyond their immediate physical environment. As a result, mages can become even more closely dependent on the notion that the fate of the world is decided by their acts. But the currently dominant worldview cultivated by Technocratic science tends to marginalize the place of humans as that of one species among many occupying a fraction of the surface of a medium-sized hunk of rock circling one of countless fireballs whirling through a void too vast to comprehend.

Mages are mortal, they are human — they must eat, crap, sleep, protect themselves from the elements and procreate their kind through biological processes. Like other members of the animal kingdom, they depend upon the energy transactions that collectively make up vast living organism known as Earth. Should these raw physical facts of existence suddenly change, can all the magic in the world save these hairless ground-apes from extinction?

Introduction: Watch the Skies

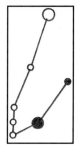

"I always find that the prospect of death contracts the mind wonderfully."
—Douglas Adams *The Restaurant at the End of the Universe*

It has been estimated that as much as 100 tons of interplanetary material falls to Earth every day. During the last three decades, over a hundred air bursts — most measured in megatons — were detected throughout Earth's upper atmosphere. Scientists who have calculated the entire heat content of the Earth over the course of its existence believe that the planet might have frozen over by now were it not for the additional warmth that the occasional collision with asteroids and comets generates.

In short, space debris collides with our world all the time. Most of it burns up or blasts apart from air friction. Objects large enough to reach the surface intact become a cause for what surface dweller Professor Richard Binzel of MIT defines as "concern." By his reckoning and others, a meteorite large enough to ruin a prime piece of real estate comes down approximately once every thousand years. Every hundred thousand years or so, something large enough to change a lot of people's religion hits. And around every couple hundred million years, we catch something big enough to knock the top dozen rungs off the planet's evolutionary ladder.

The following story concerns just such an event. The characters learn that a large meteoroid is on a collision course with Earth. Is there time to avert it, and what methods must be deployed to do so? And what can be done should these methods fail?

Theme and Mood

The asteroid aimed at Earth is a juggernaut several kilometers wide and thousands of tons in mass, practically a small planet, with a momentum that few forces at humanity's command can affect. A trajectory change of only a few degrees is all that is necessary to avert it at first, but the sluggishness of both Sleeper and Awakened authorities to acknowledge and respond to the threat makes this unlikely. As the moment of impact draws near, more and more methods of preventing it fail. It becomes clear that the home of humanity will unavoidably experience what some scientists call an "extinction-level event." The problem becomes less a matter of whether disaster can be avoided, and more of whether a breeding population of humans (and other terrestrial species) can be protected and provided with a place in which to survive. The theme is inevitability; the mood is mounting desperation.

The Celestial Ball

Concurrent with the story in the physical world runs a parallel plot line involving the reverberations of the impending impact in the Umbra. Storytellers might wish to downplay this spiritual aspect of the very physical problem — at least in the early chapters. Although they are presented as interstitial scenes bridging the physical chapters, you can run "The Celestial Ball" all at once as prelude, interlude or denouement, depending on how you choose to pace the story — fast-paced action in a race against time or a drawn-out process of mounting intellectual discovery.

The spiritual shock wave of the collision could come all at once on a single Umbral voyage foreshadowing the event long in advance, or it could unfold in brief glimpses through dreams and visions that increase in frequency and intensity as the event becomes imminent. Conversely, the Storyteller might find that the Umbral subplot gradually eclipses the deteriorating situation in the material world as the characters focus their efforts on interacting with the planetary intelligences rather than dealing with the mounting panic and natural disasters on the material plane (acting globally rather than locally, so to speak.) In either case, the Umbral subplot should not be ignored entirely, as it is ultimately the Umbra that will provide the safest haven against the coming Armageddon.

About Asteroids
(With a Digression upon Their Occult Significance)

Between the orbits of Mars and Jupiter whirls the Asteroid Belt, a broad ring of tumbling stones ranging from several kilometers in diameter to mere dust, commonly regarded as the scrap heap of planetary creation. In addition to the main belt, many thinner, less populous rings intertwine through the inner solar system, some following orbits that intersect Earth's yearly path. On average, asteroids move at about 45,000 miles per hour. A retinue of smaller rocks invariably accompanies large asteroids, and Storytellers should remember that, even if the characters successfully avert a major collision, their chosen method might not prevent any number of smaller impacts.

Those asteroids that have been identified and analyzed are grouped into classes based on their composition and orbital distance. Farthest away, orbiting beyond the main belt, are the P- and D-type asteroids, of which little is as yet known. (The body that threatens Earth is, in fact, one of these types — huge, but too distant to have been previously detected, and of undetermined composition.) C-type asteroids make up most of the outer belt, dark rocks rich with carbonaceous chondrites, complex organic compounds. The center of the belt is dominated by S-types, composed of stone and silicates. Those closest to Earth, the M-types on the inner edge of the belt, are twice as dense as any earthly matter and highly reflective thanks to their nickel-iron composition, believed to be the remnants of primordial planetary cores.

Some occult lore holds that the Asteroid Belt was once a planet until its natives developed a destructive technology that blasted their world apart. Alan Moore of Northhampton, England, proposes that the belt may be identified with the lost or hidden Sephira, *Daath* or "Knowledge," on the Kabbalistic Tree of Life. Some Hermetic and Batini Kabbalists find this "Northhampton Interpretation" intellectually and esthetically satisfying for a few reasons. Each of the Sephiroth are identified with a planet (including the sun and moon, as Ptolemaic cosmology defines these as planets) except for the uppermost three, the Supernal Triad of Understanding, Wisdom and the Crown. (In modern times, some have identified these respectively with Uranus, Neptune and Pluto, which were not visible from Earth at the time the Tree of Life was formulated.) *Daath* is situated in the Abyss of Unreason that separates the Triad from the rest of the Tree, just as the Asteroid Belt marks the division between the Near Umbra and the Deep Umbra. Although the Abyss is above Jupiter (*Chesed*, "Mercy") and Mars (*Geburah*, "Strength") on the Tree, *Daath* lies along the Middle Pillar with the other two on either side. While *Daath* is generally designated as the 11th Sephira, the Northhampton Interpretation suggests that the Arabic numeral "11" is a misreading of the two upright strokes that form part of the Greek letter pi, used for the mathematical constant denoting the ratio of a circle's circumference to its diameter. Pi is an irrational number close to 3.14, and *Daath* lies directly between the third and fourth Sephiroth.

And how do these ideas relate to the present story? When calculating orbits and the dynamics of spherical bodies, the constant pi is frequently used. This irrational number is necessary to the rational process of calculation, just as Knowledge is necessary to cross the Abyss and approach the Supernal. The characters must *know* the specifics of the current situation, its origin and potential result (and what they can do about it) in order to bridge the gap between survival and extinction.

(Storytellers who wish to incorporate this idiosyncratic kabbalistic lore into the story are encouraged to check out Alan Moore's *Promethea* comics. The *Daath*-asteroid connection is described in issue #20. The series as a whole constitutes a good primer on many occult topics. Any inaccuracies in the preceding text, however, are entirely the fault of the present author, as his copy of #20 mysteriously vanished shortly after he read it. Appropriate for the "Lost Sephira," ain't it?)

Variations on the Theme

Comets are the most well-traveled and visually spectacular planetesimals, careering in broad elliptical orbits with their tails stretching away from the sun as they swing through the inner solar system. Comets tend to be much larger than most asteroids, and they travel over twice as fast as they near the sun. Not much is specifically known about them. A 1986 flyby mission showed the core of Halley's comet to be pitted and faulted with numerous crevices and pockets filled with water and gases. As a comet's orbit brings it near the sun, these materials evaporate and blow off dust to form the characteristic tail, which can stretch up to 60 million miles in length — nearly two-thirds of the distance from the Earth to the sun. These eruptions of dust and steam can be forceful enough to actually change the comet's trajectory, making tracking and avoiding them exceedingly difficult. Presently, only two types of comet are distinguished. Short-period comets remain with the planetary orbits of the solar system, passing adjacent to Earth every few years; long-period comets fly well beyond the orbit of Pluto, spending most of their existence in a deep space zone called the Oort Cloud, falling inward to visit the inner solar system once every few decades or centuries.

Occult lore relates that the appearance of a comet inevitably heralds a world-changing event. More modern speculation suggests that comets act as "chemical messengers" that convey matter between planets and possibly even star systems. Some variations of the Panspermia hypothesis credit a comet for "seeding" the nascent Earth with the organic molecules that made life here possible. Both of these ideas relate to modern Traditional belief, in that long-period comets pass from the Near Umbra to the Deep Umbra and back again at regular intervals and might thus be used by spirits from the farthest reaches as transport into the inner solar system. (Likewise, mages or nomadic Near Umbral entities might theoretically use a comet to travel into the Deep Umbra. Those who have attempted to do this, however, have yet to return to tell their tale.) Though some would attribute human behavior when a comet appears to mere superstition and fear of the unknown, Umbra-savvy mages know that the arrival of beings from beyond in the Near Umbra can have much the same effects on the collective psychology of humanity.

Besides the known planetesimals, other bodies could emerge from space to threaten life on Earth. The orbits of asteroids can be calculated with some fair degree of precision, and comets, while moving erratically, can be seen from a great distance. Objects that have not been scientifically observed and studied, however, are less predictable. Some meteors are believed to be planetary ejecta, debris blasted off by earlier impacts on other worlds. Certain geological samples are thought to have originated on Mars, for example.

Looking beyond our own solar neighborhood, even more incomprehensibly vast menaces loom, such as the black hole scheduled to pass through our part of the galaxy over the next 700,000 years. (It might be more correct to say, as David Ossman once pointed out, that our part of the galaxy will pass through it.) Debris from a primordial nova could conceivably strike Earth after a 1,000-year plummet through interstellar space. Such condensed star-stuff might be hundreds of times denser than any terrestrial matter and travel much faster than anything in the solar system. It would be extremely difficult to determine the existence of such an object, much less predict its trajectory, until it was too late.

There is also the Andromeda galactic collision to consider, though our nearest next-door neighbor galaxy is not calculated to intersect with the Milky Way for another four billion years. While stars are too small and far apart to ever actually come into direct contact when galaxies collide, their gravitational interplay can lock them into mutual orbits, wrenching stars from their parent galaxy to be captured by another or flung into the intergalactic void. Such events are, of course, well beyond the time scale of a present-day **Mage** chronicle, but Storytellers might still find such lore applicable.

Furthermore, much of the universe's total estimated mass is now thought to consist of exotic new theoretical substances like dark matter and antimatter, which might have profoundly different properties than regular matter, moving through space in nonsensical ways or exhibiting strange and surreal effects in response to heat, light, impact, et cetera. While much of the matter in the cosmos is bound up in stars and planetoids, even more remains as gigantic clouds drifting across the galaxies, some invisible with dark dust, others colorfully lit by nearby stars. Depending on the cloud's density, passage by the Earth through such a cloud could be imperceptible or cataclysmic. A rain of inert dust could enshroud the world in cosmic winter, or an excess of raw hydrogen — very common in interstellar nebulae — could combine with Earth's oxygen to ignite the entire atmosphere in a worldwide flash.

Chapter I: Considerations

…from L considerare, *to examine carefully, prob orig a term in augury and therefore deriving from* sidus *(o/s* sider-*), mostly in pl* sidera, *the stars…*
—Eric Partridge, *Origins: A Short Etymological Dictionary of Modern English*

In this first chapter, the characters become aware of the meteoric menace through an unlikely pair of amateur astronomers, Abner and Whitney Tripplethorpe (described on pp. 125-126), who have observed the asteroid, calculated its path and are now attempting to alert the authorities both political and scientific to its presence. If one of the characters is into astronomy, she might learn of the Tripplethorpes through any number of amateur publications, message boards or chatrooms through which they have tried to make their findings public. Otherwise, the characters could bump into them by chance meeting as the pair travels around seeking any important personage who will hear them out. (It is assumed that most of the action takes place in or near a major population center within the continental United States. Washington DC, MIT, NASA offices at Langley, Virginia, Houston, Texas or Pasadena, California, Mount Palomar Observatory near San Diego or any other observatory will be on the Tripplethorpes' itinerary. Their quest for acknowledgement might take them farther afield, however, as any scientist or politician they contact will likely dismiss them as doom-saying crackpots.)

The Tripplethorpes have fallen on hard times in their quest and chosen to approach the characters for help. While Abner's life savings and Whitney's child-support/allowance from her parents enables them to travel, they are not rich, and their money could run out at any time. Alternatively, the mages might be attracted to the pair by either the aura of fate that surrounds them or the psychic waves of growing desperation they emit. Or the characters might simply be impressed by the determination and sincerity exhibited by these two "salt of the earth" Middle Americans. While not new to the big city, they will seem out of place. Abner and Whitney are normal — if slightly atypical — folks, with something very, *very* important to say to the world.

If the characters choose to help the Tripplethorpes, it will soon become clear that, while most of the world wants nothing to do with them, *someone* is definitely taking an interest — and their intentions are not good. They will be assaulted. And, if the characters have spent any substantial amount of time with them, they too might be attacked, together with the Tripplethorpes or separately. If the characters choose not to help them, they might be attacked anyway (just to draw the characters into the story). Troupes who like to start out their stories with a good old-fashioned fight scene could meet the Tripplethorpes by rescuing them from such an assault. The attackers are Sleepers, but mages catch a whiff of tainted magic upon them. Investigation yields the fact that the attackers are members of a sort of doomsday cult, the First Church of the Unidentified Flying Object, headed by one Leland Chin, a Marauder.

The fact that the Tripplethorpes are traveling can be exploited for both dramatic and thematic effect. Airplanes and railroad trains are especially intense settings for combat, being enclosed and isolated from the world at large. Jumping or being flung from a moving train is dangerous; exiting a plane in flight even more so. Trains reinforce the idea of a juggernaut speeding along a predetermined course, while planes echo the motif of a large object streaking across the sky. And what if other passengers overhear the subject of the Tripplethorpe's conversation? Abner and Whitney are not so foolish as to spark panic among the general public, but will the characters show as much discretion?

Abner and Whitney Tripplethorpe of Ten Sleep, Wyoming

Background: Abner Tripplethorpe learned to navigate by the stars while he was a young seaman during the War in the Pacific, and he has taken comfort in stargazing ever since. He keeps to himself out in his small Wyoming home, where there is a minimum of light pollution at night. His great-granddaughter Whitney, 12, was sent to live with him two years ago by her parents in Los Angeles, who sent her off to Middle America to get her away from the big-city drug scene.

Some Technical Jargon

Storytellers who wish to focus upon the hard scientific aspects of this story will probably want to use some actual astronomical nomenclature. Here are a few terms that apply, along with suggestions for naming the story's impactor (a general term for something that hits something else).

The terms planetoid and planetesimal signify bodies of varying sizes orbiting the sun. Asteroids are also called meteoroids. If one enters a planet's atmosphere, air friction causes it to heat up and give off light, whereupon it is called a meteor, and if it strikes the planet's surface before burning up, it is known as a meteorite. An asteroid that passes close to the Earth is called a Near-Earth Asteroid, or NEA. (Other bodies, such as comets, can also approach closely, so the more general term Near Earth Object, NEO, is also used.) If it is going to pass close enough to be considered a collision risk by NASA's Jet Propulsion Laboratories, their Near-Earth Asteroid Tracking program gives it one of three designations according to its angle of approach. If it is coming from outside Earth's orbit, heading inward toward the sun, it is designated Amor. One that approaches along the line of Earth's orbit, at right angles to the sun, is called Apollo, while that which comes from within Earth's orbit heading away from the sun is labeled Aten. Anything with a diameter of 200 meters or larger is labeled a PHA, or Potentially Hazardous Asteroid.

NEAs, like other celestial bodies, often receive names from mythology — which means their names have strong magical connotations as well — and/or a numerical designation based on the date of discovery or of its closest approach. The astronomers who identify the NEA heading toward Earth in this story will call it 2004 Typhon. ("2004" can be changed to whatever year the story is taking place.) If the characters are able to ensure that the Tripplethorpes get credit for its discovery, it might be named after one or both of them (in a vulgar display of insensitivity on the part of the scientific community). If Abner and Whitney are actually present to participate in the naming, however, both will insist that their own private name for it be considered: "Agnes," after Abner's daughter, Whitney's grandmother, a foul-tempered and abusive old battleaxe whom nobody in the family liked.

Image: Abner is over 70, but he will not disclose his exact age since he lied about it to join the Navy at the start of 1942. He is barrel-chested, rugged and grizzled, with a full gray beard and thinning hair pulled back in a small ponytail. Though hampered by arthritis, he is quite strong for his age. Whitney is rosy-cheeked with curly blond hair, but she has the sharp savvy smile of a street urchin. Both wear flannel and dungarees unless they have donned their new conservative suits for an appointment. (Whitney actually favors the provocative pre-teen fashions and makeup of her native LA, but she seldom dresses this way since Abner says it makes her look like a "goddamn Bangkok hooker.")

Roleplaying Hints: Whitney and Abner have grown close, especially as her great-grandfather has instilled in her a love of astronomy. They might look like a couple of yokels, but they are intelligent, tough-minded and very devoted to each other. Abner seldom speaks unless it is necessary, while Whitney is gregarious. Both are straightforward and well mannered, but they can swear and fight like longshoremen if provoked.

Abner Tripplethorpe

Nature: Pedagogue
Demeanor: Curmudgeon
Attributes: Strength 4, Dexterity 2, Stamina 3, Charisma 2, Manipulation 3, Appearance 2, Perception 2, Intelligence 3, Wits 4
Abilities: Brawl 3, Craft (Carpentry) 3, Cosmology 1, Dodge 1, Drive 3, Firearms 3, Intimidation 2, Law 1, Medicine 2, Melee 2, Science (Astronomy) 4, Streetwise 1, Survival 4
Backgrounds: Allies 1 (son of a navy buddy, now Junior Science Correspondent at a major news network)
Willpower: 7

Whitney Tripplethorpe

Nature: Loner
Demeanor: Child
Attributes: Strength 2, Dexterity 4, Stamina 2, Charisma 3, Manipulation 3, Appearance 4, Perception 2, Intelligence 3, Wits 3
Abilities: Alertness 3, Brawl 1, Computer 2, Etiquette 1, Dodge 4, Science (Astronomy) 3, Stealth 2, Streetwise 3, Subterfuge 2
Backgrounds: Contacts 2 (amateur astronomers' webring)
Willpower: 4

The First Church of the Unidentified Flying Object, Reformed

This "saucer cult" originally formed in southern California sometime during the 1950s around a married couple who claimed to have been contacted by tall red-haired humanoids from the "Olympia Galaxy." Typical of contactees from this era, they issued dire warnings against the Cold War and the arms race through sloppily printed pamphlets that attracted lonely and disaffected souls eager to believe in a better world "somewhere out there." Over the next few decades, this group remained intact, refining its outlandish dogma while fading into obscurity.

When the couple died in 1990, Leland Chin took over the cult, building it into a well-organized and cohesive underground society, while maintaining the front of a harmless crackpot "church." The old pamphlets have evolved into poorly produced pirate radio and television broadcasts and virus-riddled email spam, and many of the disaffected recruits have been trained as capable and potentially dangerous undercover operatives. Though the "congregation" is small, it has branches in many major cities, it includes a few moderately wealthy and influential individuals, and it has infiltrated rival cults, UFO affinity groups, some universities and even a few major intelligence agencies.

Under Chin's almost messianic style of leadership, the church has developed a doctrine of what might be called "extraterrestrial rapture," wherein the most devoted members can expect to be rescued from the failing Earth and the corrupt human race, and taken to Olympia. There, they will live in a perfect society engaged in enlightened artistic and scientific pursuits. Until that time, they go about the Church's business with the aid of "Olympian tech" — technomantic devices — such as ray guns and x-ray goggles.

Leland Chin

Background: In 1978, business school dropout and recently Awakened Orphan Leland Chin, a derelict unable to cope with his new abilities and perceptions, was taken in by the original contactees. Convinced that Leland was some sort of emissary from Olympia, the couple groomed him for leadership of their group. Initiating Chin into the "Olympian Mysteries," they gave him an ideological framework for his magic but inadvertently divorced his mind from reality, making him as mad as any other Marauder.

Image: Forty-five, well-groomed and of mixed Asian descent, Chin usually wears a stylishly tailored business suit over his church "uniform," a silver spandex leotard with a flying saucer insignia on the breast.

Roleplaying Hints: You know that the Earth will be destroyed soon, but you plan to be gone by then. You believe that 2004 Typhon is actually the Olympian mother ship coming to take you home. You learned of the Tripplethorpes — and of Typhon — through their efforts to alert the world, and you understand that if they succeed, your "rapture" will be aborted by attempts to deflect the asteroid. Therefore, the Tripplethorpes must be silenced immediately. (If the characters figure out how your mind works, however, they can deceive and manipulate you into sharing your allies and contacts with them, which would make their own attempts to alert the authorities and other important factions — such as the Independent Spacers — easier.)

Faction: Marauder
Essence: Questing
Nature: Perfectionist
Demeanor: Autocrat
Attributes: Strength 2, Dexterity 3, Stamina 3, Charisma 4, Manipulation 5, Appearance 4, Perception 3, Intelligence 2, Wits 2
Abilities: Awareness 3, Computer 2, Cosmology 3, Dodge 3, Etiquette 3, Firearms 2, Intimidation 3, Investigation 2, Leadership 4, Occult 3, Subterfuge 4, Technology 2
Backgrounds: Allies 2, Contacts 2, Influence 1, Resources 3
Arete: 5

Spheres: Forces 3, Mind 4
Willpower: 7
Quintessence: 5
Paradox: 3
Resonance: (Dynamic) Absurd 1, (Static) Cold 4
Quiet: 2

Chin lives in a world of bubble-gum space opera wherein he is a messianic alien emissary in human form, collecting Earth's few worthy souls for translation to his plane before they destroy themselves. He sees other mages and supernatural beings as rival aliens and considering hostile Sleepers their mind-controlled dupes. His church is pure Golden Age sci-fi kitsch, with banks of instrumentation set in sweeping lines of polished chrome. Members wear silver spandex leotards with a flying saucer emblem on the breast, even under regular clothes in the outside world. Chin's most capable — and deeply deluded — operatives might be equipped with ray guns and two-man hover disk Devices built from stolen Technocratic (read "Olympian") plans.

Meanwhile, in the Umbra...

What follows is a general description of the spirit world from around the time that the Tripplethorpes first make their discovery through their first contact with the mage characters. The Storyteller might use these scenes and images either as foreshadowing before actually running this story or to alert mages who are already engaged in some Umbral journey that something big is afoot in the material world. If the characters do not enter the Umbra until after meeting the Tripplethorpes, they might pass through these scenes as they proceed toward the later Umbral chapters.

While the inhabitants of the physical remain unaware of the threat, the spirit world darkens with foreboding. Vistas appear that show events to come (but not their ultimate cause): large scale disasters, earthquakes, tidal waves, volcanic eruptions, cities blasted into ruins, black clouds that fill the sky and blot out the sun. In the Low Umbra, mass movements and migrations are underway as the wraith populace makes room for a great influx of the newly dead. In the Spirit Wilds, the animal and vegetable kingdoms seem to be going insane, as herds stampede for no discernable reason and predators either launch into berserk killing sprees or flee in blind terror with their tails between their legs. Ancient trees uproot themselves to join in the panic, while smaller plants shrivel and shrink back into the ground, as if trying to hide from the sun. Spirits of the inorganic — mountains, clouds, etc. — become uncharacteristically active or dismissive, and some even show overt hostility to visitors, confronting humans with reminders of their ecological crimes and hinting that mankind's "dominion" over nature will soon come to an abrupt end. (Organic life is faced with extinction, while the inorganic earth will enter into a period of high-energy activity unseen since the planet's youth.) Mages who are normally on friendly terms with such spirits can engage them in conversation and learn that some major change is coming, though no spirit knows its exact nature or cause.

Because the Tripplethorpes are the only people initially aware of the threat, their identities appear in the Astral Reaches, but only obliquely. Their faces and/or figures might be seen in the constellations of the astral sky or carved on the underside of huge rocks that swoop down through the Epiphamic clouds and swing across the Vulgate, inciting panic among the spirits below. (More on these rocks in Chapter II…)

The name "Tripplethorpe" suggests a few arcane visual puns that could manifest in Idea Space: "thorp" is from Old English, related to "troop" and "tavern," with a complex of meanings involving groups of people (or herds of animals), enclosed spaces and buildings, beams used in buildings, villages or small communities, fields, farms and sections of land. Visions of the Three Umbrae (three "lands" or "plains") coming together in violent clashes might haunt the characters' dreams. Umbral travelers might see familiar edifices in the Vulgate appearing in triplicate and find the architecture reorganized around a roof consisting of three beams in a triangular formation. (This also recalls the triangulation method of determining the spatial positions of distant objects like meteors.) Mages who have visited the Tavern of the Four Winds (from **The Infinite Tapestry**) might find its co-locations within the Vulgate reduced to three personally significant places. If the Storyteller is prepared to expand the Umbral scope of her chronicle, her characters might find that the Tavern now connects to all three levels of Astral Space (Vulgate, High Umbral Courts and Epiphamies) or even to the other two Umbrae. (This would, of course, lead characters far from the thread of this story, but it might be appropriate for the Storyteller who plans a long slow buildup to this admittedly abrupt Apocalypse.)

Chapter II: Confirmations

… from L confirmatus, *pp of* confirmare *(int* con- *+* firmare, *to strengthen, from* firmus, *firm, solid…)*

—Partridge, op. cit.

Chapter II concerns the characters' efforts to confirm the existence of the approaching asteroid and locate its orbit with enough precision to intercept and avert or destroy it. A powerful computer can refine the Tripplethorpes' calculations to a sufficient degree of exactitude, but their observations ought to be corroborated by other, more experienced astronomers in order for the world to take note.

Abner and/or Whitney could conceivably die in Chapter I if the mages fail to save them, murdered by Chin's fanatics. If so, the Storyteller must make sure that the Tripplethorpes have a chance to tell the characters of their quest and to pass along the information they have accumulated. This information takes the form of meticulously recorded astronomical observations of the meteoroid headed for Earth. Whitney' computerized records date back almost two years, and she carries a number of disk copies, with back-up files on her hard drive back home in Wyoming and stashed in various semi-secure locations on the Internet (thus accessible through the Digital Web). Abner's observations go back over four decades but are handwritten in a naval logbook he keeps strapped to his torso. Entries from the last 25 years are difficult to read and impossible to scan digitally, as his advancing arthritis makes his writing increasingly illegible. This information can be crucial in later chapters.

Ideally, the Tripplethorpes should remain a part of the story, especially if the characters have no close ties with the Sleeper community, such as family or friends. The Awakened might forget that they too were once Asleep. Though they can work wonders and travel to other worlds, their own species and the very world that sustains them faces extinction. The mages must have some constant reminder that it is the very survival of the human race at stake here, and that, if they fail, billions of ordinary people — as thematically represented by Abner and Whitney — will die.

Ancient History

No amount of data is too great in this endeavor, and even the copious data compiled by the Tripplethorpes can be supplemented for greater accuracy. Typhon's current orbit is an astronomical anomaly, initiated thousands of years ago by forces yet unknown. Storytellers who wish to draw out this chapter might want to consider the following.

While astrology is often depicted as a muddled superstition left over from an antiquity when slack-jawed troglodytes gaped in dull awe at the night sky, examination of ancient history reveals that, starting around the third millennium BC, charting the movements of the lights in the heavens in order to determine future events becomes a matter of intense concern for all levels of society, not only in Chaldea, but in India, China and South America as well. The comparatively sudden emergence in such diverse regions of such a specific idea, so assiduously subscribed to and practiced by so many, has prompted some to speculate that Earth had a particularly momentous encounter with an NEO at this time.

By collating a vast amount of excerpts from history and mythology around the world in his book *Worlds in Collision*, Immanuel Velikovsky determined that the event that spawned so many legends of floods, wars in Heaven, shadowy clouds of death and seismic upheavals that ended previous civilizations was the near passage of a comet (which then became the planet Venus). Velikovsky was not a professional astronomer, and his theory strained the credibility of many, involving as it did such cataclysmic side effects as significant alterations in the rotation and orbit of the Earth that many feel would have wiped out humanity along with much of Earth's surface life at the very least.

Mages seeking to learn more about the current threat, however, would do well to follow up on Velikovsky's leads. At the very least, predicting the path of an NEO becomes much simpler and more accurate the more data one has to work with, and many ancient sources of astrological data were quite exacting and stretched back in time for centuries. The exhaustive measurements and observations that modern computers require to do their jobs might indeed be found inscribed upon lacquered bamboo strips in the undiscovered tomb of the legendary Chinese Emperor Yao, on cuneiform tablets preserved in the cavern-cities of Cappadocia, on papyrus scrolls hidden in the library reached through a secret door in the right paw of the Sphinx or carved in un-deciphered glyphs upon the walls of sunken cities on the Pacific floor.

Doctor Comet

If the Storyteller wants to use the flavor of this lore but does not intend to pursue an ever-increasing number of globetrotting adventurous subplots, all relevant information can be condensed in the character of Bernhardt Mueller, known to the Sons of Ether as Doctor Comet. Anyone familiar with recent Etherite history might remember Mueller as something of a doomsday prophet who went missing after leaving a New Year's Eve party at the dawn of the year 2000. Insiders speculate that the aging Mueller was so intent upon seeing his doomsday come to pass that he projected himself forward in time to the end of the world. Etherite wags jocularly report "Doctor Comet sightings" as proof of a coming Apocalypse.

In point of fact, this is just what the doctor has done, with the aid of some Ecstatic timesmiths. Doctor Comet could emerge into the time-space continuum at any point — walking down the street, sitting next to the characters in a waiting room, tumbling out of a closet, a lavatory or a piece of luggage. He has no control over when and where, but he knows only that he will reenter the time stream shortly before the world ends. He will be synchronously drawn to the characters and/or the Tripplethorpes because they were the first to become aware of the threat.

Background: Born in 1937, Mueller traveled extensively throughout India and Central Asia while he was still a young man, cultivating a deep love for natural philosophy and ancient lore, as well as the rigors of mathematics and research. Excelling in astronomy in a number of German, Japanese and English schools, Mueller worked with Immanuel Velikovsky through the 1960s and early 1970s until they finally parted over a difference of scientific opinion. A rare defender of Velikovsky from within the ranks of academic astrophysics, Mueller lost all professional status in the mid-1990s when he publicly predicted that a "hyperdimensional supercomet" which he named Mirzaba would pass close enough to Earth to be a collision risk at the end of the year 2012. (If this story is to be set — or run — after 2012, the Storyteller might decide that Mirzaba never appeared, or that it did not pass close enough for comment.) The Sons of Ether further distanced themselves from him when Technocratic agents leaked the information that Mueller's parents were members of the Nazi party during WWII. (Unaware of the war atrocities, they actually spent the entire era in Central Asia engaged in ethnic and anthropological research.) Were Mueller ever to show his face in the halls of legitimate science, such as NASA or a government advisory board, these facts would immediately surface to discredit him — and anybody with him.

Image: At midnight, January 1, 2000, Bernhardt Mueller was 62 years old, short, pudgy, with streamers and confetti suspended in his wispy iron-gray hair, wearing a disheveled and stained rented tuxedo, and he was extremely, extremely intoxicated. This is how he reappears when he meets the characters.

Roleplaying Hints: You hardly consider yourself a mage, eschewing the practice of magic for theoretical metaphysics. You expected to reappear sometime around December 2012, so you assume that that is the current year until learning otherwise. Once you have a chance to sober up, you can confirm the Tripplethorpes' calculations, adding information culled from your extensive travels and occult readings. Furthermore, you are familiar with the red tape and office runarounds involved in reporting scientific matters to world authorities, though your information in this regard is several years out of date. If this story takes place before 2012, you have a classic Etherite motivation to help: You must save the world in order to be proven correct about its destruction later on. (If 2012 has already passed with no sign of the supercomet Mirzaba, you can always shrug and say, "It was only a theory…")

Faction: Sons of Ether
Essence: Questing
Nature: Visionary
Demeanor: Rebel
Attributes: Strength 2, Dexterity 2, Stamina 2, Charisma 3, Manipulation 2, Appearance 2, Perception 4, Intelligence 5, Wits 3

Abilities: Academics 5, Computer 3, Cosmology 5, Enigmas 4, Etiquette 3, Firearms 3, Linguistics 5, Occult 4, Science (Astrophysics) 5, Technology 4

Backgrounds: Contacts 4 (old friends among the straight scientific community), Destiny 5 (to be present when the world ends)

Arete: 8

Spheres: Correspondence 2, Entropy 1, Forces 2, Matter 2, Spirit 1, Time 2

Willpower: 4

Quintessence: 1

Paradox: 11 (Doctor Comet, having just appeared out of nowhere after traveling through time, cannot completely synchronize himself with the present moment. Sometimes he will speak or move in reverse; clocks run backward around him, and occasionally even characters in his presence might be caught up in his Severe Paradox Flaw, unaware that they are reliving the same segment of time while the world outside continues at its normal rate.)

Resonance: (Entropic) Aging 3, (Static) Foreboding 2

Facing the Face

Abner and Whitney continue their quest to alert the leaders of the world to its peril, presumably with the aid of the characters and/or Doctor Comet. Old classmates might be looked up, favors called in, strings pulled, palms greased, backs scratched, hands washed, anything to push the news up the top-heavy chain of command. Allies and Contacts Backgrounds, not to mention social and bureaucratic capacities, must figure heavily into the action here, and rounds of tiresome appointments might be condensed into a series of rolls based on appropriate traits.

Local politicians or professors might be induced to listen, perhaps even become convinced, but they will not lend their support unless doing so somehow contributes to their own agenda and interests. (For example, a fundamentalist religious leader might be glad to have hard evidence of an approaching Armageddon to galvanize his constituents, or a military supporter might use the news to call for increased spending on missile technology.) All access to the highest levels of government, however, remain well beyond the reach of the Tripplethorpes and their friends, as they never get past the elaborate security screening process (except perhaps through opportunities the players' characters themselves create). No federal officeholder is willing to commit to a response unless it comes from a superior.

If the characters grow loudly strident or persistent, conventional security measures will be used to keep them at a distance. Any criminal record, political impropriety, legal entanglement or questionable business dealing will be cited against them. Abner's Drunk-and-Disorderly charges from his early navy days will be brought up, along with the fact that Whitney's parents were recently arrested in LA for possession of cocaine. (For drama's sake, neither Whitney nor Abner knew about this arrest.) Any documented association with other known crackpots (such as Leland Chin) is also used. If the characters choose to circumvent the proper channels to meet with an especially important person, they will be treated as criminal stalkers by Sleeper guards. If the person they were getting at is involved with the scientific community, agents of the Technocracy might become involved and learn of the mages' true nature. Technocrats would be particularly interested if Bernhardt Mueller's name or image were to come up.

After a few rounds of this activity, the mages will find that their names and faces are already known to agencies, bureaus and universities that they have not yet visited, as if somebody were warning these institutions…

The Celestial Ball: Invitations

Turmoil erupts across the Vulgate as the Astral Umbra experiences the first insubstantial bombardments from space in its own surreal way. Out of the distorted sky tumble huge rocks in horrifying slow motion, pushing through the Epiphamies and hanging among the Spires like drifting islands of stone. Where they come closest to the ground, their pocked undersides crack open, disgorging marauding packs of monsters. Sites sacred to earth goddesses are especially threatened in this way. All over the land there are skirmishes to be fought, damage to be repaired and injured beings to be cared for. Visitors will be hard pressed to take more than two steps without being hounded to help refugees and victims of the attacks.

In the spiritual remnant of the Library of Alexandria, Chief Librarian Aristarchus invokes the aid of Urania, the Muse of Science, to determine the cause of this invasion, while Chief Astronomer Hypatia marks its progress from the Mouseion observatory. Their chief aid, Spearman Kydas, rides the land in search of any who might possess knowledge of these events (such as the characters). Those who oppose or resist him earn not only his enmity and suspicion but the distrust and hostility of all local resident spirits. Mages who have had favorable dealings with the Library in the past

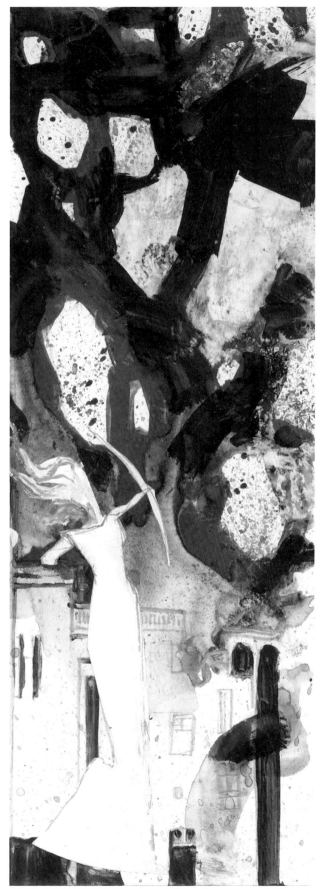

could be approached and called upon by name to help in the crisis. Hypatia will ask any experienced Umbral traveler to journey to the Epiphamy known as the Continuum Orrery, a sort of programmable interactive planetarium, to see what can be learned there. (More info on the Alexandrian Library, the Mouseion and the Continuum Orrery can be found in **The Infinite Tapestry**.)

Meanwhile, a beautiful silver-haired woman rides a bluish-white mare throughout the lands of the Vulgate, pursuing a quest of her own. She claims to know the cause of the invasion, so she will show up at the Library eventually, but the characters might cross her path at any point. She gives her name as Diana, and she has the glamour of a very powerful spirit — perhaps even an Incarna. According to her, the stones in the sky are an advance force sent by a cold and dark entity from beyond the Horizon; this spirit is desirous of Diana's mother and has come to take her by force if she does not give herself to him willingly. Diana seeks allies to secure her mother's freedom.

Diana

Diana is slender and pale, with long silvery hair framing a round face. She might appear young or old, depending on how the light strikes her. Her personality, too, tends to shift between lighter and darker phases — warm and friendly one moment, bitter and scornful the next, or shifting from grim determination to hopeless resignation and back again with little apparent cause. She will tell but little of her life or origins, but her aristocratic bearing and her given title of "Princessima de Lune" enable the spirit-savvy to recognize her as a moon spirit of high rank. (Three successes on an Intelligence + Occult or Spirit Lore roll.) She is equally coy about the exact identity of her mother, saying such cryptic things as, "She is all around you — you have known her all your life."

Willpower 8, **Rage** 6, **Gnosis** 9, **Essence** 23

Charms: Appear, Cleanse the Blight, Flood, Influence, Open Moon Bridge, Arrows of Lunacy (An arrow from Diana's silver-stringed bow, charged with two Essence points, will derange the sensibilities of any hit by it. Targets have the difficulty of all Mental rolls increased by two for the duration of the scene.)

Sphere Charms: Mind 5, Spirit 5

Meteoric Golem

Most of the invading force from the sky-stones consists of near-mindless ogres seemingly composed of solid rock. Once unleashed, they cause untold mayhem, smashing buildings and chasing people away. They move slowly and are easy to avoid, but are virtually impossible to stop. They tend to focus their rage against places and groups where veneration of earth goddesses is openly practiced, but they have no special sense to detect earth-centered magic or earth-aligned people.

Willpower 4, **Rage** 7, **Gnosis** 1, **Essence** 12
Charms: Armor, Blast Flame

Chapter III: Conflagrations

Cpd conflagare *(int* con-*), to catch fire, be on fire (esp with flames)…*
—Partridge, op. cit.

This chapter primarily concerns the powers that be, how they finally acknowledge and respond to the meteor's presence. If the Tripplethorpes and/or their friends were especially successful in alerting a world leader or academic authority to the danger, they might be allowed into the corridors of power to participate in the defense of Earth. They might also have some degree of fame — be it celebrity or notoriety — thrust upon them. This creates an interesting irony. Whereas, in the first two chapters they were going to great lengths to get the world to pay attention to them, now they are faced with an unwanted surplus of attention and might need to go to even greater lengths to go about their business unhindered.

Beyond the world of Sleeper politics, the leaders of the Awakened community respond in their own way. Some older mages see Typhon as an agent of their own hubris, sent as their punishment for losing the Ascension War — or for daring to wage it in the first place. While these mages retire to their chambers to await the end, the younger leaders (who have yet to learn the full meaning of hubris) seize the opportunity to take a more proactive stance.

Wake Up Down There!

The details of Traditional politics are best left to the Storyteller, who can best characterize the leaders of mage society in accordance with the events and tone of the chronicle to date. Yet a sampling of notable opinions, reactions and plans to save the world — beyond what the characters might come up with on their own, of course — is definitely in order. Although those opinions are presented here by Tradition, any individual mage or cabal can support and help with any plan they choose.

Dreamspeakers

While most latter-day shamans naturally abhor any major disturbance to Earth's ecosystem, some younger Dreamspeakers (with a modern education) and some older ones (claiming to speak from the deepest wells of planetary memory) say that a collision with the asteroid cannot be prevented, and, indeed, *should* not. Meteoric impacts, catastrophic though they are, are a natural part of the planet's evolutionary process, adding to its total energy and clearing away old growth to make way for the new. (Many Euthanatoi and even some Hollow Ones concur on this point.) If the human race is to survive at all, however, a breeding population must be transported to the Umbra in advance, they say. Nobody cares to hear this idea. Proponents of this view, a minority even among their own Traditions, are shouted down and denounced as fatalistic misanthropes trying to hide from harsh physical realities.

Order of Hermes

The "holders of Heaven's keys" see this crisis as the ultimate opportunity to prove their magical supremacy. Their preservation of the antiquities means they have the greatest access to the astrological lore mentioned in Chapter II (though not the more detailed recent observations of the Tripplethorpes — unless the characters choose to share it with them.) And their command of the Sphere of Forces would seem to be the natural tool to use against the oncoming juggernaut. News of Typhon's approach has a galvanizing effect on this Tradition, as most of the warring Houses cease their intramural bickering to focus on the problem at hand. The greatest of all Great Workings is needed to focus and amplify the current conjunction of large outer planets. Ancient and powerful Enochian invocations must be employed to contact, negotiate with and command the celestial intelligences. Doing so involves a large number of tightly coordinated and synchronized rituals performed worldwide, so the Order's usual efforts toward Traditional solidarity — under their leadership, of course — kick into high gear. Hermetic representatives canvas the leaders of the other Traditions and smaller mixed cabals of note (including that of the characters), attempting to convince them of the absolute necessity of adhering to the Order's plan. These attempts are professionally diplomatic and largely successful in garnering a majority of Traditional mages, but the Hermetics are so deeply convinced of the correctness of their approach that they have no qualms about employing darker means of leverage — such as bribery, coercion and blackmail. Such maneuvers will be kept secret, of course, but mages who know about them find them unconscionable, even in the face of extinction. While many old feuds might be forgotten in the general rush to join the Hermetic working, some deepen and new enmities can develop. The Celestial Chorus, for instance, agrees with the basic tenets of this working, but insists that the planetary intelligences must be approached in prayerful supplication rather than haughty authority.

Sons of Ether

Like the Order of Hermes, the Etherites see this as their chance to be proven right; unlike the Order, the Sons have no single plan of action to unify them. Every Scientist has her own idiosyncratic theory. Most utilize various means of generating a current or "wind" in the luminiferous ether to deflect the asteroid. Others call upon the gravitational influence of dark matter or the propagation of dark energy, while some even suggest that a massive inversion of Earth's electromagnetic polarity would repel Typhon (which they believe to have a predominantly metallic composition). Still others propose targeting the body with a scalar "death ray" based on the designs of Nikola Tesla. The Virtual Adepts are fervently courted as allies, both for the digital precision of their tools and their facility at magically altering spatial relationships. Nearly all of these plans, feasible or not, involves a reaction that would be catastrophic for Earth's environment, an aspect of the calculations that their proponents downplay — or fail to mention entirely. A small but growing group, however, feels that this is unavoidable. Convening under the name "Archimedes' Fulcrum," they have resigned themselves to the inevitability that much of humanity and its ecosystem might need to be sacrificed to stave off global obliteration. Separately or in small groups, the Fulcrum has committed to equipping Etherships and training laboratory crews to enact various schemes.

Verbena

Faced with the elimination of the life they hold so dear, the Verbena have dug up an ancient rite long thought to be a barbaric relic from their own dark past. Called the "Mensis Mutandis," it involves the unthinkable act of actually shifting the moon from its established orbit, so that it can be used as a physical shield (or at least a gravitational deflector) against Typhon. The specifics of the plan sound absurd, even by magical standards, but they actually have some slight basis in current scientific theory. Just as the moon affects the tides on Earth, so too does the movement of Earth's hydrosphere have a slight reciprocal gravitational effect on the moon's orbit. By artificially altering the tidal cycle through means both magical and physical (damming rivers and tidal pools, hastening or delaying the opening and closing of major canal locks, using Correspondence, Forces, Matter and Time Effects), the moon can be sped up or slowed down until it is in a position to interfere with Typhon's trajectory. Female Verbena are even risking their personal health to viscerally reinforce this pattern, changing their own internal lunar cycles through herbal means. Although the Verbena are convinced of the efficacy of this plan, they will admit that there might not be enough time to bring it to fruition, so they are making concerted efforts to enlist the aid of the Cult of Ecstasy, whose mastery of the Sphere of Time would be most beneficial. Strangely, most of the Akashic Brotherhood seems to agree with this method, somehow finding it consistent with their martial philosophy of redirecting forceful blows with gentle touches. Critics of this plan, however, deride it with the epithet "Canute's Folly Revisited."

Obviously, time is of the essence. An even more significant consideration is scale. Many mages might not even realize the true magnitude of the impending event. The greatest willworkers have extended their reach over whole countries and Umbral Realms, but Typhon is over a thousand kilometers in diameter, weighs upward of a million tons, and is traveling at a velocity measured in thousands of miles per hour. Desperate need for unprecedented amounts of Quintessence leads to some of the hardest-fought Node Wars in occult history. If the characters' cabal has its own Node, any faction with whom they are not already aligned will target it. Many doubt that all the magic in the world is sufficient to the task. Some secretly fear that the dissenting Dreamspeakers are correct, and they have begun preparing their closest family and friends for an exodus into the Umbra. The characters themselves might choose this option for their own Sleeper companions, possibly including Abner and Whitney. Note that any Sleeper entering the Umbra unprepared is likely to believe that he is hallucinating or has gone completely mad. Ideally, a crash course in astral navigation and Umbrood etiquette would be called for in advance.)

"Nucular" Diversions

Even if the Tripplethorpes fail to alert the authorities, the major world governments will learn of the asteroid by Chapter III through the diligence of NASA's Near-Earth Asteroid Tracking program (NEAT) or through the European agency known as Spaceguard. For the purposes of this story, the response of the geopolitical superpowers is essentially that of the Technocracy, a pragmatically hard-nosed countering of raw physical force with raw physical force. Of course, the Void Engineers will be at the forefront of this effort (raising the question of how a couple of amateurs from the fly-over were able to identify the threat from space before the Enlightened Scientists entrusted with this very job).

News of the threat will not be officially announced to the general public until the next chapter, in order to avoid worldwide panic. For years the people have been assured repeatedly that astronomers across the globe would identify and track any large body approaching from space well in advance of any possible collision. One or more thermonuclear devices would then be deployed to change its trajectory or blast it apart into smaller pieces that would pose no global threat. (This line of reasoning has been peripherally cited — complete with the now-standard official mispronunciation of the word "nuclear" — to justify the extremes of the arms race, despite queries as to how chemical and biological weapons can be used against a meteoric impactor.) This plan now commences, under the auspices of the United States government with the aid and cooperation of the world's industrialized nations. Only top officials and those scientists directly involved are briefed on the full extent of the situation, but even most of them are unaware that the Technocracy is actually in control of the operation, and that the explosive devices and delivery systems are, in reality, far more powerful and sophisticated than anything available to the modern Sleeper military.

Depending on the outcome of the Tripplethorpes' efforts to alert the authorities, the characters might be able to involve themselves in this particular endeavor. Of course, if the Technocrats recognize them as Tradition mages — reality deviants — they will bar access. Alternatively, the characters might decide to abandon the Traditions and put their trust in the Technocratic solution. Whether the Technocrats accept the characters' help is up to the Storyteller, but even if they do so, there is still one among their ranks with an entirely different agenda.

Seymour Glass

One of the most influential members of the president's scientific advisory staff is an astronomer named Seymour Glass. Unbeknownst to the government, Glass is also a Void Engineer and has been instrumental in guiding the world's greatest superpower

in accordance with the Technocratic agenda. Unbeknownst to the Technocracy, Glass has fallen under the sway of a dark power from beyond the Horizon. He is, in fact, a Nephandus who secretly desires the destruction of the world. It was he who kept foiling the Tripplethorpes' attempts to get a fair hearing, using his security clearance to poison all ears against them. Furthermore, his executive oversight of NASA's NEAT program and his rank within the Void Engineers enabled him to bury, destroy, distort and misdirect any data and reports that could have led to an earlier discovery of Typhon's approach. He might have even manipulated Leland Chin into trying to kill them (if the Storyteller wishes to thicken this part of the plot). He has also followed the characters ever since they made contact with Abner and Whitney, and he can call upon the services of other *barabbi* to foul the plans of the Traditions.

Background: Emerging from his upper middle class roots, Seymour displayed a prodigal genius for mathematics and science at an early age, along with a workaholic drive that propelled him through an accelerated curriculum and found him with several scientific degrees while he was still in his mid-20s. His Awakening came when he inherited an antique telescope that enabled him to see aspects of the heavens that were previously beyond his comprehension. Recruited by the Void Engineers, Glass exhibited a number of health problems that exempted him from off-world duties, but he rose through the ranks to become one of the Technocracy's most important political liaisons. Meanwhile, his telescope — a cursed Talisman from a previous century — put him in mental contact with a vast slug-like *thing* inhabiting a neutron star in the farthest reaches of the universe. This entity fervently desires the destruction of all Creation in unthinkable gravitational collapse, and it sees the impact of Typhon with Earth as but a tiny step in that ultimate goal. To this end, it has instructed Glass to sabotage any effort that might prevent the collision.

Image: The stereotypical scientist, Seymour is skinny, pale and pencil-necked, in his mid-40s, with slicked-down thinning brown hair and small round glasses with thick lenses that lend his stare a goggle-eyed reptilian aspect.

Roleplaying Hints: Cold and aloof, you maintain your double-layered façade with a soft-spoken deadpan reserve. Never raise your voice or display any emotion. Avoid being the center of attention in all situations.

Faction: Void Engineer *barabbus*

Essence: Questing

Nature: Monster

Demeanor: Loner

Attributes: Strength 2, Dexterity 3, Stamina 1, Charisma 1, Manipulation 5, Appearance 2, Perception 5, Intelligence 5, Wits 4

Abilities: Academics 5, Awareness 3, Computer 4, Cosmology 5, Dodge 2, Enigmas 3, Etiquette 1, Firearms 2, Law 2, Science (Astronomy) 5, Subterfuge 5, Technology 4

Backgrounds: Allies 4, Arcane 3, Influence 5, Resources 4

Arete: 8

Spheres: Correspondence 3, Entropy 4, Forces 2, Matter 2, Mind 3, Time 1

Willpower: 7

Quintessence: 3

Paradox: 1

Resonance: (Entropic) Jhor 2, (Static) Accurate 4

The Celestial Ball: Arrivals

Diana brings the characters to a grove far from the more heavily inhabited regions of the Vulgate, back along the River of Language toward the Spirit Wilds. Crouched between the roots of an impossibly large tree is an old woman dressed in rags, weeping silently. Even those who have already met with Mother Earth in her various guises (such as Ummaugh Daanau from **The Infinite Tapestry**) would probably not recognize this wretched creature. No traits will be given for Mother Earth, as she will not act on her own behalf — at least for the purposes of this story. While she might go along with whatever Diana or the characters suggest, she seems hopelessly resigned to her fate as the bride of some dark monster from outer space. Though she remains at the center of the action to follow, she is not so much a person or even goddess in her own right, but more of a holy relic to be protected, or a trophy to be won.

Her initial reaction to human visitors will not be friendly, and she might even be outwardly hostile, depending on how the characters act when first seeing her. In Astral Space, the earth goddess is conscious, intelligent and aware. She will treat members of the human race as would any mother who has been exploited and abused by her own children, with loathing and contempt — or even fear. (Of course, she does not include Diana — the moon — in her blanket condemnations, nor does she blame any other species for her pathetic state.) Her attitude toward the "marriage" being forced upon her is one of resignation to an inevitable fate. "It was nice while it lasted," she might say, "but all things must come to an end. Whatever must be, must be." Those who manage to get close to her might even catch a note of relief as she says, "I don't know how much more of this I can take!" (Referring to the depredations heaped upon her by mankind.)

Diana wishes to hide her mother by keeping her out of sight from the open sky, either under the foliage of the Spirit Wilds or within a building of the Vulgate or a cave under a Spire. Diana is open to any suggestions the characters make, and her mother will go along with the group whatever they do, moaning and kvetching all the way. (If they enter the Spirit Wilds, Mother Earth will take on a slightly more pleasing aspect, being surrounded by what she now considers her finest creations. Her sorrow and bitterness will be replaced with melancholy nostalgia.)

At an especially dramatic moment, the sky above darkens as the invader arrives in full force. The stones hanging in the air drift aside to make way for a veritable floating continent that descends to blot out the astral sky. Its pitted, cratered underbelly nearly touches the ground in places, engulfing or crushing the tallest Spires and triggering terrible storms and earthquakes across the Vulgate. Over the uproar, an impossibly loud masculine voice booms: "I HAVE COME TO CLAIM MY BRIDE. BRING HER TO ME AT ONCE OR SUFFER MY FULLEST WRATH!"

Now, the characters might choose to face this threat head on by traveling straightaway to the aerial continent, or they may stay to defend the mother from whatever comes to get her. (More Meteoric Golems, larger than their brothers, with a Rage of 9, Essence of 14 and the additional Charms: Lightning Bolt and Umbraquake.) If the Storyteller wishes to draw out this scene, a battle to defend Mother Earth from the Meteoric Golems can be played out in full. The Fortress of Government is probably the most defensible position in the Vulgate, a massive monolith of a building with relatively small entrances and a near-endless internal maze. Ultimately, though, the defenders will lose to brute strength and force of numbers; the characters will then be seized and taken to the floating continent. Alternatively, the characters might elect to leave Diana and her mother behind while they meet the incursion head on, with whatever other forces they can muster — such as other mages, spirit allies or even Patrons. In this case they will still be captured, and will not know what befell the two ladies until the next chapter.

Chapter IV: Catastrophe

… katastrophe, *a lit overturning* (kata, down), *hence a fig upsetting, hence a conclusion, esp in drama, of a tragedy, hence ruin, a great misfortune…*
—Partridge, op. cit.

Chapter IV covers the period of time during which Typhon becomes visible to the naked eye, just days before the projected impact. Plans to divert or destroy the rogue asteroid play out while panic sweeps the world as everyone can see with their own eyes the approach of doom. Mad with fear and enraged by the governments' attempts to keep the situation secret, rioters and looters fill the streets. Societal infrastructures begin to collapse, and the characters must depend upon their own private means of support and transportation (unless they are still in with the government, of course). Any action or movement in a public space will be hampered by the chaos erupting amid the swift decline of civilization.

And that's not all. Typhon is now close enough for its gravity to affect the very substance of the Earth itself. By the end of the chapter, the entire atmosphere will be alive with raging storms. Earthquakes, tidal waves, tornadoes, hurricanes and volcanic eruptions start to appear across the globe, even in places that have not known such disasters for millions of years. Smaller asteroids orbiting Typhon begin to reach Earth, lighting up the skies with bright streaks and tearing up the ground with waves of lesser impacts. ("Lesser" being a relative term. Chapter IV commences with white-hot pebbles punching holes in a few roofs, and could culminate in the flattening of a major city. Let the Storyteller exercise dramatic license here.) Simply avoiding a hail of meteorites can consume much of the action. Those with Correspondence, Entropy and Time senses should maintain a constant watch.

Chapter IV could be subtitled "Murphy's Chapter," in that everything that can go wrong does. Any faction that has access to the Tripplethorpes' observations and Doctor Comet's calculations might achieve some marginal degree of success — with results to be delineated in the final chapter — but only if the characters can fend off Seymour Glass's sabotage (and, possibly, Leland Chin's continued interference). Ultimately, however, the collision is unavoidable, and the best that can be done is to decrease the scale and long-term effects of the impact.

Wars in the Heavens

Characters directly involved with any of the plans described in Chapter III will naturally see its results for themselves. The progress of the other plans can be reported through Traditional channels, by scrying mages or even independent astronomers (for events taking place on the physical plane). Divergent efforts will undoubtedly conflict with each other, with Hermetics and Verbena clashing over Nodes and sacred sites while Etherite and Void Engineer vessels battle for control of the skies and the right to save the world in their own way — dodging the smaller asteroids that form Typhon's retinue the whole time. Any diplomatic skills the characters possess could lessen these conflicts, and new alliances could develop on their own. Like politics, the threat of extinction can make for strange bedfellows.

Running a magical casting on this scale by the book would be enough to drive any Storyteller insane — hundreds of cabals trying to coordinate their efforts worldwide? Forget about it. Given Typhon's mass and distance, at least 1,000 successes would be needed. Die-hard purists are certainly welcome to spend the week before the game session rolling dice and keeping tally. Some might wish to condense this mass working into a few representative rolls or merely narrate whatever results best suit the tone and action of the game thus far. If the characters are personally participating in one plan or another, they should naturally be allowed to play out their own efforts. The effectiveness of any given method requires pinpointing the exact location and trajectory of the asteroid in space — just seeing it up there in the sky is not enough, since both it and the Earth are in constant motion. This is where the Tripplethorpe-Mueller data really comes into play. The base difficulty for each plan starts at 9, reduced by one if the characters studied the Tripplethorpes' records, and by another one if Mueller had at least a day or two to work out all the math. Any additional corroboration or computation, like researching ancient texts or employing a modern supercomputer, reduces the difficulty by one more.

Even if each faction is armed with the Tripplethorpe-Mueller data, the various endeavors serve only to foul each other, giving the Storyteller a number of options to arrive at the same doom. The asteroid becomes the center of an astronomical tug of war in which different forces cancel each other out to varying degrees, leaving Typhon to follow its own overwhelming momentum. The Hermetically amplified gravity of the outer planets conflicts with the pull of the nearest body, the moon, itself drawn closer by the Verbena ritual. Technocratic super-bombs fail to reach the meteoroid's surface, pulled off course by the etheric currents generated by Archimedes' Fulcrum. These currents are in turn disrupted by the misplaced atomic detonations in the Void. Ultimately, the Earth's own gravity, the most powerful local force, drags Typhon toward its destination, even as the orbital stability Earth-moon system itself is disrupted by all this tampering with celestial harmony. At best, the inevitable might be delayed, with the asteroid caught in a temporary orbital entanglement with the moon or even the Earth itself, looming in the sky for another day or two before plunging to the surface. At worst, the side effects of each operation worsen the environmental turmoil at ground level, with nuclear fallout from space, irregular tides, orbital and axial interference that alters the length of the day or changes the seasons overnight.

Regardless, Earth will be hit, and hard. Does this mean that the Storyteller has to look her players in the face and tell them that they fail no matter how well they play? Not entirely. Even a marginal success deserves some reward. A best-case scenario would be that Typhon is blasted apart, or torn apart by gravitational turbulence, leaving at least one kilometer-wide chunk on a collision course, if not a number of larger pieces. A direct hit on the moon will still cause a similar-sized piece of lunar debris to detach itself and continue along the same path. Depending on events in the Celestial Ball, another hitherto unnoticed meteoric body can swoop in, "out of nowhere," and shatter Typhon. The Umbral causes for this will be described forthwith. The Technocratic and Etherite methods might still be used to clean up some of the debris causing these secondary threats if there is still time (Storyteller's discretion — it would take Typhon itself about five hours to cross the distance from the moon to Earth), but the Hermetic Great Working and the Mensis Mutandis will have spent themselves by the time any potential impactor passes within the lunar orbit. The difference between such marginal victories and total failure will be described in the final chapter.

If all else fails — or, rather, succeeds — and the Storyteller still intends to finish his chronicle with an Armageddon that is decisively final, Typhon or its largest fragment has one last ace up its sleeve. Being from the outer Asteroid Belt, its structure and composition are still largely unknown. It is a "proto-comet," containing numerous large pockets of ice that boil out in large jets of steam when exposed to vacuum or heated by nearby explosions. These jets are powerful enough to change its trajectory, as with comets, turning Typhon into a guided missile capable of evading all attempts to deflect it. As will be seen in the last segment of the Celestial Ball, this hurtling planetesimal is not simply a dead rock following a mathematically predetermined course, but a deliberately crafted weapon directed by a hostile intelligence.

The Celestial Ball: The Dance

Atop the floating continent is a desolate landscape of jagged rock and glaciers, with the occasional seismic upheaval or volcanic eruption for color. At its center is a tall circular mesa, its plateau wreathed in dark clouds within which whirling, strangely colored lights can be glimpsed. The characters will be taken (or escorted, if they came willingly) to the top via rough-hewn steps that wind around the mesa counterclockwise. The plateau surface is even larger than it appeared from below, lit by an immense orb of burning yellow. The whirling lights are also huge, spherical and impossibly distant, occupying places around the perimeter; as they spin, each presents a roughly humanoid face or figure that might seem familiar to the mages. A veritable sea of smaller man-sized figures mills about the surface, drifting and swaying in time to strange unearthly music and booming spirit-voices. (*The Planets* by Gustav Holst would be appropriate music for this game session.)

Because of the immensity of the scene, a few rolls are required for the characters to gain any notion of what they are seeing. Any success on a Perception + Performance roll (difficulty 5) shows that the smaller figures are actually dancing, with additional successes revealing the overall pattern in which figures wearing the same color as one of the spheres cycle outward from that sphere, intermingle with the figures from other spheres and eventually return to their source. With at least three successes on a Wits + Occult or Science roll (difficulty 7; 5 for those with a specialty in Astrology or Astronomy), it can be seen that the spheres are actually the planets, with their respective moons in attendance, displaying the images of the deities for which they were named and calling the moves of the dance in booming voices. (For most observers, these deities would be from the Roman pantheon, but each mage sees whatever god or goddess is appropriate to her own cultural paradigm.) Practicing astrologers or astronomers with more successes on this same roll will note that each planet occupies a position analogous to its current position in the physical world. (Characters who look behind them will see the Earth looming at the edge of the plateau where they just entered.) Five successes on an Intelligence + Science roll (difficulty 8) shows that the overall pattern of the dance is actually a geometrically precise representation of the gravitational relationships between the bodies of the solar system. Mages already familiar with the Epiphamy known as the Continuum Orrery (**The Infinite Tapestry**) can guess that it has somehow become continuous with the mesa top. Astronomical markings can be glimpsed on the surface between the dancing bodies, and the monuments of ancient stargazers, such as the trilithons of Stonehenge, ring the perimeter. The orrery mechanism itself is at the center, directly beneath the sun, hidden by glaring light and heat haze.

The characters will immediately join the dance, either through their own volition or by being swept up in the press of bodies. Those who do not keep up with the swirling movement around them risk getting trampled, while those who try to fight will, after being buffeted about by the other dancers, be flung from the plateau to land on the jagged rocks below or plummet all the way back to the Vulgate. Characters who choose to participate will find that they actually have quite a bit of freedom of movement due to the scale and complexity of the overall dance, as partners and teams come together, exchange places and part. Every two successes on a Dexterity or Wits + Performance roll (difficulty 6) enables them to master such moves as the

"Minuet of Mutual Attraction," the "Epicyclic Quadrille," the "Gravitic Gavot," the "Orbital Fling" or the "Perihelion Polka." Learning the steps of the dance means that the mages can interact socially with the other planetary dancers, and thus understand a little of the intentions and thoughts of the planetary intelligences themselves — interacting with these vast and distant entities by proxy, as it were.

The other dancers can be identified by color and by mythic attributes they share with their parent planet, although some take the form of their planet's putative inhabitants as described in popular science fiction and occult lore. Diana and the other moons are central figures in areas closest to their parent planets. Meteoric golems can also be found, stumbling through the affair while maintaining their places in the overall gravitational patterns. By conversing, flirting or even antagonizing the other dancers, the characters can learn of the social undercurrents, the alliances, enmities and intrigues of the solar court. The representatives of the inner planets will receive them favorably. Venus and Mercury feel sympathy for Earth's present situation and oppose the upcoming "marriage," considering it tantamount to cosmic rape. Mars and Jupiter, however, seem to feel that the Earth deserves what is coming. In fact, 10 or more accumulated successes on any Social rolls for conversing with their representatives reveal that Mars is especially jealous of Earth's proficiency at spawning and supporting life. Saturn and the outermost worlds are more aloof, awaiting the outcome of the event with detached bemusement — unless the Enochian calls of the Order of Hermes have roused them, in which case their many moons and other dancers will be found all over the dance floor.

If the characters persist, the details of the planetary plot will emerge. The spirit of the Asteroid Belt, a fragmented, schizophrenic entity, was once a vital planet itself, with an evolved population of sentient creatures. Their technological advancement outgrew their ability to live together in peace, and they destroyed their home in a cataclysmic war. Seeing the humans of Earth approaching a similar stage in their evolution, the surviving spirit of that shattered planet wishes to save the Earth from the same fate by hitting it with one of its largest remaining fragments, a giant "planet-killing" meteoroid — Typhon. (Gossip among the outer planets holds that the spirit of the belt, like that of Mars, is also bitterly jealous of Earth's vibrant and beautiful ecosystem.) Jupiter and Mars were accomplices in this act, using their gravity to help draw Typhon in toward Earth's orbit, with Mars hiding the first stage of its approach from Earth's view by keeping the asteroid in its shadow. Mars was actually "paid in advance" for this "favor" long ago, in the form of its own tiny moons, former asteroids each.

In acting as the gravitational "slingshot," however, Mars developed a slight orbital irregularity that will eventually result in its destruction as it spirals away from the sun and is finally engulfed by one of the massive gas giants. If this fact can be proven to Mars (through its two ill-tempered moons and dancers), it might change its alliance and do what it can to help Earth by flinging one of its tiny moons into Typhon's path at the last minute. (Never mind the time realistically required for this to come about. The dance takes place in an Epiphamy, effectively happening outside of time. While events already played out in the physical world cannot be changed retroactively, this particular astronomical action will not have been noticed by Earth's astronomers who were not expecting or looking for it, especially after Typhon's presence is known.) The whirl of the dance will not permit complicated mathematical demonstrations, but if the characters can reach the orrery controls beneath the sun — using a combination of the "Ecliptic Fling" and the "Aphelion Hop" along with some magical protection against the sun's blinding light and searing heat — they can switch the orrery to its "Ptolemaic" mode. (The sun does not act, or have dancing representative spirits; it is the solitary unmoving pivot around which the whole dance revolves.) The planets' orbits will then be seen as concentric crystalline spheres, in accordance with ancient cosmology, and a large cracked hole in the crystal sphere of Mars — left by Typhon when it crossed Mars' orbit — will be obvious to all.

Additional astronomical data can be gleaned from the geometry of the dance [Intelligence + Science: Astronomy (difficulty 8)], but ultimately there is nothing to be done. This plot was hatched eons ago — for the planets could see thousands of years in advance what road humanity was taking — and its momentum is nigh unstoppable. Furthermore, Mother Earth subconsciously desires this union. She has secretly renounced her favorite children, ungrateful mankind, and wishes to be rid of them. Even Diana's feelings could change if anyone reminds her that she owes her own existence to a primordial impact, or if the Mensis Mutandis causes too radical of an alteration in her orbit. While successful participation in the Celestial Ball can offer the characters a brief glimmer of hope, in the final summation the asteroid's path cannot be changed.

Chapter V: Cataclysm

…LL *cataclysmus, the Biblical Flood*: Gr *kataklusmos, from* katakluzein, *to inundate*: kata-, *down* + kluzein, *to wash*…
—Partridge, op. cit.

If one of the plans for saving the world enjoys overwhelming success, or if the various Awakened factions can put aside their hostilities in time to coordinate their efforts, the Storyteller might judge that Earth escapes with only a few minor impacts and environmental upheaval that stabilizes within a generation or two. Humans and other large animals could thus avoid extinction, even decimation. "The Earth Will Shake" might then serve as a prelude or subplot for a different kind of apocalypse described elsewhere in this book (or of the Storyteller's own devising). But this is a story about the end of the world.

What follows are best- and worst-case scenarios, respectively. The Storyteller can adjust or combine elements from each as she deems appropriate.

Civilization-Ender

If the efforts of the characters and other mages amount to any sort of victory, this means that at least one smaller body hits the Earth — a "civilization-ender" only a few kilometers wide rather than a larger "planet-killer." It strikes the North Atlantic Ocean with enough kinetic energy to create a fireball that is many miles across at its brief peak and is as hot as the sun's surface, igniting forest fires all over the planet. Nearly a thousand cubic kilometers of water instantly evaporates in a pillar of steam miles high and causing a tidal wave that eventually sweeps over all the land on Earth (although it is mostly spent by the time it reaches Central Asia, the planet's farthest inland region). A tower of pulverized earth and dust from the coasts of Europe and America rises to fill the stratosphere, cloaking the world in a haze that blots out the sun. Combined with the soot from the worldwide forest fires, this cloud creates the equivalent of the dreaded nuclear winter, lasting up to six years and dooming every agricultural effort by survivors to failure.

Would there even be survivors? At best a handful, in Mongolia, Paraguay and Antarctica, the places farthest from both the impact site and the southeast corner of Australia, where the worldwide tidal wave converges. The tidal wave is preceded by a shock wave that triggers earthquakes, but reinforced bunkers in the most seismically stable parts of these regions could endure. Their occupants need enough stored food to last out the biospheric winter, since no plants could be cultivated and any surviving game would soon suffocate or starve. Additional collisions with other "ender"-sized bodies prolong and intensify the environmental effects, but they endanger only remaining surface dwellers by the proximity of their impact sites. Any people who have left the surface of the planet can avoid all this, of course, but they will be subjected to bombardment by smaller meteors and fragmentary debris.

> ### The More You Know…
> Velikovsky notwithstanding, some respectable scientists believe that an impactor close to the size of a "civilization-ender" struck the desert of Iraq or Arabia around the third millennium BC. Stones falling from the sky figure prominently in much of the local folklore. Even the Kaaba, the Black Stone circumambulated by Muslim pilgrims in Mecca, is reputed to have dropped from Heaven in ancient times.
>
> Extinction-level impacts might mark many of the major divisions of geologic ages, such as the Devonian and Permian-Triassic extinctions or the end of the dinosaurs in the Cretaceous-Tertiary impact, which has been positively identified with the 120-mile-wide Chicxulub crater off the Yucatan coast. This impactor was only a fraction of Typhon's size.

Planet-Killer

Collision with a body 10 kilometers or more in diameter constitutes an "extinction-level event," or, informally, a "planet-killer." The resultant shock wave encircles the planet, a rolling earthquake well off the Richter scale, and converges at Australia. Even the most strongly reinforced subterranean bunker anywhere in the world would collapse. The tidal wave is as tall as the ocean is deep, and it moves at over half the speed of sound, leaving behind a crater five kilometers deep where the Mid-Atlantic Ridge used to be. Meanwhile, the very chemistry of the biosphere would be disrupted, with nitrogen oxides precipitating in the form of acid rain over the next 10 years, poisoning every body of water on Earth. All life on the planet is wiped out, with the possible exception of simple anaerobic organisms

Chapter Four: The Earth Will Shake

inhabiting the deepest points of the South Atlantic, North Pacific and western Indian Ocean floors.

If even a quarter of Typhon's mass hits as a single body, the impact propels the Australian continental plate and a significant amount of Earth's mantle into space, where it eventually coalesces into a smaller second moon. The oceans are instantly vaporized, and the tectonic plates surrounding the impact site are melted back into magma. All others are utterly shattered, bobbing on the magma sea. Earth's evolutionary clock is almost completely reset. The last time it looked like this was just under four and half billion years ago, shortly after its formation from interstellar gas and dust.

Epilogue: The Umbral Exodus

As it turns out, those Dreamspeakers had the right idea after all. When worlds collide on the material plane, the safest place is undoubtedly the Umbra.

This is not to say that physical changes have no consequence in the lands of spirit, however. A mage in the Penumbra might experience a major global impact only as a distant blast of light and heat followed by a slow rolling quake. Nearing the Spirit Wilds, the resulting storms, earthquakes and other geophysical effects might be felt with the same deadly intensity as in the physical world, but they can be avoided by those who know the ways of the Wilds. The chaotic energies of global disasters strengthen the Spirit Wilds and erode the Gauntlet in places where the world has gotten more dynamic. Every individual death swells the borders of the Dark Umbra, and it stands to reason that an extinction-level event could force a sudden interpenetration of the three Umbrae.

The Vulgate can suffer from similar effects, but it remains stable enough to be rebuilt as long as human beings remain alive and thinking. The mass destruction of material stores of data, whether in the form of books, recordings or electronic media, causes the landmass of the Vulgate to erode, however. The obliteration of a culture causes the Low Umbra to "seep upward" into the corresponding region of the River of Language, with hordes of slavering zombies clawing their way from the ground to overrun all the places of tongues that will never be heard again.

If Typhon was reduced to "civilization-ender" size, any humans that survive in the Umbra might wish to return to the material world before disembodiment claims them. Life Sphere Effects might be required to survive the soot-blackened atmosphere, and some means of sustenance not dependent upon replenishing plant and animal species in the conventional agricultural manner must be found. (Unless suitable food can be imported from the Umbra.) The rate of disembodiment itself varies, however, since the lunar orbital period was probably changed during the course of this story.

In the event of complete extinction of the human race in the physical world, the Vulgate cannot last, as the very land erupts with the hungry dead and dissolves into the Great Ocean, which itself is now seen to be spilling over a bottomless drop that moves ever closer until everything below the bare roots of the Spires has fallen into oblivion. The Spires themselves gradually crumble away from the bottom, as High Umbrood revert to non-humanoid forms and recede into the Epiphamies or abandon the Astral Umbra for the Spirit Wilds. Disembodied humans who reach the Epiphamies will, in effect, abide therein throughout eternity. Though they might see all of Creation, from the ancient past to distant future, they might never again enter into it, existing only as the long-forgotten ideas of themselves. Hypothetically, any other species that evolves a capacity for complex abstract thought could eventually reach the Epiphamies and interact with these notions of extinct humans, who would appear alien, unfamiliar and possibly even threatening to them.

A Possible Denouement

If you set "The Earth Will Shake" before 2012, and if Bernhardt Mueller lives through it all, then toward the end of that year, the characters — and the Tripplethorpes, if they are still around — receive an invitation to join the old Etherite, either at the Mouseion observatory or somewhere on Earth where the skies have cleared enough to present a view of the heavens. Mueller directs their gaze to a new and unfamiliar body looming close in the night. An irregular pitted core spurts gouts of brightly colored gases, iridescent dust and water vapor that stretch out into space, twisted into a corkscrew shape by the body's spin and curved by the solar winds.

It is Mirzaba, the cosmic wanderer returning from its long hyperdimensional voyage to pass harmlessly alongside an Earth recently jogged from its orbit. No longer a harbinger of doom and evolutionary crisis, it now appears as a thing of awesome beauty, beckoning the remnants of the human race upward and outward, encouraging them not to abandon their dreams of studying and exploring the unending wonders of the cosmos.

Jabbing a pudgy finger triumphantly upward, Mueller cries, "I was right about the comet!"

Chapter Five: A Whimper, Not a Bang

*More distant and more solemn
Than a fading star…
This is the way the world ends
Not with a bang but a whimper.*
—T. S. Eliot, *The Hollow Men*

Introduction

Great threats are sometimes shrouded from mortal eyes. A deadly disease might linger unseen, waiting for microscopic viruses or bacteria to enter the human body. Unstable material can make a man's hair fall out, skin burn and flesh die with radiation lying outside of the visible spectrum. A political plot brewed in the back room of a German beer hall might foreshadow the deaths of millions.

Or a violent storm the size of the Earth could threaten the world's very spirit while inhuman things appear in forsaken skies and shanghai secluded victims.

What if the end of the world came and nobody noticed? In the World of Darkness, it isn't unusual for players and Storytellers to consider that even the most heinous acts occur without the common man on the street taking notice. When you spend every day surrounded by an oppressive and depressing atmosphere, without even the slightest hint of relief, it is very difficult to raise your head above the clinging smog to see the light on the horizon. When the morning sun casts its hopeless pall on yet another dismal day of servitude to a faceless corporation or burdensome civil service, and the blackness of night promises horrors that you pretend are nothing more than childhood nightmares, it is hard to care about anything. Unfortunately for us, unseeing eyes do not defend mankind from danger any more than falling asleep saves a drunk driver from crashing through a guardrail and drowning in the river below.

In this vision of the end, your characters either overcome threats invisible to the public eye or earn unmarked graves for their efforts. If they achieve Ascension, the accomplishment is something that eludes the Masses. Should they fail miserably, their violent passing from the world remains unnoticed by the Consensus.

They Are Here

From July 1947 until December 1969, the United States Air Force pursued an intensive investigation called Project Blue Book with the explicit purpose of tracking Unidentified Flying Object (UFO) sightings and verifying whether such claims had any truth or threat to them. Centered at the Wright-Patterson Air Force Base in Ohio, the Air Force project examined 12,618 sightings reported to the operation. 701 of those cases are still classified as "unidentified." Military sources maintain that even the unexplained incidents provide no evidence of principles beyond modern science or of an extraterrestrial origin. Conspiracy theorists don't buy that. They consider the hundreds of unsolved cases as evidence of a covered-up alien presence.

Two obscure groups of radicals have turned up evidence of something bigger than anything paranoid intelligence officers or quixotic UFO nuts ever imagined. Unfortunately, the two factions distrust each other and neither is likely to ever solve the puzzle without certain pieces held by their rivals. Blinded by an unbending scientific viewpoint, they would be unlikely to see the truth even if they were to work together. Nevertheless, through obstinate investigation and paranoid theorizing, both have stumbled upon the existence of an enemy that has proved enigmatic beyond the ken of mage society. Unaware of the scope of the find, they have discovered traces of the seemingly incomprehensible race from elsewhere, the Zigg'raugglurr.

The Star Council

The first of these two organizations is the Star Council, a gathering of eccentric intellectuals who share beliefs and studies of UFOs. Numbering less than 50, the Star Council would likely have faded away when the '60s ended, had it not made a remarkable discovery. Following the trail of reported sightings and cracked government files, a handful of members managed to break into a restricted hangar in Area 51 in 1969. They made off with ultratech devices of both Technocratic and alien origin and have been studying them ever since. The pillaging of the famed Technocratic Node has earned the group the unwanted attention of the Union, and only its inherent paranoia, unconventional tactics and occasional amazing breakthroughs with the stolen devices have forestalled the members' capture.

Storytellers can find greater details of the Star Council in **Sorcerer, Revised Edition**. If you do not own that book, or if you prefer the use of dynamic mages over their sorcerous brethren, then treat Star Council members as the equivalent of Sons of Ether whose paradigm provides for scientific advances that duplicate all of the various elements of traditional UFO stories. Star Council members include discredited professors of astronomy, linguistics and physics. A few members are hackers who spend their time trying to crack the government's hidden databases of UFO secrets. A couple of the members are lawyers who have been disbarred and yet do their best to protect their brethren.

Thal'hun

Even paranoid groups of UFO-chasers have crackpots they refuse to acknowledge. For the Star Council the Thal'hun are these crackpots, fringe radicals who joined the Council in the early '60s and led many of those who believed in them into destruction. The Thal'hun believe that an ancient alien race advanced so greatly in science that it was like unto a pantheon of gods, but its world was destroyed in a terrible plague. The aliens, which they call Hui:xa, supposedly spread across the universe, hoping to discover those with whom they could share their enlightened science and rebuild their greatest city once again.

According to the Thal'hun, the science of the Hui:xa transcended the physical and could be transmitted through the sounds of their special linguistics. They claimed to be in contact with the entity Khuvon, who descended to Earth somewhere in Mesopotamia thousands of years ago. All of this might seem quite preposterous were it not for the fact that they can indeed muster their own sorcerous effects and that the expedition they convinced the Star Council to send to the Middle East was virtually destroyed by unknown forces.

The Thal'hun are mentioned in **Sorcerer, Revised Edition**, but their original, and more detailed, appearance was in **World of Darkness: Sorcerer**. As in the case of the Star Council, Storytellers who either don't possess these sources or would prefer to represent them as dynamic mages might find them best duplicated with Etherite magic. Thal'hun base their willworking upon a paradigm of hyperscience, in this case predicated upon the idea that the universe is controlled by specific harmonics. In recent times, the inner council of the Thal'hun has vanished, taking its most loyal followers and leaving the clueless or untrustworthy to search for another cult to join. The characters will hopefully discover that the Thal'hun have found their Khuvon and truly taken up its cause.

Stage Zero: Red Flag

Willie Spring has been hunted by UFOs as long as he can remember, or *not quite* remember, to be more accurate. He has been a member of the Ku Klux Klan (albeit only because his stepfather dragged him along as a teenager), Alcoholics Anonymous, the United States Army, the Star Council, the Thal'hun and half a dozen ragtag Internet-based help groups for the "abducted." Willie "Red" Spring is detailed in **The Fallen Tower: Las Vegas**. Be it through happenstance and sheer desperation, or through unexpected Internet revelations, Red decides to contact the characters of your troupe.

If any of the characters are active on UFO bulletin boards or similar conspiracy-oriented Internet groups, then this contact is his lead. Virtual Adepts or other mages with a hardcore computer bent might simply have come to his attention inadvertently through one of his various hacking attempts. If none of these options seems viable, the Storyteller could have a Virtual Adept or Son of Ether contact send Red in the players' characters' direction. Ralph Cannon, also from **Fallen Tower**, might be a good choice, particularly if the characters have contacted him before. Alternatively, characters investigating Technocratic equipment might be pointed toward Red by a frustrated colleague. If any member of the cabal has participated in assaults or investigations of Area 51 or the Advanced Energy Commission Construct, Red might have witnessed or heard of their work. Enterprising Storytellers can even conspire to have Red meet the characters by having him join them during an expedition into a super-secure Technocratic Construct.

It would be constraining and awkward to read a transcript of what Red says to the characters, so present the following generalities in your own words instead.

1. Red has been abducted by "aliens" more than once. He has very sparse memories of these incidents.

2. He is sure that there are two different types of aliens. One is the typical "Gray" described by most UFO believers. The other is some sort of yellow-scaled reptile.

3. He doesn't know why he is sure.

4. He also believes that the two alien species are at war with each other, but again is unsure why he thinks this.

5. He remembers hearing alien sounds during his abduction, which happen to mirror those sounds emitted by devices he's seen from Area 51. He doesn't purposefully reveal that such things are still in the hands of the Thal'hun or Star Council.

6. Some fruity occultist types (no offense intended) he met in San Francisco claimed that yellow-scaled reptiles attacked them.

Ideally, Red can convince the players' characters that he is serious despite his lack of solid information. Mages are likely to subject him to detection magic, and such will reinforce the idea that he is telling the truth as he knows it. Attempts to restore his lost memories should fail, or succeed only to the slight degree that the Storyteller needs to keep the story moving forward. With further conversation, Red will hopefully feel that the cabal is trustworthy enough to reveal information about the Star Council, Thal'hun or his occult acquaintances from San Francisco.

The Zigg'raugglurr

The first recorded sighting of these entities is claimed by representatives of the Order of Hermes in San Francisco. Hermetic scholars describe them as appearing as yellow floating blobs, sporadically changing size from a few inches to a few yards across, covered with reptilian scales and pulsating veins. Their fairly unwieldy name, Zigg'raugglurr, was assigned by Hermetic mages who recorded the first attempt to communicate with these beings — mages less worried about formality often just call them "Zigg." Repeat encounters with the same Zigg proved remarkably easier to resist, with mounting evidence suggesting that specimens actually possessed more knowledge of our world in early meetings and less later. The prevalent theories in the Order propose that these creatures exist beyond the Horizon, are capable of operating in the reputed fourth dimension, and are allied with the Nephandi.

The Order is only partially correct. The Zigg'raugglurr inhabit an alternate dimension outside this universe. Whether they were expelled from Creation or never a part of it remains unknown. Due to their existence outside our world, they interact with reality in a bizarre fashion. The alien Zigg might enter the timestream, step out of it and return at some other point. Similarly, they can enter the physical world, depart and return. Alternatively, they can manipulate the portions of their bodies entering three-dimensional space, seemingly changing shape or size. The Zigg do not possess Avatars, so they do not perform dynamic magic, yet their extradimensional natures and alien technology allow them to perform miraculous feats that can draw the wrath of Paradox spirits. Indeed Paradox spirits, when they do appear, seem particularly vicious and antagonistic toward the Zigg, probably because the outsiders are completely alien to reality.

While individual Zigg have certainly worked with Nephandi in the past, there is no true alliance there. The Zigg are not infernal beings — they are alien. The Order would be very surprised that the yellow-scaled beings have far more contact with the Technocracy than they have ever had with the Fallen Ones. The Zigg'raugglurr have devised methods of extracting an Avatar and harnessing it as a source of energy, but they can do so only in their own dimension. Paradox makes it dangerous for them to enter reality, so they have only done so rarely, but the rise of the Avatar Storm seems to have attracted their attention. Hermetics who encountered the Zigg in the early '90s claimed to have detected a mental impression from the aliens that there was a great change in the fabric of reality. Given their existence outside normal space-time, perhaps some of their early appearances were missed attempts to enter our universe during the Storm's eruption.

Zigg'raugglurr

Willpower 7, **Rage** 5, **Gnosis** 6, **Essence** 30
Charms: Airt Sense (physical world and "fourth" dimension only), Appear, Armor, Blast, Call for Aid (to other Zigg'raugglurr), Control Electrical Systems, Create Fire, Create Wind, Disable, Ease Pain, Iron Will, Materialize (costs one-half normal Essence), Mind Speech, Quake, Shapeshift (always has yellow reptilian appearance), Short Out, Spirit Away, Track
Materialized Attributes: Strength 1-10, Dexterity 2, Stamina 1-10 (always equal to Strength), Social and Mental Attributes equal to Gnosis
Abilities: Science (Dimensional) 4

Materialized Health Levels: 1-10 (same as Strength and Stamina)

Image: Zigg'raugglurr move in strange unison, due to the fact that they operate and perceive dimensions outside the One's creation. They can also vary their size by extruding differing degrees of themselves into physical space. Their favored shape is an uneven sphere with a thick hide, covered by yellow reptilian scales and pulsating veins. By manipulating their physical form's interaction with three-dimensional space, Zigg can assume other shapes, including a roughly humanoid one. Every form, however, is encased in ivory-yellow scales and thick veins.

Notes: Generally, Zigg can use their extradimensional natures to perceive beyond barriers and to communicate with each other outside the physical realm. If circumstance, or countermagic, demands a system for this ability, roll Gnosis for the alien, and contest it with the blocking mage. Individual Zigg vary in power, but the most common abilities exhibited are represented by the profile listed. Not every Zigg will be this powerful, and some prove much more so. Zigg are not spirits, so these powers should be presented as psychic or technological in nature as much as possible. Movements through time or space require the Zigg'raugglurr to exit reality and return at the new locale. The aliens appear to float or fly, but they are actually interacting with unseen forces in their own dimension. Clever mages might also discover this and figure out a way to interfere.

Ka Luon

The "Grays." Modern pop culture and UFO nuts around the world have embraced the vision of an alien species that has plagued humanity in secret for the past five or six decades at very least. As with many things in **Mage**, the truth of the matter is both shrouded and subject to one's point of view. The Void Engineers have encountered beings during their space and dimensional travels which certainly fit the model — gray humanoids with large black eyes and thin spidery limbs. These beings have been observed abducting and experimenting upon humans, and at times, they have come into direct conflict with the Void Engineers, particularly the Border Corps Division. Nevertheless, more questions arise with each answer that seems apparent.

The Psychopomps, described in **Manifesto: Transmissions from the Rogue Council** and **The Infinite Tapestry**, appear to a person as he unconsciously expects them to be, so they have been directly responsible for some of the sightings of "aliens" fitting the description of the Grays. Since the rise of the Avatar Storm, the Border Corps has been largely grounded or cut off from Control, so contact with the Grays has been restricted primarily to Earth. Void Engineers don't have detailed knowledge of the Psychopomps, though, so there is no basis for comparison. Additionally, mystic-minded mages would point out that spirits spawn in the Umbra according to human dreams and thus "coincidentally" prove legends to be true. Some of these mages refer to the spiritually spawned images of the aliens as Ka Luon. It is possible that all three explanations are equally valid. Some contacts with the Grays have been with an actual alien race, others with spirits who take the form of human images of that same race and a few with Psychopomps appearing as the "alien presence" the witness expects.

Whatever the complete truth of the matter is, the Void Engineers have been engaged in conflict since just after World War II with an alien race that certainly fits the description of the Grays. While officers of the Border Corps have certainly attacked vessels they believed were operated by the Grays, one could only call this a "war" in the sense that one uses the word when referring to the War on Drugs or the War on Terrorism. The Grays are hard to catch and armed with incredible technology, and those who have traveled this far seem to be small in number.

> ### Enough with the Aliens
>
> For some **Mage** players, any acknowledgement that the Grays are anything more than spirits tapping into human experience might damage the feeling of the game. Others might even be offended if the aliens of pop culture show up at all. Try to anticipate whether this applies to your troupe, and adjust accordingly. Remember that there is a great deal of opportunity here to utilize the tricks of Lovecraft, Hitchcock or *The X-Files*, and hint at greater things without showing them. On the other hand, this is an end-of-the-world chronicle. If some of the secrets of the universe don't come out now, then when?
>
> The Zigg offer another way to approach this problem, as well. They are unfamiliar and therefore unlikely to invoke any of the jokes or silly references the Grays might. The unknown is generally scarier than what we think we understand. Don't ignore the presence of the Psychopomps either. The soul guides are firm reminders that even amid the technological slant of the world, a mystic force is at work.

DEALING WITH RED

Willie "Red" Spring would like for the characters to meet some friends of his in San Francisco. He will fervently try to get help, though he really doesn't know precisely what help he needs. "They are after me" and "The truth must get out" are phrases he repeats a lot. As the characters speak to Red, he continuously checks his watch, fiddles with a pager, idly taps his ring (set with a small piece of metal from a UFO site) on the table and performs various other fidgety seeming actions. Although he doesn't consciously realize it — and neither do the characters unless they check for such — Red is enacting magic in defense against an oncoming assault. Outside, the clouds roll in and the wind picks up. Before the conversation comes to end, the rumble of thunder is clearly audible in the distance. Red grows more concerned, "They can control the weather with satellites, you know. Sometimes they do it just before big operations."

With a crash, lightning strikes a nearby power transformer and the lights surge brighter and then flicker out. Let the characters fumble around in the dark for a few moments, perhaps taking out lighters or invoking magic. When the lights come back up, whether due to your characters' actions or simply when they recover from the surge, Willie is gone. His laptop rests on the table, and even though it is currently closed, it is turned on and emitting a strange series of high-pitched beeps.

Red seems to have vanished without a trace. Appropriate Correspondence Effects suggest that he ran out during the blackout, was pulled into the sky about 100 yards and then disappeared entirely. Anyone physically giving chase will find a spot some distance from where the troupe met Red where the asphalt (or grass or whatever is nearby) is burning in a perfect circle approximately three feet across.

Try not to completely frustrate your players. The characters cannot reach Red because he is beyond reality for the time being, but give them as many clues as you can without ruining the story. In particular you might want to use the laptop as a way to provide further information along the way. Who knows what encrypted files Red has set to deliver to certain Internet addresses in case he disappeared, *again*?

Also, try to prepare yourself for the innumerable ways that mages will try to get more information before and after Red's disappearance. Mind Effects could read his thoughts, but he is being truthful enough anyway. His mind is truly missing chunks of memory, which would require Mind 4 to repair with at least a success or two per scene recovered. Perhaps the most pertinent new piece of information that might be discovered is that he knows, but is *not* mentioning, that the Star Council has actual technological artifacts from Area 51 in its possession. If pressed on this issue, Red will insist that he has seen such things but would prefer not to reveal their precise locations. Even if someone forces him to do so, the best he can do is to give the addresses of closed offices in San Francisco where the devices once rested. Prime scans suggest that the circle of fire was actually created by Willie, perhaps as a subconscious attempt to defend himself. Reconstructing the disappearance with suitable Time and Forces Effects in order to see what happened in the dark suggests that Red passed through the door as he fled, though it is unclear whether this is an Effect he somehow triggered or one created by whatever took him.

Finally, if the players dawdle too long, they might discover that a single Zigg has taken interest in just what its compatriots' prey was doing. It hovers above the structure, observing for a time. If the Storyteller desires, the Zigg might decide to try to seize one of the members of the cabal if it witnesses any evidence that they possess Avatars. Tailor the alien's strength to that of the characters, but lone Zigg are generally more capable of handling themselves and therefore more dangerous. If the troupe seems pretty hot on the trail to San Francisco, you might avoid revealing the Zigg at this time in order to keep its appearance from derailing the characters' plans.

STAGE ONE: EARLY WARNING

As the characters begin to investigate the clues left or given by Red, the first true signs that something is wrong manifest. Magic becomes more difficult and the players likely have little or no idea why yet. Should they just want to mock or ignore Red, then perhaps this will prove the seriousness of his claims, or at least indicate that he deserves investigation. A number of routes suggest themselves, but the majority of them point to San Francisco. The Star Council, Thal'hun and Red's occult acquaintances all hail from there.

Alternatively they might decide to investigate Area 51, but this is certainly the more dangerous path. Eventually you are going to want to point them in this direction, but without the knowledge of what they

150 ASCENSION

really seek, they are not likely to benefit greatly from taking on the Advanced Energy Commission Construct in Nellis Air Force Base (see **The Fallen Tower: Las Vegas**). Red's laptop might contain addresses or phone numbers in San Francisco. It might also be downloading wireless emails, including UFO enthusiast mail lists abuzz with word that black planes have been seen flying north of Las Vegas, near Area 51.

More important, though, is the rash of emails insisting that someone the individual writer knows has been abducted. This is reflected in odd news stories as well. The cabal might hear a couple of missing person's reports on legitimate news stations, while crazy late-night radio shows claim that dozens of abductions have occurred all around the world. Depending on the time frame of your game, the next day's supermarket rags and questionable papers across the country carry stories of aliens capturing subjects who disappear without a trace. Legitimate news organizations do have a very slight increase in kidnapping stories, but nothing particularly extraordinary. If people are indeed disappearing, they must be isolated madmen and loner eccentrics… but isn't that what people think about mages already?

What's Really Happening?

Unless you, as the Storyteller, alter the plot to suit your purposes, the disappearances in this story are not merely kidnappings or false stories of alien abduction told to garner attention on the behalf of some lonely freaks. The population of Earth is losing Avatars one by one. Two competing factions are capturing mages and stripping away their Avatars, each faction doing so for its own reasons. The secret thefts of humanity's spiritual shards of Prime have been going on for some time. Now they are happening with unprecedented frequency and purpose. The very fabric of magic in the universe is being unraveled one thread at a time, or perhaps it would be more accurate to say that it is being spun onto a new spindle held elsewhere. Of course this is occurring beyond the public eye, except perhaps in media venues traditionally perceived as fraudulent or absurd. The end of the magical world approaches steadily and quietly.

The Exceptional Antagonists

As it weren't bad enough that the cabal's magic is impeded in the physical world, that of their primary foes in this story is less affected. The alien Zigg have harnessed a number of Avatars already, and as they realize that the physical world is becoming more difficult to affect, they begin to transmit some of the captured Quintessence back through dimensional links to their

The Death of Magic

Portraying the death of magic as a story is all well and good, but this is a game. If there are no mechanics to reflect its passing, then some players simply won't take the story as seriously. Even if your troupe really enjoys the theatrics of the end of willworking, you might want some systems to reflect the changes as they occur. Each stage of this story includes proposed changes to the standard rules, each representing a further deterioration of the ability of mages to enact magic. Of course, you are the Storyteller, and you might wish to change these suggestions slightly should some detail not match your personal vision of magic fading away. Gauge how the decline of willworking might have progressed differently than proposed herein and employ the suggested rules accordingly, or change them altogether.

Stage-One Magic Alteration

The pattern of the Tapestry weaves a bit tighter, or perhaps its mystical weaving becomes a bit threadbare, and magic becomes noticeably harder to perform for the first time in the modern era. Add a +1 penalty to all magical difficulties and increase the threshold (see **Mage: The Ascension** pg. 219) by one. Remember that any target number raised above 9 by difficulty modifiers stays at 9 and adds an additional threshold for each point above 9. In general, most Effects will increase in difficulty by one and lose one success in effectiveness. This increased difficulty affects Technocrats as well, as they discover that their hyperscience is as hampered as the magic of their Tradition foes. The creative spark of mankind is suppressed, regardless of paradigm. This increased magical difficulty similarly thickens the Gauntlet, raising the difficulty of Spirit effects by the same +1 penalty and requiring an extra success.

Zigg compatriots. At the first stage, the yellow-scaled aliens send enough Quintessence to reduce their invading forces' magical target numbers and threshold by one. At the second stage, they boost this energy in order to reduce magic target numbers and thresholds by two. At stages three, four and five, they increase the reduction to three. Of course at stages one through three, this merely evens out the penalty caused by the death of magic. At fourth and fifth stages, it only partly erases that penalty. At the sixth stage, they are cut off entirely, unable to transmit. By that time, however, the Zigg have already succeeded at their goal or been defeated by the cabal.

The other faction likely to be antagonistic to the cabal is not so readily protected. The Thal'hun have contacted their mysterious patron Khuvon and joined its efforts to rebuild the mystic realm of Zoraster. Consisting of mages (sorcerers) and spirits, the Thal'hun leadership, self-styled Disciples of Zoraster, are as harmed by the reduction in magic as your characters are. They have time on their side, however, and they merely need to continue their capture of Avatars in order to realize their goals. Therefore, while magical acts are more difficult, this difficulty only slows their work rather than stopping it entirely. It is even possible that they will recruit enough new members that their rituals continue unabated in the least.

The Golden Gate

Everything Red and his laptop had to say hints at San Francisco. Here in the Crown Jewel of the Pacific, the cabal can find hints related to the Star Council, the Thal'hun and the Hermetic cabal that first encountered the Zigg. The particular order of investigating those links is not important, and it is even possible for a troupe to follow the story to the end without ever following all of these leads.

The Star Council

Scarred by interactions with the Thal'hun and the various Technocratic and government agencies that have hunted it, the Star Council has gone underground. Though of its membership still resides in the San Francisco Bay Area, the organization has no public offices there anymore and does not operate in the open. As such, the characters might have difficulty locating any of the UFOlogist brotherhood. Storytellers may let players roll a number of dice equal to the portion of their rating in *Contacts* or *Allies* that reside in the Bay Area in order to get a lead on the Council. Alternatively, Correspondence Effects might be employed, especially if they are conjunctional with various clues the cabal possesses. For example, Correspondence and Forces combined could search for copies of the alien sound files on Red's laptop. Should anyone have scanned the metal on Red's ring, she might compare its Pattern with those scanned through a Correspondence-Matter Effect.

Despite the difficulty involved, a cabal of mages worthy of its salt is likely to discover the information it seeks somehow. Unless the Storyteller prefers some other locale, the cabal probably finds one of the warehouses wherein the Star Council has stashed one or more of its alien artifacts for study. Provided they don't set off the alarms, which call various councilors' cell phones rather than calling the police, or if they knock peaceably and convince the trio of their good intentions, the characters can manage a meeting with the Zero Chips. Annie Thomason, her boyfriend Todd Campbell and their friend Melvin "Meltdown" Dawson practically live on junk food smuggled into the warehouse while they surf the Internet and study the Council's most promising artifact. If the cabal insists upon violence, the Zero Chips probably can't handle them, but they are more resourceful than mages might initially credit.

Andy Thomason

Background: Annie is 24 years old, and the child of a Haight-Ashbury hippie family that moved there during the '60s. Pulling herself up by her bootstraps, she put herself through college while working various electronics retail sales jobs. Annie was almost finished with college when she joined with the Star Council and soon realized that she couldn't risk continuing school. Technically a dropout, Thomason could have held down any number of high-tech, high-paying jobs. Instead she lives in a warehouse hoping to find the secrets of the universe in a stolen device.

Image: Annie is dark haired and attractive in a geeky way. She tends to dress in cheap polo shirts (left unbuttoned) and loose khakis, but at least they are clean.

Roleplaying Hints: Okay, so you fucked up, but this thing you're working on is the wave of the future. Meanwhile, at least you and Todd are getting along well. Maybe someday you can give him a good home.

Faction: The Star Council
Essence: Pattern
Nature: Architect
Demeanor: Director
Attributes: Strength 2, Dexterity 3, Stamina 2, Charisma 3, Manipulation 3, Appearance 3, Perception 2, Intelligence 3, Wits 2
Abilities: Academics 3, Alertness 2, Awareness 1, Computer 3, Crafts (UFO scams) 1, Drive 1, Enigmas 1, Investigation 1, Law 1, Science (Electronic Engineering) 3, Stealth 1, Subterfuge 2, Technology 2, UFO Lore 1
Backgrounds: Allies 2 (Todd and Melvin), Arcane 1, Contacts 2 (Star Council), Resources 2 (occasional computer consulting)
Arete: Linear Mage (per **Sorcerer**)
Paths: Conveyance 2, Hellfire 1
Willpower: 5
Quintessence: 0
Paradox: 0
Resonance: (Static) Keeping it Together 1

Todd Campbell

Background: Todd met Annie in college and has been in love with her ever since. How she got him into this crap, he still doesn't really know, but here they are. It all makes sense in a funny way, too. Though technically inclined, Todd is not one of the Awakened.

Image: Somewhat muscular, somewhat overweight, attentive and caring. Todd wears loose black jeans and often-grease-stained shirts. Though he is comfortable with computers, Todd sometimes feels pushed into the "simplicity" of auto mechanics by the things that Annie and Melvin manage to do. Of the three Zero Chips, Todd is the only one who carries a gun — specifically an unregistered 9mm automatic.

Roleplaying Hints: You don't understand a lot of what Annie and Melvin talk about, but you know it isn't because you are intellectually inferior. Somehow they just have the knack for things you don't quite grasp yet. Sometimes it pisses you off, but you know that Annie tries to keep you in her life and someday the two of you just might figure out how to have a normal one.

Nature: Caregiver
Demeanor: Conformist
Attributes: Strength 3, Dexterity 2, Stamina 3, Charisma 3, Manipulation 2, Appearance 2, Perception 2, Intelligence 3, Wits 3
Abilities: Academics 1, Alertness 2, Athletics 2, Brawl 1, Computer 2, Crafts (Mechanic) 2, Dodge 1, Drive 2,

Firearms 1, Intimidation 1, Investigation 1, Occult 1, Science 1, Streetwise 1, Technology 2
Backgrounds: Allies 2 (Annie and Melvin), Arcane 1, Contacts 2 (Star Council), Resources 1 (part-time jobs)
Willpower: 4

Melvin "Meltdown" Dawson

Background: Melvin is only 19. He's been arrested twice for hacking, and he sincerely believes that he will never see his third strike. He lost his scholarship due to his criminal record, so he never went to college at all. For Melvin, the ultimate school is the World Wide Web, which has given him a cold and bleak image of the world.

Image: When Melvin remembers to change clothes at all, he puts on another pair of perfectly matched black jean shorts and some obscure band T-shirt. He always wears his "The Truth is out There" button and is never more than arm's reach from a laptop, computer or PDA — and all of them have to be wired to the Internet.

Roleplaying Hints: The universe is abuzz with electromagnetic signals of every kind. From the sounds of alien cultures trying to communicate to the dying screams of supernovas, everything speaks on the same wavelength. All you gotta do is listen. Mankind is the same, only we're still stuck on this primitive Internet. Maybe you can crack the device and teach the whole world to speak in a new tongue.

Faction: The Star Council
Essence: Questing
Nature: Visionary

Demeanor: Deviant

Attributes: Strength 2, Dexterity 2, Stamina 2, Charisma 1, Manipulation 2, Appearance 2, Perception 3, Intelligence 4, Wits 3

Abilities: Academics 2, Alertness 3, Awareness 2, Crafts (Computer Components) 3, Computer 4 (Hacking), Enigmas 3, Investigation 1, Science (Mathematics) 2, Subterfuge 1, Technology 3, UFO Lore 2

Backgrounds: Allies 2 (Todd and Melvin), Arcane 1, Contacts 2 (Star Council), Resources 2 (stolen credit card numbers)

Arete: Linear Mage (per **Sorcerer**)

Paths: Conveyance 3, Hellfire 2, Weather Control 2

Willpower: 5

Quintessence: 0

Paradox: 0

Resonance: (Dynamic) New Approach 1

If the characters identify their connection with Red, or establish an alternate connection to the UFOlogists, the Zero Chips are friendly. The Zero Chips are not likely to turn over the Star Council's alien artifact, but they might be convinced to allow the cabal to examine it. The techno-trio has determined that the flat metal object, scored with silvery markings, might be some sort of computing device, but it cannot discern what it is designed to do. Appropriate Effects could discover that the device is a control panel for an alien craft, and that it serves as a special guidance system. Correspondence-Spirit conjunctional Effects might show that the device could potentially control a vessel with extradimensional capabilities.

If the characters can convince the Zero Chips of the importance of letting them use the device (through roleplay and appropriate Social rolls), or if they overcome the trio, the device can be transported with relative ease, provided one doesn't use airports. The panel is about 18 inches wide by 42 inches long, and it will readily set off nearly every alarm at an airport security terminal. The electromagnetic field projected by the panel will also set off police radar and the like, though a simple shield against this field can be created with a Forces Effect or some sort of Matter shielding.

If the Storyteller deems that the cabal needs help, members of the Zero Chips might be willing to tag along. Alternatively, they might betray the cabal to the Thal'hun (if necessary to progress the story). Should the troupe need other clues, or prodding, it is possible that members of the Zero Chips might be "red shirts" slain in dramatic or informative manners.

The Thal'hun

Finding the Thal'hun offices requires similar magic or *Contacts* rolls as discovering the Star Council did. The difference is that the Thal'hun are no longer in residence. Mundane investigations (Intelligence + Investigation, for example) might reveal that the cult's lease expired five months ago and that the leasing party did not leave a forwarding address. Depending on which Spheres are employed, additional information

No Sorcerers

The Star Council and the Thal'hun are sorcerers — also called linear mages or hedge mages by various supplements for the World of Darkness. They are best presented as factions of the same order found within the pages of **Sorcerer, Revised Edition** or **World of Darkness: Sorcerer**. If you do not possess either of those White Wolf publications, then you can easily present the two UFOlogist groups as independent, but similar, to the Sons of Ether or Virtual Adepts. Just substitute foci related to their UFO/alien-studies paradigm and plan their use of rotes accordingly.

Alternatively, you can follow the static path presented for various spirits. Simply invent a number of Charms or individual Effects your sorcerer practitioners can perform. Each one of those powers is part of a limited catalog of magic the character can wield, yet each clearly puts the sorcerer beyond the ken of mortal man. This approach is certainly less ideal than that presented by **Sorcerer, Revised Edition**, but **The Infinite Tapestry** and the **Mage Storytellers Companion** cover it in varying detail.

might be obtained via magical means. The Thal'hun leadership finally managed to contact the spiritual icon Khuvon and embarked upon a new mission to meet its goals. The inner circle and its followers have taken to calling themselves the Disciples of Zoraster, after the invisible city of light reputed to be the goal of their spiritual master. Extremely clever and successful magical investigations might even discover that the Thal'hun Disciples have taken to fomenting smaller splinter cults that specialize in tracking and kidnapping obscure figures of the occult.

The Hermetics

When the cabal starts to search for the Hermetic cabal of San Francisco, alerts are very likely to go off unless the mages take extreme precautions to ensure otherwise. Assuming that they do not remain exceedingly careful, or that at least one of their attempts fails, the Hermetics become aware of the search and manage to convince the visiting semi-pariah Mark Hallward Gillan to appear on their behalf. As the cabal closes in on the Bay Area Order of Hermes chantry, Gillan closes in on them. Ultimately he contacts the characters before they pinpoint the Hermetics, and he tries to arrange a meeting to warn against interference.

Gillan is detailed in the **Tradition Book: Order of Hermes** though he also appeared in a previous edition of **Mage: The Ascension**. If you do not possess either of those resources, assume that he is a powerful Adept who specializes in Forces and Correspondence. Gillan is known as a bit of a loose cannon among old-school Tradition mages, and the fact that the chantry called upon him might be a sign that they feel threatened and want to discourage outside contact. Gillan will introduce himself as a "Sentinel" of the Hermetic cabal that the characters seek and insist that he has been chosen to represent the cabal's interests and security.

Prepared by the Hermetic cabal, which has no desire to meet the characters' cabal or any other force in these dangerous times, Gillan will answer a number of questions. Yes, the characters did encounter an alien presence. They termed this alien race the Zigg'raugglurr. The species seemed to exist in the fourth dimension and did not pass through time necessarily in a forward, linear direction. The Zigg'raugglurr varied in size from a few inches across to a couple of yards in diameter, and they were covered in yellow reptilian scales and pulsating veins. Currently two members of the Hermetic cabal are missing without a trace, and the cabal believes that the Zigg'raugglurr are somehow connected despite the fact that they haven't encountered the alien spirits in years. The yellow-scaled creatures are somehow connected to the Nephandi. (This "fact" is a red herring produced by misjudgments on the Order's part.) Of course you are invited to have Gillan provide additional information if you feel it is necessary to propel the story forward.

Gillan's screening of the cabal, in his role as Sentinel, is intended to help invoke a sense of increased paranoia and distrust. If your cabal simply won't cooperate with such an approach, feel free to have the characters meet the actual San Francisco members of the Order of Hermes. Their statistics are not provided here, though you can easily assemble a suitable membership from the **Tradition Book: Order of Hermes** sample characters. If you can do so without wrecking the sense of story line reality, have Gillan ultimately decide to offer his assistance in the future should the characters need it. They will indeed require his help all too soon if they can get it. Whether he offers a mystic link or a cell phone is up to you.

Stage Two: Insufficient Data

Thus far, the characters are probably still equipped to figure out the plots of the Zigg or the Thal'hun, and they are at least on the trail. Of course the opposition doesn't know this, and it has potentially already been turned onto their existence. If the mages have not yet faced a Zigg attack, then you should consider invoking the lone alien observer from Stage One as it seeks to capture and abduct one of the Avatar-bearing specimens it spotted in contact with Red previously. The timing for this particular event is best left to you, but it should occur preferably at some point when it is late and lonely, or when the cabal is investigating a depressed and broken area of the city or its surroundings.

The Thal'hun Attack

The Thal'hun on the other hand, are turned onto the cabal by a snitch who observes the mages snooping around the abandoned Thal'hun offices. If the characters never do so, then perhaps the snitch instead spots the cabal visiting the Star Council warehouse. Should neither of these incidents occur, it is always possible that the Thal'hun is busy tracking Gillan and discovers the cabal in this fashion.

Chapter Five: A Whimper not a Bang

Stage-Two Magic Alteration

It is up to you when you invoke this level of trouble with magic, but it should ideally occur at some point during the second stage of the story. Mages experience significant trouble enforcing their will upon the universe. Add a +2 penalty to all magical difficulties and increase the threshold by two. The thickening of the Gauntlet begins to affect sources of magic in the physical world. All Nodes decrease by one point, and Wonders require an extra point of Quintessence each time they operate.

Whatever path proves to be the primary link to the cabal, the Thal'hun mean business. Luckily, they do not understand the power they are contesting against. Generally, the Thal'hun are used to exceeding the occult and scientific expertise of anyone with whom they contend. An attack against the cabal will consist of one or more sorcerers and a handful of cultist thugs.

The Thal'hun are no longer content with the pursuit of knowledge of their alien masters. The inner council has established contact with their ancient spiritual leader Khuvon and currently strives to aid it in the conquest of occulted Earth and the rejuvenation of the hidden dimensional city of Zoraster. Although they have lost some of their less fervent adherents, the Thal'hun have gained a purpose that inspires strength and energy. In honor of their new role, many of them now call themselves the Disciples of Zoraster. Of course most of the cultists do not truly understand what precisely they are accomplishing. Nonetheless, provided it performs the correct harmonics at the appropriate time, the Thal'hun leadership is able to turn its efforts toward powerful ends.

Currently, the Thal'hun has essentially devolved into a kidnapping cult, intent upon forcing its abductees into becoming new cult members or living out their lives in mental rehabilitation. They exist primarily to provide new subjects for their spiritual leader Khuvon and to hopefully ensure the empowerment of the new city of spirituality, the new Zoraster.

Where precisely the Thal'hun attack takes place is up to the Storyteller, of course. The Disciples of Zoraster, long suffering as relative loners themselves, recognize the value of isolating victims and taking them when they have the least protection. Hotel rooms, stalled cars on the freeway (perhaps purposefully arranged somehow), lonely stretches

of countryside and creepy back-alley neighborhoods are favored kidnapping grounds. If you are running a particularly social or political game, you might even seek to bring the characters in via recruitment to a San Francisco social club for the mystically inclined, which happens to be a front for the Thal'hun. If the cabal is on its way to Area 51 from San Francisco, then the desert highway along which they travel should serve as a perfect ground for ambush.

Whatever the circumstances are, the attack consists of one Thal'hun for every two mages in the cabal, rounded down, and one cultist thug for each cabal member. If, for example, the cabal consisted of four members, then the Thal'hun would send four thugs and two Disciples of Zoraster after the group.

Thal'hun Thug

Background: These people have found purpose in the Thal'hun. Preaching of the harmonics of the universe, the cult's message seems to be the perfect blend of technological futures and metaphysical promise. The Disciples of Zoraster insist that the great Khuvon will bring its city of light into this world with their assistance.

Image: The thugs are not particularly good at thinking for themselves. They are physically oriented, desperately seeking some sort of salvation. Many are heavy set, unkempt and poorly dressed. Thal'hun thugs are armed with pistols of varying caliber, though most of them are equally handy with their fists.

Roleplaying Hints: Khuvon promises New Zoraster; The masters heed the words of Khuvon. You have but to satisfy their wishes to please Khuvon.

Nature: Conformist
Demeanor: Bravo
Attributes: Strength 3, Dexterity 3, Stamina 3, Charisma 2, Manipulation 2, Appearance 2, Perception 2, Intelligence 2, Wits 3
Abilities: Alertness 2, Athletics 2, Brawl 2, Cosmology 1, Dodge 1, Drive 1, Firearms 2, Intimidation 2, Linguistics 1 (Luz'at), Lore (Thal'hun) 1, Medicine 1, Melee 2, Occult 1, Science 1, Stealth 1, Streetwise 1, Survival 1
Backgrounds: Contacts 3 (Thal'hun), Resources 2 (day job)
Willpower: 4

Disciple of Zoraster

Background: The Disciple of Zoraster, whether man or woman, has belonged to the Thal'hun for years. She has spent untold hours studying the secret harmonic tongue of the Hui:xa and learned to invoke its power. The 1,000 words of Luz'at barely scratch the surface of Khuvon's power and the Disciple dreams of conquering the remaining secrets of the ancient Hui:xa.

Image: The Disciple of Zoraster dresses in loose, comfortable business-casual clothes. These are the outfits seen in a typical office on Friday, but unacceptable the rest of the week. Pastels with circular or mathematical patterns are preferred.

Roleplaying Hints: The Hui:xa are the secret masters that every mystical cult has hoped to contact. You have the edge because you have realized that there is nothing mystical about the scientific masters of the universe's harmonics. Khuvon is the race's representative on Earth and you desire nothing less than to help it restore the ancient city of Zoraster to its ancient and universal glory.

Faction: Thal'hun
Essence: Dynamic
Nature: Bravo
Demeanor: Visionary
Attributes: Strength 2, Dexterity 3, Stamina 2, Charisma 2, Manipulation 2, Appearance 2, Perception 3, Intelligence 3, Wits 3
Abilities: Academics 2, Alertness 2, Awareness 2, Computer 2, Crafts (Sound Equipment) 2, Enigmas 2, Investigation 1, Linguistics 2 (Luz'at, Spanish), Meditation 1, Science (Harmonics) 2, Subterfuge 1, Technology 2, UFO Lore 2
Backgrounds: Allies 2 (Thal'hun cultists), Arcane 1, Contacts 3 (Thal'hun), Resources 2
Arete: Linear Mage (per **Sorcerer**)
Paths: Conveyance 3, Hellfire 3, Weather Control 3
Willpower: 5
Quintessence: 0
Paradox: 0
Resonance: (Dynamic) Sonic 3

Should the Disciples of Zoraster succeed in capturing the characters, they individually subject each of them to a ritual hoping to give Khuvon a chance to turn them to its needs. Khuvon will eventually strip the Avatar from the mage's being and entrap it within the hidden realm of Zoraster.

If the characters defeat the Thal'hun, they discover evidence that suggests that the Disciples of Zoraster are busy planning various illicit operations against Area 51 in the Nellis Air Force Base north of Las Vegas. The level of detail is up to the Storyteller, but it should be sufficient to point the characters toward the Void Engineer stronghold. Perhaps more important to the themes of this story, the troupe should find suitable evidence that the Thal'hun have abducted dozens of mages for unknown purposes.

Stage Three: Yellow Desert

If all goes well, the characters should be headed across California into the Nevada desert, on their way to the Area 51 region of Nellis Air Force Base. Thus far they have gained access to a strange alien control panel combined with the fact that the Thal'hun and the Star Council both have interest in Area 51. If they are paying especial attention, the characters might even have figured out that the Zigg'raugglurr are aliens who might require special means, perhaps even an Area 51 spaceship.

As the cabal travels through the desert, the Zigg'raugglurr try to take advantage of its isolated position. Whether you enforce the Stage-Three Magic Alteration before or after the assault depends upon your sense of timing. Whichever option you choose, one Zigg'raugglurr alien per mage in the cabal attacks. See the earlier statistics for the Zigg attackers.

Initially the Zigg circle the cabal like distant UFOs on the horizon. As they gather information about the cabal, the Zigg close in and begin their attack. If possible, the Zigg will grab any mage they can and transport him to their extradimensional realm.

Stage-Three Magic Alteration

Static reality grows frighteningly strong. Add a +3 penalty to all magical difficulties and increase their threshold by three. Penalize Nodes and Wonders as per Stage Two. At this level, physics begin to dampen other mystic traits of the mage. Treat all *Avatar*, *Arcane*, *Dream*, *Destiny* and magical Backgrounds as one point lower. Familiars are reduced one point in rating as well, and if they are reduced to 0, they become mundane creatures. Other mystical ratings similarly reduced to 0 become ordinary and non-magical as well. More subtly, but perhaps more dangerously, the mundane paradigm expands. At this stage and higher, cameras and other digital or mechanical recording media count as witnesses for the purposes of determining "vulgar with witnesses." All one-point supernatural Merits are lost. Fortunately one-point supernatural Flaws fade away as well. Merits and Flaws worth more points, with a magical origin, decrease by one point at the Storyteller's discretion. If the description of the Merit or Flaw is not already scaled in effect, try to describe to the player what the reduced rating means.

Stage Four: Key to the City

Having crossed the desert of Nevada, the cabal comes upon the outer reaches of the Nellis Air Force Base. The district that every map calls "Area 51" beckons from beyond barbwire and chain link fences. Storytellers with access to **The Fallen Tower: Las Vegas** should seriously consider pitting Major Thomas Houston and his Void Engineer cyborgs (Corporals Liz Smith and David Harrison) against the cabal. For Storytellers who do not possess that supplement, consider Houston to be an Adept Void Engineer who specializes in Forces, Correspondence and Spirit (Dimensional Science) Spheres. His followers are armed with built-in Wonders that provide infrared vision, increased strength and lethal razor claws. They are armed with X-5 Protectors and submachine guns.

The outer fences are electrified such that they cause three bashing levels of damage each turn of contact unless the mage uses magic, or perhaps a Technology roll, to bypass them. Physically crawling across the barbwire requires a successful Athletics roll, with the paired Attribute being the lesser of Dexterity or Stamina. Once inside the installation, the mages must succeed on at least three Stealth checks to avoid patrols of five-20 military personnel. Such personnel are mundane mortals, but heavily armed and authorized to shoot without asking questions.

Getting into an armed fortress that is funded by the vast wealth of the United States military and bolstered by the hyperscience of the Technocracy is probably impossible for most cabals. Without some sort of aid, they just aren't going to be able to get past the security that is likely to face down their efforts. Luckily, they might have gained some help before they came. If Gillan is amenable to helping them, he draws upon his contacts in nearby Las Vegas, and they cause numerous problems in the City of Sin's metropolitan area. As the cabal watches from the scrub bushes beyond Area 51's fences, soldiers and Technocratic agents depart to suppress Gillan. Whether he survives the attack is up to the Storyteller, though the end of the chronicle might render the point moot depending upon player and Storyteller tastes. Whatever the case, Gillan helps turn the tide for now. From mysterious, suspicious-looking "bomb" packages to metamathematical manipulation of the gambling wheels of as many casinos as possible, Gillan and his contacts in Las Vegas put the screws to the Technocracy and its desire for a quiet sense of normal. Gillan doesn't even hope to defeat the Union in a single pitched battle, but his operations do succeed in giving the characters the opportunity to sneak past the remaining guards.

Base Soldiers

Attributes: Strength 3, Dexterity 3, Stamina 3, Charisma 2, Manipulation 2, Appearance 2, Perception 3, Intelligence 2, Wits 3

Abilities: Alertness 2, Brawl 2, Computer 1, Dodge 1, Drive 1, Firearms 3, Intimidation 1, Melee 1, Specialized Knowledge (Military Procedure) 3, Stealth 1, Streetwise 1, Subterfuge 1, Technology 1

Willpower: 5

Equipment: hvy. pistol, assault rifle, radio, military uniform, Kevlar vest (3 armor protection, -2 to Dexterity dice pools)

If the characters rely on exceptionally absurd measures to break into Nellis, or particularly loud ones, they might attract the attention of even more powerful mages who are part of the Construct that actively manages the air force base. A worst-case scenario might involve attracting the attention of the Master Technocrat, Brigadier General Oscar Martin and/or the Syndicate representative who stays in the Nellis Federal Prison Camp in Area 2, George Carreau. Both individuals appear in **The Fallen Tower: Las Vegas**, though Storytellers without that book might simply wish to present the pair as Master-level Technocratic mages of the appropriate Conventions.

Provided they follow clues found in Thal'hun or Star Council data, the characters will hopefully find themselves headed toward Hangar 7 of Area 51. There they will find a heavily guarded alien vessel. Heavily guarded means anything from a dozen to a score of soldiers armed with assault rifles, and potentially anything from a jeep or two to an armored vehicle or attack helicopter.

The vessel's guidance system has been stripped from it, but if all has gone well, this item will happen to be the panel the troupe gained earlier in the story. Intelligence + Technology rolls providing at least five successes allow the characters to install the panel. Alternatively, magic action rolls, involving mostly Forces or Matter (potentially paired with Correspondence or the like), can prove effective in determining what happened. Ideally, the cabal manages to hijack an alien vessel, armed with the appropriate controls, and it catapults into the extradimensional spaces where Zoraster lies.

> ### Stage-Four Magic Alteration
> The whole of the physical world becomes extremely static and dangerous for mages who continue to thwart it. Add a +3 penalty to all magical difficulties and increase their threshold by four. Reduce Nodes, Wonders, Familiars and all mystic traits by two points in rating. For all vulgar Effects, add two points of Paradox in addition to any points that would otherwise be received. Supernatural Merits and Flaws worth two points or less fade from reality, with higher ratings reduced by two points.

Stage Five: The Final Assault

Screaming through the spiritual or dimensional barriers, the cabal arrives in the vicinity of the city the Thal'hun called the New Zoraster, by harnessing the Star Council's control panel. If all goes well, the cabal learns a number of great secrets here. Ideally the characters discover that the "Zoraster" of the Thal'hun is a Horizon Realm wherein the powerful spirit called Khuvon has been putting Avatars in order to save them from the Avatar Storm and to keep them from the clutches of the Zigg'raugglurr. Zoraster does happen to resemble a vast alien city, as described in Thal'hun legend, but this is not coincidental — the Thal'hun have been receiving transmissions from Khuvon *and* the Zigg'raugglurr for a long time. Bits and pieces of the truth are actually lodged in their pseudo-science cult.

If the characters fail to stop the Zigg'raugglurr from breaching Zoraster, the entities burst through the sky barriers of the city in order to steal the collected Avatars of Khuvon and escape beyond the walls of Creation. With so many potent Avatars draining the Prime Essence of the universe into the Void beyond, and more being added until it is ultimately too late to reverse, magic continues to die without anything gained. The characters have truly failed.

If the characters enter Zoraster, they have a chance to foil the Zigg'raugglurr. Tremendous gems as large as a man accentuate the vibrating metal structures of the city. Each of these massive jewels contains at least one trapped Avatar within its depths. The sky is the crackling blue of an ozone-rich generator of writhing electrical arcs, and occasionally blurry yellow shapes grow large against the force field sky. The cabal will eventually realize, via the use of Sphere Effects or mundane investigation, that the center of this new Zoraster is a great dome seemingly crafted of a single "man-made" star sapphire. Within the structure, crystalline and intricate metallic rods echo the harmonic commands of Khuvon and move Avatar/Quintessence energy throughout the citadel-fortress. Although it will be difficult to achieve without mastery of Thal'hun harmonics, it is possible to control the Effects of the crystalline and metal rods and thereby grasp control of the entrapped Avatars.

Harnessing the power of the Horizon, the characters can thwart the Zigg'raugglurr by essentially using their own trick against them. Using the Sapphire Dome of the city of Zoraster, the cabal can alter the dimensional qualities of the city-realm's entrapped Avatars so that they gather in a place far beyond the bounds of this universe. A botch or intentional act could lower the blue ozone sky barrier, but to do so would leave the cabal open to attack by the Zigg that are already struggling to assault the city.

Far beyond the walls of Creation, in some other place, the shards of the One are joined together to begin a new universe. Alas the soul of the current one is left to die, and the power of the Prime flows into a new place. It will take a long time to complete, but the characters are in on the ground floor of the next cycle, even if it does come at the expense of a whimpering end to this one.

Ka Luon

At any time throughout the story, the aliens commonly called the Grays might choose to become involved. They have an antagonistic rivalry with the Zigg'raugglurr that is not understood by human agencies. Do the Ka Luon sense that the Zigg's activities are slowly destroying their technology? If so, that would explain a lot. Certainly the Grays are likely to lose their grand mastery of technology, just like the Technocracy will. The Ka Luon have been helping Khuvon thus far into the story, if only because its goals are antithetical to those of the Zigg. It is only a matter of time before they realize that Khuvon's plan is likely to be equally devastating, however. When the cabal enters Zoraster, there is a strong possibility that a few of the Ka Luon are currently in residence. Depending on how things progress, the Grays might prove to be horrible enemies or unexpected allies. Unfortunately, either outcome screws the Grays, but they might not see this coming.

The Grays

Willpower 5, **Rage** 2, **Gnosis** 7, **Essence** 25
Charms: Entirely dependent upon technological devices
Materialized Attributes: Strength 1, Dexterity 3, Stamina 2, Social Attributes equal to Rage, Mental Attributes equal to Gnosis
Abilities: Science 4, two other Abilities at 3 each (for example Firearms and Medicine). Remember that beings using the spirit rules (even if they are not really spirits at all) add their Ability ratings to their materialized Attributes. A rating of 7 in all three Mental Attributes is rather potent.
Materialized Health Levels: 7
Image: The Grays are thin and spindly with gray skin and singularly colored black eyes. They seem fragile, yet they wield incredible technological power.
Notes: The Grays do not actually have any Charms, but they wield technology that is arguably superior to that of the Technocracy. As such, you might either give them high-tech devices (even Wonders) from various Technocracy source materials or assign Charms with a technological basis. Whether they actually come from the Umbra or from the physical universe (albeit far away) the Grays always seem to appear materialized and yet never have to expend any Essence to do so. Stranger yet, due to the way their technology works, they are "materialized" even if they appear in the Umbra or various Otherworlds.

The Void Connection

The Void Engineers have been engaging in a quiet war against the Grays since the end of World War II. Whether the atomic blasts over Japan attracted their attention or it was simple happenstance, the Engineers first came into contact with the Grays then. In 1947, Border Corps pilots shot down a Gray offworld vessel in such a manner that it became publicly known. Control freaked out and gave the Void Engineers explicit instructions to put their little war on hold. The Border Corps protested in private to the Engineers leadership and essentially was told, "We won't ask if you don't tell." The Border Corps continued its operations primarily in extraterrestrial space.

Unknown to anyone outside the Void Engineers, the Convention has long been in touch with seemingly friendly aliens who ultimately proved antagonistic to their Grays enemies. The Zigg'raugglurr saw the developing Engineers as an approachable faction among a growing network of individuals who shared their general principles. The Technocracy wanted to dispatch magic from the universe, and the Zigg wanted to do so as well. Their motivations aren't precisely the same perhaps, but the goal was. A few Zigg managed to somehow communicate with some Enlightened Void Engineers, and a rough, vague, indeterminate alliance seemed to be struck. At least the Zigg seemed to work against the Grays, and so did the Border Corps.

It is likely that the Void Engineers will give chase when the characters' cabal seizes the fallen alien vessel from Area 51 and catapults into the realm of Zoraster. How you handle this as Storyteller is ultimately up to your personal taste. You could conduct high-action space battles en route to Zoraster or even among the ozone layered crystalline and metal towers of the extradimensional city. On the other hand, the fast alien vessel might simply leave its lesser human trackers far behind with no hope of catching up. Alternatively, the Void Engineers might catch up, only to find themselves engaged in battle with the Grays who are currently within Zoraster. If Major Thomas Houston has not yet made an appearance, this is the sort of thing that gets him up in the morning. He wouldn't miss it for the world.

New Zoraster

In case it need be said, the realm of Zoraster is probably not the mystical locale that the Thal'hun believe it to be. Khuvon is almost certainly a powerful spirit, somehow related to the Psychopomps, which has latched onto the Thal'hun pseudo-science cult as a ready source of power and inexorably found itself as caught up in their paradigm as they are in its influence. Whether Zoraster is the ancient ruins of Atlantis — either cast into another realm by its destruction or thrust across the dimensional barriers as it slipped beneath the waves — or some other mythical city, is up to you. Mu, Lemuria, El Dorado and any number of other legendary cities could be the source for the realm. Of course, it is also possible that somehow the Thal'hun have been right these past five decades while the rest of the world has been wrong for thousands of years.

Whatever the truth of the matter is, the city of "Zoraster" has become immensely important. It is the home to untold numbers of Avatars drawn here by Khuvon. Currently it lies outside of the world, resting upon the barriers between Creation and elsewhere. This completely frees Khuvon of the rigors of the Avatar Storm, yet unfortunately it also opened the city to the scrutiny of the Zigg. As the characters descend in their vessel to the city streets, the Zigg seek to enter through the sky barriers as well. Indeed, the cabal might even have to contend with Zigg who appear as large as possible while nearing the borders to the city.

Khuvon

Willpower 8, **Rage** 8, **Gnosis** 8, **Essence** 75

Charms: Airt Sense, Appear, Armor (adjusts to match incoming molecular vibrations), Blast (harmonics), Influence, Insight, Iron Will, Materialize, Mind Speech, Re-form, Seize Avatar, Spirit Away

Materialized Attributes: Strength 4, Dexterity 4, Stamina 4, Social and Mental Attributes equal to Gnosis

Abilities: Academics 3, Alertness 3, Awareness 4, Cosmology 4, Etiquette 2, Intimidation 2, Occult 4, Subterfuge 2

Materialized Health Levels: 7

Image: Due to its growing association with the ideas of the Thal'hun, Khuvon appears to have blue skin and an alien appearance. When it speaks, it makes harmonizing sounds rather than words.

Notes: Khuvon's Seize Avatar Charm allows it to literally strip the Avatar out of a target, be it living foe or imprisoning object. Khuvon must take an action to use its Seize Avatar power, and it must be able to touch its target. Depending on the situation, touch is either automatic or it requires a physical attack. Activating the power costs one point of Essence per point of the target's Willpower + Arete + *Avatar*, and it pits Khuvon's Gnosis of 8 in a resisted roll against the Willpower of its target. Each point of Arete gives the target mage one

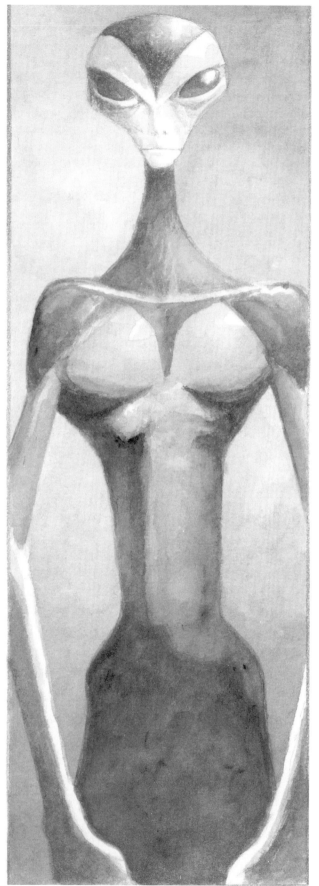

extra die to resist, but each point of *Avatar* Background actually subtracts one die. Therefore, if Khuvon assaulted a mage with Willpower 5, Arete 3 and *Avatar* 2, the player would roll [(5 + 3) – 2] = six dice against Khuvon's dice pool of 8. Things do not look good.

Khuvon's materialized traits are unlikely to be required in the extradimensional space of new Zoraster, but they are included in case the actions of your characters make them necessary. Should Khuvon seize an Avatar, it will place that Avatar into a suitable object, such as the harmonic crystals of Zoraster or let it float freely to be snatched up again. Putting an Avatar back into a mage who has lost it is a Prime 5 Effect.

Stage-Five Magic Alteration

The Gauntlet has grown so thick that magic is being choked from the world. Add a +3 penalty to all magical difficulties and increase their threshold by five. Reduce Nodes, Wonders, Familiars and all mystical traits by three points in rating. Supernatural Merits and Flaws worth three points or less cease, and those worth more are appropriately reduced. As the spirit of the world is cut off from its body, it becomes nearly impossible to avoid witnesses when performing magic. Every crawling insect in the corner or invisible satellite overhead enforces the mundane paradigm. Even veteran mages begin to doubt their own power. All vulgar magic is treated as "*with witnesses.*" The Gauntlet grows so strong that mages who attempt to return to the physical world from any of the various spiritual realms discover that they suffer Paradox even if they fail to pierce it.

Stage Six: This Is the Way the World Ends

Whatever the characters have accomplished, magic is almost entirely gone from the world at this point, and it is fading away completely as time passes. If the Zigg have triumphed, then they have garnered the majority of the Avatars of the universe and its magical forces have inexorably drained away. Locked away in the Zigg'raugglurr's parallel universe, the Avatars of our reality drain the Prime energy into an alternate existence. The Avatar Storm drains away as the shards of which it consists are inevitably drawn to join the rest of the One in the elsewhere inhabited by the Zigg. As the Quintessence builds and the Zigg improve their control of it, all but the mundane lose the ability to continue. Even the Enlightened Science of the Technocracy and the Ka Luon fails. Everything of wonder, inventiveness and magic fades away and becomes a possession of the Zigg. It is questionable whether their alien minds actually take joy in this or it is merely the logical conclusion of millennia of work.

Should the cabal succeed, things are more exciting, even if they still represent a loss of magic to the current universe. If the cabal wins out against the Thal'hun rulers and their leader Khuvon, the dimensional city of Zoraster spirals out of control. If the characters act with foresight and wisdom, they gain control over the city's pathway and save it from destruction. Alternatively, even if they fail to right the tumbling domain, it still sails into a new place by luck alone. Beyond the might of the Thal'hun and Khuvon, the city either crashes into some alien locale or is guided to a new extradimensional home by the cabal. In the new universe, it is highly likely that the great city will assume legendary stature as the founding place of all magic, at least among those practitioners that remember. In future ages, the cabal might be remembered as mythical willworkers or even as godlike figures.

Khuvon

In case it is not obvious, Khuvon is a spiritual aspect of the Thal'hun dominance of the mystical realm. Khuvon is a powerful spirit similar to a Psychopomp — one whose being has been thoroughly corrupted by the cult that worships it. In order to garner the highest access to our world, and expand its power, Khuvon joined with the Thal'hun. As befits the appearance of the leader of the Thal'hun, the master spirit who has usurped their leadership exhibits blue skin and exotic features. The spiritually enhanced powers of Khuvon allow it to direct the passage of Avatars. The Thal'hun have perfected a harmonic ritual that allows them to loosen an Avatar from its Awakened soul, such that Khuvon might guide it into its dimensional city. This ritual, in combination with Khuvon's recruitment of unattached souls, has stockpiled a dangerously large collection of Prime reservoirs in one place — so concentrated that the Zigg cannot help but try to seize them for all time.

New Zoraster

The city between the dimensional barriers is certainly not the New Zoraster of the Thal'hun cultists' faith. Nevertheless, it is a potent construct of Primal

> ## Stage-Six Magic Alteration
>
> There is no turning back now. Magic breathes its last gasps and begins to disappear completely. Add a +3 penalty to all magical difficulties and increase their threshold by six. Those rare places or items of potency surviving thus far begin a rapid decline. Reduce Nodes, Wonders, Familiars and all of the mage's mystical traits by an additional point per month until they are nothing but mundane in nature. Vulgar magic becomes impossible. No mage can perform any magic except for coincidental Effects and even those are subject to the increased difficulty. Notably, this means that it is too late to escape Earth or return to it, as spiritual barriers like the Gauntlet are now impenetrable. Particularly unlikely coincidences require a Willpower point to invoke. If you are running a crossover chronicle with **Mage** being the dominant setting, you will probably wish to have all of the supernatural aspects of vampires, werewolves and Bygones vanish as well. With the miracles of faith and science banished beyond the Gauntlet, and the human spirit along with them, the world is left to languish on borrowed time as it begins its millennia long descent into the sun, while the spiritual realms slowly wither.

power. The godlike spirit Khuvon has guided numerous Avatars to the place, and this number has vastly increased since it gained the aid of the Thal'hun and the Disciples of Zoraster. The Prime Energy, or Quintessence, that has been gathered by this reservoir of souls is unprecedented. The draw is so incredible that the magical Tapestry of the universe is disrupted, for the energies of the Prime are to be found in greater concentrations here than anywhere else in Creation.

The Zigg

The Zigg have been watching the Horizon Realm the Thal'hun call Zoraster for decades, if not centuries. For years they have raced Khuvon to seize majority control over the Avatars of Creation. Originally their success seemed assured, given that Khuvon was relatively inactive when compared to their own operations. Nonetheless, the Thal'hun expansion to the power of Khuvon overturned the Zigg plans. That is, until they discovered that the stronghold of Khuvon might be subverted. Provided the characters do not intervene, the Zigg break into the city and burst through its barriers. They steal the magic of the universe away, and it is never seen again.

The Cabal

If mage society is to win in this great contest, the cabal must defeat Khuvon and scores of the Thal'hun cultists who plot against physical reality. Should this occur, with the cabal defeating the powerful leader Khuvon, then the stockpile of Avatars that Khuvon has been gathering is set free.

The dimensional city of Zoraster bursts free from the barriers of the universe and finds a new, unfettered home. Though they are now caught outside the boundaries of reality, the characters find that they have transported the will of the One to another place. They have the building blocks of willworking a new universe at their command, and they only need heed it. It is possible that they forge a new Cycle in a new universe, or that they simply force magic to abandon this one. If the Avatars they carry elsewhere forge a new universe, then they leave the current one to slowly die, bereft of any magical force. Even the Enlightened Science of the Technocratic Union ultimately fails. Inspiration, magic and nature are all that persist in the new world. Perhaps the new universe will be indelibly marked with the archetypal imagery of a great city, or of its ruins.

Paradox in a World Gone Mundane

The forces of Paradox act in an inscrutable fashion to enforce the ruling paradigm of reality in the face of overzealous willworkers. Whether left over from the Mythic Age or spawned by a universe imprinted with a sense of irony, many aspects of Paradox are as disruptive as the forces they seek to quell. Unearthly fires scourging a mage are no less unbelievable than the blazing fireball she cast down the street. Being plucked from the time stream by the sinister white-suited Paradox spirit Wrinkle is more frightening than hurling yourself forward in time, and it arguably wreaks greater havoc upon the Consensus. Nonetheless, mages have grown somewhat accustomed to Paradox being louder than the magic that called it, as it seeks to subtly plunge them into internal Quiet.

When trying to evoke the slow whimpering death of magic, being interrupted by thunderous punishments for the prideful or rash mage is counterproductive. Consider making Paradox in this particular endgame subtle, and color it with a tone of finality and terrible loss. The standard forms of Paradox and its resulting Backlash can be presented as evocative of the dying wonder of the world without actually changing the rules behind them, and this is probably a desirable route at least in the early stages of the quiet apocalypse.

When a mage suffers direct damage from Paradox, describe it as feeling her body turn deadly cold accompanied by a heart-chilling fear. Specifically avoid flashy displays of Backlash damage that would be unbelievable to the eyes of the typical Sleeper. Focus upon methods of harm that invoke imagery of draining or loss of energy, such as cold, darkness, vacuum, suffocation or lethargy. When you have the chance to convey mental impulses, don't hesitate to use them as well. The mage senses that the forces of magic are slipping away. Mages entering Quiet might experience visions that seem to suggest that magic will soon pass from the world. Alternatively, you can avoid giving them obvious signs in favor of personal horror. Portray Quiet episodes in which the mage loses control over her magic rather than having it disappear from the face of the Earth. Leave her standing in a world within her own mind in which her power has gone and she must rely entirely upon mundane means. If lesser Paradox spirits arrive to punish the mage, you might even have them warn her of their impending victory over deviant activities while enacting their relatively minor defenses against her Effects. Foreshadowing is the mood at this stage.

As you move the timeline further in your story, have the seeming loss of magic begin to manifest in quantifiable fashion by choosing Backlash effects that suggest such. When a mage suffers the effects of a Paradox Backlash, have one point of Quintessence dissipate into the Backlash per point of Paradox expended. As the Quintessence of the universe becomes more and more static, its Primal Energy is soaked into a hardening reality. If the mage lacks a powerful Avatar and possesses only meager supplies of Prime Energy, then have the Backlash steal them from her Wonders, or maybe even starve her Familiar of the sustenance it requires. If extremely potent Paradox spirits are drawn to the mage's acts of hubris, try to temper their efforts to the eye of the Sleeper. Consider the spirit's ability to conceal attacks within the mundane. More than one mage has died in a fiery automobile wreck originating with an unexpected Backlash. Although certain spirits are known to act with extreme disregard for the Consensus, give them a newfound care for it. If a Paradox spirit catapults a mage beyond the ever-strengthening Gauntlet in order to remove her from the physical world, see to it that the spirit leaves a realistic corpse to assume her place or a treacherous trail of documents suggesting she fled into obscurity of her own volition. At this point, the threat to the very existence of magic has become powerful and yet more bound by its own opposition to the wonder it seeks to end.

Finally, in the latter stages of your tale, Paradox becomes unable to violate the precepts of the reality it defends, and it ultimately fades as surely as magic. Paradox spirits are left outside the Gauntlet or transformed into quiet minions of static reality. A powerful spirit like Wrinkle might be banished to the Umbra. Alternatively, its vast skills could be limited to doctoring timecards, paychecks, alarm clocks, bus schedules, email date stamps and other coincidental time-based events that might negatively affect a mage who continues to try to invoke magic in the face of its end. Backlash of a direct physical nature becomes increasingly rare. When it does manifest, it is exclusively of a believable, realistic source. Ignoble, commonplace threats such as slipping on the soap in a bathtub or heart trouble are the most common forms of Backlash damage now. As time passes, Paradox grows weaker, until it suffers the same degree of pitiful death as the magic that fosters it.

Chapter Six: Hell on Earth

Unspoken, the promise dies stillborn. This is what they have chosen. This is the fate they have invited us to forge for them. This is the path to peace and unity. Long days have I struggled, my brothers and sisters, and now we stand upon the edge of victory. We have given them leave to play the games of state, and they have served us admirably, rearing many fine lambs to sate our hunger. Let us feast, then, for the time of celebration is nigh…

—The Unnamed, First among the Fallen, addressing the council of the Aswadim

What if reality's slow, inexorable slide into decay picks up some steam and the Nephandi find themselves poised to attain victory over Creation itself? Just as Ascension can, theoretically, be achieved by humanity as a whole, so, too, can Descent. But what happens when the Consensus betrays the promise of its own inner divinity? What happens when mankind chooses darkness over light, death over life?

Killing Creation

This is the endgame, when the stakes are high and the prize is the fate of everything. Despite what anyone might believe, the Nephandi currently have the upper hand in the War for Reality. They need only prod here and guide there, and they will be in the position soon enough to sunder hope itself and scatter its ashes in a cold, meaningless tomb.

If you choose to walk this way, be careful. You are about to betray everything you ever believed about the Ascension War and humanity's place in the world of the Awakened. Are you still reading? Good, because this is more than just the story of Ascension's most terrible and merciless enemies. It is the tale of humanity's weakness and the dismal failure of the Awakened to champion the cause of enlightenment and give Ascension to the Sleepers.

But where to begin?

The Futility of Sacrifice

One of the most critical (and counterintuitive) things to do in portraying the End is to demonstrate that, sometimes, fighting — and even dying for — the Good Fight makes no difference. Sometimes, a heroic end is futile and pointless — a light extinguished in the dark that inspires no one and leaves only despair in the wake of its passing. Whole cabals of mages will make heroic last stands and die without accomplishing anything. Friends, allies and the characters' loved ones will die or even fall to corruption (without the chance of redemption), and no one will be able to prevent it from happening.

Storytelling Hopelessness

Of course, no one wants to play a game with no themes beyond relentless depression, failure and misery. There is great potential for amazing roleplaying within the context of a losing battle (just look at the premise of **Werewolf: The Apocalypse**), but players want to feel as though their characters' actions can and do make a difference.

Unless you believe that your players would be perfectly comfortable with the notion of a character dying or otherwise falling for no good reason and without even the chance of getting something worthwhile out of that sacrifice (and there *are* players out there who would be all right with this), try to at least bestow some meaning and, perhaps, a kernel of hope and possibility in the demise or corruption of any character. Even if it is something that cannot be realistically capitalized upon during the character's lifetime, the sense that those who will carry on the fight in the future might be able to glean some strength from the characters' loss can help allay the sense of disappointment that comes with an unpleasant end for someone's character.

No Mercy, No Quarter: The Heroism of Desperation

Now, it is important to remember that, despite the fact that so many sacrifices will go unnoticed in the eternal night of Descent, there should be meaningful victories, even in the midst of defeat and great loss. Those with the will, the conviction, the power and the savvy can strike telling blows against the Nephandi, even as the world literally goes to hell. Though these inspiring souls might not be able to turn back the tide, or even lead others to do so, they will leave legends that echo down through generations, proving that, as long as there is life, there is hope.

Indeed, during "Hell on Earth," many Traditions will fall almost entirely, leaving only a scattered few stragglers to carry on the fight. Those Traditions most willing to die to a man (the Akashic Brotherhood, Celestial Chorus, Euthanatoi and Order of Hermes) are apt to get just such a fate. (Indeed, the Order falls in Chapter III, but other Traditions might also meet their doom during the periods of time provided in "Hell on Earth," during which you can unleash your own plots and subplots.) In such a case, perhaps any of your characters who are members of those Traditions become literally the only survivors of those Awakened mystic paradigms (save perhaps for a handful of *barabbi*).

Other, more individualistic, Traditions are more likely to put up a disorganized resistance in places and to simply look for cover in others, though you shouldn't hesitate to skew what the players expect is dramatically appropriate. (A daring final stand by a truly unified Dreamspeaker Tradition, for example, can be a painfully poignant moment.) Still, just as heroism knows no gender, race, religion or creed, it knows no Tradition (or even Convention). Anyone with the will to fight can make a stand and, with sufficient skill and conviction, a difference. It is important to satisfy expectations of both pointless and heroic sacrifice in the Fall, so that mages can never be sure if their own sacrifices will mean anything, but they know that torment and even death *can* have meaning.

Men of Dust

Above all else, it is important to portray Descent as much a product of humanity's failure (on the part of the Sleepers and the Awakened alike) as it is the result of Nephandi success, if not more so. Descent can result only when the overwhelming majority of the human race loses all concern for the world, the people in it, the sanctity of the human soul and the possibility of something better. Only a feast of apathy and spiritual atrophy can produce victory for the Fallen. In many ways, Descent will come about because humanity deserved nothing better, because it chose to die, rather than to feel, try or care.

Don't forget to illustrate the human hubris, selfishness and folly that *earn* mankind the sentence of Descent. As the haves step over the have-nots in the street (with perhaps only a snide "Get a job" to indicate any awareness that a sentient being is slumped in the gutter); as the weak and innocent are preyed upon in mind, body and spirit by the malevolent strong; as hope is drowned amidst a sea of layoffs, sex scandals and conflicts born of political ambition and the desire for profit; as people do *nothing* to reverse this tide it becomes clear how all of this came to pass. The Traditions are fighting an admirable battle, but they are doing so for a human race that has, for the most part, not done much to warrant such support.

Every faction on every side of the Ascension War fights for something, but the Sleepers, who are both the battlefield and the object of contention, by definition, stand for nothing special. Without any kind of spiritual forcefulness or conviction to their existence, *they* become the primary architects of Descent. While the Nephandi profit by it and grow fat on its spoils, it is — and only could ever be — the un-Awakened who give the Fallen the strength and the power to make it happen, by dint of their own withering souls.

Where Shadows Run Thick and the Walls Grow Thin

As the End approaches, the worlds of flesh and spirit begin to grow closer and the Gauntlet shudders, preparing to give up the ghost. In a scenario where the glorious redemption of Ascension is nigh, this will be a frightening though ultimately rewarding time. In a world caught in the throes of Descent, however, such a merger of planes is an occurrence to be dreaded. The corruption and degradation of the material world is reflected bodily in the Umbrae, and all that is darkest and most loathsome in humanity is free to incarnate.

The "brighter" aspects of the various Umbrae will be devoured almost entirely by the final darkness. Doubtless, the Penumbra will be the first place to succumb completely, growing fetid with spiritual taint before bleeding into the physical world through the dissolving Gauntlet. Whole realms will probably follow suit, and the world's Awakened will need to begin making hard choices. As the reflection, among other things, of human hopes and dreams, the Umbrae are indisputably worth at least *attempting* to save, but can it be done? Is there enough time left to try? Is it better to seek to abandon Earth for the Umbra or vice-versa? These are painful choices and, in the Fall, there are no easy (and maybe even no correct) answers.

The Avatar Storm

In the Fall, the Avatar Storm plays an entirely different role than the one envisioned in the more "standard" **Mage** cosmology. Just prior to the fall of the Gauntlet, Fallen magic unleashes this nightmare torrent upon Sleeper and Awakened alike, a singular moment of untold worldwide destruction. The rent and tattered souls become a new kind of widderslainte Avatar when the worlds of flesh and spirit bleed together. Or perhaps it is more accurate to say that the spirit-shards even bond with Nephandi to become the Fallen equivalent of Anakim, a new nobility among the damned.

One Hell of a Downer

Normally, you're not supposed to railroad characters along or make them feel that their actions have no value. Unfortunately, that's kind of the point of Descent. No matter what you do, things aren't going to turn out well. It's a sad fact, but a fact, nonetheless. "Hell on Earth" allows the characters to make some choices along the way and even to make a potential positive impact here or there, but they can't set things right, no matter how hard they try. They can only attempt to make things a little *less* shitty. That said, enjoy.

The Tenth Sphere and the March to Armageddon

Virtually every Mystic Tradition, Technocratic Convention and Disparate Craft has its own pet theory on what, exactly, constitutes the "Tenth Sphere." These ideas have ranged from Self to the Unified Field Theory to the much-touted Unity. All of these theories were well-thought-out, diligently researched and actively propounded.

Of course, all of them were also wrong.

The Tenth Sphere does not exist. There is no "final truth" that leads to perfection, no easy answer to the innumerable problems that have plagued humanity since it first looked to the world and knew that something more could be. It would be convenient if there were, but Creation rarely conforms to expectations and certainly doesn't go out of its way to make things make sense for the human race. It was up to the Awakened to reconcile these paradoxes for themselves but, instead of accepting that Reality makes its own rules, they made up stories and convinced themselves over the course of generations and centuries that those stories were true. In the case of the Traditions, many did so in order to lay claim to the Tenth Seat at Horizon, the one that mysteriously appeared years ago, before the devastation of the Reckoning. This delusion made them easy prey for a cunning hunter, for the Tenth Seat belonged to one and one alone, and none could challenge his dominion over it.

Master of the Tenth Seat

Over the course of millennia, he has worn many names. In medieval Europe, they called him the Black Man, patron of witchcraft and devil-worship. (Some believed that he *was* the Devil.) In the Arabic world, where he abided for many years in days long ago, he went by the name of al-Aswad, the name he gave to those who followed after him as Fallen Oracles. To the Sumerians, he was Ut-Napishtam, the primordial man who was chosen by the gods to survive the Great Flood and was thereafter granted immortality but made to abide apart from all lesser creatures. In truth, he was all these things and none, the anointed champion of the darkness from beyond Creation, and his True Name is lost to the deep memory of time. Perhaps the most far-thinking human being ever to exist, he was chosen not for his power or his knowledge — for with life enough a man might develop these qualities — but instead for his wisdom, patience and sense of strategy. The gods who raised him up remembered being outcast from the endless shadow in which they abided, shoved away by the hateful presence of something new — existence. They looked on it and were pained by jealousy, for they, though powerful and terrible, could never truly *be*. That privilege was reserved for all that existed within the hateful light.

Still, these elder things were cunning and resourceful, and they knew many secret paths into Creation, the furrows they had left when they were fragmented and greatly lessened in power through their forceful expulsion. Shards of themselves, the barest fractions of their essence, they poured into the world, seeking those who could hear them and be moved by them. At last, one living thing heard and answered.

What began was a dialogue, perhaps the first bargain forged between man and spirit (if spirits they could be rightly called, who were the avatars of all that which did not exist and yet hungered and hated). In exchange for his aid in helping the elder darkness to achieve *being* within Creation, they would exalt him above all other creatures. The man sealed the covenant by sacrificing his Name. Carving it upon a stone, he cast his Name into a fire and, as the stone blackened, so too did his skin, his hair and even his eyes, becoming like unto pitch. The shattered fragments of the One who had driven out the elder darkness saw this and were terrified. Acting in fear, these shards descended through the planes, from their high places of power, to unite in just the same fashion with other mortal men. The one who was Nameless, grown much in awareness through his pact, felt this change and, inwardly, he laughed. The so-called "Pure Ones" had sown the seeds of their own destruction.

The Hundred Centuries Campaign Begins

What began thereafter was the lengthy crusade to set the pieces in place for the final, devastating coup upon reality itself. Some key events in the history of the Awakened and the Sleeping alike were of his artifice; some, but by no means all, most or even many. Instead, he acted as he had to, coming out of seclusion only when necessary and otherwise allowing the evils to which humanity was prone to do his work for him. When he found others who were worthy, he offered them his covenant, transforming them into the incarnate vessels of the Darkness Beyond. Including himself, six in all rallied to his cause, the first six widderslainte, poisoned souls who had infected Creation with its unmaking.

It would be many years yet before the Hebrews named them the Qlippoths, the shells of the Sephiroth

170 ASCENSION

and the embodiments of the "virtues" of the Tree of Death, but they were now the living reflections of all that which dwelled Outside. The Unnamed had his council of lords and ladies, his hands and eyes, just as he was the hands and eyes of those Beyond.

With clever manipulations, gentle prodding, brutal threats and occasionally a precise application of mind-numbing violence, the six Fallen Oracles, the first Nephandi, worked to sculpt the progression of human history. Still, as the Unnamed himself told the rest, it was important only to guide, rather than force. Men were capable of ruining Creation on their own and needed only the barest direction in doing so. The Unnamed preferred to think of himself as a father, helping his children, all of humanity, to achieve its full, destructive potential.

So it went, as years became decades, centuries and even millennia. The Unnamed and his fellows watched the rise of Sumer and Egypt, Greece and Rome. All those they found worthy of the "gifts" of their lords, they took to hidden places, the tunnels carved by the ferocious expulsion of those Outside, and anointed them in blood, rending their souls and piecing them back together inside-out. This they did in order to teach their disciples the suffering that the primordial ones had endured, and to flense away their human weakness and failing. Those who were strong emerged changed — cruel, hateful, cunning and powerful. Those who were weak did not emerge at all, having wandered out into the vast labyrinths of those furrows, rotting arteries spiderwebbing through Creation, and met those they would call master. None survived the gnawing hunger of those elder beings.

Most importantly, the Unnamed established the standards of the Fallen covenant, whereby human beings might accept the Outer Darkness into their souls and thereby become avatars of its power. In fact, through careful bargains with his masters, the Unnamed made it so that he, of all human creatures, would wield control over the very fabric of the Pact. Whether they knew it or not, from that day onward, *all* Nephandi everywhere would be subject to the will of one alone. Though he sacrificed much in order to make it so, he felt the trials he endured were well worth it, for his lords were vast and terrible beings, not much given to offering their attentions to such small creatures as mortal men. It suited them well to have a caretaker for their menagerie, and the Unnamed, first among their slaves, was perfect for this purpose. In the end, he became the sole arbiter of their good graces and the hand responsible for dispensing their power. Such authority would later serve the Unnamed well.

The World Changes

As time and times changed, the Unnamed gradually found himself barred farther and farther away from even the most distant shores of Creation. So saturated with his masters' power was he that he was now more a creature of the Void than the Tapestry. Still, he could, when needed, exert his will and walk the dark and forlorn paths of the Earth in order to pass along some shred of hidden and blasphemous knowledge to a promising apprentice of his foul arts. At last, reluctantly, however, he realized that the Fallen Oracles would eventually be all but barred entirely from the world. It was time to pass along the knowledge of the Pact to others, that they might be able to forge the unspeakable bond and deliver unto the Masters their tithe of souls.

The Unnamed chose several men and women for this purpose and gathered them up in the ruins of Ur. It had been 313 years since the birth of a carpenter's son in Galilee. Twenty in all had he chosen, and all were called to stand before the Unnamed in turn. He stared into the eyes of the others and, by daybreak, six yet lived, all of them now knowledgeable in the ways of the Pact. Tired beyond reckoning through the great expenditure of energy he had made in order to show these children the secrets of his power, the Unnamed retreated into the Void, there to recuperate and rest. While it would be many decades before he would awaken again and trouble the world of men with his tread, he was joyous in the knowledge of the one secret he kept for himself. No matter what else might happen, his victory was now assured.

Those who would bend knee to the service of the Unnamed were many and they hailed from many shores. Some called the darkness "Shaitan," "Ildabaoth," "Ahriman" or "Lucifer." They saw those Outside as gods (or, in many cases, as one god) and prayed to them for power. Many, turning away from the rise of the power of Him who was martyred for mankind, embraced the Pact as a means of denying the Cross. Others, who hailed from quarters far removed from Rome, Persia and the other bastions of civilization, came to understand the darkness as a myriad of spirits. Some worshipped it as ghosts, returned from the Underworld to plague the living with their hatred and their jealousy. In the end, the pure adulation of the Void was tarnished, blasphemed by giving Names to that which existed outside of Adam's knowledge and had never been shaped by the Will of his Word.

So it was that the power of the Fallen diminished even as it grew, for, in Naming their masters, the Fallen gave others the ability to know them and to gain power over them. It was a grievous hurt and one from which the Fallen would not soon recover, but all it really did was prolong the inevitable. The Pure Ones — those who were the scattered remains of the One who had sprung up out of the Nothingness and broken Itself upon the hard armor of those who came Before — began to diminish through the long process of passing themselves along to greater numbers of magi, priests and philosophers. In all things, there was equilibrium and order. This was just as the Unnamed would have it.

The One and the Many

The only true fear that the Unnamed harbored within his cold heart was that the scattered heirs to the power of the Pure Ones might unite as one and, as their spiritual ancestor had before them, drive the Darkness out, this time with such thoroughness as to bar the Void forever from Creation. As the Unnamed awoke to discover the fractiousness that had overpowered his children, he was enraged and horrified. Further, he looked with great wrath upon the Names they had given and those they had taken upon themselves. Stumbling in the long darkness of their masters' sleep, they had lost their way. Many now had no true sense of what it was they served. Only a few kept alive the essence of the Pact and remembered its lessons. Worst of all, many of them accepted a single Name as their own: Nephandi. The only thing that kept the Unnamed from despair was the change he saw taking place in Rome.

Magi and philosopher-scientists, unaware that the one thing was the other, and vice-versa, squabbled over their beliefs. They had proven themselves, thankfully, no more wise or understanding than the chattels that were not gifted with the power of Will. Indeed, within his sanctum far beyond the kingdoms of men, he laughed aloud to see them strike at one another and, as he had done unto his initiates, anoint themselves in blood. While his own children had become mired in ignorance, his enemies had become engrossed in petty struggles to prove the superiority of their beliefs. And then, in the midst of this folly, something both miraculous and terrible happened. One magus, pushed beyond grief by the slaughter of his family and apprentices, strode beyond the boundaries of simple Will and into an unfettered madness from which there was no return. He existed, within his own mind, in a world in which his loved ones yet lived, and nothing could make it otherwise for him. Those who tried to show him otherwise were annihilated by his insanity. The Unnamed pondered this occurrence, for such things could be dangerous weapons against his chosen, but it was all but assured that such madmen would never be able to unite with the other willworkers against his cause. So it was, the One had become Many, none of which could find concord with one another. As Rome fell, truly and finally, into the barbarism of the Dark Ages, the Unnamed could not help but feel a great joy.

A Betrayal

By the point at which the Nephandi stood on the brink of victory during the Second World War, the Unnamed considered himself an entity at least on par with many of the very beings he served. Over time, newcomers had stuck their noses where, in his estimation, they did not belong. Such unfortunate happenings had always been turned to his advantage, however. The conclusion of World War II was just such an event.

With the Nephandi strong and growing stronger, it seemed that even the temporary alliance of the Traditions and Technocracy combined was insufficient to the task. Still, at the seeming moment of their victory, the Nephandi lost their powers, their prayers and supplications falling upon deaf ears. Many potential answers have been put forward in the years sense, ranging from the sage to the ludicrous, but none was *the* answer.

It was the Unnamed and his Aswadim who laid low the Nephandi that day.

Why? Because, despite his devotion to the cause, the Unnamed could not bear to be upstaged, especially not by interlopers like the "demons" of the Cross and the evil spirits feared by wild shapechangers who rutted with beasts. Further, he saw the many flaws in their designs. It was a plan of great zeal and little forethought, but such had always been the downfall of the Fallen. Therefore, using his mastery of the Pact, the Unnamed struck at the source of the power of the younger Nephandi, severing the bonds of spirit that tied them to the masters to whom they had sold their souls. When the Traditionalists and Technocrats opened wide that door to the Beyond, he waited on the other side of it, harvesting the ripest and most powerful souls for his own. Others, he slew for their power, harvesting the Quintessence in their bodies and spirits like a sweet honey and storing it for later use. Then, by means of the secret paths known only to those who dwelled in the Outer Dark, he made the long and arduous journey back into Creation, now fattened with many strong Avatars. These he devoured and reconciled within himself, growing in might until he became something more than human, Nephandus or even Oracle.

Satisfied with all that had transpired, the Unnamed began to walk the Earth again, this time concealing his gifts and offering them to but few. The end was growing close, and he had no wish to offer his Pact to simpletons or madmen. Enough of those were coming into the Power on their own — the unfortunate byproduct of a wasted age.

The Last Few Steps

Finally, after millennia of struggle, the Unnamed was in the position to win his war. It was, however, no time for celebration. Only a fool counts his enemies slain before he himself has crouched over their cooling corpses and seen their souls escape with their final breaths.

The Taking of Mus

While the Hermetic College Covenant at Mus seemed like a trivial goal to most of the Fallen, enough of them could be cowed into submission through various emissaries to force them into battle. While the Technocracy fortuitously assaulted the chantry, the Unnamed dispatched his servants to defeat both sides and drive them out. The Fors Collegis Mercuris was important in his endgame, but he could not yet allow any to know how or why, not even his Aswadim. Too much hung in the balance to trust anyone but himself. Even the dark and brooding masters of the Unnamed went uninformed in their fitful deathlike slumber.

The Great Deception

The board was set, though most of the pieces upon it fancied themselves players. One final play needed to be made. The rest would fall into place on their own. Using the vast power he had harvested from the defeat of the sleeping Nephandi Lords in 1945, the Unnamed transported his own throne into the heart of the Traditions, Horizon itself, as well as opening a vast rift in its landmass. Surely, the foolish children would argue among themselves, each seeking to claim the chair, each trying to expand their power at the expense of their fellows. Sadly, the Traditions proved the Unnamed right and fell to petty bickering.

Most importantly, though, was the fact that they did not question whence the seat came. The Traditionalists accepted the Throne of the Unnamed into their midst. This would prove most significant, since, in doing so, they essentially invited him into Horizon, indeed, into the heart of Concordia itself. It was a dangerous gambit, for the seal of the Unnamed was graven upon the chair and, by it, the Traditions might know him, but he was confident in his ruse and his power, and he knew that the time for half-measures had passed. It was a perilous gambit, but the Unnamed was quite certain that even the mightiest of Traditions mages would prove unable to decipher the sigil according to anything other than their own pride and self-congratulatory worldviews.

The Traditions, the only enemies who could conceivably mount a credible offense against the Unnamed, were lost in their own games of state. Even those who touted the Tenth Seat as Unity could not swallow their pride long enough to bring that ideal about by shutting their mouths and letting someone else's beliefs win the day. It was no less than he had expected. Arrogant and contrary to the end, the Traditions would never see the deathblow coming.

As for the Technocracy, the Marauders and the Disparates, the Unnamed spared no time or effort. Such foes were, to his thinking, weak, foolish and clumsy. They would fall when the time came, but no special effort would be devoted to them, so profound was the Unnamed's disrespect for these willworkers.

The Reckoning

The heavy weight of bleak destiny fell at the waning of the millennium. Masters fell, realms withered and brother turned upon brother. It was, to the thinking of the Aswadim, perfect. Such cataclysms were set in motion by the hubris of other mages. The Fallen needed do nothing to make it happen, though they saw all the signs of it upon the Horizon and laughed with glee to see the hammer finally fall. In a matter of two years, all potential resistance had been crushed, reduced to a pathetic few, incapable of long holding out against the unleashed power of the Unnamed and his Fallen.

The stars were right. It was time to finish the game.

The Rogue Council

So, who's been sending those messages, telling the Traditions to get in gear and fight the good fight? The Unnamed, of course, from his Fors Collegis Mercuris, located within the Shard Realm of Correspondence. With the ability to send anything, anywhere, untraceably, the Unnamed and the rest of the Aswadim have been trying to get the Traditions to shake off the lethargy of recent centuries. This will cause them to move more openly and expose themselves. Further, such activity among the Awakened can only lead to more Awakenings, fattening Creation with a bevy of ripe and potent souls on which Those Beyond might feast.

Perhaps most importantly, though, the Unnamed understands well that the heirs of the magi and philosophers of long-ago days, the Traditions and the Technocracy, will set their sights upon one another in these grim final hours, allowing him and his chosen to operate unimpeded by unfortunate entanglements. Freed from the threat of conflict with their two greatest enemies, the Fallen are liberated to lay siege to Creation itself.

Important to note is the fact that this scenario assumes that you have been using the events portrayed in **Manifesto: Transmissions from the Rogue Council**, or, at the very least, that the Rogue Council phenomenon exists and that your characters are aware of it. If not, you'll need to make a couple of adjustments to "Hell on Earth," but doing so shouldn't be too problematic.

Chapter I

The Lead-Up

Before the final chapter is told, the stage must be well and truly set. In the sessions leading up to Descent, remember to portray events as turning darker, more futile and hopeless. Let the mages feel that things are coming apart at the seams due to the failings of Sleeper and Awakened alike.

After all, "Hell on Earth" should not come as a total surprise when it begins, so much as it should seem a grim but logical conclusion to Reality's troubles.

Side Trips

While "Hell on Earth" presents a linear series of events, nobody but you knows what the individual needs of your troupe are. That in mind, there's a lot of intentional "dead air" in this scenario, spans of time ranging from weeks to months in which you can insert events pertinent to your chronicle. After all, you're probably not reading this so you can be told exactly what to do, step by step, to end the World of Darkness in pain and horror. We just don't have the room in one chapter (or even one book) to print that sort of thing, anyway.

Claiming the Prize

The first phase of the Unnamed's final plan involves the capture of Horizon, there to eventually exploit the powerful Nodes connected to the realm in order to spread the taint of his masters to the farthest reaches of the Earth. Fortunately, little but magic stands in his way. Horizon has been sealed since Lord Gilmore barred all from entry (or exit) by means of powerful wards. The Aswadim, however, are arguably the most powerful individual mages within or without Creation. With a few hours worth of rituals, the Unnamed shatters the seals holding Horizon shut and unleashes a terrible conflagration, killing all spirits and disembodied mages who yet reside therein.

Triumphantly, the Unnamed enters into the blasted ruins of Horizon. There, he begins to strip the realm of its Quintessence stockpiles and uses his mastery of the Qlippothic Spheres to send connections back along the ley lines that connect the realm to its anchoring Nodes on Earth, nine of the world's most powerful. Through these channels, he will pour out his corruption and thereby defile the Earth. In the Council Chamber, he sets his left hand upon the Saxum Oculorum (the "Stone of Eyes" which records all that has ever been said within the heart of Horizon) and it burns black, run through with cracks. Closing his eyes and swaying for just a moment, the Unnamed has just absorbed the knowledge of all that has ever transpired within the Council Chamber, the deepest secrets of his greatest enemies.

Signing Off

The last transmission from the "Rogue Council" is sent from Horizon. Now, the Unnamed feels no need for secrecy, safe within the walls of the most powerful manmade realm ever to exist. Sending his message to the Hierophant of Winds (see "The Other Aswadim," pp. 186-187), the Unnamed allows the following message to reach Traditionalists, Disparates, Orphans and even Technocrats, seemingly at random. It is strongly suggested that the characters' cabal (or at least a significant portion of it) be privy to the message as it is transmitted.

I am the one who came before and shall follow after. I am your father and your destroyer, architect of your destiny. I am him who is come in glory to crush the thrones of the Earth beneath my tread. You have known me by many names, O my children, but you know not the slightest part of my power. Submit to me and know the bounty of my love. Defy me and suffer the agonies of my boundless wrath. It is for you to decide, but choose quickly. The Final Hour is nigh. I wait for you at the heart of your strength.

Naturally, the Unnamed anticipates that the world's Awakened will come after him in numbers and with great force when "the heart of your strength" is deciphered as meaning Horizon. This is as planned, for it allows his other agents to work in what secrecy they require, while he and the remainder of the Aswadim fend off a new siege upon Horizon.

The Attack

Naturally, virtually every Tradition mage on Earth, as well as no small number of Technocrats and scattered others, will want to launch an assault against the Aswadim. Battling the Nephandi has, over time, been one of the only things that virtually everyone else can agree upon. Even those who realize that a frontal assault is likely a bad idea don't know what else to do. Hastily, the Traditions convene at the Hermetic House Quaesitor's ancestral chantry in Stuttgart, Germany. Of course, your characters are among those who receive an invitation, by whatever means.

The council gathered there consists of many of the few remaining earthbound Masters and Adepts, with a larger number of young, less experienced mages on the fringes, as well as the occasional Orphan or Craft mage. Bickering is the order of the day, with none of the power-players in attendance able to sort out for themselves what should be done. As the day wears on, the consensus seems to support an attack upon Horizon, though mages are divided over how best to do so. Finally, three separate forces resolve to enter the realm by various means and there attempt to wrest control of it from the Fallen. Notably, most of those who hold out against this obviously foolhardy plan are the Traditions' most and least experienced willworkers.

In the midst of this model of poor planning, the characters are taken aside by a hooded and cloaked figure. The individual, a man of seemingly middling years, places an elaborate key into the hands of one character and tells her to "seek the *Parma Magica* in the ruins of Doissetep." He tells the characters that they must go to Horizon with the ill-fated attackers, there to use the back door found in the Tomb of La Salle (the Hermetic Master who is largely credited with the formation of the Traditions) to enter the Shard Realm of Forces at the site of the annihilated chantry. At that, he walks away and all but disappears. Within seconds, the character can't even remember which direction he went in. All that is left are his instructions and his key.

The battle at Horizon is fierce and desperate. Let the characters see only as much as they have to in order to get to the tomb. Leave them confused as to what was taking place and with nothing more than the most vague descriptions of those who lay waste to the Traditionalists (and others) present. They seem to be drawn to the tomb and instinctively know where it is (a gift from he who gave them the key). Make the characters sweat a bit in the Shard Realm of Forces, but don't punish them too harshly; they have a lot of hard work coming up.

Searching through the ruins, one of the characters eventually finds a charred book titled *Bonisagus' Parma Magica*. A quick glance reveals it to be a text about the quest to unify the Houses of Hermes and that journey's reflection in the formation of the Nine Mystic Traditions; uplifting, perhaps, in better days, but now seemingly useless. No other trace of a "*Parma Magica*" is to be found among the rubble, and the characters might eventually grow frustrated. Just as the cabal is about to give in to despair, the key given over to one of the mages begins to grow warm and, of its own accord, floats into midair, passing harmlessly through any container it is stored in. The key "unfolds," warping along its spatial axes to become a golden gateway, beyond which a battered but still beautiful realm can be seen. The cabal has an open invite to Balador, courtesy of Akrites Salonikas and Marianna.

DAMAGE CONTROL

So, what happens when nothing goes according to plan? Players invariably find some way to have you ripping out your hair by the fistful because they just won't open that first door on the right, no matter how many times you've tried to spell out the fact that what they're looking for is in that room. (Or whatever.) "Hell on Earth" is not likely to be much different in that regard.

These questions and their answers obviously can't address everything that could possibly stray from center, but they are there to attempt to take into account some of the more likely twists of the plot. So, without further ado:

• **The characters don't go to Stuttgart**. This is a strong possibility, especially if the cabal has had to deal with a lot of stupid Traditions politics and has the feeling (and rightly so) that whatever "meeting" is about to occur will just degenerate into, "My Will is bigger than yours; let's do it *my* way." Also, if the cabal has a large number of Craft mages or Orphans (to say nothing of what to do if you're running a Technocratic amalgam, in which case, they won't get the invite in the first place), it's increasingly likely that the characters just won't go. In such cases, you need to get the right note into the characters' hands by different means. The important part is that Akrites Salonikas approaches the characters (and, as an archmage, he has the ability to do so and make the meeting peaceful, whether the you're dealing with a cabal of lackadaisical Traditionalists or staunch Technocrats), tells them that the attack upon Horizon is doomed to failure and suggests the new course of action.

• **The characters decide to stay at Horizon**. This is a tough one. Feel free to do what you have to in order to highlight the absolute futility of fighting the Aswadim, even if it means killing a character or two. Surrounded by enormous reserves of Quintessence and powerful beyond mortal reckoning, the Fallen Oracles are unassailable. In the end, if the characters *insist* upon remaining, you can always have the *Parma Magica* come into their possession in others ways (such as through the auspices of a Hermetic Master who did not go on the foredoomed attack) after casting them out of the realm, forcibly if necessary, and back to Earth.

CHAPTER II

THE STORM IS LOOSED

As the wash of energy from Horizon floods out into the Tellurian, the Unnamed contends with the wills locked within the Avatar Storm. A great instinctive dread hangs within these miserable soul-fragments, a beast's terror at the thought of being forced out of its den. By strictest mental fortitude, the Unnamed "pulls" the Storm out of the Gauntlet and unleashes it upon both the world and the Umbrae at once. Everywhere, people — the Awakened especially — are ravaged by the Storm. Those Awakened who do not have protections against both Prime and Spirit assaults die horribly. Most Technocrats, Orphans and Craft mages perish in agony, flayed to their souls and then into nothingness. Even a majority of Traditionalists, who did not benefit from Salonikas' warning (most of whom would not have heeded it, anyway) die.

THE AEGIS

Armed with the knowledge they gleaned from Salonikas' quest and the open gate to Balador, the characters can begin to establish the Aegis (otherwise known as the *Greater Parma Magica*) that will, hopefully, help a number of the world's Awakened weather the coming storm alive. When they arrive at Balador (causing the gate to collapse behind them), the characters discover that, despite any rumors they have heard or evidence they have seen to the contrary, the Pleasuredome is still very much alive. A Prime matrix (corresponding to Earth's own resonance) has kept the mages here alive and embodied. The "ghost town" of mages-cum-spirits that many recent Umbral travelers have encountered was actually an elaborate illusion created by Marianna and several others at Salonikas' insistence, in order to give the Traditions somewhere secure to retreat to when his visions came true. Marianna approaches, her eyes alight with joy, and kisses the mage holding the book, gently slipping it out of his hands. She smiles broadly and says, "Hopefully, it will be enough."

At this, Lord Edward Gilmore, standing behind Marianna, takes the book from her, studies it for a moment and then speaks elaborate command words in Enochian, the Order's mystic secret language. He reaches *into* the book and withdraws a sphere of blinding golden light, which slowly congeals into a small, orichalcum buckler, graven with the sigils of the Spheres. Gilmore looks it up and down and mutters, "The Seer was good for his word. It will suffice."

The shield holds extraordinarily powerful enchantments in it, designed to create a two-way ward with *all* nine Spheres. Nothing comes in or goes out once the *Parma Magica* is activated. As trusted confidantes of the Tradition luminaries who are present (Marianna and Gilmore, as well as Senex, Dante and Tasygan), the characters will be asked to help with the preparations. (If they ask *what* the preparations are for, the characters are told that there's no time to explain and to just please work as quickly and thoroughly as they can. It will all be quite apparent soon.) Huge amounts of Tass have to be fed to the *Parma Magica* when it is in place, and circles and seals must be placed in the proper configurations. Hermetics and any others with an eye for detail especially will be asked to draw the proper signs on the walls of Balador. Just as the work is finished, the wisdom of Salonikas' counsel is revealed.

As the Avatar Storm strikes, it is apparent that the Aegis will hold if nothing goes wrong. Of course, something does go wrong. Having defeated the would-be invaders and sensing the flaw in his plan, the Unnamed leaves the other Aswadim to continue with the ritual that keeps the Avatar Storm in flux (and, thus, attacking the worlds of spirit and flesh) and comes to Balador to attend to the Aegis personally. His arrival is heralded by a cataclysmic shaking of the realm's foundations. Some of the Storm slips in, probably killing mages standing just paces away from the characters before dissipating. As this happens, the Unnamed can be seen outside the Aegis, hurling terrible sorceries at it.

Allow perhaps one character to notice Senex, heaving a sigh, running his gnarled old hands through his gray hair and walking away. If the character attempts to talk to the Old Man, he will gently lay a hand on her shoulder and put her to sleep with a word. Moments later, Senex appears outside the Aegis, behind the Unnamed, where all can see him hold high a dagger and what looks to be a human thighbone. He slashes deeply into the bone, even as the Storm rends and tears his body and spirit, and the Unnamed recoils in obvious pain, ceasing his assault upon the Aegis. The Fallen Oracle's blood seeps from his wounds and hangs in the ether, as though it were floating in microgravity. Some of it strikes the Aegis, which hisses and smokes but holds. The Unnamed does not turn his attentions to Senex but instead resumes his attack on the Aegis. Characters skilled in Prime and/or Spirit might wish to attempt to shore the Aegis up. Allow them to do so. Senex cuts the bone again and this time the Unnamed's left arm dangles limp and useless by his side, his robes soaked in his own blood. Reluctantly, the Unnamed turns from the Aegis to attend to the Old Man.

At this point, note that *nothing* will save Senex. This is a battle between Oracles, and the Old Man has chosen to embrace his fate with honor and courage, for the sake of those who must survive him to carry on the fight. The magics they loose are grim and terrible, and both are already badly wounded — Senex by the Storm; the Unnamed by his enemy's sorcery. Sadly, though, the fight is decided before it ever begins. Worn away by the Storm and the Unnamed as one, Senex must eventually fall, ravaged by dark powers until he is unrecognizable as the kindly Old Man. Leaving his foe's body floating there, the Unnamed turns back to the Aegis, looking like he just jumped into a grain thresher and only barely made it out alive. As he gathers his remaining might for one last assault, however, the roiling tempest around him begins to die, its power at last exhausted by the foul enchantments that bound it.

The Aswadim have just run out of Avatar Storm.

Showing fear for the first time, aware of the fact that there are Masters and perhaps even an archmage or two within the Aegis, the Unnamed flees, in no shape to take on even the lowliest Initiate. Shortly after the Fallen Oracle departs, the Aegis is dropped (to conserve the remaining stockpiles of Tass) and the Old Man's body is recovered. An enterprising character may grab his long-bladed dagger, which is overlooked by those wishing to give Senex a hero's honors. It is an *extremely* powerful Wonder and will likely aid the cabal greatly in the dark days to come.

Senex's Blade

15-pt. Wonder

This heavy, long-bladed dagger is forged of matte black iron with a grip of bone. Its blade is etched with pictograms that are now worn by time and use to the point of being unrecognizable. After being used to wound the Unnamed, the blade also bears wet-looking irregular spatter marks on it that no amount of time or magic can erase, as well as a heavy *Purifying* Resonance. The weapon has tasted the blood of a Fallen Oracle and comes away from the experience as a potent artifact against the Nephandi.

System: Senex's Blade inflicts Strength + 2 aggravated damage with a successful strike and contains within it the following Effects; **Locate Disorder and Weakness**, **Rip the Man-Body** (which can be activated only by cutting into a human bone) and **Lambs to the Slaughter** (which works only upon Nephandi killed by the blade's wielder, altering the Resonance of the Quintessence gained to *Purifying*, which immediately goes to refueling the Wonder). The blade uses six dice of Arete for its Effects, and if its **Rip the Man-Body** Effect is successfully used upon a Nephandus, it is treated as though one additional success had been rolled in its activation.

The Storm-Born

As the Avatar Storm is released, many of the Unnamed's favorites stir within the depths of the world's most powerful Labyrinths; beneath Crete, Chernobyl, Dachau and the like. As the fragments seek them out, these Nephandi, surrounded by wards and circles of protection, are able to slowly and methodically incorporate the soul-shards into their own inverted Avatars and, through them, feed their masters. Promised as much by renewed Pacts, each becomes a mightier vessel for the Outer Darkness.

Virtually all Nephandi everywhere seek refuge from the coming Storm in their Labyrinths (and are thus protected from the worst ravages of the Avatar Storm), but only a very few are specially selected to grow in might and become the court of the Unnamed in the world to come.

The Gauntlet Falls

Overwhelmed by human fear and the belief in what is impossible and yet plainly true, the Gauntlet crumbles, allowing the Umbrae to wash into our world. Sprits of pain, death and torment, drawn close by the suffering

The Change

Most of the Nephandi empowered by the loosing of the Storm become quite potent, having channeled the essence of dozens (or even hundreds) of people into themselves, expanding their Awakened abilities thereby. Consider those Nephandi who partake of the dark sacrament of the Storm (a select few, perhaps only 10% of all Fallen) to benefit from the following changes; +5 dots to Attributes, +15 dots of Abilities, +2 to Arete (to a maximum of 8), +5 Qlippothic Spheres and +2 Willpower (no maximum).

These alterations, however, also put a strain on the sanity (such as it is) of the affected parties. All such Nephandi gain a permanently active derangement to reflect the psychic shock of so gruesomely and forcibly incorporating the tormented souls of others into one's own being. Naturally, as none of the Aswadim particularly need the boost (and the Unnamed forbids any of them to get it, given the probably of insanity), they refrain from the rite, instead choosing to remain beyond the Tapestry, in the Outer Void.

Damage Control

• **For whatever reason, the characters didn't hide from the Avatar Storm.** Hey, it could happen. If any character isn't within the Aegis (or a similar construct) while the Storm rips through the material world and the Umbrae, he will suffer three levels of aggravated damage per turn of exposure for approximately 10 minutes (the length of time it takes for the Storm to dissipate). Lesser wards than the Aegis can mitigate the punishment and really clever thinking might serve to prevent the damage entirely. Just don't let a character walk away unscathed, however, if he doesn't floor you with the brilliance of his plan.

• **The characters attempt to attack the Unnamed.** It just won't work. By the time the Aegis is brought down, he's long since gone.

• **Someone accepts the Unnamed's offer.** Congratulations! You've got a brand-new Storyteller character to use. Unless, of course, you're feeling truly evil, in which case, you can allow the spiritual cancer to fester within the cabal and let the other characters attempt to survive with a traitor in their midst. (This latter option works really well if you isolate the players from one another during their "temptation" scenes, so that no one can ever be 100% certain that anyone else *didn't* accept the Fallen Oracle's bargain.)

inflicted by the Avatar Winds, are among the first into the world. Humanity's shield against the terrors of its dreams has just failed and nothing will ever be the same again. Ghosts walk among the living and demons crawl free from the pits of countless hells, eager to feed on warm blood.

Conversely, however, mages no longer need fear disembodiment or acclimation effects, and previously disembodied mages can walk on Earth as if they were material.

An Offer You Can't Refuse

The world's number of Awakened constitutes the barest fraction of its total population. Even as the number of human beings has grown, the vital spark of the Pure Ones has waned, fractured into ever thinner slivers, trying to expand the minds and open the eyes of increasingly blind Sleepers. That being the case, the Unnamed has no problem with offering a slice of the pie to any Awakened person who will hear his pitch. Normally, intermediaries make the pitch, but your characters are somehow different or special. He will want to offer them their hearts' deepest desires personally. Even as the Gauntlet crumbles and all hell breaks loose, the Unnamed will find these young heroes who so courageously acted to save the mages at Balador, seeking them out in private, when they are far out of earshot of any powerful Awakened who might aid them.

Whether the Unnamed appears in all his dread majesty or takes a more innocuous form is really up to you and should be tailored to your players and their characters. In any case, he will offer to fulfill their fantasies, no matter how base or grandiose, if only they will submit to being branded with his seal and call him master. Answers such as, "I accept on the terms that you die/leave Creation/stop what you're doing/etc." will be met with laughter and polite refusal of such terms. The Unnamed will leave such characters believing that he is more amused by the request than offended. Those who are clever in their bargaining but, in the end, hold out against him, earn his esteem. He might even do something "nice" for such a character: returning a slain loved one to life (no strings attached, but don't let the player know that) or leaving a legendary Wonder at the character's feet, all without asking for anything in return. If the character is truly moral (and, if she held out against the Unnamed, she is almost doubtlessly moral), the "gift" will feel cheap and corrupt.

Chapter III

A Brief Respite

For a while, things grow quiet again, as the Unnamed takes stock of his situation, recovers his strength and compensates for unexpected casualties. Give the characters enough time to do some errands of their own during this lull. Also, you might have some plot threads that you'd like to tie up. Don't feel pressured to do so with all such plots right now (other opportunities will arise down the line), but it might be helpful to you to deal with a few loose ends at this point.

Some far-thinking characters will want to make preparations for when the shit really hits the fan (which it will). Let them. Some of these plans might work, and others definitely will not. In general, only the most innovative contingencies have any chance of proving useful in the days to come. Anywhere from a week to a month can pass at this phase, depending upon the needs of your game. The Unnamed has time on his side and feels no need to rush now that victory is well within his grasp. His next move will be a devastating one.

The Withering of the Tree

Now that the Umbrae are peeled back and revealed to humanity at large, just about anyone can wander to the Alder Bole and find a way up or down, into the highest or lowest realms of the spirits. More importantly, some of the few remaining Oracles and archmages, who exist in distant corners of Creation, can more readily make manifest their will in the world, sending their magics through the Axis Mundi to wherever they wish. Naturally, the Unnamed has no desire for this to happen, so he plans to undertake what is doubtlessly the single most abhorrent act of mystic will in the history of the human race. He means to strike down the Tree, severing the worlds from one another in chaos (making Earth the only place in which they intersect) and leaving a great, bleeding wound at the center of the Universe.

Using yet more of his stockpiled Tass and blasphemous rituals scribed on the outer walls of Creation, the Unnamed sends his Aswadim to the Axis Mundi bearing a cauldron of venom, which they pour into a wound in the Tree. Within a week, it withers and topples, dropping dying branches throughout the worlds. Some might even end up on Earth. A few live long enough for people to find them and save them, meaning that hope is not *entirely* lost. The characters might be able to recover some branches from the Alder Bole. Kept alive and enchanted properly, such remnants of the Tree can allow for travel between worlds and contact with the surviving Oracles (if any) as well as serving as potent weapons against malevolent spirits.

Branch of the World Tree
4-10-pt. Wonder

These powerful Talismans are made from the still-living branches of the Axis Mundi. Such Wonders vary in potency. A small branch might have a minor power or two, while a huge, stout one might enable a mage to do many things. Life 3/Prime 2/Spirit 2 is necessary to keep a branch alive. A mage with Prime 4 can keep the branch alive indefinitely, without the need to continually renew the Effect.

It is possible that one of these Talismans, if planted deep in the heart of the Dark Umbra and tended carefully by at least one mage of each Avatar Essence, will eventually grow, sprouting up through the Umbrae and creating a new Axis Mundi. Given the many dangers inherent in such an attempt, however, it is highly unlikely that anyone will ever have the opportunity to find out.

System: The 4-pt. Branch is the least powerful. A character using one might move between levels of the Umbrae *if she possesses the ability to do so*. Such a branch inflicts the character's Strength in aggravated damage upon a spirit of any sort. The 6-pt. Branch is identical to the 4-pt. Branch, save that the character might bring others along with her (even if she only has the Spheres necessary to move herself between the Umbrae), and it inflicts Strength + 1 aggravated damage against spirits on a successful hit. The 8-pt. Branch is identical to the 6-pt. Branch, save that it also allows a character who normally cannot move between Umbrae to do so at will (rolling three dice of Arete to do so, though the character cannot bring others along with her when using this Effect) and it inflicts Strength + 3 damage against spirits. The 10-pt. Branch is identical to the 8-pt. Branch, save that it allows a character to move herself and any number of other people between Umbrae at will (rolling five dice of Arete to do so) and inflicts Strength + 5 aggravated damage against spirits.

The Oracles Severed

Now that the Alder Bole is dead, those Oracles and far-flung Archmasters who have removed themselves from Earth are virtually incapable of returning. Dispatching legions of ghosts, spirits and Unspeakable Horrors (supplemented by a handful of truly frightening Storm-Born Nephandi) along the hidden paths of Creation, the Unnamed eliminates all but a few of them, one by one. Though he loses many resources in the process, it is far more important to his cause to see the most powerful mages in Creation slain, lest they rally their lessers at some inopportune moment.

The Order's Last Stand

While the Oracles and Archmasters are being hunted very nearly to extinction, the Unnamed burns out the last of his Quintessence stores at Horizon, at last unleashing his poisoned magic into the Nodes that power the realm. From them, spiritual corruption (made real and physical by the lack of a Gauntlet) saturates the planet. Within three days, the sun and moon are lost in a roiling tempest of clouds that looks like nothing so much as a churning mass of dying embers. Lord Gilmore hatches a final, desperate ploy, but one that will cost the Awakened dearly.

It is at the now-polluted Node of Alexandria, where once stood the greatest library of the ancient world, that the Order of Hermes makes its final stand. Summoned by Lord Edward Gilmore, the mages of the Order have come from far and wide to strike what blow they can against the tyranny of the Nephandi before all ends in ashes and shadow. Many mages of other Traditions (and even a few Crafts and Conventions) stand with the Order of Hermes, knowing full well the futility of their endeavor but able to think of no other way to do what must be done.

At least, that's the ruse. Lord Gilmore has other ideas in mind, but he knows that the lives of the mages of the Order, himself included, must be forfeit in order to see it happen. He is aware that the Fallen have no choice but to respond to this gathering, since the mystic might assembled there could reasonably disrupt the Unnamed's plans if directed properly. In order to do so, though, the Unnamed will need to commit an army, and he will still lose many of his most loyal and powerful. The Order of Hermes does not sell its life cheaply, and Gilmore has more tricks than mere attrition up his sleeve.

The Subterfuge

This is a brutally dangerous mission, and the characters are among those elite forces selected to undertake it. The strike force is assembled in northern Canada, far from the massed forces of the Order. Shortly before the anticipated moment of the Nephandic response to the Order of Hermes'

> ### Jessica Schmidt, "Grand Mistress" of Mus
> **Faction:** Orphan *barabbi*
> **Essence:** Pattern
> **Nature:** Autocrat
> **Demeanor:** Autocrat
> **Attributes:** Strength 1, Dexterity 2, Stamina 6, Charisma 1, Manipulation 5, Appearance 0, Perception 4, Intelligence 6, Wits 5
> **Abilities:** Academics 4, Alertness 3, Awareness 4, Brawl 1, Computer 2, Cosmology 3, Dodge 1, Enigmas 4, Etiquette 3, Expression 2, Firearms 3, Intimidation 5, Investigation 3, Law 2, Leadership 4, Linguistics 4, Medicine 4, Occult 5, Science 4, Stealth 1, Subterfuge 5, Technology 3
> **Backgrounds:** Allies 3, Arcane 4, Avatar 2, Contacts 2, Destiny 1, Library 5, Node 5, Resources 4
> **Qlippothic Spheres:** Correspondence 2, Entropy 4, Forces 1, Life 2, Matter 2, Mind 3, Prime 3, Spirit 2, Time 1
> **Arete:** 5
> **Willpower:** 8
> **Quintessence:** 12
> **Paradox:** 6
> **Resonance:** (Entropic) Degenerate 2, (Static) Tenacious 1

defiance, Gilmore appears to wish the fighters good luck. Any members of the Order of Hermes in the cabal are taken aside by Lord Gilmore, who says the following:

I never would have imagined that I would live to see the death of our Tradition, yet that is what now awaits us. Still, we are the heirs to the Thrice-Great and nothing, not even death itself, can undo our Path of Gold. I need you now to do something for me. Mus was once mine and a fine realm it was. Now, it serves as the maggot-den of the Fallen. I shudder to think of their "teachers" defiling my Sanctum with their unholy rites. Still, what is done is done, and I cannot be the one to avenge my students and my friends. You are my hands now. Destroy them all, lest our fall be for naught. Avenge Mus and the Order. Keep our ways alive in the long darkness to come.

At this, Gilmore embraces the mage or mages as he would a son or daughter and, with a stern, resolute face, returns to the ranks to face his demise.

The Siege of Mus

Dante opens the Correspondence gateway to Mus, easily breaking the wards placed upon it by some of the Unnamed's most trusted Nephandi. The Fallen are completely unprepared for the attack and their armies are absent, having been sent to deal with the massed army of the Order of Hermes. Still, there are some defenders there, and they quickly recover their wits. Tailor the number of Nephandi present to the power of the cabal. The siege should be extremely difficult, but possible.

The "Grand Mistress" of the chantry is the gilledian Jessica Schmidt, once the wife to an SS officer. Now, she is a powerful Nephandus who looks like the mummified, ambulatory corpse of a woman in her mid-60s.

Afterward

If Mus is to be retaken, it will happen because of your characters' actions. If the cabal makes the right moves, then the realm can be restored to the Traditions, giving them a stable base of operations from which to strike against the Nephandi, who will be unable to mount a second attack upon a reclaimed Mus, regardless of their power. If the characters do not make the right choices (or have a run of bad luck), however, the endeavor will be a failure and Gilmore's gambit will be proven folly. In any case, virtually everyone who made a stand at Alexandria will die, leaving only a very few to limp home. Still, by the time Lord Edward Gilmore perishes in battle, he has seen scores of Nephandi and their foul servants feed the desert with their lives.

> ### Damage Control
> • **The characters aren't fighters.** No problem; if the characters can't fight, don't try to make them. Instead, give them jobs on the sidelines, coordinating the offensive and making sure the lines of communication stay intact. If, on the other hand, the characters *want* to fight, this is commendable. Foolish, but commendable. Don't hesitate to let them die if members of the cabal can't cut it, but try to give them some small measure of vindication for standing up and doing the right thing.
> • **The characters refuse to take part in the siege of Mus.** This, on the other hand, *is* a problem. If the cabal chickens out, feel free to give the characters what they deserve. The Order falls and the Fors Collegis Mercuris is not retaken.

Chapter IV

The Death of the Machine

With faith in the power of science and technology to protect the world at an all-time low and no Gauntlet to hold back superstition, the Technocracy's paradigm falls apart. Money ceases to have value in such a world, medicines do not cure plagues, and machines will not stop those swarms of flies that feed on spinal fluid and distilled terror. Stasis falls apart, but not in any good way. The Umbrae wash over the world, dissolving 10,000 years of human progress and reducing mankind to barbarism. Laws that were once true are no longer so. Friction on a dry branch might cause it to shudder and bleed, but it will not start a fire.

Science and technology based in wonder and possibility (Dynamic Science and technology) still function, since such innovations are based in reliance upon the self, rather than reliance upon things. A scarce few Technocrats manage to survive the fall of the Union with their abilities intact, and these are the ones who are capable of reconciling the enigma of Will versus Reason. Virtually to a man, the New World Order, Iteration X and the Progenitors fall. With a bit more ethical and philosophical flexibility, small numbers of Syndicate operatives and a larger number of Void Engineers walk away from the end of Reason still capable of performing Enlightened Science.

Shortly afterward, the Void Engineers approach remaining Tradition authorities (such as they are) — the characters among them — and ask for succor from the Nephandi, in exchange for what resources they can help bring to bear (including some bizarre alien technologies and stores of Tass from off-world sources) in the final hours of the conflict. Allow the characters to be among the policy-makers here. They have treated with some of the Traditions' most powerful, influential and respected, and now, regardless of how mystically weak or powerful they are, they are looked to as voices of guidance. It is probably best in the long run to accept the Void Engineers' proposal, but, in the end, it's really up to what's best for your game and what seems wisest to the characters' cabal.

This chapter is more of a period of time than a series of events. The Fallen entrench themselves, just as the remaining mages of Earth do. (If Mus was retaken in the previous chapter, then they might hole up at the For Collegis Mercuris; if not, they'll have to make do with whatever they can find.) Anything from a week to a couple of months can pass at this point. The Unnamed wants to allow the Umbrae to do his work for him for a while. As terrible spirits wander the world, desperate mages strike out on quests — some potentially useful but most futile and doomed to failure. The cabal might number among these mages, or it might be one of the nerve centers of the slowly coalescing resistance. (Or, if you are feeling particularly cruel, the characters might be compelled to do double duty, searching for scattered Masters, Wonders and the like while at the same time being looked to for tactical advice.)

> ### Damage Control
> - **The characters are Technocrats.** The best option here is to allow the characters to be among those select few members of the Union who can somehow manage to "grow beyond their programming," as it were, and realize that it is will as much as next-generation science that makes such procedures function.

Chapter V

Salonikas' Lesson

Akrites Salonikas has one final lesson to impart. He has by now realized that the prophecy of Moloch could not be averted and that, in trying to prevent it, he has helped to bring it about. In the end, he has learned that, sometimes, there *is* no victory. He has played his part to the end and now, overwhelmed by guilt and remorse, he feels he must show the children of magic the fate that awaits them.

Mages everywhere are gripped by terrible cries of psychic anguish. Salonikas' voice rings out, clear despite its torment, even as the Aswadim, whom he has dared to challenge directly, rend him to shreds.

Sometimes, even the best of intentions fail. Sometimes, there is no right answer. Sometimes, you do what is good, only to find that the flames consume the just and the wicked with equal abandon. Remember this always and fight on. I am so sorry.

At this, the message ends, along with the life of Akrites Salonikas, student of Sh'zar the Seer.

Waiting for the Worst

On that depressing note, Descent truly comes to Earth. The spiritual ruination sown by the Unnamed (though Horizon's Nodes) has devoured the purity of the world. The Traditions are a frail shadow of their former power and the Technocracy is fallen entirely. Perhaps 10% of the world's (non-Nephandic) Awakened have survived this holocaust.

Mages will have to fight hard to survive during this dark time, and it might take months for all of the terrible consequences of recent times to fully come to light. By now, the characters are certainly pivotal figures and are looked to by many. They feel hopeless, but they've got to try to put up a confident front, for the sake of those who now rely upon them. They might be considered leaders by both Sleepers and Awakened. Even as Descent claims untold lives, the undeniable truth of magic spurs no small number of Awakenings, and such lost Orphans, adrift in a world gone mad, need guidance.

Now, there is nothing left to do, save fortify one's position, gather up what stragglers are to be found, wait and try to survive whatever comes next.

Chapter VI

The Descent of Creation is come, and the Unnamed stands triumphant, the architect of mankind's history — from its promising beginnings to its terrible end in fire and torment. The Nameless Lords bestride the Earth like titans, and the ruination of reality reaches its crescendo.

The Scourging of the Earth

Now that the Gauntlet is no more, the Traditions and the Technocratic Union have fallen and the other willworkers of the Earth are scattered in fear and fractiousness, the Unnamed raises high his ultimate weapon, ready to end the war forever and break humanity to his yoke.

In a ritual held at the new site of his rule, in the blasted wasteland that was once Eden, the Unnamed summons his masters to Earth, giving them leave to incarnate physically within Creation. As they do so, pockets of the Tapestry dissolve forever, unable to support the weight of the chthonic titans. Here and there, around the world, pregnant women miscarry children, finding horribly misshapen things that crawl away of their own accord, animals bleat and howl, with some of them going mad and rabid and others just dying, and bodies of water turn to blood and venom. The order of Creation is broken, and Those Who

Chapter Six: Hell on Earth 183

Came Before are given dominion over all that is. Finally, their jealousy finds its satisfaction and they learn what it is to have substance and existence, to the lamentation of reality itself.

Divvying the Spoils

Of course, the Unnamed keeps his word to most of those Fallen who supported him in his rise and subsequent conquest. Each of the Aswadim is given an abode from which to exert his or her will, though most of the day-to-day affairs of running Creation fall to the lesser Nephandi, the gilledians and adsinistrati, supported by Storm-Born shock troops. Unless killed (or otherwise put out of commission) by the characters, for example, Voormas accepts the truth of his Fall and graciously takes up the mantle of rulership over the remains of India and Pakistan. Jodi Blake governs everything from Los Angeles to Las Vegas, and Anson d'Arcangelo takes up residence in Vatican City, there to lord over Italy.

The Nephandi are virtually unstoppable at this point, and victories (when they are had at all) are small and come only through hit-and-run tactics. None can now delude themselves into believing that the Ascension War persists. For now and perhaps forever, it is ended. Beneath a sky of seething molten crimson and choking black mists, the Fallen sit in judgment over the desert wastes once known as Earth.

> ### "Anson Who?"
> You might not know who some of the various Nephandi given one-line cameos in "Hell on Earth" are. That's fine. All of them can be found in **Mage** books of varying levels of antiquity, and for the most part, their names are mentioned only for flavor. If you've got a Nephandus antagonist of your own in mind for the Governor of Sin, Patron of Las Vegas, then by all means feel free to boot Jodi Blake's skank ass out of town.

The End of It All

When all is said and done, the world writhes in the throes of Descent, damnation seemingly everlasting. Magic still lives, though the numbers of its practitioners are much diminished, save for the Fallen. Demons, dark spirits and Unspeakable Horrors from Beyond walk the Earth with impunity, and some lord over scattered enclaves of miserable survivors as dread taskmasters and cruel barons. The Fallen revel in what they have wrought and settle in to enjoy an eternity of ruling over a helpless human race largely reduced to Iron Age civilization and subject to depredations unknown since the worst excesses of the priests of the demon-gods of the ancient world.

If the characters have done well, then some manner of resistance lives on, surviving another day to bring the fight to the Aswadim once more and topple them, so that the centuries-long (at least) process of driving out the dark can begin anew. For now, however, it is enough to know that the End has come and gone, and Ascension has proven to be a lie, a feast of ashes supped upon in sorrow by a failed human race.

The Unnamed

This is the Unnamed, in his final incarnation as god-king of the smoldering ruin of Creation.
Essence: Primordial
Nature: Incomprehensible
Demeanor: Tyrant/Visionary
Attributes: Strength 4/15, Dexterity 6/9, Stamina 10/20, Charisma 9, Manipulation 10, Appearance 8/0, Perception 10, Intelligence 9, Wits 9 (numbers after the slash indicate the Nameless' battle-shape)
Abilities: Assume that the Unnamed possesses virtually *all* Abilities, save those pertaining to modern technologies (say, those developed within the past thousand or so years), at between four and nine dots.
Backgrounds: Arcane 6, Avatar 10, Destiny 10, Dream 10. The Unnamed possesses virtually all other Backgrounds save Mentor (which he no longer possesses or needs) at effectively limitless levels, since the resources of the entirety of Creation are his to command
Qlippothic Spheres: Correspondence 6, Entropy 10, Forces 5, Life 5, Matter 5, Mind 7, Prime 8, Spirit 8, Time 5
Arete: 10
Willpower: 20
Quintessence: Limitless
Paradox: N/A
Resonance: (Entropic) Ruin 10

Image: In his human form, the Unnamed is a tall, slender, painfully handsome man with skin, hair and eyes like polished obsidian. Only the striking whiteness of his perfect teeth offsets the relentless blackness of his form. He dresses in elaborate black robes, befitting the lord and master of Reality itself, covered in silver-stitched sigils of such malevolence as to sear themselves temporarily onto the eyes, like lights stared at too long. He speaks in a calm, measured, seductive voice that seems kind and wise, but within its depths lurks a forcefulness so intense as to render disobedience virtually unthinkable.

Roleplaying Hints: You are always in control of yourself and the world around you. More or less nothing fazes you, and you always project exactly the image you wish to others, having become quite a capable student of human nature over the course of your long millennia. You give the impression of a benevolent father, even when you are heaping unspeakable torments upon those who displease you. You simply accept as fact the notion that you can break anyone, achieve anything and meet the price of any man's soul.

Notes: The Unnamed can expend a Willpower point to cast more than one magical Effect in a turn, with no limit to the number of points of Willpower, other than his current temporary total, that might be spent in this fashion in one turn. He also possesses 10 dice of inherent Countermagic, though these apply only to Effects that target him directly. (Of course, he may still attempt to Unweave any magical Effect within his sensory range.) At the cost of a point of Willpower, he might assume his battle-shape, a nightmarish tapestry of whirling madness, flailing pseudopods and glimpses into the vast gulfs of Beyond. All who gaze into its depths must make a Willpower roll (difficulty 9, three successes required) or be driven stark, raving mad (Storyteller's discretion as to what form the madness takes, though it will be extreme). The Unnamed can also assume many other shapes, changing race, gender and even species if it suits his needs. These other transformations, however, are handled as a function of his Qlippothic Spheres.

From his bleak throne, the Tenth Seat, as he still affectionately calls it, the Unnamed rules Creation — or what remains of it, at least. Physically, the center of his power is located in Mesopotamia, where once was found the cradle of civilization. In terror and pain, millions of slaves labor to heap glory upon his name, living and dying at his command. He is the face of the Void, incarnate upon the Earth, architect of the Universe's despair.

The Other Aswadim

The Unnamed still enjoys the support of the first five people to accept his offer (maintained through canny politics, incentives and, of course, the threat of their destruction). The youngest of them hails from Pharaonic Egypt, and all are vastly powerful. Naturally, all have their own agendas and each has accepted a lesser position only because the Unnamed is so much more mystically potent than any one or two (or perhaps even three) of them and none trust each other enough to attempt to depose him. Still, it *is* possible to turn one Fallen Oracle against another, given time, effort and planning. Perhaps, it is even possible to turn all of the Aswadim, including their founder and master, upon one another. Whether such an act would allow the world to be freed from the grip of terror or would only set the stage for a tyrant yet more terrible, however, is a question none can answer.

There are six Aswadim in total (and have been so for thousands of years). During all that time, their membership has never changed. Each of the non-Pattern Spheres (Correspondence, Entropy, Mind, Prime, Spirit and Time) has a Fallen Oracle associated with it. Forces, Life and Matter were considered too "base and fleeting" to be worthy of their own exemplars, though all six of the Aswadim are quite proficient in the use of *all* of the Qlippothic Spheres. All of the Fallen Oracles have sacrificed their Names to Those Beyond, so, like the Unnamed, they are known by titles of their own choosing. The meanings of these monikers are now remembered only among the Aswadim.

The other five Aswadim are as follows (the Unnamed is the lord Entropy):

• **The Hierophant of Winds, Fallen Oracle of Correspondence:** In his presence, distance and space mean nothing. The Hierophant of Winds walks the dangerous paths of the Fallen Earth always, messenger and herald of the Unnamed, even as he broods within a tower of broken angles and fragmented planes in the heart of what was once New York City. Wherever he goes, enemies grow closer and help becomes ever more distant, while evil tidings travel swiftly and good news never arrives. The Hierophant of Winds is a handsome man, with a long, sweeping mane of brown hair, fine-boned and dusky features and resplendent robes that always seem to ripple in an unfelt breeze.

• **The Stillborn King, Fallen Oracle of Mind:** The Stillborn King now exists only within his own tormented dreams. Still, the echoes of those nightmares seep into Creation, infecting others with his demented fantasies. He has been granted no one demesne over which to lord, for such concepts as physical space and corporeal existence have ceased to have value to him. Instead, his nightmares roil across the Earth like a storm, raining down deranged hallucinations that cross the boundaries between illusion and reality, eroding the value of the walls between sleep and wakefulness, sanity and madness. In the rare instances when he is seen, his form is protean, conforming to the ebb and flow of his own mutilated self-perception.

• **The Harlot Empress, Fallen Oracle of Prime:** When asked, she happily confesses that she was once a priestess-whore of Babylon. The Harlot Empress sits upon an undulating throne of intertwined human bodies in orgiastic celebration, deep within her citadel in what used to be Bangkok. Her embrace leaves men and women alike as statues of ash, their faces frozen into expressions of ecstatic pain. Hers is the selfish love that devours the object of its affection (or obsession). She has a ripe, voluptuous body and the face of a goddess. The Harlot Empress disdains clothing entirely, using desire as her first and foremost magic and thereby ensnaring all those who look upon her in webs spun of their own lusts.

• **The Angel of Ghosts, Fallen Oracle of Spirit:** The Angel of Ghosts makes her home in what was once Central Africa. The living and dead alike coexist in torment under her watchful eye; life and death have, therefore, ceased to have meaning. She kills with a look and suffers none to see her naked face without being consumed to sate her hunger for souls. Her form is that of a shapely woman in her late teens or early 20s, with chalk-white skin and ashen hair. Her eyes are lost in the shadows of her alabaster mask, carved into a visage of coldly beautiful perfection, and she wears robes of tattered rags that are strips of rudely tanned human flesh, woven and stitched into a gruesome patchwork.

• **The Laughing Fool, Fallen Oracle of Time:** Neither dead nor alive, the Laughing Fool dwells only in those spans between breaths, in the few seconds when life ends and death begins, in the moment of fear and dread wherein time ceases to have meaning and every instant expands to become an eternity. An empty palace, built of moments frozen in time, stands deep within the Siberian taiga, at the edge of the Arctic Circle. Those who walk its frigid halls hear distant sounds and see fleeting sights of times and places and people who never were or will be. Among them is the Laughing Fool, garbed in rich purple robes with a face that seems neither old nor young, but instead long since dead or waiting to be born.

Naturally, all of the Aswadim are phenomenally powerful. None has an Arete less than 7, and each one has his or her Qlippothic specialty Sphere at the highest possible rating. In general, consider each of them to be roughly half as powerful as the Unnamed, with a bit of variation on both sides of the curve. Each alone is more than a match for all but the most powerful cabals of mages, and such potent Fallen are almost never found alone, being surrounded at virtually all times by flocks of servitors and mystically bound slaves. Some, such as the Harlot Empress, have followers who would willingly die for them, while others, like the Angel of Ghosts, hold vast armies in unbreakable bondage. Each is, literally, a demigod upon the Earth.

Aftermath

"Salt Lake City once stood there," the hooded figure asserted quietly, as though those words should mean something to those who stood before him, the children of Armageddon's aftermath. He gestured out over the glassy black pyramid in the center of the city, atop which burned an angry red flame. Even from this distance, the wailing of the naked souls that fueled it could be heard.

"So what?" the young woman who seemed to speak for the band asked. Her eyes were hard, so out of place in a face that could not have seen more than eighteen years. She ran a callused hand through the red-brown tangle of her hair and muttered acidly, "The World Before ended over a hundred years ago. Man had his chance. Now, They rule here, and that's all there is. Thanks for the history lesson, though, old man."

The cloaked figure shook his head in sorrow, the mane of white-streaked light brown hair spilling from beneath his cowl catching the breeze. As the youths turned to leave, his eyes narrowed to slits and he inhaled slowly and methodically, focusing the vitality of his spirit upon his Crown Chakra. His consciousness split the air between himself and the young men and women, entering each of their minds with the force of an avalanche.

YOU ARE MORE THAN YOU DARE IMAGINE. GIVE UP YOUR WILL TO BE BLIND. OPEN YOUR EYES AND SEE. YOU ARE HUMAN, AND YOUR BIRTHRIGHT IS FREEDOM. CAST OFF THE CHAINS OF SLEEP AND RISE UP TO BECOME WHAT YOU ARE.

The young vagabonds reeled with the force of the contact, but the redheaded girl was the first to regain her footing. She shook her head to clear it and gasped, "How did you do that? Who are you?"

The man brought his hands up and drew back the hood of his cloak, revealing a face still young and handsome, despite the lines of care that now creased it. A devilish smile crossed his lips and he spoke, "As to how I did that, it's nothing that you won't be able to do, given a little training. I have seen the destiny of your souls, and I know that each of you is struggling to Awaken. As to who I am; that's a complicated question. For now, you can just call me Julian…"

Of course, while the world as we know it ends with Descent, the Earth doesn't crumble and fade into nothingness. There is still reason enough to fight against the tyranny of the Fallen. After all, perhaps, as some who are now dead might have said, the Wheel turns — sometimes, it is at its zenith and, at other times, it is at its nadir. All things have their time, and any apocalypse you can walk away from obviously isn't final. While the Awakened now have on their hands the greatest uphill battle in the history of the human race, it is during such times that heroism thrives and the mettle of great men and women is proven.

Hopefully, at least a few of the characters are still alive, as are at least some of the influential and experienced mages of the Traditions, Crafts and Conventions. You can tell any number of stories in the aftermath of "Hell on Earth," whether shortly after the end of humanity's Descent or, as in the example, decades later. Perhaps you want to *begin* your chronicle after Descent, and who are we to tell you otherwise? It's up to you, after all, for endings are almost never as final as they seem…

Chapter Seven: Designing Ascension

Sooner and later you will see great changes made,
dreadful horrors and vengeances.
For as the moon is thus led by its angel
the heavens draw near to the Balance.
—Nostradamus' Quatrains, Century 1, Stanza 56

It's not easy to end the world. Even if your finale is a little quieter, it's important to plan the end of your game with care. This chapter uses some ideas from **Mage**'s metaplot to help Storytellers bring their game to a satisfying conclusion. Then we'll talk about how to define your World of Darkness and present concepts and systems to help you use the classic, epic devices common to such finales.

On Stage for the Last Act

Mage's development promotes a universe centered upon the players' characters. Their cabal is at the hub of things. On the other hand, it's important to provide a context for this. The fact that the characters are the most important participants in the game world doesn't automatically make them the most powerful. It doesn't make things easier for them. Your game's cabal is important because it overcomes challenges and acts as a fulcrum for change. Whether or not that means giving the characters leadership positions is up to you.

For your cabal's efforts (and the players') to have any meaning, they have to be contrasted with the backdrop of the setting and its antagonistic elements. The Traditions don't get along. The Technocracy struggles with internal schisms while marching forth to suppress reality's dissidents. Nephandi and Marauders prowl the dark and mad corners of the universe. Other supernatural beings point to undiscovered cosmic secrets.

These elements *don't* exist to make the characters feel small. They're there to underscore how important — how improbably accomplished — the cabal is against a host of adversaries and a huge backdrop. The World of Darkness story line is something that the characters grow to encompass. We don't belittle that goal by shrinking the universe into an economical, easy-to-conquer package. The purpose of metaplot is to make greatness worth striving for.

Let's survey where the game's setting stands circa 2004. Division rocks every alliance, but these differences aren't incurable. Cabals and amalgams can mend things or splinter their enemies into rival factions. Of course, they can make mistakes and do the reverse, too.

The Traditions

Without the grand chantries of the past, Tradition cabals are left to their own means, but the strange fruits of desperate innovation lead to new kinds of magic and new ways to undermine dominant paradigms. It's an exciting time to be a Council mage — but which Council? Two factions claim the nine thrones. They aren't enemies, but renewed conflict with the Technocracy has strained diplomacy.

Scions of the Phoenix

Relying on an ad-hoc network of Heralds, five regional Tribunals and word of mouth, the *New Horizon Council* connects mages who want to exchange ideas and protect the Traditions without sacrificing their personal projects. New Horizon is more of an idea than a place. In 2001, the new Council gathered in Los Angeles to trap the Nephandi. Jodi Blake's minions were decimated, and cooperating mages used this success to unite the Traditions. That utilitarian spirit still holds true, and the new Council now gathers whenever and wherever it can do the most good. LA is still a general locus for New Horizon activity, especially after the "angel sightings" of 2003 relaxed the local paradigm (see **City of Angels** for **Demon: The Fallen**).

Because the New Horizon Council emphasizes individual goals and does not pursue conflict with the Technocracy, it's a popular affiliation for Guardians, a faction that opposes the influence of Rogue Council transmissions. The Guardians don't dominate the New Horizon Council, but they do have a significant voice.

Timelines and Triggers

The metaplot's official timeline roughly corresponds to the release dates of each product. Yet the story line isn't so chained to White Wolf's release schedule that a book that comes out on July 1st has its effect from that precise date forward. Also, new books include history, which might extend into the past to set up what is to come.

It's important, however, to realize that, in the end, the story happens when you say it does. It's never too late to run Doissetep's intrigues or the Second *Massasa* War.

It's very easy to plot out a timeline prior to your game, but keep it vague. Leave room for prequels and unexpected history. At some point, it might be convenient for you to decide that Porthos Fitz-Empress was a secret Infernalist, so you don't necessarily want to add extra detail to his personal history. You aren't married to set dates, either. Doissetep can fall in 2002. The Avatar Storm can hit in 1980.

After the chronicle's in-game start date, you can lay out subsequent events using a system of triggers. Make these triggers vague. For example, you could declare that the Second *Massasa* War (see **Blood Treachery**) happens whenever the Order of Hermes suffers a catastrophic loss of influence or magical lore. You determine the degree. In your game, the Avatar Storm might not exist, or it might have little effect, but your cabal might torch a key Hermetic college, triggering the war.

Doing so takes the metaplot and puts it firmly in your chronicle. Some triggers can lead to a domino effect, and not always in the "official" direction. The Euthanatos might destroy House Janissary because of a Rogue Council transmission, leading to the *Massasa* War. This violence wakes up an ancient vampire-god in India, the Technocracy destroys it, and storms wrack the Umbra. See each story as a modular affair. Adapt them for consistency, and tie them to your game.

It isn't necessarily desirable to tie every event to a trigger. To keep the epic scope of the setting, allow some events to proceed on their own. This gives the players a sense of being caught up in the history of a wider world. Otherwise, they might get the sense that they need to kick something over to move things forward at all.

The New Horizon Council

The following Councilors are the default choices from the 2001 Los Angeles gathering, but you needn't cling to them. In fact, it's possible that your characters are actually members of the Council. Unlike the old Council of Nine, they take seats by Tradition, not Sphere. One of the New Horizon Council's ideals is democratic representation, in which less experienced mages (even Disciples!) can run for positions. In fact, each Tradition keeps its own counsel about how members are selected. Some Traditions have embraced this idea, appointing mages with fresh ideas to Council seats. Other Councilors are mere mouthpieces for their Tradition's remaining Masters. If you haven't stocked the Council with your own characters, the following mages hold the Council's seats:

Chancellor Pro Tempore: Mark Gillan bani Hermes (Adept, though he has never revealed his rank). A new position, the temporary Chancellorship was created to cut down on internecine bickering and scheming. Despite his vocal protests, seven of the nine new Councilors (Lord Gilmore abstained) voted for his appointment. Naturally, Gillan accepted. True to their hopes, Gillan's tenure has been marked with swift, efficient decisions. The alleged ex-Hermetic doesn't trust the Emissaries, but he mostly tries to direct discussion elsewhere. Besides, he'll quit any day now. He doesn't want to be here. Really.

Akashic Brotherhood: Sifu Nu Ying ("Raging Eagle") of the Shaolin Diaspora (Master). The monk accepts his new duty with equanimity, but the warrior in him picks apart recent Technocracy movements for weakness as a form of reflexive meditation. He's not apt to take sides, but he can offer valuable advice to anyone who asks.

Celestial Chorus: Reverend Simon Pain of the Monist Church (Disciple). This ex-Technocrat is the least trusted member of the entire Council. A strong believer in eventual reconciliation with the Technocracy, Pain opposed the recent destruction of House Janissary. Tensions between the Chorus and the Euthanatos haven't been this high in over 100 years. Consequently, the Chorus wields the least influence.

Cult of Ecstasy: Lee Ann Milner, Joybringer (Disciple). Milner's a practical woman with an open mind, able to change her convictions in response to a good argument without succumbing to bullying. Even though she's the least skilled mage in the Council, her sincerity and open-mindedness often sways the others. Milner thinks the Emissaries are a bit rough-edged, but many Cultists took up the Sphinx banner and she feels she should say something on their behalf.

Dreamspeakers: Netsilak Raymond, Mastersmith of Spiritual Machines (Adept). The Spirit Smith has a quick mind but less of a head for politics. He deals with this shortfall by simply stating his position. When someone argues, he restates it. He does so until his views win or he's ignored. His Tradition knows the Otherworlds and spirits best, however, so Councilors are willing to compromise. Netsilak takes the Sphinx very seriously. The Invisible World is crying out; mages need to find out why.

Euthanatos: Chela Alexander Moro of the Albireo (Adept). He might be the descendant of Cygnus Moro, but everyone knows that the Euthanatoi are ruled from Pluto, don't they? In fact, common wisdom is wrong; Senex is too preoccupied with his own plans to direct his Tradition. Moro pieced together an obscure code with reports of a secret Umbral library, leading to the extermination of Janissary "secret Technocrats." Hated by the Order of Hermes and feared by the other Traditions, he uses his influence cautiously.

Order of Hermes: Lord Edward Gilmore bani Tytalus (Master). When ordered to vote by their mentors, the Hermetics naturally chose a Master. Nothing else would do! Lord Gilmore's a man who's tasted defeat and been humbled. He mixes power with restraint because he's been eyewitness to self-destructive magical excess. More importantly, Gilmore is famous for three acts: evacuating his chantry on Mus (Mercury), facing down the astral body of the Tremere Primus, and sealing the Ways to Horizon before being the last known mage to leave. The first two acts inspire admiring speeches; the last, curious whispers. Lord Gilmore claimed that he kept the realm's civil war from spilling over, but what if he was keeping something else in — or out?

Sons of Ether: Professor Yves Mercure (Adept). The professor sees this whole Council business as a pain, really. There must be a machine that could do this tedious politicking (and if he has time to return to his workshop, there will be!). In any event, as long as the Council keeps the Emissaries off everyone's back, he can get back to work and stop worrying about being an ad-hoc diplomat, judge and general.

Verbena: Hector de Xangô (Adept). The Twister of Fate is a somewhat conservative addition to the Council. He believes that his purpose is to keep the rest of the Traditions off the Sacred Branches' backs and is skeptical of any attempt to give the Council a higher purpose. For him, survival and the primal Arts are enough.

Virtual Adepts: Catherine Blass, a.k.a. X-Cel, of the Reality Hackers (Adept). Blass would describe herself as a "social guerilla." During the Ascension War, she delighted in humiliating the Technocracy instead of killing its agents. As a Councilor, she sees no reason to stop. She favors directing the Emissaries' energies into a propaganda counteroffensive and illustrates her position with impromptu holographic presentations when the mood strikes her. A known Ascension War veteran and one of Gillan's old accomplices, Blass wields considerable power.

Emissaries of the Sphinx

Composed of invisible generals and their enigmatic commands, the Rogue Council upset the defeated stability that kept the Traditions safe but left the Technocracy's rule uncontested. This Council doesn't even have a proper name; it was labeled after its *Manifesto*, a document calling on mages to fight for freedom against control. Nobody knows who wrote *The Rogue Council Manifesto*, but most mages assume that it's the handiwork of a sympathetic cabal.

The authors of the transmissions are unknown. The Council's effective representatives are the so-called Emissaries, who share transmissions, organize guerilla strikes and assemble caucuses to search for a larger pattern in Sphinx communiqués. Rogue Council mages tend to be unconventional, mobile and violent, moving from one mission to the next as transmissions dictate.

The Technocracy

Meanwhile, the Technocracy adapted to multiple crises. First, front-line amalgams learned to take on an independent role. After the Reckoning, Control lost regular contact with its earthbound operatives. Freed from scrutiny, the Conventions (most notably Iteration X) made more allowances for agents' moral scruples. At the same time, this freedom exaggerated the influence of the Union's secret societies. Neo-Arthurians, Invictus and the SPD all contended for remaining resources.

Ragnarok Command

In 1999, the Technocracy sacrificed dozens of agents in Operation Ragnarok. After containing the threat, the Conventions decided to cooperate on a comprehensive response to supernatural threats. Powered armor replaced HIT Marks. Project Sunburst formed to research anti-vampire tactics, all under the rough umbrella of Ragnarok Command.

Ragnarok Command is a loose organization run by representatives from each Convention. All of them watch Iteration X's statistics carefully, hoping to beat the odds on an over 90% chance that humanity will become extinct within a decade or less. This affiliation is less a matter of duty than personal interest. Full time Ragnarok projects never employ more than two dozen Technocrats. For most affiliates, the alliance is a matter of developing useful technologies and putting humanity's defense first.

Many Constructs concentrated on their own projects instead of collective efforts like Ragnarok. As

such, they were totally unprepared for the first wave of Sphinx terrorism — or Control's answer.

Panopticon

Shortly after the appearance of Rogue Council transmissions, orders from Control appeared on screens and in mailboxes, drop sites and psionic networks around the world. Within a month, the first Panopticon amalgams appeared. Distrusted at first, they used their mandate to rapidly acquire influence and power, modernizing old war machines and rehabilitating agents for a renewed Pogrom.

Despite the fact that it challenges their authority, most earthbound Technocrats find Panopticon useful — even comforting. It's a sign that the Union is working, unbowed in the face of the Reckoning and ready to march forward. Researchers are spared the messy work of taming the Consensus. Warriors and spies can test their abilities to the limit. Best of all, Control is still powerful enough to keep the Union on top of its hegemony — a comforting thought to the operatives conditioned to respect it.

Still, recent contact with the supernatural and three years of relative (though never complete) freedom from Control leads some Technocrats to wonder if the Union is just too corrupt to obey. Exposed to wider supernatural mysteries, they wonder if Enlightened Science is enough. Faced with Tradition mages who respect Reason, they wonder what purpose the Pogrom serves — in any form. More agents go AWOL or defect to technomantic cabals from 2002 onward.

The Nephandi

Their old masters are more subtle than ever, but new lords await. Nephandi pursue destruction through devotion; there are always new entities ready to make a bargain.

At the same time, new rulers create new conflict. Hive Dwellers are eager to seize waning resources from the old Nephandic factions. Worshippers of Grandfather Wyrm and Samael-Ildabaoth have ancient cults and Labyrinths to command. Despite the weakened presence of their masters, they still benefit from centuries of wicked cunning.

The one thing that keeps the Fallen from tearing each other apart is the Red Star. Members of all sects have seen it in vile Seekings, flaying away their weaknesses cell by cell. Their instincts tell them that it's the key to ultimate Descent; common reverence dampens their rivalries.

The Eaters of the Weak

They chant in languages that predate humanity and read crumbling man-skin scrolls from ancient Bhât itself. That is the heritage of the Eaters of the Weak: a term used by the most learned to denote Nephandi from ancient traditions. A few of them know the old atrocities of the *Nif'ur'en Daah*. All dig deeper into a pit begun by the Void's eldest servants.

Since the Avatar Storm, their Dark Lords have been unusually quiet. The K'llashaa's mad gods send fewer signs and Rex Mundi's apparitions are fainter. Even the Great Wyrm leaves nothing but its Eye to hound its Nephandi, forcing them to torture orders from lowly Banes. Old demons don't always respond to summons; requests for aid go unanswered.

One rumor that spreads through the ranks like wildfire is that their religions are nothing but the dream games of sleeping Malfeans, fading as the Neverborn awaken. Though blasphemous, it fills them with amusement to think that their faith consists of the same kinds of lies that they love to sow among the Masses. For some, this leads to a new admiration for their unknowable masters. Others go mad.

Hive Dwellers

After the Avatar Storm ravaged the Otherworlds, a few Nephandi found that new creatures were answering the old rites. These Hive Dwellers share a collective purpose: Break through to Earth as soon as possible. In exchange for help, they are all too willing to answer a summoning spell.

The Nephandi know little about these beings, save that they have a rough collective mind that portions itself into various castes. The Hive Dwellers' native realm is a twisting network of caves, tunnels and valleys. These formations appear wherever the Umbra has tasted corrupted Entropy, as if they are the interior of cracks in reality. Some Fallen necromancers note similarities with the Spectre hosts of the Underworld. In fact, it's almost as if the Dark Umbra's deepest levels now have an astral twin.

The Marauders

A dark current runs through the Mad Ones. They can taste the chance of imminent victory. The only obstacles are the guardians of the reality prison: the Technocracy and Traditions. Benign factions such as the Butcher Street Irregulars have maintained their core membership, but new Marauders are flocking to more apocalyptic groups. The moderates reach out to the Traditions to warn them of impending chaos, but Quiet keeps them from properly passing along the message.

New Marauders tend to internalize their insanity, making them harder to spot and counter. More of them work together, and these confluxes learn to translate one Quiet into another. Each believes that his personal reality is paramount, but a collective urge drives each to further a larger Dynamic agenda.

The Chaioth Ha-Quadesh

The growing ranks under General Geoffrey's banner understand that Tradition and Technocracy "archons" are about to stumble. These mages avoid direct conflict, preferring to gather resources and bide their time. By 2004, they make up the most prominent Marauder faction in the world.

Geoffrey sees himself as the last true Gnostic. The world is an illusion created by the archons and their puppet states. The Technocracy serves Samael, the blind demiurge. Under its direction, technology, architecture and culture constitute a massive ritual designed to bar humanity from its divine destiny. As unwilling participants in this rite, Sleepers are legitimate targets. To that end, his army employs terrorism and assassination based on Geoffrey's numerological findings. A plane they destroyed was actually weaving a sigil with its contrail; a smashed building was a secret standing stone.

General Geoffrey's Quiet is particularly infectious. The size of his cabal (the Sitrin) has doubled in the last three years. Allies translate his commands into their own delusions but don't necessarily believe in secret masters. Some (like the murderous Team 23) just enjoy destruction.

For more information on the Chaioth Ha-Quadesh, see **The Book of Madness**.

Other Arrangements

Naturally, you're encouraged to let your own game's needs trump the situations we've described. Never forget to use the characters' influence on history alongside or instead of what you see here. Here are some additional options:

A Trembling Monolith

The tension between the political and humanitarian aims of the Technocracy can be encompassed by the Panopticon/Ragnarok Command split, but you might want to introduce other elements of intrigue. For example, the global reach of the Union includes organizations that promote their own local agendas. Some feature a certain amount of mystical heresy. The Elemental Dragons of East Asia (see **Dragons of the East**) and Britain's Harbingers of Avalon (see **Guide to the Technocracy**) both subvert the cause of absolute Technocracy with their own cultural agendas. As such, they might even reach out to like-minded Traditionalists to preserve a common way of life. One of these factions could even defect.

The Crafts

The remaining Crafts might play a decisive part in the story to come. In Chapter Two, the Ahl-i-Batin hold a key to humanity's Ascension, but that's just one of the groups that might provide pivotal help — or enmity. The corrupt Hem-ka Sobk is only one of Egypt's magical threats. Those mages' new ties to Apophis' flesh-eating cult might bring unkillable assassins and Bane Mummies (see **Mummy: The Resurrection**) with them. The Templars are said to preserve many mystical secrets, including the fate of the lost Merovingian Craft and with it, the location of the Holy Grail. You can use these as secondary conflicts to underline how chaotic the world becomes, or you can lead your characters to resources and secrets that will help them play out your chronicle's finale.

Signs and Portents

The Reckoning and the end of the Umbral Ascension War was more than a way to refocus the game. It was also meant to create an atmosphere in which Armageddon was imminent. Recent events were designed to make the end a real concern. Mages couldn't rely on a static universe to comfort them and were confronted with the fact that their actions could have cataclysmic results.

Since then, other signs have revealed themselves. The Sphinx, Avatar Storm and other anomalies signal radical change. A wrong step could lead to Armageddon, but mages who seize the moment might find that these crises lead the way to new opportunities.

The Avatar Storm

The most notorious sign of the End Times, mages are only beginning to understand the Avatar Storm. Certain Mind, Spirit and Prime Effects can circumvent it; complex scrying spells can detect calm metaphysical spaces. Furthermore, mages have identified a minority who can bend the path of the storm to protect themselves. A few can even shield other mages. For more information, see **The Bitter Road** and **The Infinite Tapestry**.

The wisest Heralds and best connected Technocrats have heard a disturbing rumor: The Avatar Storm isn't an isolated event, but is the largest manifestation of a phenomenon that has occurred before. The stories say that over a year ago, Tradition mages sabotaged an isolated Technocracy research outpost and uncovered a Control-mandated experiment to harness the Avatar Storm's energies. The experiment was based on research from the Second World War. Apparently, scientists discovered that in the presence of tainted psychic energy, the Primal imprint of Genius did not disperse, but inflicted horrible wounds upon Awakened subjects who crossed into other dimensions — just like the Avatar Storm.

The story says that a few subjects were resistant to the Storm, and the secret experiment tried to continue Nazi research aimed at creating a "super Stormwarden." For more information, see **Manifesto: Transmissions from the Rogue Council**, which details what actually happened.

The Lash of Salvation

Spirit (and Dimensional Science) scholars still don't understand why the Avatar Storm targets mages but spares shapeshifters and Umbrood. How can the storm generate Sendings? After ravaging the spirit world, why do most Avatar shards cling to the Gauntlet?

Mages would understand the truth if they paid very close attention to a special type of spirit traveler: Sleepers. Very few mages send un-Awakened companions across the Gauntlet. In the Technocracy, only the Void Engineers make a habit of it, but even they do so too rarely to be statistically significant.

Sleepers who have been to the Otherworlds have been quietly Awakening. If mages were to observe the course of the Storm when Sleepers cross, they would see that it rushed toward them as well. If mystics tracked the course of individual Avatar shards, they would see that some of them burrow into acolytes — and *stay there*.

Although they are crippled by the trauma of being torn from humanity, every shard in the Storm possesses slightly more sentience than a Sleeper's Avatar. Each shard has been tormented into awareness. This primitive intelligence seeks out the completeness that only a human can provide. Just as Avatars complete their mages, human beings complete their Avatars. Disembodied Avatars cannot refine their consciousness, reincarnate or Ascend.

When human beings reach through the Gauntlet, shards rush to inhabit them and embody themselves. In a Sleeper, the shard encounters no resistance. It incorporates the host's dormant Primal soul into itself. This combination is often enough to jar the Sleeper into full Awakening.

Mages are not as lucky. Their Avatars are already Awake; there's no room for a second mystical consciousness. The more refined a mage and Avatar are, the less they are able to tolerate contact with the primitive shards of the Storm. The resulting psychic dissonance expels the weaker shard and the imbalance disrupts the mage's Pattern. Sometimes, the experience injures the mage's Avatar, producing Gilgul-like torment.

Avatar shards cannot always discriminate between a human being and a mystical simulation. Such simulations include Talismans, which are by nature recreations of the mage's self image. Similarly, familiars can sometimes "trick" Avatar shards by dint of their arcane ties, protecting their mages (see **The Infinite Tapestry**) from harm. The familiar still doesn't fit the criteria for embodiment, so the Avatar Storm moves on.

> ### Primal Souls
>
> One way to hint at the nature of the Avatar Storm is to introduce Avatar shards as characters in Seekings or visions, especially when these Seekings involve crossing the Gauntlet. The shard could be actually present (and the whole Seeking takes place in an instant as the mage is exposed to the Storm), or it might leave a mystical "stain" on the mage's own Avatar. The shard represents the temptation of superficial answers over deep insights and comfort over challenge.
>
> Avatar shards are unrefined, possessing just enough intelligence to yearn for something greater. In visions, they appear in such forms as Dynamic children or "wild men"; Patterns of the simple scientific formulae and unfinished statues; Primordial eggs or blind, grasping monsters; and Questing squires or wounded companions.
>
> In a Seeking, the Avatar Shard interferes by arguing for the easy solution or the simple path. Sometimes, the shard is just wrong, leading the mage into folly, or it warps the Seeking itself, creating a false lesson. Usually, the mage's true Avatar will strenuously oppose the intruder. If the shard is actually present, the mage suffers some kind of torment at these moments. The mage is actually seeing, from the Avatar's perspective, what happens when she enters the storm.
>
> For general information about Seekings, see the **Mage Storytellers Handbook**

The Psychopomps

First introduced in **Manifesto: Transmissions from the Rogue Council**, the Psychopomps are spirits with the power to direct Avatars to specific incarnations. They are mentioned in the obscure mythology of many Traditions. The rituals to summon them are nearly impossible to find.

Sometimes they were called were called Annunaki: an order of beings who once plotted the course of stars and thus, the fate of those who dwelled beneath them. Other sects committed them to occult lore as angels, Norse fetches, Persian *gallu*, and Tibetan *dakini*. While they wished to liberate humanity, these soul guides were barred from the world by a greater, nameless Power. Their judgment was lost and humankind was left to suffer. Still, the right rituals or special conditions allowed them to return to Earth. They used their power on mages' Avatars to commit them to suitable bodies and minds.

Avatars refined their connection to mages at an accelerated pace, incarnating in mortals that perfectly complemented them. The result was so powerful that by the late Dark Ages, many Avatars perfected their relationship with the mage's consciousness and no longer needed a direct voice. Writings from the period only discussed an inner "Fount" that mages could draw upon to work greater magic.

Eventually, silent Avatars worked against the Awakened. Even though a unified magical consciousness gave Mythic Age mages unparalleled power, it did so in the service of an all-too-human conscience. In some cases, mystics cloistered themselves into powerful Covenants, ignoring everything except occult study. Silent Avatars were not the sole cause of the problem, but without a challenging voice, many mages became complacent, taking sole credit for the power of their connection to a greater whole.

Many mages still maintained an interest in the world. Among them were philosopher scientists who drew their power from the study of nature. Sickened by their colleagues' hermitage and irresponsibility, they attacked the Hermetic Covenant of Mistridge, and the Ascension War began.

For the most part, the Psychopomps did their work invisibly. Most mages were totally unaware of their existence. Few noticed when the soul guides' ban from the inner realms returned. By the 15th century, Avatars reincarnated without the benefit of Psychopomp guidance, leading mages to renew their inner struggle with their Avatars' desires.

The Secret of the Phoenix

The Psychopomp called Phoenix has been the secret patron of the archmage Senex for centuries, guarding him from the madness that strikes long-lived mages. By guiding the path of the Avatar Storm, Phoenix allowed Senex to maintain an arcane connection to Earth, preventing disembodiment. Phoenix advised Senex to acquire Euthanatoi with certain powerful destinies, such as Amanda Janssen and Theora Hetirck. The Old Man owes his continued existence in the spiritual wasteland beyond the Horizon to Phoenix's assistance, but it doesn't come without a price.

The Psychopomps' ultimate purpose is to guide humanity toward its destiny, even if that includes destroying it. One day, Phoenix will ask Senex to turn away from efforts to save the world. The archmage knows that his quest to balance the world's Resonance has a time limit. Once Phoenix decides that humanity has run out of chances, Senex's chiminage forces him to step aside and leave the world to Destiny's inconstant mercy. When the time comes, Phoenix will consume the Old Man in spiritual fire, then recreate itself to move the Wheel forward again.

As one of the most significant soul guides, Phoenix is mentioned in countless prophecies and legends. The spirit visits other mages, but most seers only see it in visions or hear rumors in the Umbral Court. Therefore, visions of the end are often associated with Phoenix. The soul guide can project only the smallest fragment of itself inside the Horizon, but that shard is enough to make prophets and Spirit mages take note.

Their Nature

Because of the ban, Psychopomps can be summoned only with rituals that can surpass the Outer Horizon. Furthermore, only a small set of rituals will do. The soul guides are beyond the power of any but the mythical Archmasters to compel, and they will respond only to the appropriate spell. These spells require the caster to use a close derivative of the primal tongue of Creation; two known candidates include Hermetic Enochian and the Kaja language associated with the Wu Lung Akashic sect. These languages don't necessarily have to be understood, but using them phonetically makes the magic more difficult.

Despite their powers over the Avatar, the Psychopomps are utterly inhuman. They normally take a form appropriate to the summoner's paradigm, but only because their true forms are incomprehensible. Their power is on par with that of the mythical archangels or Incarnae, but they do not use it except to guide Avatars; attempts to attack or bind them are pointless. Regardless of the presence of the Avatar Storm, all radiate the Dynamic Resonance mages have come to identify as *Storm-Tainted*. In fact, this psychic imprint (which resembles a chorus of incoherent voices, winds and a subtle glow) is representative of their inherent connection to Avatars.

When summoned, soul guides can be persuaded to lend mages a portion of their essence. This loan confers control over the Avatar Storm, but unless the mage fulfils certain conditions, the alien power of the Psychopomp will drive her mad. In ancient times, the monstrous half-spirits were called Anakim. Their modern descendants are the Stormwardens who cross the Gauntlet without fearing Avatar shards.

Holy Union (••• Mind, ••• Prime, •••• Spirit, optional ••••• Life)

This is the true and complete ritual used to summon and merge with the essence of a Psychopomp. Occultists have developed their own corrupt versions, but Heylel's rite (see Chapter Two) is the only one that can create a balanced union between mage and spirit. See **Manifesto: Transmissions from the Rogue Council** for one example of the consequences of an incomplete spell.

The rote calls a Psychopomp and asks it to grant the summoner a part of its essence. This is a form of partial possession. The mage gains the ability to use a limited version of the spirit's soul-guiding power — a fragment of a very powerful Charm, controlled by the caster's Awakened consciousness. It reflexively protects the mage from the Avatar Storm, but it can also be used to incorporate incarnate and disincarnate Avatars. The version in Heylel's astral Grimoire adds Life magic to join the bodies of two mages, but this is only required if the caster is incorporating the Avatar of a living mage — an almost certain way to trigger the spell's corruption Effect. This combined entity is called a Rebis.

System: Spirit calls the Psychopomp from beyond the Horizon, Prime prepares the mage to assimilate a fragment the spirit's essence permanently. It is possible to cast the spell without Prime, but the duration lasts for a day or less. Any corruption effects gained during this period remain even after the *gallu's* essence is discharged. The spirit's fragment is actually sentient; the mage must communicate with it telepathically, requiring Mind.

The spell requires 14 successes to cast permanently (or 10 to last a single day), plus one per additional subject. The magic is difficult, however. The mage's

Avatar balks at the alien presence, and the Effect is mentally and spiritually taxing. Add two to the spell's difficulty. The spell is vulgar without witnesses because it is an inhuman alteration of the mage's being.

The spell ties the caster to inhuman cosmic forces, straining her psyche and Pattern. The result is a *corruption effect*. Without a properly prepared mind and spirit, the caster risks becoming a true Anakim — a monster.

The mage must call a Psychopomp compatible with her Essence and personality. Ancient manuscripts listed the corresponding True Names for each Essence and Nature, but these sources are virtually lost. In Chapter Two, mages Awakened by the Avatar Storm are sensitive to Telos, the Tenth Sphere, and can name another mage's compatible Psychopomp. The Tenth Seat of the Traditions also has this property. Failure to summon the correct Psychopomp creates a corruption effect.

The mage can influence only those Avatars (including Avatar shards) that don't oppose her will. Otherwise, she suffers corruption. Storytellers should be aware that the Storm's primitive consciousness is largely unaware of the suffering it inflicts, but living Avatars will certainly oppose attempts to pull them from the path to Ascension.

The spell's recipient gains the benefits of the five-point version of the *Stormwarden* Merit (see **Mage: The Ascension**, page 295). In addition, she can use the Psychopomp's Charm fragment to perform the following tasks. All tasks require an Arete roll (difficulty 6; the mage's enlightenment is directing a "static" power).

Control Avatar Storm: The mage can adjust the severity of the Avatar Storm by one die per success and can devote extra successes to affecting an area. This effect adds to or subtracts from the Storm's damage.

Avatar Shaping: In any area where the Avatar Storm is present (normally limited to the Umbra), the mage can expend a success to shape it into a rough form, such as a barrier, weapon or shield. As a weapon, the Avatar Storm inflicts two aggravated wounds per success on Awakened beings and creations. It can be loosed or held in one place like the **Holy Stroke** Effect. A barrier inflicts the same damage on Awakened beings and creations that pass through it. Any magic directed through a barrier is twisted by five dots of *Storm-Tainted* Resonance.

Overwhelm Sleeping Avatar: The mage can direct the Avatar Storm into a Sleeper with such intensity that it destroys the Sleeper's own Avatar and will. Awakened mages are immune to this attack. The mage must score more successes than the target's Willpower. If the target is a living supernatural being, it eliminates all of its supernatural attributes, leaving it bereft of a soul or spiritual power, but in this case, successes must also exceed any supernatural power source (such as Gnosis or Conviction). This power always invokes a corruption effect. Victims are the mage's mindless thralls, and they eventually duplicate her physical corruption.

Assimilate Avatar: The mage can meld an Avatar with her own.

In the presence of the Avatar Storm, the mage's mind and Pattern can host Avatar shards. These are cause for strange dreams and visions, but they provide no immediate benefit. Over time, however, she might treat these newcomers as extensions of her own Avatar. The player can increase the character's *Avatar* Background by spending (new/current level) x 3 experience points on the new rank. The mage's *Avatar* rating cannot exceed her Arete.

The mage can also absorb the Avatar and consciousness of a living mage. Doing so almost always invokes a corruption effect. Storytellers should note that characters are, by default, innately opposed to having their souls devoured. You should allow your characters to give up their Avatars only to one another without invoking corruption on very special occasions. As with the Storm, the mage can increase her *Avatar* Background, but only to a limit of the victim's *Avatar* rating or one higher than the character's current rating, whichever is better. As abhorrent as it is, devouring souls always provides a little benefit. The mage can also learn the victim's Spheres and associated foci by purchasing them at half cost. Unlike the system for switching Traditions in the **Mage Storytellers Handbook**, the character can even purchase Spheres she doesn't know with the victim's foci, but are limited to those foci unless she pays the other half of the experience cost.

The victim's consciousness perishes unless the caster absorbs his body with Life. The Mind Sphere then creates a permanent telepathic bridge between the two mages. Each consciousness can willingly cooperate, but in case of a struggle, a contested Willpower roll determines who controls the combined entity's body and Avatar in a given scene. A Rebis may use Mind Arts to control her rebellious half.

The power requires five successes per new *Avatar* level, plus three successes per level of Arete when used on a living mage.

Corruption Effects

Using a soul guide's essence against the greater ethos of Ascension twists a mages body and psyche. Every two successes converts into one level of corruption. If the spell is cast without the appropriate protections, the mage automatically gains seven corruption traits. Corruption manifests itself according to the mage's paradigm, as the character struggles to reconcile her worldview with the alien drives of the Psychopomp fragment. The Storyteller determines what traits manifest. When the character attains 10 corruption traits (Flaws) she becomes a true Anakim and is no longer run by the player. Anakim are driven mad by the attempt to assimilate the Psychopomp into their native paradigm. The mage's mind is bent to the cause of calling the Psychopomps by any means necessary.

Traits are spent on Flaws. Half of the point value of these Flaws are immediately reinvested in Merits from any other category. The following are suggested as corruption traits, but need not be the only ones.

Mental Corruption Flaws: *Amnesia, Nightmares, Deranged, Phobia, Short Fuse, Vengeful.* Also: ranks of *Quiet*.

Mental Corruption Merits: None.

Physical Corruption Flaws: *Disfigured, Primal Marks, Deformity, Degeneration, Monstrous, Permanent Wound, Mayfly Curse.*

Physical Corruption Merits: *Acute Senses, Catlike Balance, Huge Size, Insensible to Pain.* Also: additional Physical traits, even to inhuman levels, Investments (see **The Book of Madness**) or for technology users, physical modifications from **Guide to the Technocracy**. These cybernetics behave just like real technological implants, but they manifest because the character's paradigm warps her self-image and Pattern.

The Rogue Council

When the Avatar Storm struck, it didn't just change the Gauntlet. The Horizon thinned and cracked under the waves of screaming shards, and the Psychopomps slipped through. Driven to fulfil their duties as soul conductors, they went to the Well of Souls — what mystics call Purgatory, Bardo and many other things. They encountered the Avatars and spirits of certain mages there and prevented them from returning to the Cycle.

Each Avatar once belonged to a mage with a passion for Ascension — one so strong that in some cases, their Avatars spent centuries resisting reincarnation in a new, less skilled human. These mages weren't necessarily close to attaining enlightenment, but all seven of them had refined their spirits by mastering their favored Spheres. Their Avatars possessed an especially strong infusion of their former host's personality, reinforced by a special arcane tie: their fame. Each of them were well known Tradition mages in life, and they possessed quiet but powerful connections to their writings, their former apprentices and legends of their acts and failings.

The soul guides prevented these Avatars from being reincarnated, then bound them to their old places of power.

Using Soul Guides

In Chapter Two, the Psychopomps are emanations of the Tenth Sphere, counterparts of the Malfeans and servants of the universal balance. Storytellers might want to use them in other roles, however.

In a game where Oblivion and the Nephandi are the ultimate threat, Psychopomps might have been banished from reality for corrupting human Avatars. In this case, Psychopomps become half-demonic antagonists who rally the Fallen for the final battle. In this case, ignore the ways to avoid Anakim corruption. These don't concern the Nephandi at all.

Speaking of demons, the Psychopomps bear many similarities to the exiled angels of **Demon: The Fallen**. In **Mage**, they are a related but separate class of entity, but you might decide that some Annunaki escaped the Abyss by traveling beyond the limits of Creation. Now they've come back with fearsome alien powers, but like the Fallen, they feel the spiritual gravity of the Abyss. Anakim are their tentative projections into the World of Darkness. You can grant Anakim additional powers and an alternative background using the **Demon** core book.

Of course, you could go the opposite route and make soul guides intercessors on the part of a benevolent power. Mages who partake of their essence become more demonic when they gain corruption effects because they've defied the One's will — but they might receive angelic modifications for obeying it. You may supplement the listed powers with True Faith. See **Tradition Book: Celestial Chorus** for systems.

As manifestations of raw mystical will, the seven Avatars set their old domains to trembling. The physical remains of Doissetep were cut from existence by an angel with a flaming sword, scattering warriors determined to ravage the ruins and leaving nothing but phantoms. Spirits drove the survivors from Concordia. In early 2001, Lord Edward Gilmore was the last to leave. Since then, every path to Horizon is impenetrable. Even if it still exists, its place in the heavens has shifted. The bridges are closed and the island has drifted away.

By keeping these Avatars discorporate, the Psychopomps granted the Awakened a great boon. The Avatars drove reluctant mystics from their personal heavens — and in many cases, eventual disembodiment. Secondly, the soul guides tempered the incredible wills of these seven Avatars. Left to return, they might have reproduced the very conflicts that destroyed the Traditions' fortresses. Now, they were forced to act indirectly — and with mortal aid.

The Rise of the Sphinx

The seven Avatars reached out, imbuing nearby spirits with their essence. These Sendings breached the Gauntlet and traveled the world on mysterious missions. Many forgot their missions when they crossed the Avatar Storm. Others hid among mortal mages, pursuing the enigmatic agendas given to them by their creators. Some searched for old servants and hidden Wonders, while others passed on messages. Other archmages noticed the Sendings and duplicated the technique, but it was never widely used. Only a handful of Sendings remained after these mages died or were changed into spirits.

One mage could see the combined effect of the seven Avatars' presence. As Dante meditated at the hidden hub of the Digital Web, he extended his perceptions beyond millions of computers to realize that the physical universe was its own luminous collection of mathematics and Trinary uncertainty. The Virtual Adept wasn't just at the nexus of computerized information, but *all* information, everywhere. As he joined the ranks of the Oracles he saw the Tellurian's secret rhythms. He picked out the predestined actions of the seven, then used the only magic capable of countermanding the Psychopomps' binding: his own. Dante was an Oracle of Correspondence now; all places were alike to him.

He brought them to Horizon, the former home of so many of their intrigues. He mediated the Avatars' wills and used the lore they remembered from several lifetimes, then created the first Rogue Council transmissions. The messages were carefully crafted to prevent attribution and even arouse suspicion. Dante understood that mages couldn't be *ordered* to Ascend. The renewed quest would die if it turned into a cult of personality.

Despite Oracular aid and the seven Avatars' wisdom, the Council wasn't omniscient. Therefore, the Sphinx served a dual purpose. Each transmission uncovered a new bit of lore, but each quest was a riddle in and of itself. Unbeknownst to the mages who received them, the communiqués' magic ensured that anything they discovered would eventually reach Horizon. Therefore, every transmission fueled the next. Mages followed them, learned about the world and passed that information back to the source.

Alternate Rogue Councils

You might wish to reinvent the Rogue Council for their chronicle. Keep in mind that the Rogue Council needs to be untraceable, able to gather information from a wide range of sources, and it has to have a compelling motive for communicating with mages. See **Manifesto: Transmissions from the Rogue Council** for a collection of suitable theories.

> ## Famous Souls
>
> By default, the seven Avatars belong to Akrites Salonikas and Marianna of Balador (who shared the same Avatar), Porthos Fitz-Empress, Bernadette of the First Cabal, Nightshade, Ihuanocuatlo, Jou Shan and Alexis Hastings. See **Mage Chronicles 1** (which compiles **Digital Web** and **The Book of Chantries**), **The Fragile Path: Testaments of the First Cabal** and **Horizon: Stronghold of Hope** for details about each mage. Naturally, you should substitute famous mages from your own game where appropriate.
>
> Keep in mind, however, that these beings are *not* living mages. They are Avatars that have absorbed their mages' driven personalities without the moderation of human frailty or desire. In a sense, the Rogue Council is ruthless; each Avatar wants to grab hold of Ascension and is willing to pit mage against mage to do it. Ultimately, the Avatar's instinct to reach for greater self-awareness trumps its morality. Characters expecting the former gentle humor of Master Porthos are in for a shock.
>
> Dante is the Rogue Council's human element and tempers its schemes and urges. If something removed him from events, the Rogue Councilors wouldn't be able to send transmissions, but they might be able to assert themselves through Horizon, reopening the portals, claiming the bodies of visitors and clutching their old seats. The old Ascension War with its hubris and flawed power could rise again — or it might not. The Storyteller should decide whether such successors could improve on the work of the old Council, but keep in mind that the old Council wasn't stupid, either. See the **Mage Storytellers Handbook** for a rundown on the old Ascension War.

What if the Council Avatars were actually captured by the Nephandi and sent to the Cauls? In this scenario, the Rogue Council is gathering mages' trust until it can safely claim to be the renewed Council of Nine. Then, the Nephandi will use renewed conflict with the Technocracy to whip up hatred, death and corruption while the Fallen Council destroys the old safeguards against demonolatry and Infernal temptation. This is an excellent option for a Technocracy or Orphan game because the Storyteller can make the Council establishment vile, black-hearted enemies without ignoring the periphery of duped mages.

If you follow the version given in Chapter Two: Judgment on the nature of Control, you might want to make the Sphinx a variation of the Union's own massmind. In this story, part of the Technocracy's collective is actually goading the Traditions to war. Without a common enemy, the Union is on the brink of collapse. The unconscious desire for an enemy generates the transmissions. Mystics who discover the truth need to stop a new Ascension War so that the Technocracy can collapse under its own inertia instead of strengthen in the face of opposition. Technocrats who learn the truth need to decide whether unity is worth eternal war. If they decide that it is, then they need to plan for battles the Union won't lose, but can never really win.

Dante: Oracle of the Last Age

The young Virtual Adept Master vanished at the end of the old Ascension War. Technocrats spread rumors of his death, but the Adepts denied it. Still, some of them sarcastically speculated that Dante was going to meet Turing. Others assumed that he was preparing to unleash some terrible revenge. After all, Dante has good reasons to hate the Technocracy. He was their genetically engineered prodigy, raised without a hint of love.

Desmond Collingsworth III refused Ascension and joined the ranks of the Oracles. His final Seeking broke the barriers between virtual and physical reality, but the Sleepers weighed heavily on his mind. He turned back from enlightenment and discovered his role among the Oracles. He would become the center point for Ascension's final movement. Therefore, the Oracle is the focus for the Rogue Council; the human counterpart for Avatars that hold the Traditions' wisdom. When he became an Oracle, he took the role of the Digital Web's Net Sphinx: the icon representing the entire database of human wisdom. This gestalt took it — took *him* — as a sign, focus and totem, and through it, Oracular magic sent the transmissions. These instructions were vague and anonymous because Dante knew that the Rogue Council risked becoming another Control. Enigma, not dogma, safeguarded it from being too accepted. Otherwise, the mages' massed wills could convert it into a new oppressive principle.

For this reason, Dante works subtly, appearing where he can to help mages and Sleepers. In fact, he's more likely to work miracles in front of the latter, saving them from the End Times' calamities. Where mages might misinterpret his actions, Sleepers just thank him for helping.

For more on Dante, see **Digital Web 2.0**.

Image: Dante is an African-American in his mid-30s. He normally wears a long trench coat and gloves lined with silver circuitry. He's abandoned the need for props, but he still uses foci as an expression of his love for the programmer's art. Now, his computer is a floating circlet of light and steel that reacts to his thoughts and gestures.

Roleplaying Hints: You know why the Tellurian is the way it is, and you almost know how to help it to its ultimate end, but there's always a balance. Use too much intervention, and you'll suffer the same fate as Control. People will look to you instead of themselves for answers. Too little, and the world could spiral into destruction. Humanity needs to come to Ascension freely. Nevertheless you do what you can to alleviate physical suffering. You can manifest anywhere, so some subtle action isn't out of the question. Still, it risks the balance. Everything you do has the look of something that you've long contemplated. You're a very careful man.

The Darkness Ends

Ascension focuses on **Mage**'s last stories, but that doesn't mean that it's impossible to incorporate the rest of the World of Darkness. In our stories we assume that Gehenna and the Apocalypse are background events. Whether its Ascension, Armageddon or final Stasis, we assume that the mages' stories are paramount.

The easiest way to cross over the games' endings is to follow suit and let the other endings reinforce **Mage**'s themes and story line. It's more challenging to synthesize a single, overarching ending that includes all the lines, but it's not impossible. Don't just throw together disparate elements. Look at it as the last story of an entire world, not an opportunity to use as much World of Darkness continuity as possible. Finally, admit your biases and discuss them with the players. If you're going to run roughshod over **Mage**'s themes because Gehenna really fascinates you, you should share that with a player who's thinking of running her Akashic Brother.

Vampire

Vampire's core scenario is quiet. The Thin-Blooded rise and the ancients fall, but they endure the changes without overturning human history. After all, the herd shouldn't see them as weak. The Antediluvians stir but seem to have learned the Ravnos Ancient's lesson: No vampire is too powerful to need the Masquerade. The Camarilla and Sabbat collapse, leaving individual packs and coteries to wend their way through a world that's forgotten the undead.

Gehenna can attract mages on several fronts. The Technocracy's anti-vampire Operation Sunburst is four years old and one of Ragnarok Command's most important projects. After Bangladesh, Ragnarok Command is *very* edgy about strange vampire activity. Union scientists know that the thing they killed was somehow related to the undead that infest every major city. Ragnarok Command's hypothesis is that creatures like the Ancient and more common vampires have a predator/prey relationship. The more powerful creatures devour the weaker ones to keep them from overfeeding and threatening their ecological niche. Therefore, Technocrats can prevent more powerful creatures from arising by managing the vampire population. It's a brilliant hypothesis based on compelling evidence — and it's wrong. It fails to pacify a single Ancient. Nevertheless, Operation Sunburst thins the Kindred population where it can, preventing insane mass Embraces from spilling over into the public eye.

Among the Traditions, the Order of Hermes benefits with each blow the Tremere clan suffers. As the Warlocks flee their chantries, Hermetic scavengers move in, pilfering anything of value. Some of the thieves die horribly (Tremere warding rituals are as effective as ever), but a handful manage to fatten the Tradition's libraries with recovered Grimoires. In Chapter Two of this book, this turns out to be a fortunate thing indeed, as their books feed the hungry minds of hundreds of new mages.

The Tremere do little to stop the thieves. Their Ancient reels from the plots of other Antediluvians and, perhaps, heeds the warning given him during the Second *Massasa* War. As the clan flounders, Hermes triumphs; the ancient balance shifts for the last time.

Werewolf

Chose the **Werewolf** scenario that best fits your story. If the Technocracy wins, you might want to have a concurrent victory for the Weaver. The Gauntlet becomes an impassable wall, severing the world's ties to the supernatural. The Nephandi could eliminate and usher in the Wyrm's reign if you decide that their lords are nothing but masks for the primeval destroyer. You shouldn't feel bound by the obvious choices, though. After the Technocracy defeats its rivals, does it have the knowledge and resources to fight a triumphant Wyrm? The Special Projects Division might fully defect to Pentex, leaving two industrial juggernauts to battle it out with Awakened super-science.

In a **Mage** scenario, Storytellers will probably want to keep the final battle against the Wyrm in the Umbra so that Awakened humanity has room to fight for Earth. Nevertheless, if the Gauntlet falls, Triatic spirits will make their mark. Chapter Two assumes that they're just three factions of a legion of Umbrood; their influence isn't pervasive enough to distinguish it from other spiritual activity. If you like, assume that the majority are deeper in the Umbra, fighting for Gaia's soul.

Umbral war can help your game by making the spirit world so hazardous that characters will focus on an Earthly agenda. Fill the Spirit Wilds with screaming Banes and Pattern Spiders to emphasize that great things are afoot, but that the characters would be better off with their feet on the ground. On the other hand, Chapter Two ends after characters explore an Umbra rent by titanic magic. You'll probably want to resolve the werewolves' war before seeking final Ascension.

Chapter Two posits that the Red Star is actually a force for balance and completion. In **Werewolf**, the Red Star could be the Incarna Phoenix, ready to cleanse the world. Is this the same Phoenix as Senex's Psychopomp? These spirits share a common purpose and power, making it very likely. Phoenix is certainly powerful enough to show Garou and mages different faces and spur them to independent quests in search of the same goal.

Other Lines

It's the end for the World of Darkness, and the fates of more obscure supernatural factions might interest you.

Demon's Earthbound didn't get there by themselves; occultists squandered the gift of magic to bring them to Earth. Now that the greatest fallen can pierce the Abyss, followers of old and new demons fight to reshape the world in their image. Strangely, the Earthbound's sorcerous cults are generally avoided by the Nephandi, who prefer to be enslaved to less comprehensible masters. Even so, they might find common cause to finish off Creation. Of the Traditions, the Hermetics are past masters of demonology. Their considerable wisdom can serve as a source of power and temptation. Still, the Hermetics have been through the cleansing fire of the Reckoning and are less likely to succumb than ever before.

The imbued are likely to move in two directions. Some of them will settle their scores with the supernatural as vigorously as possible. With little to lose, their desperation will endanger mages who happen to cross their path. Other hunters see the end as a time of final reconciliation; they'll offer a hand to Awakened that the Heralds show in a favorable light. For a twist, you might want to retain the rule that hunters are "witnesses" even after the Consensus breaks down. This limitation portrays the imbued as "anti-mages" or suggests that they could form the bedrock beneath a new Consensus.

Simplifying the Cosmology

Whether your game will be dominated by **Mage** or balances all the games equally, recognize that each game's self sufficiency leads to certain redundant elements. Some games already deal with this by interpreting another game's features though their own lenses. In **Werewolf**, Paradox is controlled by certain Weaver spirits because, like Paradox, the Weaver represents reality's imbalance toward a stagnant, sterile structure. This choice folds Paradox into **Werewolf**'s cosmology but doesn't really work in a straight **Mage** game, in which Paradox spirits are unlike any other Umbrood in the Tellurian.

As a Storyteller, you can moderate things by fitting Paradox under the Weaver but without allowing Garou or mages to influence them without a fifth-rank power. Werewolves would be right to recognize the stink of the Weaver in mages' Backlashes, but they couldn't abuse their spirit-binding Gifts to attack mages with Paradox spirits.

Look at the broader themes around the elements of each game, decide how much they overlap and whether or not you can merge them. For example, **Mummy**'s Judges of Ma'at, **Hunter**'s Messengers and **Mage**'s Psychopomps all represent similar cosmological principles. It's not too much of a stretch to decide that these entities are all aspects of a single cosmic balance that wears different masks for different tasks.

A Unified World of Darkness

Paring down the setting will help you take care of major contradictions, but you still need to wrestle with divergent histories and street-level metaphysics, like the eternal question of why werewolves and vampires can avoid Paradox.

There's no easy answer. Each game was designed to be true to itself first. What you have to do is find a common theme. Instead of deciding which game you like better, pick the option that best suits the stories you want to tell.

For example, you could decide that your game is primarily about uncovering cosmic secrets. For this reason, you decide that mages are only half right; the Consensus is a prison of delusion, but mages have only escaped by incorporating a bit of the truth into a largely false worldview. This tension causes Paradox to strike. The hidden cosmos is animistic, with a secret Triat ruling over a host of spirits. Werewolves are descended from the true spirit world, but they have no proof that Gaia unifies the Triat. Instead, it's just their species' cult. The Celestines don't appear to them, so they have to deal with millions of lesser Umbrood with diverse agendas. Vampires really are servants of Entropy, cursed by the forces of Stasis to remain in the false world of the Consensus. Because nobody has ever seen the face of the Celestines, these beings might be angels and demons.

In this World of Darkness, supernatural characters all seek out the secrets of the universe. Werewolves want to divine the true nature of the spirit world. Mages want to throw off the last shackles of human ignorance. Vampires want to escape a false world where they're forced to live as blood drinkers. In this world's Armageddon, the Antediluvians' concentrated spiritual power breaks the Gauntlet, loosing the spirits upon an unprepared populace. Mages must educate humanity so that it can flee the crumbling prison. Werewolves need to learn how to keep the Triat balanced.

A Fractured Cosmos

In **Mage**, Storytellers don't need to worry too much about forging a unified cosmology. Instead, you can decide that each game has its own universe. Let's outline such a possibility.

Science fiction and occult literature both support the idea of other universes. In Jewish Kabbalah, God created other universes, but none of them suited humanity. In one instance, He created a perfectly just universe, but absolute justice contradicted mercy and free will. Out of compassion, God created a new universe where injustice could exist, but where men and women can make meaningful choices. The prototype universes were peeled from Creation, leaving hollow shells (or Qlippoth), full of energies inimical to spiritual health. Mystics who travel the Sephiroth (the Kabbalistic Tree of Life) risk wandering into the Qlippoth and falling to corruption.

Buddhist and Hindu cosmology provides its own opportunities for alternate universes. In this belief system, time is cyclical, moving from *yugas* of thousands of years to *kalpas* and *mahakalpas* of millions and billions of years. Since time is circular, there isn't a true past or future. Each cycle has common characteristics, such as the manifestations of a great religious teacher or god. Mystics can travel from one iteration of the cycle to the next by recalling other incarnations.

In contemporary physics, the idea of alternate universes exists in the Many-Worlds (or Everett) Interpretation of Quantum Mechanics. According to this controversial idea, superpositioned particles don't collapse into a single state. Instead, every possible permutation splits off into its own, self-sufficient universe. Communicating with or traveling to these worlds is supposedly impossible, but that's a small barrier for interested Etherites and Technocrats. These universes do interfere with each other on a very small scale. In a **Mage** game, this interference can be exaggerated to allow for more robust interactions between universes.

> ### Nephandi and the Qlippoth
>
> If you use the Fractured Cosmos, Nephandic initiation isn't just about dark Resonance and self-destruction. Nephandi are literally invaders from another universe.
>
> When the Fallen go to the Cauls, their souls (and later, Avatars) are corrupted according to the laws of the Qlippoth: the corrupt shell-universes inhabited by their masters. Their magic draws upon the Spheres of those anti-worlds. Every Qlippothic spell and corrupted soul infects the Tapestry with more of the Qlippothic essence, until major intrusions such as the Red Star appear and each world is either consumed or uses its own strange laws to transform and escape. In any event, every World of Darkness changes beyond recognition.
>
> At the same time, remember that the Qlippoth might exist because of humanity's imperfection. The Qlippoth were cast away as an act of mercy, to support our free will. In this case, the Nephandi are unwittingly forcing humanity to Ascend by integrating its dark half.

Cosmic Interaction

In **Mage**, all of these theories can reflect a larger truth: The Tellurian actually consists of several connected Tapestries.

The destinies of these worlds are intertwined. When a significant event occurs in one, its vibrations transmit to the others. Sometimes, this causes the parallel universe to duplicate the event, but precise details shift. A sufficiently strong pulse can violate causality in several universes. The events of the Reckoning might have been so traumatic that cause and effect were scrambled, allowing the Ravnos Ancient to project its singular being into several worlds.

Thus, mages inhabit a Tapestry in which belief shapes reality. This property bleeds into an animistic cosmos, where Garou claim that the Awakened's alien powers come from twisting Gaia's sacred names. Vampires', werewolves' and mages' dark sides are paramount in a world where they are all rebels against the cosmic order. In this universe, the imbued fight for the rightful dominion of the Messengers and Ministers. Each game line has a Tapestry in which its rules are paramount — and they are a few drops in a sea of possibilities. Contradictions represent the interference of parallel worlds.

Travel and Duplication

Is it possible to travel to alternate Worlds of Darkness? Spirit, Correspondence, Time and Entropy magic could all help catapult a mage into another world. **Tradition Book: Sons of Ether** features one suggested rote and a story that takes place in an alternate universe.

Characters might be able to reach alternate worlds through the Umbra, but only by traveling past the Outer Horizon and into uncharted Umbral space. In the spiritual wilderness, the traveler needs to search for paths that don't correspond with physical space. Rumor has it that great cracks and portals lie in the deepest regions of Umbra, capable of taking voyagers out of the known Tapestry completely. Parallel worlds include their own Umbrae all the way to the Outer Horizon. Even the spirit world can change from universe to universe.

In the default Fractured Cosmos, we assume that the universes described in each game line are sufficiently entangled that people and objects can't duplicate themselves. A technomancer who changes her quantum harmonics to visit the world described in **Vampire** displaces her counterpart. Her counterpart will be almost exactly the same, but a few slight differences might arouse suspicion in her friends. Remember that according to this model, moving between universes is common. Most people aren't even aware of it, since the Tapestries tend to have very subtle differences.

What happens to the counterpart? The visitor's Pattern, mind and spirit might superimpose themselves over the double. Its more likely that when the visitor

> ### Creators
>
> Archmages with the ninth rank of Prime might invert a Node's flow so that it projects Quintessence away from the Tapestry. Energy streams into the Void, settling into the cycles and Patterns of an expanding cosmos. The archmages might control the cosmological constants of their universe, but they cannot transfer anything from the created universe to their native universe. It would certainly be possible for an Archmaster to create a second universe inside the next one, leading to a succession of nested Tapestries. Nodes in each universe serve as the power source for the next.
>
> A few Masters maintain that this has already happened, but they refuse to speculate about what universe they live in and who created it.

arrives, the double travels to another universe as well because she replicates the visitor's Tellurian travel. The double might switch universes with the visitor or move laterally in the same direction as the visitor. The latter option means that the double's double also moves down a universe, ad infinitum.

Radical Differences

Once you leave the local cluster of closely related worlds, you reach truly alternate worlds, like a blackened Earth where Gehenna happened in AD 1000, or a continuum where the Biscoccian Coprosperity Sphere (see the **Mage Storytellers Handbook**) spreads Etherite hegemony throughout the inner planets. In these universes, visitors won't always have counterparts. Even if they do, their doubles might lead comparatively strange lives. In these cases, it *is* possible to meet your counterpart. Dissimilarities prevent the traveler from superimposing himself over the double, or the double doesn't decide to hop to a different universe.

Escape!

Characters can't use the Fractured Cosmos scenario to escape to a familiar-looking world. Whether its Gehenna, the Apocalypse or Armageddon, each end comes at about the same time because of the worlds' linked destinies. Characters can avoid destruction only by escaping to radically different worlds. Even then, they might bring the seeds of devastation with them. A character from the World of Darkness cluster could carry his home's metaphysical burdens. A refugee could infect her new home with the World of Darkness' doom, or she might suffer Paradox for living past the death of her home universe.

Alternatively, the end of the universe might only *start* with the World of Darkness. Dimensional travelers could stay one step ahead of the metaphysical wave front by leaping to stranger and stranger worlds.

Mad Worlds, Mad Gods

The Book of Madness notes that some Marauders acquire too much Quiet to exist in the Consensus. Reality ejects them into the Umbra, where ephemera twists to support their delusions.

If you use the Fractured Cosmos, mad mages can take this one step farther. When a large enough self-sufficient universe accretes around the Marauder, the mage and his creations split off into their own Tapestry. Marauder-created worlds definitely belong to the radically different category. These worlds outlast their creators. If the Marauder still exists, she might be the supreme god of her own universe, presiding over a variant Umbra and radically different physical laws.

Storytelling

Epics and finales have some recurring elements that you can use to great effect. Don't worry about clichés; those are usually a matter of specific plotting rather than the story's familiar theme. For instance, a cliché redemption story happens when you've seen the protagonist's sins and the way he resolves them before. While there's nothing wrong with a little nonprofit plagiarism to drive your personal chronicle forward, you should keep your inspirations from being too familiar.

How do you harness classic story elements without looking unoriginal? In the final story arc of your chronicle, rely on your game's own history to make the story unique. Your redemption story won't seem familiar because it involves character histories, Storyteller characters and ongoing plots that your group has made its own.

For this reason, you should make sure that your game has matured well before you prepare for the end. Do the players reminisce about past stories? Do they justify character actions based on in-game history? If so, your game is ready to end. If not, you should rethink the idea or run the scenario as a separate mini-chronicle. Let your game continue and see if it gets to the point where the players are ready.

At the same time, you don't want to wait *too* long. Some games continue for long after most of the players have stopped enjoying it. It's better to put these games straight out of their misery instead of wrapping them up over 10 sessions. It's sad but true: You have to like your game to end it in style. Go out on a high note, but make sure that the players have accomplished most of their character goals.

In fiction, finales usually begin after a bit of a pause. The characters are recovering from dramatic events and have time to get back in touch with their everyday lives. They contemplate or demonstrate how events have transformed them while the reader braces for a last torrent of events. Players find this kind of traditional structure comforting because it gives them a chance to play out character growth. In **Mage**, the last chapter of your chronicle can begin after a season of study or a low-action, character-driven story. The players get a chance to catch their breath before plunging into Armageddon, and you have time to make some last-minute adjustments to your plot.

With that in mind, let's look at some of the characteristics of successful conclusions.

Your Basic Concerns

You shouldn't just dump the finale on players without providing some sort of context. Try to answer the following questions:

How will I foreshadow events?

The story should be woven into an ongoing chronicle, with elements appearing in greater frequency until the whole story is consumed with the end. Start with omens, wars and rumors of wars. Strangeness. The Red Star swelling in the sky. More than that, make the story your own. Let regular Storyteller characters spout portents of doom. Examples of these portents are given in Chapter One.

How will I handle the plot?

The massive scope of some events can leave players with a lot of questions. You should be prepared to work out the details. The blue and red book system outlined in the **Mage Storytellers Handbook** can serve as a way to update players on the state of the world during key events.

How will I deal with failure or unconventional plans?

Don't make your end an inexorable march to destiny. The characters *can* fail. You shouldn't give them too many extra chances, but you should prepare for an alternative chronicle. It's possible that the players will latch onto a totally different method of success. Go with their suggestions (players fruitlessly searching for the One True Solution is always a drag), but don't be too lenient. Have an open mind.

Storyteller Characters

When we talked about metaplot, we said that a story becomes important when it's set against an active backdrop. Your characters aren't the only occultists, explorers or freedom fighters out there. Antagonists have agendas that don't revolve around the players' characters' cabal.

You might think that this idea contradicts advice that tells you to make sure the characters are at the center of the story. In fact, it makes your characters' actions more significant. They are stirring a vast world full of its own plots. If the Technocracy tries with all its might to crush the cabal for the 500th time, it just means that the Union in your game is particularly incompetent. If the cabal draws Technocracy attention away from another project, that's much more interesting. For one thing, it means that the cabal's importance now outranks another Technocratic concern, making it important according to the setting's own standards. It also means that you've now introduced a possible plot complication (whatever it was the Technocracy was originally working on) that you can drop into the story later.

Plus, background events make the story larger. An epic is usually just too big to be contained by a handful of characters. Even a small story benefits from Storyteller characters and their projects and motives. A gift from a Storyteller character boosts the characters' egos. A Storyteller-run cabal that makes the wrong choices highlights the players' characters' wisdom. Those Storyteller characters' deaths emphasize danger. Active Storyteller characters and background events put your characters in a larger world.

Quiet Moments

It's very tempting to run a finale by constantly ratcheting up the danger and suspense, but you risk alienating your players. Like their characters, players need rest. They need time to assimilate what happened to the characters and change their plans and portrayals accordingly. Remember that Armageddon is bound to require some emotional in-character moments.

If you relentlessly stack action-packed or emotional scenes on top of each other, the players will eventually stop caring. For one thing, players need time to sort out how their characters feel about events. If you segue from threatening their country to threatening the world, the element of scale becomes meaningless. The players haven't had time to digest it. It's important to pause and allow enough time for the players to absorb what's going on, but not for so long that you lose tension. Quiet moments are ideal times to introduce passive elements of the plot like occult research or general news. Update your game's metaplot, let the lab and library bear relevant fruit. Introduce new omens and prophecies while your group prepares for more action.

The End and Your Characters

Despite the importance of an active, populated background, it usually all comes down to your cabal. There's a fine line to be drawn here between Storyteller character assistance and meddling. If your players readily recognize some Storyteller-run allies, you might want to leave them out of the finale. This will help keep you from overshadowing the players' actions.

Old antagonists, skeletons in the closet and obscure bits of character history should come out. This gives the players the sense that the fictional history you've built together is integral to the story. Above all, an ending that depends on your characters should rely on their personalities at least as much as it does on their powers and raw problem solving abilities. Craft stories that appeal to the characters' Natures and exploit their failings.

On the other hand, you don't have to end the story around character actions. It's acceptable — but dangerous — to have stories that underline the characters' ultimate insignificance. You can present an ending in which the cabal suffers at the whim of unstoppable, uncaring forces. This is a classic horror story ending, but it doesn't necessarily have to be negative. You can run an ending in which the universe abides. The Tellurian rights itself according to its own inscrutable laws, and the characters merely taste the underlying truth. It's a happy ending, but what does it mean? Are mages merely puppets of a higher power? This is a bit different from the conventional deus ex machina because it's supposed to question the characters' beliefs and significance as well as wrap things up. Just remember that this isn't a story for novice groups or Storytellers. Players might hate it, so choose carefully.

Tragic Endings

Ironically, Storytellers often make dangerous-seeming stories easier on the players. While there's nothing wrong with fudging die rolls for the sake of drama, you don't want to rob players of the feeling that they're risking their characters with an uncertain plan. It's too easy to visualize a terrific conclusion, then railroad the characters so that they have no choice but to arrive on time, with the final riddle, fight or dramatic moments laid before them. It might make for awesome theatre or literature, but it isn't interactive storytelling.

Plan for a defeat that's at least as cool as the cabal's victory. Once you do, you'll be less likely to soften challenges. For example, Chapter Two posits an alternate ending where one of the characters becomes Ascension's ultimate enemy. A good Storyteller will have at least one interesting defeat on hand. Never punish failure with boredom. Even when the characters can't save the universe or solve the final mystic riddle, their defeat should lead to something new and interesting.

Final defeat is difficult for even an experienced Storyteller to pull off. You might wish to give the cabal one final chance to rectify things in exchange for a great sacrifice, but you don't have to. It's hard for even very mature groups to accept failure, so you should either present alternatives or emphasize that, given the decisions they made, it couldn't have gone any other way. An unhappy ending generally calls for a quiet scene. Characters (and players) think on what could have been and the enormity of their defeat. Yes, it's a chance to indulge in grand angst, but on the eve of Armageddon, it's appropriate. Give them a peaceful moment before closing the curtains or sending them to Ragnarok and you'll find that failure isn't such a bitter pill to swallow.

Mysterious Endings

Resist the temptation to tie up every loose end. Aside from the risk of information overload, the things you *don't* tell the players can be as entertaining as what you do share. Always leave room for speculation; providing total closure makes players put the story completely behind them. A really good ending should linger in the players' imagination. Let the players wrestle with a few remaining enigmas. There's nothing wrong with sketching out several possibilities, then refusing to commit to any of them. Just point to these hidden truths, and let the players construct the best theory for themselves.

A chronicle's conclusion doesn't need to be straightforward. It can entertain by raising as many questions as it answers. Take the opportunity to decide on a few ultimate truths, but don't share them all with the players. Believe it or not, this isn't arbitrary; if they see a predictable framework behind things, you don't have to tell them what it is.

For example, you might decide that the Computer that commands Iteration X is really trying to liberate the Convention from Control. It ordered Iterators to destroy healthy brain cells and replace them with computer implants so that members of the Convention would be resistant to mind-control techniques. You never tell the players this, but you show them the results. Senior Iterators help their Traditionalist characters avoid Panopticon strikes. They recruit characters to skirmish with younger operatives. The players can see a pattern in all of this, but you keep the truth to yourself. Doing so adds depth to the story by hinting that the characters' actions affect something much larger and stranger than they know.

Obviously, you can take this idea too far. You should provide *some* answers. Even though you don't need to wrap everything up, you should account for some of the major events of the chronicle. For the most part, use the finale to reveal secrets, but hold enough back to retain a sense of grandeur and mystery.

The Denouement

Remember that you don't have to destroy the world or bring about Ascension to end your game. A game's end is defined by whether or not the things important to your players are resolved. This can be something as small as driving mystic enemies from the character's city or finding the answer to a riddle that has followed them throughout the entire chronicle. The essence of an ending is not destruction, but a fundamental transformation that affects everything the characters care about.

This book is about somewhat larger events, but the same rule applies. Perhaps Ascension doesn't swallow

Plot Coupons

Many roleplayers are familiar with the epic plots of mass-marketed fantasy literature and computer games. While there's a lot to be said about using good novels and games as inspiration, there are certain clichés that you want to avoid. One of the most common has been dubbed the plot coupon.

A plot coupon structure leads characters from one event to the next, rewarding them with the finale when they attend all the required events. Rather than make substantial choices (combat tactics don't count because characters will simply die if they fail), the characters just have to show up. Individual scenes are only significant as far as they can advance characters to the story's conclusion. One example of a plot coupon would be a supernatural guardian who defends a Wonder that the characters need to reach the finale. If the guardian or conflict is nothing but a backdrop for acquiring the Wonder, then the scene is really a plot coupon. You'll be tempted to use scenes like this in your game's finale because you'll be thinking forward to the conclusion instead of making individual moments count.

No story can avoid having some resemblance to the plot coupon structure, but there are two easy ways to avoid the problem. First of all, make sure that every scene is relevant to the entire plot. If you need the characters to steal a Wonder to counteract some nasty magic later on, make the Wonder, its hiding place and its guardians relevant to the plot as a whole. If the finale is a powerful antagonist, the guardian might be the antagonist's ally — or a disgruntled cohort who's willing to give the Wonder to persuasive characters.

Second, make sure that the scene adds complications in its own right. The purpose and outcome of a scene shouldn't always be immediately obvious. Characters need be able to make mistakes. Looking at the preceding example, the Wonder might have a destructive side effect if it's misused, or it might provide the needed power at an awful price.

If you integrate scenes and make their impact last for the whole story, you'll avoid the impression that the plot is a set of loosely connected, arbitrary events. Add this to a coherent history, and your epic story will keep the players interested.

the universe. Instead, Awakening becomes a genuine choice. Individuals can freely decide whether or not to become mages or live normal lives. Maybe the Traditions and Technocracy drive away Marauders and Fallen mages, but still have to deal with each other. Mages might form the mystical equivalent of the United Nations (with the Conventions holding disproportionate influence as its Security Council).

Storytellers can take this time to tie up any loose ends. The classic example of this kind of denouement is the (usually cut) end of *Hamlet*, where Fortinbras assumes the throne and clears up lingering plot threads. We know that he's king, Rosencrantz and Gildenstern are dead and that Denmark's history is assured.

Aside from leaving the door open for a sequel, the denouement allows players to process the ending slowly and figure out how their characters will fit into the new world. Players have an opportunity to say goodbye and imagine what could happen long after play ends. Give them a scene where they can say farewell, and don't rush it. Players always have things on their mind that you can't anticipate, and this is their time to act on them.

Epic Stories

Momentous events are intimidating. In most games, we don't worry about the fate of governments, ecosystems or the other foundations of our setting. Even after the fall of House Janissary, the United States still exists. Doissetep's destruction might have knocked over Stonehenge, but it didn't flood California. Characters might be called on to save the world, but their victories make only the smallest impact on day-to-day life. Exceptions like the Reckoning change fundamental assumptions about our setting. For example, the Reckoning signaled a change from ceaseless, hidden intrigue to a desperate measures in the face of Armageddon.

World-changing epics are challenging because they make players question everything. If the global economy collapses, how do characters get food and shelter? How will the government respond to magic on the streets?

Cataclysms

Tidal waves. Earthquakes. Comets and asteroids. Rains of blood. Our appetite for mass destruction is at least as old as Exodus. Since then, literature, film and television have portrayed disasters with a set of strategies that you can use to enhance your chronicle.

One effective way is to use cut scenes: breaks from the main action that show the players how bad things really are. In the 21st century, we look at news as a kind of endless montage. This is handy, because you can use the World of Darkness' media to do the same thing, producing quick, vivid summaries of disasters in progress. Each sound bite can be a story seed, to boot. Appending any story with the Rogue Council's sphinx icon can point characters to critical events in the global melange.

Remember that you don't want the characters to act like frightened couch potatoes. They need to be engaged with the world while it falls apart. Accordingly, don't be afraid to run side stories in the thick of a natural disaster. Even though it's an archetypal theme, humanity versus nature tends to be underused. You don't even need to use your regular characters. Run a session or scene with another group of mages or Sleepers as they try to cope with the devastation. Doing so has the advantage of allowing you to kill the characters with impunity. Let the players see the bodies and learn how bad things really are.

One other kind of cut scene is only suitable for games in which players are careful not to let out-of-character knowledge taint their actions. In these stories, you follow an antagonist or other vital Storyteller character's actions. You might even want players to run these characters for a while so that they can see a cataclysm from the eyes of other important figures. In these scenes, you can even hint at the cause of the disaster. Players can spend a session at Ragnarok Command and view the global fall of the Gauntlet, or they can play Umbra-walking Euthanatoi who see Voormas invade the Entropy Realm.

You can supplement cut scenes with facts and statistics about the disaster. This seems like a cold, modern way to show off Armageddon, but it actually has an ancient pedigree. We know that the Angel of the Lord devastates Pharaoh's Egypt by slaying every firstborn child. We've read John of Patmos' prophecy that a third of the waters will be made bitter with wormwood. Nowadays, we tend to describe events by the numbers. Use both, and remember their respective connotations. Body counts and dollar values on damage tend to be the products of modern, industrialized cultures. Poetic descriptions by area and type are associated with mystical and occult sources. You can use each style to indicate the perspective of the source or the nature of the catastrophe. These descriptions help prevent monotony and keep you from having to play out every bit of the end. Otherwise, too many gory interludes or heart-wrenching side stories can make the players stop caring, get sick of the melodrama or spin it into black comedy.

Blood is Thicker

Now is the time to get your players to sketch out who their characters' family, mundane friends and acquaintances are. It's easy to ignore a character's personal history outside the cabal, but once you detail it, players tend to embrace the idea. This is wonderful, because you've just acquired a new set of characters to threaten.

A player might be only vaguely alarmed when a supernatural typhoon in the game kills hundreds in a nearby city, but kill a character's mother, and you've added a personal touch that compels a response. Family and friends also have their attendant obligations: funerals, inheritances and other elements that you can use to introduce another plot thread or just to ratchet up the pathos. Just be careful not to overdo it

Systems for Disasters

The omnipresent threat offered by disasters might seem difficult to judge, but once you think about what you want to accomplish, it narrows the scope of your concerns down to a manageable level. Remember that you don't have to calculate the damage of the entire tornado. Let description take over your job and talk about flying cars, ruined buildings and howling, dark skies. It's best to view the disaster as an antagonist. It needs a good description, a way to avoid it and an effect that is interesting as well as punishing. Remember to consider the effects of magic. Some spells can negate the disaster entirely, but some disasters have mystical variants that enhance their lethality. Here are some sample disasters to get you started.

Major Earthquakes

Although they are normally caused by shifting tectonic plates, the shock wave from a major magical Effect, a celestial body striking, gargantuan Bygones and roused spirits of the land can also shake the earth. These rules simulate earthquakes measuring 6.1 or higher on the Richter scale.

Effect: Most earthquakes cause minor damage at best, but earthquakes measuring 6.1 or higher can topple buildings and rend the earth. In game terms, this means that characters in the area of the effect can suffer bashing or lethal damage from collapsing buildings and flying debris. They also risk being trapped under a fallen structure. Assign a dice pool to strike characters based on the size, number and resilience of nearby structures. This pool varies from one or two dice for a sparsely developed area to 10 or more dice in a downtown core. If the characters are in the vicinity of a major building

210   ASCENSION

collapsing, this pool can easily exceed 20 dice. In places where quakes are common (such as parts of Japan and California), some buildings are built to withstand quakes, reducing the threat by one or more dice.

If the debris strikes the characters, apply five dice of bashing damage, adding additional dice for the successes made on the "attack roll." If the character botches, she is also pinned by debris or snagged by a crack in the ground. The attack dice now become the number of successes the character must overcome to free herself with a feat of strength. If the threat was given 10 or more dice, the character might have to dig her way out before she runs out of breathable air.

Earthquakes also make combat movement difficult. Add a +1 to +3 difficulty penalty to driving rolls, difficulties in combat and performing athletic feats that require a steady footing.

Defense: Avoiding broken ground and debris requires a Dexterity + Dodge (difficulty 8) roll for threats of six or fewer dice (fragments or disturbed earth) and a Dexterity + Athletics roll (difficulty 7). Correspondence magic can help characters orient themselves (negating movement penalties) and teleport away from the disaster. Calming the quake is a Forces 4 Effect, and every two successes reduce the area's threat by two attack dice within the mage's line of sight. The seventh rank of Forces can halt or cause earthquakes in an area bounded by one tectonic plate per success.

Variations: An earthquake can cause a shockwave effect in the ocean called a tsunami. These disasters begin as small waves emanating from the disturbed area, but the waves grow in size until they become strong enough to strike coastlines with tremendous force. A normal human cannot evade it. On the open sea, waves can travel at speeds of 200 meters a second. As they approach land (and shallow water) they slow down, but still travel faster than a human being can run. Waves can reach 100 kilometers in width. An unnatural or exceptional tsunami could be even faster and larger. Characters should seek shelter and high ground. The impact damage is comparable to that of an earthquake, but with the added risk of drowning.

Nuclear Blasts

Harnessing the power of the atom, a nuclear weapon guarantees instant death for anyone unfortunate enough to find himself at ground zero, and a slower death from radiation burns and poisoning for many survivors. Nuclear weapon strength is measured by its equivalent in tons of TNT. Therefore, a one-kiloton burst packs the power of an explosion caused by 1,000 tons of TNT.

Effect: Characters at ground zero are disintegrated with 10 (for a low-yield tactical nuclear weapon) to 30 levels (not dice) of aggravated damage. This damage cannot be soaked by any natural (or most supernatural) means. The initial blast for a one-kiloton explosion affects a radius of 140 meters; for a one-megaton explosion, the blast radius is 3100 meters.

Milliseconds later, a firestorm created by heat and pressure envelops an area approximately two and a half times that of the initial blast. This wave of destruction inflicts the base damage of the weapon in dice of aggravated damage. It consists of ionized gas (plasma) at shorter ranges, then flash burns and flame at longer ranges.

In addition, the supersonic pressure wave (the Mach effect) inflicts an equal number of dice of bashing damage. This wave extends to about eight to 10 times the radius of the initial blast.

Then, you must consider the effects of radiation and fallout. Roll 16 dice for characters caught in the pressure wave or closer and subtract the character's Stamina score. Inflict the remainder at the rate of two unsoakable levels of bashing damage per hour. The characters who lose all of their bashing levels receive the remainder as aggravated damage instead, however. After that, fallout will have similar effects. Depending on the yield and the type of burst, the bomb's fallout might have wide-ranging effects. Characters in the vicinity of the fallout should roll Stamina + Science (difficulty 8) every hour to reflect their natural health and ability to take precautions against further contamination. These effects are left to the Storyteller's discretion, but they include cancer, chromosome damage, leukemia, cataract formation and localized cell death.

A nuclear bomb's electromagnetic pulse (EMP) radius is a factor of the burst's altitude. At very high altitudes, a bomb can affect a continent-sized area. At lower altitudes, the EMP will affect unshielded electrical systems (including the power grid) up to 30 miles away. Usually, only modern militaries have access to shielded equipment. Civilian equipment that survives the pressure wave will almost certainly be destroyed by the EMP. At longer distances, equipment still suffers mild to severe damage.

In the World of Darkness, nuclear weapons have a spiritual effect. Anything killed by the initial blast is also *spiritually* destroyed. Avatars are shattered, joining the Avatar Storm. Death also severs mystical ties, preventing contingent mind transfers, reincarnation and subsequent resurrection. The immediate area of the blast is spiritually polluted, infecting local Nodes with foul Resonance. If the blast occurred near a ley line or dragon track, the corruption spreads to any adjoining Nodes as well.

Defense: Aside from fleeing or hiding hundreds of feet underground, the only defenses available are magical; Forces 4 can protect against all aspects of the blast, providing two dice of protection per success. Conjunctional Forces and Correspondence magic can shield against EMP and radiation. In the standard Consensus, using Life magic to shrug off radiation is a vulgar Effect.

Variations: In exchange for losing some of its sheer destructive kilotonnage, a neutron bomb bathes a large area in neutron radiation, allowing it to kill more people (and inflict less collateral damage). Neutron radiation cuts through most shielding, allowing it to leave an armored vehicle untouched while killing all of its crew. A typical neutron bomb has a one-kiloton yield, but releases fatal radiation at the same distance as a 13-kiloton weapon. Treat the average neutron bomb like a one-kiloton weapon, but allow it to deliver radiation damage *all at once* (rather than every hour) over a one-mile radius. Neutron radiation dissipates faster, so Storytellers should reduce the effects of fallout.

Using Correspondence and Dimensional Science (Spirit), the Technocracy uses neutron bombs that have been designed to detonate in all three Umbral layers simultaneously. The infamous spirit nukes were used during the Reckoning to devastating effect. Ironically, the Avatar Storm has convinced Ragnarok Command to think twice about employing these weapons again, convincing them to use more surgical methods to remove major threats. Consequently, Panopticon has requisitioned these weapons for itself.

Great Enemies

In Chapter Two, the characters confront Voormas, Grand Harvester of Souls. The mage has an Arete of 9. His magical powers include the seventh rank of Entropy. He's formidable, all right — so how do you run him?

This kind of question applies to any powerful antagonist. These mages are forces to be reckoned with, but when all is said and done, it's time to be rid of them. If the antagonist is a long-running villain, the characters (and players!) will be eager to finish things once and for all. You have to work hard to create a satisfying showdown that doesn't totally outclass the characters but doesn't look like you're being merciful. You can't hand them victory on a platter without cheapening the event.

Motivations and Weaknesses

In the **Mage Storytellers Handbook** we introduced the maxim: With great power comes necessary flaws. This is the key to running a satisfying antagonist. A battle with titanic magic is fun, but without the depth provided by character motivations it can too easily boil down to a series of opposed rolls.

Mage magic is a strategic thing. Characters with enough time and competency can unleash devastating

The Mad God's Hammer

According to the Sons of Ether, the comet Mirzaba will strike the earth in 2012. Aside from that, other celestial threats exist, from the simple probability that a celestial body will eventually hit hard to the machinations of archmages and wrathful Umbrood.

Rorg, the Planetary Incarna of the Asteroid Belt, is one such threat. Its urge to cleanse the world with a massive asteroid grows daily. Aside from the danger such an act poses to Earth, it might alter the Far Horizon itself. Smashing the world with a piece of the Dreamshell's physical correspondent is bound to have some effect. Rorg might even decide to send a completely Umbral asteroid for an effect invisible to humans but devastating to the spirit world. See **Rage Across the Heavens** for more details.

A comet or asteroid strike represents a threat to all life that could inspire unlikely allies. Even the Nephandi are against such a clean cataclysm.

Meteors penetrate the atmosphere all the time, but most of them just burn up. Larger bodies like asteroids and comets can survive all the way to the ground, hitting with the force of a tremendous nuclear blast. For direct impact, use the rules for nuclear bombs but omit EMP and radiation effects. Strikes large enough to affect the entire planet will have a kill zone of dozens of miles and a shock wave that extends for hundreds more.

When a planet-killer strikes the ocean (as it probably will), it creates tsunamis large enough to destroy cities hundreds of miles inland. The strike also throws up clouds of dust, leading to years of darkness. Crops will fail and humanity will starve.

---

attacks, sense anything and create unbreakable defenses, but they can't do everything at once or can't cover everything at once. Ultimately, a mystic antagonist's strengths and weaknesses are going to boil down to his personality and goals. A mage who fears death (like Voormas), is likely to concentrate on defensive magic. An obsessed mage might devote all of her magical power to a personal project, leaving severe weaknesses in her arsenal.

Motivation also affects the villain's ability to anticipate character actions. Regardless of his intelligence, an arrogant mage is capable of underestimating his enemies' power and cleverness. He might omit a fundamental spell and use his magical reserves on flamboyant, self-aggrandizing spells.

A villain's motivations need to be understandable. The cabal needs to have a chance of learning about what makes him tick. This doesn't mean that you give away his secrets for nothing, but with effort, characters can learn vital information to help them in the battle ahead.

Remember that, in the end, even archmages are servants of their paradigms. They might have internalized certain elements (and no longer need foci), and they might have expanded the scope of their beliefs, but in the end, their apprenticeships stamp them with the kind of magic they're going to use forever. Characters can use occult study to determine what kind of tactics the enemy will use, then plan accordingly.

Portions of Power

Magical battles are won or lost before they are fought. Fast-cast battle magic plays well around the amateurs of the supernatural world, but even though a bolt of flame terrifies a vampire, it will merely annoy a mage with time to erect a Forces shield.

> ### Defining Magic
>
> One of the most important tools in the Storyteller's arsenal is the ability to enforce strict definitions of how an Effect functions. Even though the Spheres are broad, the applications are narrow unless the character takes time (and the player spends successes) to widen them. Governed by paradigms and personal preferences, a spell performs a specific function, like a "contract with reality." A rote designed to ward off werewolves doesn't necessarily affect other Changing Breeds. That's a different spell, or one that requires more successes for a broader effect. The exact scope of a spell is normally defined when it's cast. It can't be changed later unless the mage casts another one to modify it. Storytellers might want to limit "stacked" Effects so that players' characters and antagonists can't constantly reinforce critical spells. Apply a cumulative +1 difficulty penalty to attempts to modify running spells.
>
> In early games, you should be generous about magic's scope, but as time goes on, try to tighten the conditions of each spell. Apply this restriction to all characters, and you'll eventually start to see magic played like a chess game. Each Effect is a piece with strictly delineated powers, reinforced by fast-cast pawns meant to probe enemy defenses, shore up weaknesses and bluff.
>
> As a result, antagonists can be out-spelled by being out-thought. Water elementals can rip right through a **Ban** designed to block earth spirits; personal Forces shields can leave Wonders vulnerable.

Major antagonists know this and are likely to have multiple rituals prepared, but they have to strike a balance between power and flexibility. Remember that every two active spells adds one to the difficulty of subsequent magic. Protagonists and antagonists have to balance preparedness and spontaneity. Some antagonists can offset this balance with Quintessence, trusted foci and certain Wonders, but doing so opens up new avenues of attack. If the mage misses an important defense, ongoing rituals will hinder any fast Effect he uses to compensate.

Some ancient magi have constantly running spells that keep them alive. Attacking this magic is an insidious way of bypassing other defenses, but a 500-year-old wizard is likely to have devoted many, many successes to reinforcing his longevity magic against opposition. At the same time, older mages have less difficulty with fast-cast magic, and they might risk an attack that hasn't been built up over days.

Storytellers should devote a certain number of successes to pre-cast Effects. An active Adept might have 10 or so successes worth of running spells. Archmages could have 20 or more. Remember that aside from the mage's character flaws, his magic might be humbled by the sheer scope of his work. A mage like Voormas needs ongoing Effects to link him to Nodes, counter scrying attempts and deal with dozens of other concerns that have nothing to do with the players' characters. This way, you can keep very powerful mages from totally overwhelming characters without using too much sheer fiat.

Optional Rules: War

War encapsulates the essence of epic storytelling. War stories stand at the intersection between death, passion and moral dilemmas. It has a special place in **Mage**, as the game confronts the politics of violence and beliefs worth dying for. The old Ascension War collapsed when its generals didn't live up to the ideals of the war cabals it sacrificed. Now the Archmasters are almost gone; their secret fortresses contain little more than ghosts and dreams. The latest edition of **Mage** began with the devastated Traditions taking stock of their situation and building their own roads to enlightenment. The new Ascension warriors were committed to their own agendas first. Sometimes they cloistered themselves away. Sometimes they devoted their energies to local projects and mystic secrets that the old war never gave them time to explore.

Destiny can't wait. Even though the Pogrom declined, Tradition mages who tried to subvert the Technocracy's rule soon discovered that their old enemies were more than willing to crush any serious dissent. Even as they experimented with new forms of magic, the Traditions chafed under a Consensus that let humanity's potential wither on the vine. The Rogue Council turned this smoldering resentment into dozens of fires: cabals who were ready to fight for freedom instead of Tradition rule.

Mage is about magic in the 21st century, so the supernatural needs to stay subtle to avoid warping the setting — until you end the chronicle. Now, you can let the pent-up wrath of centuries loose. It's bound to be a cathartic moment for the players. The Rule of Shade dies on the battlefield. Massive spells burn through a sky filled with Technocratic aircraft. Immerse the characters in it, but don't forget that battles rarely take place in a vacuum. In any war, civilians are the first to suffer and the last to recover. The final tremors of an Ascension War are no different.

In addition to general advice, the following section introduces a very loose system for adjudicating battles. This doesn't cover every nook and cranny of 21st century warfare. Instead, it's designed to help players and Storytellers figure out the shape of the grand conflict that serves as a backdrop for their actions. As such, it should never overrule the actions of individual characters. The rules cover a large strategic scale. For smaller engagements, see the **Dark Ages: Storytellers Companion** and **Dark Ages: Spoils of War**, but remember that these sources will need adaptation to cover modern battles. Also, note that the following rules are *not* a competitive war game; they rely on Storyteller adjudication.

Command

Chapter Two puts the characters in command of the Traditions' forces. You don't have to do this to put characters at center stage just to make them important. They can always perform a decisive mission as a part of the larger force. On the other hand, military command is a rare role in a game in which characters usually rely on nobody but themselves.

Commanding an army is a daunting task; commanding an army of men and women who are so self-willed that they reject the authority of natural laws is even more challenging. Leaders need to generate respect, react to changes on the battlefield and ensure that their fighters are adequately supplied. Aside from raw resources, leaders need competent assistants to relay orders down the chain of command.

In this strategic combat system, *Command* is the dice pool used to govern the effects of offensive actions: It is normally equal to the commander's Intelligence + Leadership. If you have **Tradition Book: Akashic Brotherhood**, you may substitute the Strategy Knowledge instead. In both cases, the leader's dice pool cannot exceed her Intelligence + Academics (Military Strategy) dice pool or that of an assistant who can be easily consulted.

Control

Leaders also need to be able to keep troops together with effective communications and morale. Unless they regroup for guerilla warfare, a broken army is just as useless as a dead one. This is a delicate matter, as clever generals can keep soldiers fighting effectively until the last one dies, while distrusted or incompetent leader might ensure that her ranks break before a single shot is fired.

The art of keeping units fighting effectively is called *Control*. In the strategic system, this is a dice pool representing the force's defensive capabilities. Add the leader's Manipulation + Leadership, or substitute Abilities as you would for the Command pool. Control scores can outstrip formal knowledge, as force of personality compels units to keep fighting. This emphasis on communications and personal conviction isn't necessarily realistic, but it emphasizes **Mage**'s themes. War, like reality, ultimately plays out to serve the strongest convictions.

Force

Every decision made at the command level depends on troops to carry it out. The Ascension War's swords and shields were its mages and consors. Open warfare doesn't change this.

In the strategic system, we measure troop effectiveness in *units*. The more effective a unit is, the less people staff it. This reflects the fact that a single HIT Mark can outfight a dozen conventional soldiers. To determine a unit's strength and numbers, consult the following table:

Number of Troops	Competence
500	Untrained (no ranks in one or more relevant Abilities, average combat dice pools of two)
200	Trained (1 rank in relevant Abilities, average combat dice pools of three-four)
100	Veteran (2 ranks in relevant Abilities, average combat dice pools of four-five)
50	Elite (3-4 ranks in relevant Abilities, average combat dice pools of five-six)
20	Heroic (4-5 ranks in relevant Abilities, average combat dice pools of seven or more)

Every rank of a supernatural power (in mages' case, their highest Sphere rank) moves the unit size one line down the table. After "Heroic," each additional rank reduces the number of troops by four. Subtract one if these powers are (like sorcerous Paths) slightly less potent than equivalent Spheres. If the unit has access to Wonders or other sources of limited supernatural ability, add half of the power's rank, rounded up. Therefore, a unit of Akashic Adepts (Sphere rank 4) with average combat dice pools of six consists of only eight mages — the equivalent of 500 untrained fighters.

Of course, special troops won't always be available in large numbers, and units won't always have a homogenous composition. Storytellers should put together units based on the average strength of a given group.

Resolving Battles

Before starting, the Storyteller and players define a battle site. The strategic system is designed for large areas like entire cities. The Storyteller adjudicates how many units of the overall force can participate based on terrain features, magic and other circumstances. Movement is abstract; instead, the Storyteller and players determine the battle's objectives. These are defined as goals that a unit can accomplish while the battle still rages, such as capturing a Node or destroying a bridge.

Each turn is 24 hours. There are no initiative rolls; all actions are treated as if they occur simultaneously. Resolve the following phases with the full strength of each side, only counting losses at the end of the turn. The base difficulty for all strategic combat rolls is 7, but weapons and other circumstances can modify this number.

1. Move to Objectives: If they have the means and the desire, each side devotes at least one unit to securing an objective. These units automatically succeed unless one or more enemy units move to oppose them.

2. Resolve Objectives: Each side fighting for the objective rolls Command scores to attack and Control scores to defend. If a side rolling Command wins, the player makes a *Force* roll equal to the number of units committed to the battle plus any successes scored in excess of the number needed to win. Each success destroys one rival unit.

3. Resolve General Battle: Each side selects a number of units and declares which and how many of the enemy's units they are attacking — but they can only defend against those units in turn. Therefore, an army could devote all of its energies to a small cluster of units but suffer as the enemy's remaining forces attack undefended elements. The leaders of each side roll their Command scores to attack and their Control scores to defend. Make a Force roll for each victorious use of Command the same way as when fighting for an objective.

4. Tally Destroyed Units: Each side marks off any units destroyed in combat. The Storyteller determines the ratio of those injured, routed and killed in each unit.

5. Make Adjustments: Each side applies any modifiers for secured objectives and other circumstances. During this phase, each side chooses which units will retreat and whether or not they will move new units to the battle site. The Storyteller determines the feasibility of each strategy.

Objectives

The Storyteller determines how many objectives a battle contains. By default, every objective accomplished adds one die to either Command or Control pools (Storyteller's choice), thanks to increased morale and general strategic superiority. Here are some sample benefits for securing specific objectives:

Seized Node: Every unit able to channel Quintessence is treated as being one rank more superior. This boost normally causes each affected unit to split into two, doubling its effective strength. For example, one unit of eight elite Akashic Adepts splits into the equivalent of two units of four mages, contributing two dice to their side's Force pool.

Downed Bridge: Enemy units that travel on the ground suffer a +1 difficulty penalty to Command rolls.

Critical Success

If a commander scores at least four successes *and* twice as many successes as the opposing Command or Control roll, her affected units can perform an extra action (attacking or taking a minor objective) after all others have been resolved but before the next turn. Only similarly successful enemy units can respond to this action. No unit can perform more than one extra action this way.

Outnumbering the Enemy

The strategic system uses units as a "health" and "damage" rating, but their overwhelming force also assists offense. If the attacking side commits even one more unit than the number of enemy units it's attacking, add one die to the attacker's Command rating. Add two dice if the attacker commits twice as many units as it's attacking, and three dice if it commits triple the number of units. After this there is no further benefit for even greater numbers, reflecting the fact that a weaker force can sometimes hold out.

Communications, Weapons and Intelligence

These rules assume that each unit is equipped with the equivalent of small arms (assault rifles and minor explosives), a few wheeled vehicles and reliable radio communications to coordinate movement and acquire intelligence. Superior vehicles modify a unit's Command difficulties. Superior communications (and intelligence gathering) modifies a unit's Control difficulties, and better weapons modify Force difficulties. Average the total modifier when groups of differing units attack together. At the Storyteller's discretion, several units can share the benefits from one vehicle or piece of equipment. For example, a Technocratic fighter with air superiority can modify the Command and Force scores of nearly every Union unit on the battlefield.

Strategic weapons aren't covered by these rules. If spirit nukes or the equivalent drop on the battle site, treat it as a disaster (see pp. 210-212) and apply the average (and probably fatal) damage to units based on their described location.

Storytellers should keep in mind that these are only examples. Think of mundane and magical equivalents when consulting the following table.

Difficulty	Vehicles/Command	Communications/Control	Weapons/Force
-1	Armored Vehicles	Satellite Phones	Portable Rockets
-2	Tanks, Helicopters	GPS Uplinks	Modern Artillery
-3	Air Support	Dedicated Satellites	Missiles
-4	Teleportation	Networked Minds	Lasers, Elementals

Guerilla Warfare, Stealth and Espionage

The strategic systems don't cover these options because they are the domain of **Mage**'s conventional systems. These rules assume enough access to modern communications to see most enemy movements and direct troops out of the leader's line of site, and that soldiers are doing what they can to foil enemy intelligence. Decisive character action can remove unit equipment modifiers with sabotage, deny defensive Control rolls by covering units in magical camouflage and regroup scattered soldiers into a ragged but effective force.

Space considerations aside, these rules are here to help you answer questions about how a relevant war is going and to give players a taste of command. There's still plenty of room for individual heroism. When in doubt, let that rule the day. Mages are dynamic enough to defy the odds.

Ascension

The Universe, including the visible and the invisible, the essential nature of which is compounded of purity, action, and rest, and which consists of the elements and the organs of action, exists for the sake of the soul's experience and emancipation.

—Patanjali, *Yoga Aphorisms*

What is Ascension? **Mage** has never answered that question definitively out of respect for your games and beliefs, and because that fundamental mystery makes it that much more appealing. If you run a game to the point of personal or mass Ascension, you're going to need to confront this question, but you *don't have to answer it*. Ascension can take many forms without contradiction. You can rule that it embraces contradiction and resolves all paradoxes. After all, we're talking about superhuman wisdom: a state that we can talk about but not necessarily describe.

In Chapter Two: Judgment, we assume that Ascension allows humanity to embrace whatever destiny it wants without being chained to a particular paradigm, but you needn't be so liberal. Your convictions or story needs might dictate that Ascension comes in a very specific form. You could decide that one Tradition is right, but that would open the door to some odd questions. If, for example, the Order of Hermes' paradigm is the best path, why doesn't this make Hermetics more powerful or wiser than other mages? It's usually a better idea to create a path that transcends Tradition or Convention dogma, but that doesn't mean that it can't be specific. With that in mind, here are some sample paths to Ascension. You can incorporate some or all of them into your game.

Gnosis

Gnosticism (from *gnosis* — Greek for "knowledge") is the name of a spiritual tradition with roots in Neoplatonism and Zoroastrianism. Christianity, Judaism and Islam have all had Gnostic sects. In most cases, these sects have spun off into their own faiths and so-called heresies, but its legacy lives on in everything from mainstream theology to real world occult movements. Our main concern isn't so much with the history of Gnosticism as its ideas.

The essence of Gnostic belief is that the world is a deception — even a prison. In some schools, humanity's deluded existence is a result of its lack of wisdom. Others go further and claim that an evil agency is actively imprisoning humankind. The most extreme view is that material reality itself is evil.

Early Gnostics credited this deceiver with creating the prison-universe and called him the Demiurge. Some went so far as to say that the Bible was written about this false god. Obviously, mainstream Christianity and Judaism had a dim view of these claims. To Gnostics, the true God was a wisdom principle that some of them described as the female Sophia: the mother of wisdom. Others claimed that the Adversary of Abrahamic monotheism was the real God; the Demiurge's followers had just given him a bad reputation.

One tenet of Gnosticism is that people cannot escape the prison through mainstream religious rituals. Instead, the seeker needs to use asceticism and meditation to contact Sophia. Self-denial wears away the seeker's attachment to the impure material world, while mystical exercises help her perceive hidden spiritual realms. The Demiurge has spiritual cohorts (often called Archons), who the seeker must defeat to escape the prison. In many ways, Gnosticism resembles early Buddhism because it favors detached living and skepticism about the material world.

Mage takes some of its major inspirations from Gnosticism. The "prison-universe" is the Consensus. Mages are a spiritual elect whose abilities allow them to defy the illusion. On the other hand, the game doesn't have a position about who created the Consensus or whether it's good or evil. The Gnostic view of Ascension is one where people escape reality and defeat its demonic jailers. This view can translate into an Ascension best found in the Umbra, contending with powerful spirits. On the other hand, this quest isn't conducive to global Ascension; the real trick is finding a way to bring the truth back to Earth.

You could even take the position that the Avatar is a mage's personal Archon, throwing up obstacles to prevent the mage from contacting Sophia. In any event, you have to ask yourself who created the cosmic prison, why they did it, and how they would react to escape attempts.

Synthesis

While some forms of mysticism reject the material world, others incorporate it. In Mahayana Buddhism, reality isn't an illusion per se, but requires wisdom to see it for what it is: a transitory, unified whole, without discrete objects or entities. The synthetic path is often associated with Asian religions such as Buddhism and Taoism, but other mystics and philosophers have talked about it as well. Synthesis also has a scientific role. Once thought indivisible, the atom seems to bear a host of exotic particles. Ecology and mathematics both encounter systems that need to describe individual components as parts of a greater whole, and vice versa. Some synthesists say that this division ultimately stops at the soul; others believe that even it is an illusion that only denotes a temporary alignment of spiritual forces.

The synthesist argues that we can't really say that one object is different from another because of two qualities: interdependence and divisibility. Any object we perceive has actually existed in countless forms, so we see only one particular instant of an ongoing process. This process naturally involves other forces and objects. Extended far enough, everything that exists does so because of everything else that exists. This cycle includes division as well as conglomeration. Every object can be infinitely divided, so no object has an inherent reality as a thing in and of itself.

The synthesist's primary problem is how to live in harmony with the whole universal cycle. Philosophical Taoism prescribes passivity because human willfulness interferes with the natural course of things. Buddhism teaches its students to understand that everything is transitory and not to fixate on people, objects and emotions that will eventually pass away.

Synthesis breaks down barriers, and for that reason, it's an excellent approach to Ascension. As enlightenment nears, the Spheres and their associated concepts (such as a reality made of discrete Patterns) can dissolve, turning magic into a holistic study that encompasses everything at once. The **Mage Storytellers Handbook** provides some guidelines for transcending the Spheres (pp. 26-30). Just remember that the Nephandi and Marauders both try to defy the cosmic cycle. Are they really doing so, or are they unwittingly aiding its flow?

Salvation

Perhaps humanity can't Ascend on its own. This isn't an unreasonable proposition. Christianity, Judaism and Islam are all based on the idea that we need God's love to live fulfilling lives. Devout Sikhs, many Hindus and members of other traditional religions also believe that enlightenment requires the grace of a higher power.

Traditionally, doing so means entering into a covenant with the Creator. Sometimes, this covenant is specific to a particular group, but others believe that there is a path to God that is open to all. These covenants needn't be mutually exclusive. For example, many contemporary Christians believe that Jews keep a separate but equal covenant with God. For the most part, religions that believe in universal salvation tend to proselytize, but this isn't always the case.

Sometimes, God is said to be a part of Creation. Others claim that the Creator is separate and that it's humanity's job to return to Him (or Her). In **Mage**, Awakened legends talk about the One: a primal being

who split into the Pure Ones, who in turn spawned the first mages. Does the One still have its own consciousness, hidden in the whispers of thousands of Avatars? Did a part of it remain whole, waiting for the return of its broken pieces? You can answer these questions without having to identify the One with God. You might want to do this to avoid offending religious sensibilities, or you might want to keep the One distinct from the Creators that figure in other lines. **Vampire** assumes that the Judeo-Christian God is real on some level. **Werewolf** has its own Gaia. You could say that Ascension is the reunification of these disparate deities or keep it a mystery.

Not to put it lightly, but if Ascension requires the Creator's intercession, then you need to decide what God wants. The Creator (or the One) might want the characters to follow a particular creed. A higher power might not be as interested in ritual behavior as much as moral rectitude or a devotion to the truth. If you choose this approach, then you don't necessarily have to apply specific religious tenets.

Obviously, **Mage** doesn't have a position about which religion is right. Introducing one would be a radical shift for the setting, but it isn't necessarily a bad idea. What if there is only one true religion? **Tradition Book: Celestial Chorus** introduced the idea that faith-based magic could be intrinsically different from Awakened willworking. You can run with this idea and decide on an explicitly monotheistic chronicle. In this case, miracle workers have to convert their allies and crusade against their enemies. The Nephandi serve the Adversary and encourage "heathen" Traditionalists and Technocrats to stick to their false beliefs.

Singularity

The Singularity is a "post-historical" epoch: a time when human potential (or the products thereof) develops at an exponential rate. Even though the name was first coined by SF author Vernor Vinge, versions of the Singularity scenario have found their way to many different beliefs and fields.

The Singularity happens when human innovations spawn increasingly more rapid successors, to the point where thousands of years of development occur in months, weeks or even days. The classic Singularity scenario asks what will happen when humans invent a computer with superhuman intelligence. What's to stop that from leading to an even smarter AI? In each cycle, the inventors have the means to make a more dramatic improvement in less time, to the point where machine intelligence reaches the point of constant, near infinite improvement. The steep curve of technology-assisted innovation already affects our lives in many ways. Drugs that were inconceivable a few years are now in easy reach because we've just begun to map the human genome.

Other versions of the Singularity replace technology with spiritual or political refinement. Teilhard de Chardin postulated that as each generation seeks out a deeper relationship with God, it accelerates the pace and intensity of devotion to the point full reconciliation and salvation. Utopian philosophers postulate an "end of history" where social forces bring humanity to an earthly paradise. In Buddhism, the appearance of Maitreya (the future Buddha) leads to final enlightenment for all.

A technological Singularity could be a nightmare scenario. If machines improve themselves to godlike stature, what do they need humanity for? In **Mage**, this could be a story in which humanity doesn't Ascend, but creates a new form of life to succeed it. The machines might use their incredible intelligence to care for their creators, ignore them or treat them as pets or slaves. Sleepers might find themselves in Iteration X's position, divided between the cult of the Machine God and rebels who chafe under the AI control.

On the other hand, the Singularity can be reinvested in human development. A hyper-intelligent computer could augment human brains and supercharge the evolution of consciousness. The "posthumans" of the Singularity era have nanotechnology-enhanced bodies that never age or die and minds capable of contemplating the universe's most complex riddles. Just remember that mystic magic can perform most, if not all of these feats. In Chapter Two, the protagonists transform themselves into arcane posthumans by using the **Holy Union** rote.

Social Singularities are interesting models for global Ascension. When everyone is Awakened, does that speed the quest for Ascension? This kind of mass transformation might have happened in the past. Legends about the Anasazi and Prester John's kingdom indicate that at various times and places, entire nations have discovered their spiritual destiny, then vanished from the world.

A Final Word

Why is Ascension desirable? What makes it so precious that mages would suffer, kill and die for it?

Psychologist Abraham Maslow's famous Hierarchy of Needs puts self-actualization at the top of a pyramid of desires. He thought that after physical safety, security and social ties, human beings need to devote themselves to something outside of themselves — to follow their abstract passions. These are the desires of artists, scientists and philosophers. We could look at Ascension in that context: a creative calling that makes humanity whole.

Maslow's work is often interpreted to assert that people don't really think about their creative drives until their needs for safety and companionship are satisfied. Victor Frankl, however, noted that people who suffered the worst offenses to their safety still searched for greater meaning in their lives. He came to this conclusion while he was being marched to a concentration camp in World War Two. Examples like this show us that suffering alone isn't enough to extinguish our desire for meaning. If we look at Ascension as a quest for meaning, we can understand why it's so hard to undermine its value.

Frankl developed a school of psychology called logotherapy, which stressed that survival — our ability to live whole lives — rested upon confronting personal paradoxes. But we live in a postmodern era, where we're keenly aware of how subjective our perceptions can be and how all of our actions have multiple meanings and inherent paradoxes. Sometimes, we wonder how much of our free will is mediated through cultural assumptions, personal anxiety and the demands of powerful institutions.

Still, we muddle along, approaching our finite time on Earth with varying degrees of passion, fear, apprehension, generosity and small-mindedness. We are all tapestries composed of doubt and desire, selfishness and a higher drive. Each of us is the story of the world we know.

Yet at the same time, all of these instincts, thoughts, emotions and relationships are contained within us. There is no escape; we have to resolve these paradoxes. When pain contradicts our desire for comfort, we search for surcease. When ignorance contradicts our need to know, we learn. That's no different than what mages strive for. The paradoxes are different, but the motivation is the same. After each moment, their stories, like ours, move forward.

Mage is a game about these stories. Mages craft grand tales, taking the universe and weaving it on the looms of their paradigms. Ascension is not the end, it is the whole meaning of that story. Mages encounter Paradox when the bedrock of their beliefs clash with the rest of the universe. It's a continuity problem, a strange leap that makes the story seem less authentic. It calls the meaning of the mage's life into question.

So the purpose of Ascension — the purpose of a mage and, some would argue, the purpose of our own lives — is to integrate our strange encounters with reality and craft them into a consistent whole. As mages progress, they expand their paradigms to include new phenomena. Their personal stories open wider windows into the universe.

Who are they, if they are not that story? That's where self-actualization, meaning and Ascension come from. The Awakened want to tell a story that confronts all paradoxes — that encompasses the cosmos.

It's a worthy goal for anyone.

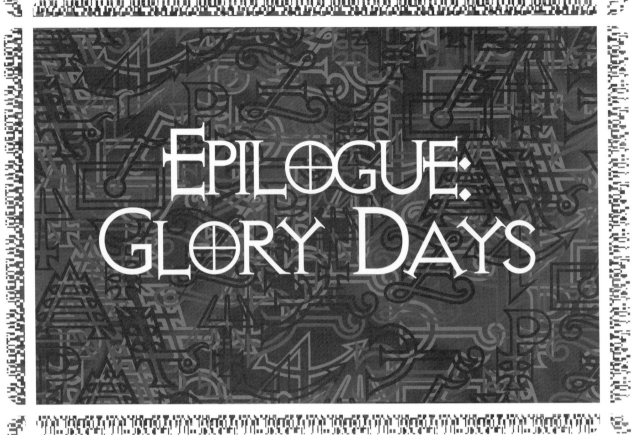

Epilogue: Glory Days

The silent and empty street did not deter Penny, even though San Francisco should have been packed with pedestrians and cars. She gracefully stepped along the empty sidewalk and did a quick twirl to look all around her before putting her face up to the glass window of City Lights Books. She peered into the darkness within and frowned.

"Nobody home," she said wistfully. "We have truly become barbarians."

"Always have been," a gruff voice said from her overlarge handbag.

Penny looked down at the bag she had placed next to her on the street and frowned. "Oh, come out already. There's nobody here. Besides, I haven't smelled a whiff of Paradox for days."

A black cat slipped out of the bag and stretched across the pavement. It then began to lick itself.

"Well, we might as well wait in Vesuvio. The door is open, but nobody's home there, either." Penny picked up her bag and walked the half-block back down the street to the bar. The cat watched her for a moment then followed.

Penny sat down at a window table and watched wistfully out the glass, wishing she'd had a cup of tea or even a glass of wine — something tragically romantic to heighten the forlorn moment of waiting. The cat jumped up onto the table beside her and continued grooming itself. It suddenly lifted its head, ears cocked, listening. "Someone's coming."

Penny frowned. "Neville?"

The cat shook its head, and then jumped from the table to hide under the chair.

Penny took a deep breath and relaxed, anxious to see who else was out on the streets besides herself and her expected cabalmate. A man walked up the street from the direction of the Transamerica Pyramid. He looked like something out of an Indiana Jones movie: cracked, brown leather jacket, jodhpurs and knee-high leather boots. All that was missing was the whip and fedora. Instead, the man wore sunglasses that wrapped tightly around his cheeks, almost as if they were goggles. He headed straight for her.

She stood up and stepped halfway outside the door, arms crossed and leaning against the frame, a look of practiced indifference on her face. Her pale makeup, dark hair tied into outdated buns, and black,

220   Ascension

spidery dress stood in sharp contrast to his adventuresome attire.

The man stopped and smiled, bowing slightly to her. "Hello, miss," he said in a deep voice, rather forthright, as if he were an old-time movie actor. "I've traveled a long time to get here. I do hope you are Miss Penny Dreadful. Am I correct?"

Penny frowned and tipped her chin up. "Yes. Do I know you?"

"Probably not," the man said, smiling. "I haven't been on Earth for some time now. Not since… 1957, I think."

Penny raised her eyebrows, not out of surprise so much as exasperation, an "Are you for real?" gesture.

"Do you mind if we sit down?" the man said. "I've been on my feet for a while."

Penny's eyes bugged out and her jaw dropped. She'd finally realized who he was. "You're not… No, it can't be you. The last book in the series said you died."

"Fiction, miss," the man said, stepping past her into the empty bar. "My Terrific Trio took a lot of license in representing our exploits to the Masses."

"So you *are* Doc Eon," Penny said, almost under her breath. She followed him inside and gestured to an empty chair across from the one she had been sitting in. He took it and she sat back down, looking at him with a smile, as if she'd just met a movie star. "What brings you here, Doctor Eon, Man of Many Tomorrows?" She barely suppressed a giggle as she said that last, well-known appellation. "And how do you know me?"

"My allies are aware of you and your cabal's deeds, Miss Dreadful. Very impressive." Doc Eon leaned back in his chair, relaxing.

"You're kidding, right? I've never been to the Hollow Earth or flown etherships to the edge of the Horizon. You can't seriously care about what I've done."

"On the contrary. Your avoidance of… shall we say, 'high adventure,' makes you all the more impressive in times like these. You've kept your feet where they belong, but your mind has never stopped imagining what could be."

"More like what should have been. I'm a hopeless Romantic, you know, as in the Lord Byron version."

Doc Eon smiled. "I'm well aware of it. My allies and I are about to attempt a gamble, one from which I'm sure none of us will return. We believe the fate of the Earth hangs in the balance."

Penny smiled. "Doesn't it always in your adventures? At least, in the old books. I used to read them, even though they were really aimed at boys."

"Sometimes it did," Eon said, chuckling. "Now, it truly does. I think you know that. If times were different, we wouldn't be sitting in a deserted bar in a deserted city."

Penny sighed and looked out at the sliver of the distant Bay she could see past the crowded skyscrapers, cocking her head at just the right angle to heighten the melancholy effect. "Yes. I suppose it really is the End of Days, isn't it?"

Eon frowned. "Perhaps. Or perhaps not. How things turn out depend on a number of factors. My allies and I aim to be one of those factors. We'd like you to consider being another."

Penny frowned, confused. "How so? I can't very well engage in the sort of fisticuffs you're so renowned for."

"That's not what we need — at least, not here. Not anymore. The fight has moved on, beyond the Horizon. But someone's got to hold the fort here at home, to make sure there's something to come back to."

"And how am I supposed to do that?" Penny looked down at her cat, who looked back up at her with a perplexed gaze.

"Don't let them win. Don't let the Technocrats round everyone up in camps. They've already started, and panic has emptied the streets. It's not Sleepers they're after, it's mages — new mages, people who have just Awakened. There are hundreds of them, from all over, Awakening spontaneously as the Gauntlet fades."

"Is that what all those roundups have been about? We've been looking into it, and the Hollow Railroad has had a lot of static about it. Are you sure? Hundreds of new mages?"

"We're sure. I wouldn't even think of asking something this dangerous of you if we didn't have hard evidence to back it up."

"Okay, let's assume it's true, because it does make sense. Why me?"

"You said it yourself: The Hollow Railroad. They'll listen to you, and they'll act. The Traditions are… caught up in their own problems. The Orphans, though… they're not tied down — or pledged to any single ideology except freedom. They'll understand, especially if you explain it to them."

"Me? Why not Neville? He's supposed to be meeting me here. Why not tell him? He's the one who's got all their respect."

Doc Eon smiled. "But he's never read my books. He's got no reason to believe me. But he *will* believe you…"

CHAPTER SEVEN: DESIGNING ASCENSION 221

Penny smiled. "Ah, I get it. If you win me over, you win Neville over. Probably true. But I'm not sure you've won me over."

"Oh? I know you've been checking me out while we've talked. I saw that distant look in your eyes, and I know it's not just an empty affectation. Your Time Senses surely tell you that I am a Master of Time. How many of those are left on Earth?"

"Time Senses? That's so… *pulp*. I just call them 'anachronicities.' And yes, you're right, I've been checking you out, and you seem to fit the description, at least. But I need more than that before I commit to a cause. Dragon slaying, as they used to call such knightly quests, is serious business. Who are these allies of yours?"

"Me for one," a man said. He sat next to her, in a chair that hadn't been there a moment before. He was black and wore a long trench coat, hiding thick gloves with glowing dials and wires. He winked at her and then was gone.

The cat hissed and leapt into her lap.

"Mistoffelees!" Penny yelled. She petted the cat to soothe him.

Doc Eon frowned. "I'm sorry if Dante startled you."

"Has he been here all along?" Penny fumed.

Eon shrugged his shoulders. "He comes and goes as needed. He can be in many places at once, just as I'm in two time zones now. You'll excuse me if I seem distracted at times; there's something coming through the… well, I'd best not spoil the surprise."

The cat climbed onto the table and stared at Doc Eon. "Who else you working with?" the cat said, no longer in any mood to wait for Penny to ask the questions.

Doc Eon didn't even blink. "I can't yet reveal my other benefactors. Trust me that their names will be known soon enough, and you'll understand everything then." He looked at Penny. "I know I'm asking for a lot. But all I can give you at this time is my solemn word."

Penny shrugged. "I guess that will do, then. You seem the chivalrous type. I will talk it over with Neville. We'll turn our attention to these camps, and see if we can't get a revolution going."

"Thank you, Miss Dreadful." As he said this, he began to fade, as if a ghost.

"Uh… what's happening?" Penny said nervously.

"This isn't my true time. I'm talking to you from the future. We realized we hadn't accounted properly for the Technocracy camps, so I went back to fix that error."

Penny's eyebrows raised again. "You… you're not just a Master anymore, are you?"

"Let's just say I've been doing this sort of thing for some time now." She could barely see his smile as his form became a trick of the light coming through the window.

"Goodbye, Doctor Eon," Penny said, and then added in a formal voice, " I hope I prove worthy of your trust."

"You will. You see, it's already happened here…"

Penny stared at the empty space for a while, ignoring Mistoffelees' attempts to engage her in conversation. She looked out the window at the empty street and smiled. She now had a quest. Chivalry wasn't dead yet.

Act Three of the Time of Judgment Trilogy™

JUDGMENT DAY™
A novel of Ascension by Bruce Baugh

ISBN 1-58846-857-7; WW11912; 352 pages; $7.99

A war for reality has raged unabated for centuries between mages of the mystical Nine Traditions and the authoritarian and rational Technocratic Union. Each side has fractured and cracked the very nature of reality in a constant quest for victory. Now, as entropy takes a final hold and forced ascension envelops the universe, there remains only for the weight of sins to be judged before all returns to its primal state. Three disparate mages are thrust center stage in this process by agents of the mysterious Rogue Council. Can the fate of Creation lie in their hands?

Available Now.